The Vineyards of Calanetti

Saying "I do" under the Tuscan sun...

Deep in the Tuscan countryside nestles the picturesque village of Monte Calanetti. Famed for its world-renowned vineyards, the village is also home to the crumbling but beautiful Palazzo di Comparino. Empty for months, rumors of a new owner are spreading like wildfire...and that's before the village is chosen as the setting for the royal wedding of the year!

It's going to be a roller coaster of a year, but will wedding bells ring out in Monte Calanetti for anyone else?

Find out in this fabulously heartwarming, uplifting and thrillingly romantic new eight-book continuity from Mills & Boon® Cherish™!

A Bride for the Italian Boss by Susan Meier

Return of the Italian Tycoon by Jennifer Faye

Reunited by a Baby Secret by Michelle Douglas

Soldier, Hero...Husband? by Cara Colter

His Lost-and-Found Bride by Scarlet Wilson
Available October 2015

The Best Man & the Wedding Planner

His ~~Carpenter~~

SOLDIER, HERO. . . HUSBAND?

BY
CARA COLTER

Printed and bound in Spain
Pl. Barcelona

MILLS & BOON

Published in Great Britain 2015
by Mills & Boon, an imprint of Harlequin (UK) Limited,
Eton House, 18-24 Paradise Road, Richmond, Surrey, TW9 1SR

© 2015 Harlequin Books S.A.

Special thanks and acknowledgement are given to Cara Colter for her contribution to The Vineyards of Calanetti series.

ISBN: 978-0-263-25173-9

23-1015

Harlequin (UK) Limited's policy is to use papers that are natural, renewable and recyclable products and made from wood grown in sustainable forests. The logging and manufacturing processes conform to the legal environmental regulations of the country of origin.

Print_ ___ _____ __ ____
by CI _ _____

Cara Colter shares her life in beautiful British Columbia, Canada, with her husband, nine horses and one small Pomeranian with a large attitude. She loves to hear from readers, and you can learn more about her and contact her through Facebook.

To the team of editors and writers who worked so tirelessly on this series:

I am proud to have been a part of it.

I stand in awe of your creative brilliance.

CHAPTER ONE

CONNOR BENSON AWOKE with a start. It was dark. And it was hot. Where was he? Somalia? Iraq? Afghanistan? Wherever he was, it was so secret, even his mother didn't know.

That feeling tickled along his spine, a sense of imminent danger. It brought him to red alert. Still not knowing exactly where he was, he was suddenly extremely focused, on nothing and everything. Each of his senses was so wide-open it was almost painful.

The tick of a clock somewhere in the room seemed explosively loud. Connor could feel the faint prickliness of the bedclothes against his naked skin, and he could feel a single bead of sweat slide down his temple. He could smell the residue of his own sweat and aftershave, and farther away, coffee.

Another sound rose above the ticking of the clock and the deliberate steadiness of his own breathing. It was a whispery noise just beyond this room, and as unobtrusive as it was, Connor knew it was that sound that had woken him. It was the sneaky sound of someone trying to be very quiet.

Connor tossed off the thin blanket and was out of the bed in one smooth movement, from dead asleep to warrior alert in the time it took to draw a single breath. The floor was stone under his bare feet and he moved across it soundlessly. His nickname on his SEAL team had been "the Cat."

At six foot five, every inch of that honed muscle, his comrades didn't mean a friendly house cat, either.

They meant the kind of cat that lived like a shadow on the edge of the mountains, or in the deepest forests and the darkest jungles, where men were afraid to go. They meant the kind of cat that was big and strong and silent. They meant the kind of cat that could go from relaxed to ready to pounce in the blink of an eye. They meant the kind of cat that had deadly and killing instincts.

Those instincts guided Connor across the room on silent feet to the door that had a faint sliver of light slipping under it. His movement was seemingly unhurried, but his muscles were tensing with lethal purpose.

Though most people would have detected no scent at all, when he paused on his side of the door, just under the aroma of coffee, Connor could taste the air. He *knew* someone was on the other side of that door. He also knew they were not directly in front of it—a hint of a shadow told him someone was to the left of the door. It was not a guess. His muscles tautened even more. His heart began to pick up the tempo. Not with fear. No, there was no fear at all. What he felt was anticipation.

Adrenaline coursed through his veins as Connor flung open the door.

He was nearly blinded by sunlight in the hallway, but it didn't stop his momentum. He hurled himself left, at the figure, back to him, rising from a crouch beside his door well. His hands closed around slender shoulders.

Slender?

A scent he had not noticed before tickled his nostrils. *Perfume?*

His mind screamed, *Abort!* It was too late not to touch, but not too late to temper his considerable strength. Instead of taking the culprit to the ground, he used the existing momentum to spin the person skulking outside his door toward him. The force of the spin caused a stumble, and as luscious curves came in full contact with him, Connor recognized the truth.

Her.

Connor stared down into the eyes of the woman he had just attacked, stunned. It wasn't that women couldn't be bad guys, but this woman so obviously was not. He cursed under his breath, and her eyes, already wide, widened more.

She seemed to realize she was still pressed, full length, against him, and she pushed herself away.

"Ma sei pazzo!" she said. Her voice was gorgeous, husky and rich, a note of astonishment in it that matched the astonishment in her huge, wide eyes. She definitely had the most beautiful eyes he had ever seen.

Eyes that, at the moment, were wide with shock. Now that she had pushed away from him, her hand went to the sweet swell of her breast, and he could see where her pulse beat wildly in the delicate column of her throat.

Connor, ever the soldier, and still in that place of heightened awareness, took in every exquisite detail of her. She had long, dark hair, luxuriously thick and straight, that was capturing the incredible morning light that poured in through the arched windows of the hallway they were in. Her hair fell in a shimmering waterfall of dark chocolate past slender bare shoulders.

At least a foot shorter than he was, the woman had on a bright, flower-patterned dress. It was sleeveless and accentuated the lovely litheness of her figure. The dress was pinched by a narrow belt at a tiny waist and then the skirt flared out in a way that made him able to picture her dancing, that skirt flying around her. She had sandals on her delicate feet, her toenails painted a soft shade of pink.

Her coloring looked as if it was naturally pale, but golden from the sun. Her skin was flawless. *Ma sei pazzo.* It occurred to Connor he was not in Iraq. Or Somalia. Not Afghanistan, either.

He cringed inwardly at his mistake. "Jeez," he said, out loud. "I'm in Italy."

It all came back to him. He was in a small town in Tuscany on a puffball mission for Itus Security, the company he and his friend Justin had started after Justin's injury had made them both leave the US Navy SEALs, though for different reasons.

"Sì, Italia."

Yes, he was in Italy. And it was not a secret. Everyone in his world, including his mother, knew exactly where he was. In fact, his mother had been thrilled for him when he had told her the Tuscan village of Monte Calanetti was on his itinerary.

Italy? she had said breathlessly. She had looked at him with ridiculously hope-filled eyes and said softly, *The land of amore.*

If anybody had a right to be soured by love, it was his mom, who'd had him when she was barely sixteen and had suffered through all it meant to be a single mother at that age.

In addition, Connor knew exactly what his years of service in the world's trouble spots and danger zones had made him. He knew only a mother could look at a battle-hardened and emotionally bereft specimen like Connor and hope love was in his future.

"Do you speak English?" he asked the young woman. He kept his voice deliberately quiet, threading it with calm. The woman was still watching him silently, with those doe-like eyes, and just like a doe, was ready to bolt at one more wrong move from him.

She nodded warily.

He deserved her wariness. "Sorry, ma'am," he muttered. "I seem to have a bit of jet lag. I was disoriented."

"You came out of that room as if you expected an assassin!" she said accusingly, finding her voice.

No point sharing with her that was exactly what he had been expecting. There was something sweetly angelic in her face that suggested that would be entirely foreign to her world.

Looking at her, it did occur to Connor that if a man was not completely hardened to life, the woman in front of him—beautiful and angelic, yet still sensual in an understated way—might have made his thoughts go to *amore*.

"I said I was sorry. I hope I didn't hurt you." Connor had tempered his strength, but even so, she was right. He had come out of that room expecting trouble of one variety or another, and his force had been substantial.

"No. No, I'm not hurt," she insisted hastily, but then she folded her hands over her shoulders and rubbed them.

He stepped in close to her again, aware of her scent

intensifying. He carefully pried her hands off her shoulders. She stopped breathing, staring up at him, her hands drifting to her sides.

If he was not mistaken, he stopped breathing, too, as he leaned in close and inspected the golden surface of her shoulders for damage. He stepped back and started to breathe again.

"There are no marks on your shoulders," he said quietly. "You won't be bruised."

"I told you I was fine."

He shrugged, looked away from her, ran a hand through his hair and then looked back. "I just thought I should make sure. What does that mean? What you said to me? *Ma sei pazzo?*"

"It's an exclamation of surprise," she said.

It was her eyes sliding away from him that alerted him to the fact there might be more to it than that, so he lifted an eyebrow at her, waiting.

"Specifically," she said, looking back at him, "it means *are you crazy?*" She was unrepentant, tilting her chin at him.

"Ah. Well. I can't really argue with that, or blame you for thinking it."

His senses were beginning to stand down, but even so, the woman's scent tickled his nostrils. Her perfume was very distinctive—it had an exotic, spicy scent that was headier than any perfume he had ever smelled. He looked once more into the liquid pools of green and gold that were her eyes and recognized a weak inclination to fall toward those pools of light and grace, calm and decency.

Instead, he reminded himself who he really was. He let his thoughts travel away from her and down the road to the sense of failure that traveled with him these days, around the globe, like a shadow.

What had just happened was precisely why he'd had to leave the only world he had known for nearly two decades. He'd started making mistakes. It was why he had left the SEALs when Justin had. In his line of work, mistakes demanded a price be paid. Often it was a huge price. Sometimes it was an irrevocable one.

And he knew, from firsthand experience, it was even harder when it was someone other than yourself who paid the price for your mistakes.

"It's all right," she stammered, and he realized she had seen something in his face that he would have preferred she hadn't seen.

And of course it was not all right to be attacking innocent civilians. Now that the initial shock had worn off, Connor could see she was trembling slightly, like a leaf in a breeze, and her eyes were wide on him. Her gaze flitted down the length of him, and then flew back to his face, shocked.

He glanced down at himself.

"Sheesh," he muttered. "Would that be adding insult to injury?"

"I told you I wasn't injured," she stammered. "And I'm not sure what you mean by insulted."

"It's an expression," he clarified, "just like your *ma sei pazzo*. It means on top of giving you a good scare, I've embarrassed you with my state of undress."

Her eyes flew to his state of undress, again, and then back up to his face. She confirmed that she was indeed embarrassed when her blush deepened to crimson.

He would probably be blushing himself if he had any scrap of modesty remaining in himself, but he did not. He'd lived in the rough company of men his entire adult life and guys had a tendency to be very comfortable in their underwear.

Still, he was very aware that he was standing in this beautiful woman's presence outfitted only in army-green boxer briefs that covered only the essential parts of himself.

Despite the circumstances he found himself in, he was reluctantly charmed that she was blushing so profusely it looked as if she had been standing with her face too close to a robust fire.

"Sorry, I'm disoriented," he said again, by way of explanation. "I've been on an insane schedule. I was in—" he had to think about it for a second "—Azerbaijan yesterday putting a security team in place for the World Food Conference. And the day before that...ah, never mind."

She struggled to regain her composure. "You're Signor Benson, of course."

"Connor, please."

"I'm sorry I was not here to greet you last night. Nico told me you would arrive late." Her English, he noted, was perfect, the accent lilting and lovely in the background of the precisely formed words. Her voice itself was enchanting, husky and unconsciously sensual. Or maybe it was that accent that just made everything she said seem insanely pleasing. Connor was willing to bet she could read a grocery list and sound sexy. He felt, crazily, as if he could listen to her all day.

"I think it was close to three in the morning when I arrived."

She nodded. "Nico told me your arrival would be very late. That's why I closed the shutters when I prepared your room. To block out the light so you could sleep in. I was just leaving you something to eat this morning. I have to be at work in a few minutes."

"Schoolteacher?" he guessed.

She frowned at him. "Nico told you that?"

"No, I guessed."

"But how?"

"You just have that look about you."

"Is this a good thing or a bad thing to have this look about me?"

He shrugged, realizing he shouldn't have said anything. It was part of what he did. He was very, very good at reading people. He could almost always tell, within seconds, what kind of lifestyle someone had, the general direction of their career paths and pursuits, if not the specifics. Sometimes his life and the lives of others depended on that ability to accurately read and sort details. This was something she, living here in her sheltered little village in Italy, did not have to know.

"I still do not understand if it is a good thing or a bad thing to have this schoolteacher look about me," she pressed.

"A good thing," he assured her.

She looked skeptical.

"You're very tidy. And organized." He gestured at the tray beside his door. "And thoughtful, closing the shutters so I could sleep in. So, I figured some profession that required compassion. A teacher. Or a nurse. But the dress made me lean toward teacher. Your students probably like bright colors."

He was talking *way* too much, which he put down as another aftereffect of jet lag. She was nibbling her lip, which was plump as a plum, and frowning at him.

"It's like a magician's trick," she said, not approvingly.

"No, really, it's something everyone can do. It's just observing details."

She looked as if she was considering having another long, hard look at all of him, as if he had invited her to play a parlor game. But then, wisely, she decided against it.

Connor glanced at the tray set so carefully by his door, more proof of a tidy, organized, caring personality. It was loaded with a carafe of coffee and rolls still steaming from the oven. There was a small glass jar of homemade preserves and a large orange.

The fact he had guessed right about her being a teacher did not alleviate his annoyance with himself over this other stupid error. He'd heard someone sneaking around, all right—sneaking his breakfast into place so as not to disturb him.

"Thank you," he said, "for taking me in on such short notice. I should have made arrangements for a place to stay before I arrived, but I didn't think it was going to be a problem. When I researched it, there seemed to be lots of accommodations in the village."

"There are many accommodations here, and usually there would be more availability," she offered. "Today looks as if it will be an exception, but it is usually not overly hot in May. That makes it the preferred month for weddings in Tuscany."

Weddings.

"Ah, signor," she said, and the fright had finally melted from her and a tiny bit of playfulness twinkled in her eyes. "You are right! Sometimes you can see things about people that they don't tell you."

"Such as?"

"Even though you are here to help with the royal wedding, you do not like weddings."

What he didn't like was being read as easily as he read other people. Had he actually encouraged this observation? He hoped not.

"What makes you say that?" he asked.

"Just a little flinch," she said, and for a moment he thought she was going to reach over and touch his face, but she thought better of it and touched the line of her own jaw instead. "Right here."

Her fright had brought out his protective instincts, even though he had caused it. Her power of observation, brought out with just the tiniest of suggestions, was somehow far more dangerous to him. He noticed she had ignored his invitation to call him by his first name.

"I'm not exactly here to help with the wedding," he said, just in case she had the absurd notion he was going to be arranging flowers or something. "My company, Itus, will be providing the security. I'm going to do reconnaissance this month so all the pieces will be in place for when we come back at the end of July. Though you are right on one count—weddings are just about my least favorite thing," he admitted gruffly.

"You've experienced many?" She raised an eyebrow at him, and again he felt danger in the air. Was she teasing him, ever so slightly?

"Unfortunately, I have experienced many weddings," Connor said.

"Unfortunately?" she prodded. "Most people would see a wedding as a celebration of all that is good in life. Love. Hope. Happy endings."

"Humph," he said, not trying to hide his cynicism. Over his years in the SEALs, lots of his team members had gotten married. And with predictably disastrous results. The job was too hard on the women who were left behind to fret and worry about their husbands. Or worse, who grew too lonely and sought someone else's company.

He was not about to share his personal revelations about the fickle nature of love with her, though. Around a woman like her—who saw weddings as symbols of love and hope and happy endings—it was important to reveal nothing personal, to keep everything on a professional level.

"My company, Itus Security," Connor said, veering deliberately away from his personal experiences, "has handled security for some very high-profile nuptials. As a security detail, weddings are a nightmare. Too many variables. Locations. Guests. Rehearsals. Photos. Dinners. And that's before you factor in Bridezilla and her entourage."

"Bridezilla?" she asked, baffled.

Some things did not translate. "Bride turned monster over her big day."

His hostess drew in a sharp breath. "I do not think you will find Christina Rose like that," she said sternly. "She is an amazing woman who is sweet and generous and totally committed to her country."

Connor cocked his head at her. He was hopeful for any inside information that might prove useful to the security detail. "You know her?"

She looked embarrassed all over again, but this time there was annoyance in it, too. "Of course not. But her husband-to-be, Prince Antonio de l'Accardi, is a member of a much-loved royal family. That has made her a very famous woman. I have read about her."

"Well, don't believe half of what you read. No, don't believe *any* of what you read."

"So, you don't believe in weddings, and you are a cynic, also."

"Cynic is an understatement. I think you might have picked up I was a bit of a battle-hardened warrior when I treated you like an assassin instead of just saying good morning like a normal person would have," he said.

There. Letting her know, right off the bat, he was not a normal person.

"Well, I choose to believe Christina Rose is everything she appears to be." Her eyes rested on him, and he heard, without her saying a word, *And so are you.*

Connor lifted a shoulder, noting that his hostess had a bit of fire underneath that angelic first impression. It didn't matter to him what the future princess's personality was. It would be her big day, laden with that thing he was most allergic to, emotion. And it didn't matter to him what his hostess's personality was, either.

"Believe me," he muttered, "Christina Rose will find a million ways, intentional or not, to make my life very difficult."

But that was why he was here, nearly two months early, in the Tuscan village of Monte Calanetti. Not to save the world from bad guys, but to do risk assessment, to protect some royals he had never heard of from a country he had also never heard of—Halenica—as they exchanged their vows.

That was his mission. The lady in front of him could fill his life with complications, too, if he was not the disciplined ex-soldier that he was. As it was, he was not going to be sidetracked by a little schoolteacher in a flowered dress, no matter how cute she was.

And she was plenty cute.

But if that proved a problem, he would just keep his ear to the ground for another place to stay. He'd survived some pretty rough living arrangements. He wasn't fussy.

"Thank you for breakfast," he said curtly, moving into emotional lockdown, work mode. "Please thank your mother for providing me with a place to stay on such short notice, signorina."

"My mother?"

"Signora Rossi?"

A tiny smile, pained, played across the beautiful fullness of her lips.

"No, signor. I am Signora Rossi. Please call me Isabella."

So he had made another mistake. A small one, but a mistake, nonetheless. Looking at Isabella, after she made that statement, he could see, despite his finely honed powers of observation, he'd been wrong about her. She was not as young as her slender figure and flawless skin had led him to believe. She might have been in her thirties, not her twenties.

No wonder Justin had him on wedding duty. Connor was just making mistakes all over the place.

And no wonder Justin had said to Connor, when he gave him this assignment, "Hey, when is the last time you had a holiday? Take your time in Monte Calanetti. Enjoy the sights. Soak up some sun. Drink some wine. Fall in love."

Justin really had no more right to believe in love than he himself did, but his friend was as bad as his mother in the optimism department. Justin had even hinted there was a woman friend in his life.

"And for goodness' sake," Justin had said, "take a break from swimming. *What* are you training for, anyway?"

But Justin, his best friend, his comrade in arms, his brother, was part of the reason Connor swam. Justin, whose whole life had been changed forever because of a mistake. One made by Connor.

So giving up swimming was out of the question, but at least, Connor told himself grimly, he wouldn't be falling in love with the woman in front of him. After having felt her pressed against him, and after having been so aware of her in every way this morning, it was a relief to find out she was married.

"*Grazie*, Signora Rossi," he said, trying out clumsy Italian, "for providing me with accommodation on such short notice. You can reassure your husband that I will not begin every morning by attacking you."

His attempt at humor seemed to fall as flat as his Italian. He spoke three languages well, and several more not so well. Connor knew, from his international travels, that most people warmed to someone who attempted to use their language, no matter how clumsy the effort.

But his hostess looked faintly distressed.

And then he realized he had made his worst mistake of the day, and it wasn't that he had accidentally propositioned her by mispronouncing a word.

Because Isabella Rossi said to him, with quiet dignity, "I'm afraid my beloved husband, Giorgio, is gone, signor. I am a widow."

Connor wanted to tell her that she of all people, then,

should not believe a wedding was a symbol of love and hope and happy endings.

But he considered himself a man who was something of an expert in the nature of courage, and he had to admit he reluctantly admired her ability to believe in hope and happy endings when, just like his mother, she had obviously had plenty of evidence to the contrary.

"I'm sorry for your loss," he offered, grudgingly.

"My husband has been gone six years, and I miss him still," she said softly.

Connor felt the funniest stir of something he did not like. Was it envy? Did he envy the man this woman had loved so deeply?

Stupid jet lag. It seemed to have opened up a part of him that normally would have been under close guard, buttoned down tight. Thoroughly annoyed with himself and his wayward thoughts in the land of *amore*, Connor turned from Signora Isabella Rossi, scooped up the tray and went into his room. Just before he shut the door, her voice stopped him.

"I provide a simple dinner at around seven for my guests, when I have them," she said, suddenly all business. "If you could let me know in the mornings if you are requiring this service, I would appreciate it."

Connor, a man who was nothing if not deeply instinctual, knew there was some dangerous physical awareness between them, a primal man-woman thing. Eating her food and sitting across a table from her would not be an option.

On the other hand, he did not know the lay of the land in the village, and he would have to eat somewhere today until he figured that out. Besides, Isabella Rossi had shown she was unusually astute at reading people.

He did not want her to know he perceived her as such a threat that he was willing to go hungry rather than spend more time with her.

"Thank you," he said, keeping his tone carefully neutral. "That would be perfect for tonight. I hope the rest of your day goes better than it began, signora."

CHAPTER TWO

ISABELLA STOOD IN the hallway, feeling frozen to the spot and looking at Connor Benson, balancing the tray of food she had provided for him on the jutting bone of one very sexy, very exposed hip. She felt as if she had been run over by a truck.

Which, in a sense, she had. Not that Connor Benson looked anything like a truck. But she had been virtually run down by him, had felt the full naked strength of him pressed against her own body. It had been a disconcerting encounter in every way.

His scent was still tickling her nostrils, and she was taken aback by how much she liked the exquisitely tangy smell of a man in the morning.

Now she'd gone and offered him dinner. Everyone in town knew she occasionally would take in a lodger for a little extra money. She always offered her guests dinner. Why was it suddenly a big deal?

It was because her guests were usually retired college professors or young travelers on a budget. She not had a guest quite like Connor Benson before. In fact, it would be quite safe to say she had never met a man like Connor Benson before.

"I hope my day goes better, too," she muttered,

and then added in Italian, "but it is not looking hopeful."

This man in her house, who stood before her unselfconscious in his near nakedness, was the antithesis of everything Isabella's husband, Giorgio, had been.

In fact, Isabella had grown up in Florence and walked nearly daily by the Palazzo Vecchio, where the replica of Michelangelo's statue *David* stood. The statue represented a perfection of male physique that had filled the frail Giorgio with envy, and at which she had scoffed.

"Such men do not exist," she had reassured Giorgio. She had swept her hand over the square. "Look. Show me one who looks like this."

And then they would dissolve into giggles at the fact the modern Italian male was quite far removed from Michelangelo's vision.

And yet this nearly naked man standing in the doorway of the room she had let to him made Isabella uncomfortably aware that not only did perfection of male physique exist, it awakened something in her that she had never quite felt before.

That thought made her feel intensely guilty, as if she was being disloyal to her deceased husband, and so she rationalized the way she was feeling.

It was because she had been pulled so unexpectedly against the hard length of him that her awareness was so intense, she told herself.

Her defenses had been completely down. She had just been innocently putting his breakfast beside his door when he had catapulted out of it and turned her around, making her stumble into him.

And now her whole world felt turned around, because she had endured a forced encounter with the heated silk of his skin, stretched taut over those sleek muscles. She had been without the company of a man for a long time. This kind of reaction to a complete stranger did not reflect in any way on her relationship with Giorgio! It was the absence of male companionship that had obviously made her very sensitive to physical contact.

It didn't help that Connor Benson was unbelievably, sinfully gorgeous. Not just the perfection of his male form, but his face was extraordinary. His very short cropped light brown hair only accentuated the fact that he had a face that would make people—especially women people—stop in their tracks.

He had deep blue eyes, a straight nose, high cheekbones, a jutting chin.

He was the epitome of strength. She thought of his warrior response to her outside his door, that terrifying moment when she had been spun around toward him, the look on his face, as if it was all *normal* for him.

There was something exquisitely dangerous about Connor Benson.

The thoughts appalled her. They felt like a betrayal of Giorgio, whom she had loved, yes, with all her heart.

"I've become pathetic," Isabella muttered to herself, again in Italian. A pathetic young widow, whose whole life had become her comfy house and the children she taught. She found love in the mutual adoration she and her students had for each other.

Why did it grate on her that her houseguest had known she was a schoolteacher? What would she have wanted him to think she was?

Something, she realized reluctantly, just a little more exciting.

"I'm sorry?" Connor said.

She realized she had mumbled about her self-diagnosis of being pathetic out loud, though thankfully, in Italian. She realized her face was burning as if the inner hunger he had made her feel was evident to him.

Well, it probably was. Men like this—powerfully built, extraordinarily handsome, oozing self-confidence—were used to using their looks to charm women, to having their wicked way. They were not above using their amazing physical charisma to make conquests.

He'd already told her how he felt about weddings, which translated to an aversion to commitment. Even she, for all that she had married young and lived a sheltered life, knew that a man like this one standing before her, so at ease with near nakedness, spelled trouble, in English or Italian, and all in capital letters, too.

This man could never be sweetly loyal and uncomplicated. Connor Benson had warned her. He was not normal. He was cynical and hard and jaded. She could see that in the deep blue of his eyes, even if he had not admitted it to her, which he had. She would have been able to see it, even before he had challenged her to look for details to know things about people that they were not saying.

"I said be careful of the shower," she blurted out.

That exquisite eyebrow was raised at her, as if she had said something suggestive.

"It isn't working properly," she said in a rush.

"Oh?"

"I'm having it fixed, but the town's only plumber is busy with the renovations at the palazzo. I have to wait for him. Now, I'm late for work," she choked out, looking at her wristwatch to confirm that. Her wrist was naked—she had not put on her watch this morning. She stared at the blank place on her wrist a moment too long, then hazarded another look at Mr. Benson.

The sensuous line of Connor Benson's mouth lifted faintly upward. The hunger that unfurled in her belly made her think of a tiger who had spotted raw meat after being on a steady diet of flower petals.

Isabella turned and fled.

And if she was not mistaken, the soft notes of a faintly wicked chuckle followed her before Connor Benson shut his bedroom door.

Outside her house, Isabella noted the day was showing promise of unusual heat. She told herself that was what was making her face feel as if it was on fire as she hurried along the twisted, cobbled streets of Monte Calanetti to the primary school where she taught.

Yes, it was the heat, not the memory of his slow drawl, the way *ma'am* had slipped off his lips. He sounded like one of the cowboys in those old American Western movies Giorgio had enjoyed so much when he was bedridden.

Really? The way Connor Benson said *ma'am* should have been faintly comical. How come it was anything but? How come his deep voice and his slow drawl had been as soft as a silk handkerchief being trailed with deliberate seduction over the curve of her neck?

She thought of Connor Benson's attempt at Italian when he had tried to assure that her mornings would not begin with an attack. That accent should have made that comical, too, but it hadn't been. She had loved it that he had tried to speak her language.

"*Buongiorno*, Signora Rossi. You look beautiful this morning!"

Isabella smiled at the butcher, who had come out of his shop to unwind his awning, but once she was by him, she frowned. She passed him every morning. He always said good morning. But he had never added that she looked beautiful before.

It was embarrassing. Her encounter with Connor Benson this morning had lasted maybe five minutes. How was it that it had made her feel so uncomfortable, so hungry and so alive? And so much so that she was radiating it for others to see?

"Isabella," she told herself sternly, using her best schoolteacher voice, "that is quite enough."

But it was not, apparently, quite enough.

Because she found herself thinking that she had not told him anything about his accommodations. She could do that over dinner tonight.

Isabella was *never* distracted when she was teaching. She loved her job and her students and always felt totally present and engaged when she was with the children. Her job, really, was what had brought her back from the brink of despair after Giorgio's death.

But today, her mind wandered excessively to what kind of meal she would cook for her guest.

Candles, of course, would be ridiculous, wouldn't they? And they would give the wrong message entirely.

She had not made her mother's recipe of *lasagne verdi al forno* for years. Food, and finally even the smell of cooking, had made Giorgio sick. Isabella was shocked at how much she *wanted* to cook, to prepare a beautiful meal. Yes, lasagna, and a fresh loaf of ciabatta bread, a lovely red wine. School in many places in Italy, including Monte Calanetti, ran for six days instead of five, but the days were short, her workday over at one. That gave her plenty of time to cook the extravagant meal.

So, on the way home from school, she stopped at the grocer's and the bakery and picked up everything she needed. She had several beautiful bottles of wine from Nico's Calanetti vineyard that she had never opened. Wine opened was meant to be drunk. It had seemed silly and wasteful to open a whole bottle for herself.

From the deep silence in the house, Isabella knew that Connor was not there when she arrived home. Already, it occurred to her she knew his scent, and her nose sniffed the air for him.

She began unloading the contents of her grocery bags in her homey little kitchen. She considered putting on a fresh dress. One that would make him rethink his assessment of her as a schoolteacher. It was then that Isabella became aware that it wasn't just the idea of cooking that was filling her with this lovely sense of purpose.

It was the idea of cooking for a man.

She stopped what she was doing and sat down heavily at her kitchen table.

"Isabella," she chided herself, "you are acting as if this is a date. It's very dangerous. You are out of your league. You will only get hurt if you play games with a man like Connor Benson."

She was also aware she felt faintly guilty, as if this intense awareness of another man—okay, she would call a spade a spade, she was attracted to Connor Benson— was a betrayal of the love she had had with Giorgio.

Everyone kept telling her it was time to move on, and

in her head she knew they were right. Six years was a long time for a woman to be alone. If she did not make a move soon, she would probably never have the children she longed for.

But no matter what her head said, her heart said no. Her heart had been hurt enough for this lifetime. Her heart did not want to fall in love ever again.

Slowly, feeling unreasonably dejected, she put everything away instead of leaving it out to cook with. She would bring anything that would spoil to school tomorrow and give it to Luigi Caravetti. He was from a single-parent family, and she knew his mother was struggling right now.

She opened a can of soup, as she would have normally done, and broke the bread into pieces. She would invite Connor to share this humble fare with her when he arrived. She needed to go over things with him, make clear what she did and did not provide.

It wasn't very much later that he came in the front door. She felt she was ready. Or as ready as a woman could ever be for a man like that.

"I have soup if you would like some," she called out formally.

"*Grazie*, that sounds great."

Isabella wished Connor would not try to speak Italian. It made her not want to be formal at all. It made her long to teach him a few words or phrases, to correct his pronunciation. She listened as he went up the stairs. She heard the shower turn on. Her mind went to the memory of touching that perfect body this morning, and something shivered along her spine. It was a warning. If she was smart there would be no language lessons with Connor Benson.

A little while later, he came into the kitchen. Oh, God. He was so big in this tiny room. It was as if he took up all the space. Her eyes felt as if they wanted to go anywhere but to him.

But where else could they go, when he was taking up all the space?

He was freshly showered. He had on a clean shirt. He smelled wonderful. His hair was dark and damp, and towel roughened. He had not shaved, so his whiskers were thick, and she could almost imagine how they would feel scraping across a woman's skin.

"I hope you don't expect homemade," she said. Her voice sounded like a croak.

"I didn't expect anything at all, ma'am."

There was that *ma'am* again, slow and steady, dragging across the back of her neck, drugging her senses.

"Isabella." Her voice sounded like a whisper. "Please, sit."

He took a seat at her table. It made her table seem ridiculous, as if it had been made to go in a dollhouse.

"Isabella," he said, as if he was trying it out. Her name came off his tongue like honey. She wished she had not invited him to call her by it.

"It smells good in here," he said conversationally and then looked around with interest. "It's quaint, exactly what I would expect an Italian kitchen to look like. That stone wall must be original to the house."

She felt tongue-tied but managed to squeak, "Don't be fooled by its charm. This house is three hundred years old. And it can be quite cranky."

"I think I noticed the crankiness in the shower just now," he said.

"I warned you about that." She did not want to be thinking about him in the shower, *again*.

"No big deal. Woke me up, though. The water was pouring out and then stopped, and then poured out again. I'll have a look at it for you, if you want."

"No," she said, proudly and firmly. She did not need to give herself the idea there was a man she could rely on to help her. "You are a guest in this house. I have already called the plumber, but I'm afraid with the renovation at the villa, my house is not a priority for him."

"I don't mind having a look at it."

Some longing shivered along her spine, which she straightened, instantly. "Signor, this house is three hundred years old. If you start looking at all the things wrong with it, I'm afraid you will not have time to do the job you came here to do. So, please, no, I can manage."

He looked faintly skeptical about her ability—or maybe the ability of any woman who was alone—to manage a three-hundred-year-old house, but wisely, he said nothing.

She dished out soup from the stove, gestured to the bread, took a seat across from him. She felt as if she was sitting rigidly upright, like a recent graduate from charm school.

"Relax," he said softly, "I won't bite you."

She was appalled that her discomfort was so transparent.

"Bite me?" she squeaked. She was also appalled at the picture that sprang to mind. And that it involved the cranky shower!

"It's American slang. It means I won't hurt you."

Wouldn't he? It seemed to her Connor Benson was

the kind of man who hurt women without meaning to, and she didn't mean by attacking them outside the bedroom door in the morning, either. He was the kind of man who could make a woman think heated thoughts or dream naive and romantic dreams that he would not stick around to fulfill.

"This morning excepted," he growled.

"You didn't hurt me!"

"Not physically. I can tell you're nervous around me now."

She could feel the color climbing up her face. She wanted to deny that, and couldn't. Instead, she changed the subject. "How was your day?"

"Uneventful," he said. "I met with Nico and had an initial look around. It's a very beautiful village."

"Thank you. I like it very much." Her voice sounded stilted. What was wrong with her? Well, she'd married young. Giorgio had been her only boyfriend. She was not accustomed to this kind of encounter. "Would you like wine?"

"I'm not much of a drinker."

"You might like to try this one. It's one of Nico's best, from his Calanetti vineyard."

"All right," he said. She suspected he had said yes to help her relax, not because he really wanted the wine.

The wine was on the counter. Isabella was glad her back was to him, because she struggled with getting it open. But finally, she was able to turn back and pour him a glass. She could feel a dewy bead of sweat on her forehead. She blew on her bangs in case they were sticking.

He sipped it carefully as she sat back down. "It's really good. What would you say? *Buono?*"

"Yes, *buono*. Nico's vineyard is one of the pride and joys of our region." She took a sip of wine. And then another. It occurred to her neither of them were eating the soup.

Suddenly, it all felt just a little too cozy. Perhaps she should not have insisted on the wine. She took rather too large a gulp and set down her glass.

It was time to get down to business. "I will provide a simple supper like this, Mondays to Saturdays, the same days that I work. On Sunday, I do not. I provide breakfast every day, but I don't usually leave a tray by the bedroom door."

"I wouldn't risk that again, either," he said drily. She had the uncomfortable feeling he was amused by her.

"It's not a hotel," she said sternly, "so I don't make beds."

"Understood." Did he intentionally say that with a military inflection, as if he was a lower rank being addressed by a superior? Was he perceiving her as bossy?

Given how she wanted to keep everything formal between them, wouldn't that be a good thing?

"I also do not provide laundry service." Thank goodness. She could not even imagine touching his intimate things. "I have a washing machine through that door that you are welcome to use. There is a laundry service in the village if you prefer. Except for sheets, which I do once a week. I provide fresh towels every day."

"I can do my own sheets, thanks."

"All right. Yes. That's fine. The common areas of the house are yours to use if you want to watch television or cook your own meals, or put things in the refrigerator."

The thought of him in her space made her take another rather large and fortifying sip of the wine.

"I don't watch television," he told her, "and I'm accustomed to preparing my own meals. I don't want you to feel put out by me. I can tell it is a bit of an imposition for you having a man in your house."

He was toying with the stem of his wineglass. He put it to his lips and took a long sip, watching her.

She tilted her chin at him, took a sip of her own wine. "What would make you say that? It's no imposition at all, Signor Benson."

Her heart was beating hard in her throat. He shrugged and lifted his wineglass to his lips again, watched her over the rim.

She might as well not have bothered denying it was any kind of imposition for her. She could feel her discomfort snaking along her spine, and he was not the kind of man you could hide things from.

"Connor, please," he said. "We're not very formal where I come from."

"Connor," she agreed. He had caught on that she was being too formal. Didn't he know it would protect them both? But she said his name anyway, even though it felt as if she was losing ground fast. She was using his first name. It felt as though she was agreeing, somehow, to dance with the devil.

But the question was, was the devil in him, or was it in her?

"And where are you from?" she asked. This was to prove to him she was not at all formal and stuffy and could hold a polite conversation with the best of them. She hoped it would not appear as if she was desperately eager for details about him, which she was not! She still had not touched her soup. Neither had he.

"I'm from Texas," he said.

"I thought the accent was like that of a cowboy."

He laughed at that. His laughter was deep and engaging, relaxing some of the constant hardness from his face, and she found herself staring at him.

"Ma'am—"

"Isabella," she reminded him.

"Isabella—"

Him saying her name, in that drawl, made her feel the same as if she had drunk a whole bottle of wine from the Calanetti vineyard instead of taken a few sips out of her glass.

Well, actually, her glass was empty, and so was his. He noticed, and tipped the wine out over both their glasses.

"Most people hear that drawl and automatically lower my intelligence by twenty points or so."

"I can tell you are a very intelligent man," she said seriously.

"I was just trying to make the point that regional accents can lead to judgments in the United States. Like you thinking I'm a cowboy. I'm about the farthest thing from a cowboy that you'll ever see."

"Oh! I thought everybody from Texas was a cowboy."

He laughed again. "You and the rest of the world. I grew up in a very poor neighborhood in Corpus Christi, which is a coastal city. I started picking up a bit of work at the shipyards when I was about eleven, and occasionally cattle would come through, but that's the closest I came to any real cowboys."

"Eleven?" she said, horrified. "That is very young to be working."

Something in his expression became guarded. He

lifted a shoulder. "I was big for my age. No one asked how old I was."

"But why were you working at eleven?" she pressed.

For a moment, he looked as though he might not answer. Then he said quietly, "My mom was a single parent. It was pretty hand-to-mouth at times. I did what I could to help."

"Was your mom a widow?" she asked. She and Giorgio had not had children, though she had wanted to, even with Giorgio's prognosis. Now she wondered, from the quickly veiled pain in Connor's face, if that wouldn't have been a selfish thing, indeed, to try and raise a child or children without the benefit of a father.

"No," he said gruffly. "She wasn't a widow. She found herself pregnant at sixteen and abandoned by my father, whom she would never name. Her own family turned their backs on her. They said she brought shame on them by being pregnant."

"Your poor mother. Her own family turned away from her?" She thought of her family's reaction to the news she was going to marry Giorgio.

Life has enough heartbreak, her mother had said. *You have to invite one by marrying a dying man?*

Isabella could have pointed out to her mother that she should be an expert on heartbreak, since Isabella's father, with his constant infidelities, had broken her heart again and again and again. One thing about Giorgio? He was sweetly and strongly loyal. He would *never* be like that.

But it had seemed unnecessarily cruel to point that out to her mother, and so she had said nothing. And even though they were not happy with her choice, Isabella's family had not abandoned her. At least not physically.

Connor lifted a shoulder. "My mother is an amazing woman. She managed to keep me in line and out of jail through my wild youth. That couldn't have been easy."

"I'm sure it was not," Isabella said primly.

He grinned as if he had enjoyed every second of his wild youth. "Then I joined up."

"Joined up?"

"I joined the navy as soon as I was old enough."

"How old is that?"

"Seventeen."

She drew in her breath sharply.

"I served in the regular navy for two years, and then I was drawn to the SEALs."

"SEALs? What is this?"

"It stands for sea, air, land. It's an arm of the navy. Combat divers."

She could tell there was a bit more to it than what he was saying.

"And your mother? Was she heartbroken when you left her to join the military?"

He smiled wryly. "Not at all. Once she didn't have to expend all of her energy keeping me fed and in line, she married a rich guy she cleaned for. She seems deliriously happy and has produced a number of little half siblings for me."

"You adore them," Isabella guessed.

"Guilty."

"I'm glad your mother found happiness."

"Me, too, though her luck at love has made her think everyone should try it."

"And shouldn't they?" Isabella found herself asking softly.

He rolled his shoulders, and something shut down

in his face. "A man who seeks danger with the intensity and trajectory of a heat-seeking missile is not exactly a good bet in the love department. I've seen lots of my buddies go down that road. They come home cold and hard and damaged. Normal life and domestic duties seem unbearably dull after the adrenaline rush of action."

"That sounds very lonely," Isabella offered. *And like a warning*. Which she dutifully noted.

Connor studied her for a moment. Whatever had opened between them closed like a door slamming shut. He pushed back from the table abruptly. "Lonely? Not at all," he insisted coolly. "Thank you for dinner."

But he hadn't eaten dinner. After a moment, she cleared his uneaten soup off the table and cleaned up the kitchen.

Really, he had let her know in every way possible that any interest in him would not be appreciated.

After putting her small kitchen in order, she retreated to her office. She hesitated only a moment before she looked up navy seals on the internet. She felt guilty as sin doing it, but it did not stop her.

It was actually SEALs, she discovered, and they were not just combat divers. Sometimes called Frogmen because they were equally adept in the water or on land, they were one of the most elite, and secretive, commando forces in the world.

Only a very few men, of the hundreds who tried, could make it through their rigorous training program.

Isabella could tell from what she read that Connor had led a life of extreme adventure and excitement. He was, unfortunately, the larger-than-life kind of man who intrigued.

But he had told her with his own words what he was. Cold and hard and damaged. She was all done rescuing men.

Rescuing men? something whispered within her. *But you never felt you were rescuing Giorgio. Never. You did it all for love.*

But suddenly, sickeningly, she just wasn't that sure what her motives had been in marrying a man with such a terrible prognosis.

And fairly or not, looking at her husband and her marriage through a different lens felt as if it was entirely the fault of Connor Benson.

Even knowing she had been quite curious enough for one night, she decided to look up one more thing. She put in the name Itus Security. There was a picture of a very good-looking man named Justin Arnold. He was the CEO of the company. Beside his picture was one of Connor, who was the chief of operations. There was a list of services they offered, and a number of testimonials from very high-profile clients.

Their company was named after the Greek god of protection, Itus, and their mission statement was, "As in legend, Itus is sworn to protect the innocent from those who would do them harm."

Intrigued, she went and read the mythology around Itus. A while later, Isabella shut off the computer and squared her shoulders.

A month. Connor Benson was going to be under her roof for a month. After one day, she was feeling a terrible uneasiness, as if he could, with just his close proximity, change everything about her, even the way she looked at her past.

"I have to avoid him," she whispered to herself. And

it felt as if her very survival depended on that. She went to bed and set her alarm for very early. She could put out his breakfast things and leave the house without even seeing him tomorrow. There were always things to do at school. Right now, she was preparing her class to perform a song and skit at the annual spring fete, and she had props to make, simple costumes to prepare.

She had a feeling with Connor under her roof and her badly needing her schoolroom to hide out in and something to distract from the uncomfortable feelings she was experiencing, she was about to produce the best song and skit the good citizens of Monte Calanetti had ever seen!

CHAPTER THREE

CONNOR RETREATED TO his room, annoyed with himself. He was not generally so chatty. What moment of madness had made him say yes to that wine? And why had so very little of it made him feel so off balance?

Intoxicated.

Maybe it hadn't been the wine, but just sharing a simple meal with a beautiful woman in the quintessential Italian kitchen, with its old stone walls and its deep windows open to the breeze, that had brought his guard down.

He had told Isabella things he had not told people he'd worked with for twenty years. Justin knew about his hardscrabble upbringing on the wrong side of Corpus Christi, but no one else did.

The soft look in Isabella's eyes as he had told her had actually made him feel not that he wanted to tell her less, but as though he wanted to tell her more, as if his every secret would be safe with her.

As if he had carried a burden alone for way too long.

"Stop it," Connor snapped grimly at himself. He acknowledged he was tired beyond reason. You didn't unload on a woman like her. She, cute little schoolteacher that she was, wouldn't be able to handle it, to hold up to it. She'd buried her husband and that had sent her into full retreat. That's why someone so gorgeous was still unmarried six years later.

So there would be no more wine tastings over supper that loosened his tongue. No more suppers, in fact. Tomorrow, rested, his first duty would be to find a nice little place to eat supper every night.

With none of the local wines. That one tonight had seemed to have some beautiful Tuscan enchantment built right into it.

And if avoiding her at dinner proved to be not enough defense, he would go in search of another place to stay.

Not that he wanted to hurt her feelings.

"The Cat does not worry about people's feelings," he said, annoyed with himself. What he needed to do was deal with the exhaustion first. He peeled off his clothes and rolled into bed and slept, but not before grumpily acknowledging how hungry he was.

Connor awoke very early. He knew where he was this time. Again, he could hear the sounds of someone trying to be very quiet. He rolled over and looked at his bedside clock.

Five a.m. What the heck? He had the awful thought Isabella might have gotten up so early to make him breakfast. That made him feel guilty since he knew she had a full day of work to put in. Guilt was as unusual for him as worrying about feelings. Still, he needed to tell her not to bother.

He slipped on a pair of lightweight khakis and pulled a shirt over his head, and went downstairs to the kitchen.

She had her back to him.

"Isabella?"

She shrieked and turned, hand to her throat.

"Sorry," he said, "I've startled you again."

She dropped her hand from her throat. "No, you didn't," she said, even though it was more than obvious she had been very startled.

"Whatever. I think we've got to quit meeting like this."

The expression must have lost something in the translation, because she only looked annoyed as she turned back to the counter. "I just wasn't expecting you to be up so early."

"I wasn't expecting you up this early."

"I'm preparing for the spring festival," she said. "I have extra work to do at school."

"And extra work to do here, because of me?"

She glanced over her shoulder at him, and then looked quickly back at what she was doing, silent.

"I wanted to let you know not to fuss over me. A box of cereal on the table and some milk in the fridge is all I need in the morning. And coffee."

"I'll just show you how to use the coffeemaker then—"

He smiled. "I've made coffee on every continent and in two dozen different countries. I can probably figure it out."

She looked very pretty this morning. Her hair was scraped back in a ponytail. It made her look, again, younger than he knew her to be. The rather severe hairstyle also showed off the flawless lines of her face. She had on a different sleeveless dress, and her lips had a hint of gloss on them that made them look full and faintly pouty.

"All right then," she said, moving away from the coffeemaker. "So, no breakfast?"

"I don't need supper tonight, either. I'm kind of used to fending for myself."

And he did not miss the look of relief on her face.

So he added, "Actually, I probably won't need dinner any night. Instead of letting you know if I won't be here, how about if I let you know if I will?"

The look on her face changed to something else, quickly masked. It only showed him the wisdom of his decision. The little schoolteacher *wanted* someone to look after, and it would be better if she did not get any ideas that it was going to be him!

"I actually like to swim before I eat anything in the morning. This is the perfect time of day for swimming."

"It's not even light out."

"I know. That's what makes it perfect."

Whenever he could, Connor had begun every morning of his life for as long as he could remember with a swim. That affinity for the water had, in part, been what made him such a good fit for the SEALs. But when he left the SEALs, it was the only place he had found where he could outrun—or outswim, as it were—his many demons. Despite Justin's well-meaning advice to take a rest from it, Connor simply could not imagine life without the great stress relief and fitness provided by the water.

"You'll wake people up."

"Actually, Nico invited me to use the pool at his private garden in the villa, but I'd prefer to swim in the river."

"The river? It's very cold at this time of year."

"Perfect."

"And probably dangerous."

"I doubt it, but I already warned you about men like me and danger."

"Yes, you did," she whispered. "There's a place on the river where the boys swim in the summer. Would you like me to show it to you?"

"You aren't trying to protect me from danger, are you, Isabella?" he asked quietly.

"That would be a very foolish undertaking, I'm sure," she said, a little stain that confirmed his suspicions moving up her cheeks. "It's hard to find, the place where the boys swim. That's all."

"Yes, please, then, show it to me," he heard himself saying, though he had no doubt he could find good places to swim all by himself. He didn't want to hurt her pride. "Yes, I'd like that very much."

And so he found himself, with dawn smudging the air, painting the medieval skyline of Monte Calanetti in magnificence, walking down twisting streets not yet touched by the light beside Isabella to the river.

And enjoying the pink-painted splendor of the moment way more than he had a right to.

Isabella contemplated what moment of madness had made the words slip from her mouth that she would show Connor the way to the river. By getting up so early, she'd been trying to avoid him this morning.

Instead, she was walking through the still darkened streets of Monte Calanetti with him by her side.

And despite the pure madness that must have motivated her invitation, she would not have withdrawn it had she been given a chance. Because that moment, of unguarded impulse, had led to this one.

It was unexpectedly magical, the streets still dim, the

brilliance of the dawn that was staining the sky above them not yet reaching into the cracks and crevices of the town. The occasional light was blinking on in the houses and businesses they passed.

Isabella was intensely aware of how it felt to have this man walk beside her. He was so big, his presence commanding. He had gone back up to his room for a moment, and when he came down he carried a small black bag and had a white towel strung around his neck.

He had a way of walking—shoulders back, stride long and confident and calm—that gave a sense that he owned the earth and he knew it. Isabella had never felt unsafe in Monte Calanetti, but she was aware, walking beside him, of feeling immensely protected.

"I can't believe the light," he said. "I've never seen anything like it."

"It's part of what makes Tuscany famous, that quality of light. Artists throng here for that."

"How would you say this in Italian?" he said, making a sweeping gesture that took in everything—the amazing light and the twisting streets, still in shadows, dawn beginning to paint the rooflines in gold.

She thought a moment. Wasn't this exactly what she had longed to do and had decided was dangerous? The morning was too beautiful to fight with herself, to be petty about what she would and wouldn't give. She would give him a few words, nothing more.

"In tutto il suo splendore," Isabella said.

He repeated it, rolling the words off his tongue. Mixed with his drawl and the deepness of his voice, it was very charming.

"And the translation?" he asked her.

"In glory."

"Ah," he said. "Perfect."

After that neither of them attempted conversation, but the quiet was comfortable between them as they moved down the narrow streets. It gave a sense of walking toward the light as they left the last of the buildings behind and followed the road past the neat row of vineyards that followed the undulating green of the hills.

"There it is," she said, finally, pointing at the ribbon of river that had become visible up ahead of them. "When you come to the bridge, turn right and follow the river. You'll see a tire suspended on a rope where the boys swim."

"Thank you. *Grazie*."

"You're welcome." She should have turned back toward the town, but she did not. She recognized a reluctance to leave the simple glory of this moment behind. He must have felt that, too.

"Come with me." His voice was husky.

Come with him? Where?

"Swimming?" she asked. Her voice felt very squeaky. It felt as if he had asked something far graver. To tangle their lives together, to follow the thread of magic that had led them through the town in the enchanted light of early morning.

When he said nothing, she rushed to fill the silence. "I couldn't possibly. I don't know how to swim. The water will be cold. I—I—I don't have proper bathing wear."

"Don't come this far and not at least put your feet in the water."

It felt as if he was saying something else altogether. He was inviting her to wake up instead of sleeping. He was inviting her to really live instead of going through the motions of living.

"I have to tell you a little secret," she confessed. "I've never learned to swim because I am a little bit afraid of the water."

"All the more reason to say yes instead of no," he said.

It occurred to her Connor Benson was that kind of man. Being with him would challenge you to be more than you had been before. She had always been perfectly content with who she was before!

"Maybe another time," she said uneasily.

"Putting your feet in the water is the first step to swimming, to overcoming that fear."

"It's not as if it's a crippling fear—it's not as if it changes my life," she said defensively, already sorry she'd confided in him that she was afraid.

"Fear can be a gift," he said, his voice calm and low. "It can show you that you are in very real danger. But an irrational fear can change your life in ways you don't even understand. If you give in to it, it can expand. So, one day you're afraid of swimming, the next you're afraid of everything."

Did he see her as afraid of everything? And how much truth was there in that? She looked at the safe little world she had created for herself. Maybe, even if it was annoying, maybe he was right. She needed to stretch just a tiny bit out of her comfort zone.

What would it hurt to get her feet wet?

"All right," she whispered, and was rewarded with a tentative smile. The smile put the dawn to shame and warned her exploring new territories and experiences was always going to be fraught with hidden dangers.

That's why she had chosen life as a schoolteacher in a small town. Her choices had given her a life with a reassuring sameness to everything that made her feel safe and secure.

Though in this amazing dawn, she saw things in a new and less flattering light. Had she allowed herself to become utterly boring? Apparently. Apparently she had become the kind of woman who you could tell in a single glance was a schoolteacher.

They came to the bridge and stood on it for a moment. The water was flowing underneath it like liquid gold, stained by the rising sun. They stood there in silence, watching morning mist rise off the vineyards all around them.

"Everyone should know how to swim," he said sternly, as if he was deliberately moving away from the magic of the shared moment, as if he was making sure she was not mistaken about his motivations in asking her to join him.

"Really? Why?"

He frowned at her, as if the question was too silly to deserve an answer.

"Most of the world's population, including you, lives near some sort of body of water. You could be in a boat that capsizes. You could fall in."

"I suppose," she agreed, but looking at him, she recognized what was at his very core. He protected people. It was more than evident that was his vocation and his calling. His shoulders were huge and broad, but broad enough to carry the weight of the whole world?

He broke her gaze, as if he knew she had seen something of him that he did not want her to see. Connor moved off the bridge and found a path worn deep by the feet of hundreds of hot little boys over many, many years.

The path was steep in places, and her footwear—a pair of flimsy sandals, fine for town—was not very good for scrambling over rocks.

"Oh," she gasped at one point, when she nearly fell.

He turned, took it all in in a breath, and his hands found her waist and encircled it. He lifted her easily over the rough spot and set her down. But his hands remained around her waist for just a hair too long, and then he turned away just a hair too quickly.

Her sensation of being with a man who would protect her with his life, if need be, strengthened.

It made her feel exquisitely feminine to be the one being looked after, for a change. Giorgio had never looked after her. It had always been the other way around.

A touch of guilt rippled along the perfect mirrored surface of the morning. But it evaporated like the mist rising all around them as they arrived at the swimming hole. Her awareness of Connor seemed to fill up every crack and crevice in her, just as sunlight would be filling every crack and crevice as it poured into the town.

The river widened here, gurgling on both sides of a pool that was large and placid. A tree leaned over it, and from a sturdy branch, a tire swung on a frayed rope.

Connor kicked off his shoes and shucked his trousers and his shirt and stood before her much as he had yesterday, totally unself-conscious in bathing trunks that were the same cut and style as his underwear had been, and every bit as sexy. He bent over his bag for a moment and fished out something that he held loosely in his left hand.

He stepped to the water's edge.

"Is it cold?" she asked.

"Oh, yeah," he said with deep pleasure. He reached back his right hand for her. "It's a bit slippery."

Crazy to accept that invitation, but really, it was much too late to stop accepting the crazy invitations now. She kicked out of her sandals and reached out. His hand closed around hers, and he tugged her gently to the water's edge. She was not sure anything in her entire life had felt as right as accepting the strength of that hand, feeling it close around her own, with a promise of strength and protection.

"The first step to swimming," he encouraged her.

She stuck a toe in, shrieked and pulled it back out swiftly. She tried to loosen her hand from his, but he just laughed and held tight until she put her toe back in the water.

"Come on," he said, patiently. "Just try it."

And so, her hand held firmly in his, she stepped into the icy cold water and felt her eyes go round. The mud on the bottom oozed up between her toes.

It felt wondrous. She didn't feel the least bit afraid. He tugged her hand and smiled. What could she do? She could say yes to life. Isabella bunched up her skirt in her other hand and lifted it. The morning air on her naked thighs felt exquisite. She saw his eyes move there, to where she had lifted her skirt out of the water, and felt slightly vindicated by the flash of deep masculine heat she saw in them. That was not the look one gave a boring schoolteacher.

He led her deeper into the water—it crept up to her calves and to her knees—and he smiled at her squeal that was part protest and mostly delight. And then she was laughing.

The laughter felt as if it was bubbling up from a hidden stream deep within her; it had been trapped and now it was set free.

Connor was staring at her, and his gaze added to the sense of heightened awareness. She was entering another world, a foreign land of sensation, his hand so warm and strong guiding her, the cold water tugging on her feet and her bare calves, licking at her knees, storming her senses. She was not sure she had ever felt so exquisitely and fully alive.

Something sizzled in the air between them, as real as getting a jolt from a loose wire. Connor Benson was looking at her lips. She allowed herself to look at his.

A knife-edged awareness surged through her. If she took one tiny step toward him, she knew he would kiss her.

Was this what she had given up when she had chosen Giorgio? Was this what her mother had tried to tell her she would miss? The thought was an unexpected dark spot in the brightness of her unleashed spirit.

She felt the laughter dry up within her, and Isabella let go of Connor's hand and took a step back instead of toward him.

"What?" he asked.

She backed away from his touch, from the exquisite intoxication of his closeness. It was clouding her judgment. It was making her crazy.

Ma sei pazzo, she chided herself inside her own head, backing away from the delicious craziness that beckoned to her.

But he did not allow her to escape. For every step

back she took, he took one forward, until she was up against the slippery bank and could not move for fear of falling in the water. He came to her and lifted her chin, looked deeply into her eyes. "What?" he asked again, softly.

She could feel the strength in his hands, the calm in his eyes. She could smell the scents of him and of the morning mingling. She could lean toward all of this...

But she didn't.

"Nothing," she said. "I have to go. I can't—"

Can't what? she asked herself. Enjoy life? Be open to new experiences? She broke away from his gaze—a gaze that seemed to know all her secrets, to strip her of everything she had regarded as truth before. She gathered her skirt, shoved by him, waded up the river to where it was easy to find the bank and left the water.

"You can use my towel to dry off your feet," he called.

She did that. She grabbed his towel and her shoes and found a dry place on the bank to sit and towel off her feet.

She dared to glance at him. He stood, watching her. He was so extraordinarily attractive, those strong legs set in the water, the morning light playing with the features of his face, so comfortable in his own skin. Italians had an expression about men like this.

Sa il fatto suo.

He knows what he is about. He knows himself.

And then this man who knew himself so well, who knew his every strength and his every weakness, lifted a shoulder, dismissing her. He dipped the mask and snorkel he held in his left hand into the water. He slipped them on, resting them on his forehead. Then he casually saluted her, adjusted the mask and snorkel, and dived neatly into the water and disappeared.

She held her breath. Where on earth had he gone? It seemed as if he could not possibly be down there for that long without something having happened. Was he tangled in a branch under the water? Had he hit his head on a rock?

But then the water broke, at the far edge of the pool, where faster water fed it. He broke the surface, and without looking back began to swim against the current.

It would always be like this if you were with a man like him, Isabella told herself sternly. *You would always wonder what danger he had managed to find.*

And still, she could not tear her eyes away from him. She watched in utter amazement as Connor propelled himself through the water. His strength and his grace were utterly awe-inspiring. It was as if there was no current at all, his body cutting through the water at high speed. If she didn't know better, she would think he had flippers on, but no flippers had come out of that bag. She watched him swim until he reached a bend in the river, swam around it and disappeared.

She finished drying her feet and put her shoes on. It was harder navigating the tricky path back to the bridge without him.

But it was what she had to do. She had to navigate without him—she had to go back to the way her life had been before they took that walk into a world of enchantment, this world where fears evaporated like the morning mist was evaporating under the Tuscan sun.

Isabella had to be who she was before.

A few minutes did not alter the course of an entire life. But she of all people should know that was not true, because the entire course of her life had been altered the second she had said *I do* to Giorgio.

And it felt like the worst kind of sin that these few minutes this morning had filled her with regret, for the first time, at what the choice to say those words had made her miss in life.

But one thing about saying that to Giorgio? If she ever did say those words to a man again—and that was a big, big *if*—it would be to one who would grow old with her.

And there would never, ever be a guarantee of that with a man like Connor Benson.

The river was amazing to swim in, and Connor quickly made morning swims a part of his Monte Calanetti routine. His time in the military had made him move toward a structured approach to life. He loved routine and order. From firsthand experience, Connor knew when the world turned to chaos—which it could do in the blink of an eye—that was when an investment in discipline paid dividends.

And so now he developed a schedule for his days. He rose early, before Isabella was up, walked to the river and swam against the current in the cold water until his muscles ached but his mind was sharply clear and focused.

It was all working out quite nicely. By the time he returned, Isabella had left for work.

Isabella. The clear mind made Connor uncomfortably aware, especially after that magical morning together, that this time Isabella could well be the chaos waiting to unfold in his life.

And that kind of chaos was way more dangerous than

the sudden crack of a sniper's rifle, or a bomb going off on the side of the road.

Oh, she seemed innocent enough, the last place a man would expect chaos to come from, but that would be a man who had not felt her hand close around his, who had not heard her unexpected shriek of delighted laughter split the silence of the morning as her toes touched ice-cold water. That would be a man who had not, for one crazy, glorious moment, looked at her lips and wanted to taste the promise of them, wanted to see if they tasted like the nectar of life itself.

The answer was simple. No more dawn encounters. No more walking through streets so quiet he could hear her dress swishing against her bare legs, no more putting his hands around her narrow waist to lift her over the rocky parts of the trail. No more wading in icy cold water with her. No more encouraging her to explore the world of sensation.

And especially no more looking at the sweet plumpness of her lips!

A man—one not as disciplined as Connor knew himself to be—could live to see the light that had come on in Isabella's face that morning by the river.

And so, he was avoiding her. And his avoidance had helped him develop a routine that he was comfortable with. There were no more tongue-loosening little chats over wine, and no more shocking morning encounters in the hallway or kitchen, and most of all, no more morning strolls through a predawn town.

Isabella seemed to enjoy routine as much as he himself did, and so it was proving easy to avoid her. He, an expert on figuring out people's habits, had her routine down pat in no time. It fit perfectly with his lifestyle.

By the time he returned from his early morning swims, Isabella was gone. He used the kitchen and did his laundry when she was at school. A lot of his work could be done on his computer, and he took advantage of her absence and the coolness on the lower floors of her house to do that when she was not there.

When she was at home in the evenings, he went out to eat and did reconnaissance. It was cooler then, anyway, and he made sure never to be back until her house lights—and her bedroom light, which he could see from the street—were out.

Even with all that effort, it was hard to ignore the fact he was sharing a house with a woman. No, it seemed his avoidance strategy had made *more* awareness, not less, tingle along his spine. Her little touches were everywhere in that house: an exquisite painting, a fresh vase of flowers, the smell of toast and coffee in the morning. Her scent was in the air.

And by now it had become apparent to him that all the while he was congratulating himself on his avoidance strategy, the truth was it was so successful because she was avoiding him!

By the fifth day of living under her roof, after succeeding with zero encounters of the Isabella-in-person kind, Connor was not at all sure what his success meant, because he was fairly certain he had never been more aware of another person.

Connor came into the house. It was much earlier than he usually arrived in the afternoon, but he felt a need to change clothes before he went and found a place to eat tonight. It had been another scorching day in Monte Calanetti and he thought he might head to the river for the second time that day.

He paused and listened. Had he managed to get in before she got home from school?

Today, for the first time, he realized he had not been successful in avoiding sharing the house with his appealing roommate. He could hear the one and only shower running upstairs.

Well, that was okay. He would nip into his room and get his swim things and a change of clothes. Isabella wouldn't even know he'd been in the space. The thought of bumping into her in the hallway, fresh out of the shower, made him hurriedly gather his swim things from his room.

His escape was nearly complete when the sound of an explosion, followed by a woman's shriek of terror, came from the bathroom. There was a loud *thunk*.

And then there was the worst thing of all.

Complete and utter silence.

CHAPTER FOUR

WITHOUT EVEN THINKING, doing what came as naturally to him as breathing, Connor threw down his things and ran into the hallway, straight toward the now silent bathroom.

"Isabella? Are you okay?"

There was no answer. He pounded on the door. There was still no answer. He tried the door. It was locked.

"Isabella?"

When there was still no answer, he put his shoulder to the door. The old wood cracked with ease and the door fell open.

He was hit in the face by water. He threw his hands up over his face and peered out between two fingers. Water was spewing out of the pipe where the showerhead had been, going in every direction, drenching the walls in water. The showerhead was on the floor under the sink.

Isabella was on the floor, soaked. The shower curtain had been ripped from its rod, and it was draped across her naked body. Turning his back to the spraying water to protect her from the worst of it, he crouched down beside her. Her head was bleeding and a lump was already rising.

"Isabella," he said, touching her wet arm.

She opened her eyes, dazed. Her brows knit as she looked at him in confusion.

"I—I—I don't know what happened."

"I think the showerhead blew off and hit you." He rose quickly, turned off the water at the handle, and then crouched back beside her.

"Please don't tell me, 'I told you so.'" Her eyes were wide on his face, all those greens and golds mixed together like the shades of an exotic flower.

"I won't."

"I should have let you fix it when the plumber wouldn't come. Didn't want to be dependent." Her voice was slightly slurred. It sounded like a bit of a confession. Her eyes suddenly widened even more. "Are you in my bathroom?"

"Yes, I'm afraid so."

She went very still. If it was possible, she grew whiter. "Am I naked?" she whispered.

"Ah, I'm afraid so."

"I have never been so mortified." She clenched her eyes shut as if she was hoping when she opened them this would all go away.

"Now we're even," he said, trying valiantly to put her at ease. "Though I think I've mentioned before that we should stop meeting like this."

She groaned weakly—at his attempt at humor or because of pain and humiliation, he wasn't so certain.

"We're not even," she decided. "We'd be even if you had ever been embarrassed about being unclothed, which I suspect you never have been."

He didn't say anything.

"In your whole life."

He still didn't say anything.

"Have you?" she demanded.

"Uh, well, you're not exactly unclothed. You must have pulled down the shower curtain when you came out of the shower enclosure. You're decent."

"My shower curtain is transparent," she said through clenched teeth.

"I'm not looking."

Of course her eyes flew open just as he looked. "Just for injuries!"

She clenched her eyes tightly shut again.

"I'm going to help you get up."

"No, you aren't!" She tried to tuck the transparent shower curtain tighter around her. It had the unfortunate result of becoming even more transparent.

"Ah, yes, I am," he said, keeping his eyes on her face. Chaos had struck. And all that discipline was paying off, after all. He could look just at her face. Couldn't he?

"I can get up myself." She wiggled ineffectually this way and that, trying to figure out how to get up on the slippery floor and keep the small protection of the shower curtain around her at the same time. She gave up with a sigh.

He reached out to help her.

"Don't touch me." She slapped at his hand, but it was halfhearted.

"You can trust me." His hand closed around hers, and this time she surrendered. "I have pretty extensive first-aid training."

"Yes, I know."

He lifted an eyebrow at her.

"I read about it. On the internet. The SEALs."

"Oh." She had read about what he'd done for a living. He contemplated that.

"Not that I was spying."

"No, of course not."

"Just intrigued."

"Ah."

"It seems like you have done very dangerous things."

"Yes."

Her voice suddenly went very soft. "Things that make a man very lonely."

Her eyes felt as if they were looking deep within him, as if she could see his soul, as if she could see the vast emptiness that was there. Her hand tightened marginally on his.

"Maybe," he said, telling himself he was only agreeing because he didn't want her to get riled up.

"I feel lonely, too, sometimes." And then, just like that, she was crying.

"Hey." He patted her shoulder clumsily, realized how very naked she was and pulled his hand away. He stared at it as if it was burning.

She seemed to realize how awkward this situation really was. "You need to leave me alone," she sobbed. "I'm not even dressed."

What *wasn't* happening? He wasn't leaving her alone. What *was* happening? He was going to try and make her okay with this.

"Don't worry about it," he said, pulling his attention away from his hand and ordering himself to buck up. "You've had a bit of a shock. People say and do things they wouldn't normally say or do. I'm a trained professional. I deal with stuff like this all the time."

Even as she scrubbed furiously at her tearstained

face, she looked dubious. She slid a look down at her thin covering of a shower curtain. "Like a doctor?"

"Sort of," he agreed.

"And you deal with unclothed, crying, lonely women who have been assaulted by exploding showers? All the time?"

"I just meant I deal with the unexpected." He tried for a soothing note in the face of her voice rising a bit shrilly. "It's what I'm trained to do. Let's get you up off the floor."

He reached for the nearest towel rack and tugged a towel off it, and then, as an afterthought, another one. He put both of them on top of her, trying to fasten them, without much success, around the sopping, slippery, transparent shower curtain.

Tucking the thick white terry towels around her as best he could, he slipped his arm under her shoulder and lifted her to a little dressing table bench. It was the first time he had touched her since he had held her hand at the pool in the river. Awareness quivered along his spine, but he could not give in to that. He needed to be professional right now, as he never had been before.

Connor guided Isabella to sitting and tucked the towels a little tighter around her.

Professional, he told himself grimly.

"Let's just have a look at that bump on your head." *That was good*, he told himself of his neutral tone.

"Why are you lonely?" he heard himself growl as he parted her hair and dabbed at the bump with a wet cloth.

What was professional about that? *Distracting her*, Connor told himself. He turned from her for a moment and opened the medicine chest over her sink. He found iodine and cotton balls.

"I suppose you find me pathetic," she said.

Distracting her would have been talking about any-thing—the upcoming royal wedding, the grape crops—not probing her personal tragedies.

She grimaced as he found the cut on her head and dabbed it.

"I don't find you pathetic," he told her. "You were married. Your husband died. It seems to me you would be lonely."

"Thank you," she said softly.

Leave it, he ordered himself. "I mean, of course I've wondered why such a beautiful woman would stay alone."

"You wondered about me?"

Just as she had wondered about him, going online to find out about the SEALs. All this curiosity between them was just normal, wasn't it? They were two strang-ers sharing a house. Naturally they would have ques-tions.

"Did you love your husband that much?" Connor asked. "That you are prepared to stay lonely forever? To grieve him forever?"

"Yes," she said. It came out sounding like a hiccup. "Where there is deep grief, there was deep love."

And something about the way she said that made his radar go up. He realized he didn't believe her. It was none of his business. He ordered himself not to probe. He was, at heart, a soldier. He would always be a sol-dier. That's what he did. He obeyed orders.

So, why did he hear his own voice saying, in direct defiance of the command he had just given it, "Tell me about your husband."

It was not, as he would have liked himself to believe, to provide a distraction for her while he doctored her head.

"No one, least of all not my very traditional family, understood my decision to marry him," she said, sticking her chin up as if daring him to reach the same conclusion.

"Why's that?" he asked, keeping his voice carefully noncommittal.

"He was very ill when we married. We knew he was going to die."

He had to work to keep his face schooled.

"My mother was begging me, on the eve of my wedding, not to do it. She said, *Life has enough heartbreak—you have to invite one by marrying a dying man?*"

It seemed to Connor her mother had a point, but he didn't say anything. He pretended intense concentration on the small bump on her head.

"Giorgio was part of the fabric of my life from the first day I started school."

Connor could just picture her starting school: little dark pigtails, a pinafore dress, knee socks and a scraped knee.

Something that had never happened to him happened—he wondered what Isabella's daughter would look like, if she had one someday. He felt it was a tragedy that she had said no to her own little girl somewhere along the line.

"Giorgio was never good-looking." Isabella looked at Connor critically. He was pretty sure she found *him* good-looking, but not nearly as sure if she saw that as a good thing or a bad thing.

"He wasn't even good-looking as a child, though his

eyes held such depths of beauty they took my breath away from the first moment I looked in their liquid dark depths."

He had to bite his tongue from saying cynically, *How very poetic.*

"He was always sickly—perhaps seeds of the illness that killed him had been growing since we were children."

Connor did not like the picture she was painting of the man she had married. Good grief. What had she been thinking?

She seemed to sense his judgment, because she tilted her chin at him. "He took the fact he was different from all the other boys and made that his greatest strength."

"Oh," he said flatly, not a question. But she took it as a question.

"Giorgio was able to use such a simple thing as a word to spin entire worlds, enchanted kingdoms. He could see what others missed—the pure magic in a ladybug's flight, the whole universe residing in the center of an opening flower. While other boys were crass and full of frightening energy, Giorgio was sensitive and sweetly contemplative."

Connor hoped he wasn't scowling. He himself had been one of those crass boys, full of frightening energy.

"When he asked me to marry him, I didn't even have to think about it, I just said yes."

What kind of man, knowing his prognosis was fatal, would ask someone he supposedly loved to share that with him?

"I've never even been on a real date. Giorgio was not well enough to go out for dinner, or to the movies. Certainly not dancing."

She'd never been on a date? That last— certainly not dancing — seemed to have been offered with a bit of wistfulness.

"I still have the poems he wrote for me, and the splendor of them is still wrenching enough to make me weep."

Connor looked at her lips. If she hadn't dated any other men, she probably hadn't kissed any other men, either. He had the irreverent feeling he could make her forget the splendor of those poems in about twenty seconds flat. He made himself focus on the small cut on her head.

"At sixteen I declared my love for him. At twenty I married him, over the protests of my entire family. He had already been diagnosed with his illness. At twenty-six I laid him to rest. In my heart is nothing but gratitude for the amazing time we had."

She seemed to be expecting him to say something, so he said, "Uh-huh," when what he really wanted to do was take her by those slender, very naked shoulders and shake some sense into her.

"Now in me is an empty place that nothing—and no one—can ever fill."

Her tale made Connor want to kiss the living daylights out of her, to wake her up from her trance, to show her maybe that empty place inside her could be filled. But he recognized he was treading on dangerous and unfamiliar ground if he thought he would be the one who was up to the challenge of filling her empty places. Isabella apparently liked the sensitive type. Which, if the way he felt about her husband was any indication, Connor most definitely was not. The man had been sick. That wasn't his fault. And yet Connor felt aggravated, as if Giorgio had taken advantage of Isabella's soft heart to give her a life of looking after him.

"You think I felt sorry for him," she gasped. "You think I didn't love him at all."

"Hey! I didn't say that."

"You didn't have to. I saw it in your face. You think I don't have a clue what love is."

He was the one who had told her to be observant, but he hadn't been expecting this. "I don't know what you think you saw in my face, but it wasn't that. You did not see that in *my* face, because you are looking at a person who truly does not have a clue what love is."

"Humph." She seemed unconvinced. She seemed unfairly angry at him.

"Maybe," he suggested carefully, "you said out loud the doubt you've been nursing inside since the day you married him."

With speed that took him by surprise, she smacked him hard, open-handed, across his face, hard enough to turn his head. He looked slowly back at her as she stood up. The towel fell to the ground, leaving only the shower curtain around her. Gathering her shower curtain, regal as Christina Rose could ever hope to be, as confident as the emperor with no clothes, Isabella got up and walked by him and out of the bathroom. He watched as she walked down the hallway to her bedroom, entered it, sent one damning look back at him and slammed the door.

Connor Benson stood frozen to the spot, absolutely stunned. He touched his face where her palm had met his cheek.

Jeez, for a little bit of a thing she packed a better wallop than a lot of men he'd known.

* * *

Isabella lay, wrapped in her shower curtain, on her bed in a pool of dampness and self-loathing. She could not believe she had struck Connor. She was going to have to apologize. It was so unlike her!

It was only because she had hit her head. He'd said it himself. She'd had a bit of a shock—people did and said things they wouldn't normally say under those circumstances.

Isabella would not normally confess all kinds of things to him. She had told him she was lonely in a moment of dazed weakness. It was also in a moment of dazed weakness that she had given in to his encouragement to talk about Giorgio.

What a mistake that had been. She had seen in Connor's face that he thought her marriage had been a sham.

Or was what he said more accurate? That bump on the head had removed a filter she had been trying desperately to keep in place, and her own doubts, not Connor's, had spilled out of her.

She got up off the bed. Enough of the self-pity and introspection. Yes, she was lonely, but why had she confessed that to him instead of just looking after it herself?

People had to be responsible for themselves!

Tonight was a case in point. She had been invited to the sixteenth birthday party of one of her former students. As a teacher, she was often invited to her pupils' family events, but she rarely attended. So, who did she have to blame but herself if she was lonely?

It wasn't Connor's fault that he had made her aware of the loneliness as if it was a sharp shard of glass inside her.

She went to her closet and threw open the door. She

wasn't going to the party as a demure little school-teacher, either. She wasn't wearing a dress that would label her prim and tidy for all the world to see.

She was not dressing in a way that sent the message she was safe and boring, and not quite alive somehow.

Way at the back of the closet was a dress she had bought a long time ago, on a holiday she had forced herself to take a year or two after Giorgio died. The purchase had really been the fault of one of those pushy salesclerks who had brought her the dress, saying she had never seen a dress so perfect for someone.

It was the salesclerk's gushing that had made Isabella purchase the dress, which had been way more expensive than what she could afford. When she brought it home, she had had buyer's remorse, and dismissed it as not right for her. Still, it hung in her closet, all these years later. Why had she never given it away?

She took it out and laid it on the bed, eyed it critically. Not right for the old her. Perfect for the new her.

The dress was red as blood and had a low V on both the front and back, which meant she couldn't wear it with any bra that she owned.

It was the dress of a woman who was not filled with unreasonable fears.

Feeling ridiculously racy for the fact she had on no bra, she slipped the dress over her head, then looked at herself in her full-length mirror. She remembered why she had purchased the dress, and it wasn't strictly be-cause of the salesclerk gushing over it.

The dress gave Isabella a glimpse of who she could be. It was as if it took her from mouse to siren in the blink of an eye. She looked confident and sexy and like a woman who was uninhibited and knew how to have fun and let go. It was the dress of a woman who had the satisfying knowledge she could have any man she wanted.

Isabella put makeup on the bump on her head and then arranged her hair over it. She dabbed mascara on her lashes and blush on her cheeks. She glossed her lips and put on a little spray of perfume.

She found her highest heels, and a tiny clutch handbag, and a little silver bracelet. Taking a deep breath, she marched out of her room. Connor's bedroom door was closed. Summoning all her courage, she knocked on the door.

After a long moment, long enough for her heart to pound in her throat as if it planned to jump out of her, the door opened. He stood there looking down at her. He was wet, still, from the water from the broken shower spewing all over him, from helping her. Awareness of him tingled along her spine.

She was so glad she had put on the red dress when Connor's mouth fell open before he snapped it shut. Something flashed in his eyes before he quickly veiled it. But even if she had led a sheltered life, Isabella knew desire when she saw it.

He folded his arms over his chest.

"My, my," he growled.

She tossed her head, pleased with the way his eyes followed the motion of her hair. "I'm going to a birthday party. I wanted to apologize before I left. I have never hit a person in my whole life. I'm deeply ashamed."

"Really?" he growled doubtfully.

"Really," she said, lifting her chin.

"That's kind of not the dress of someone who is deeply ashamed."

"The dress has nothing to do with this!"

"I think it does."

"Explain yourself."

He lifted a shoulder. "All right. I think you're a boiling cauldron of repressed passion."

"Maybe it's not repressed," she snapped.

His eyes went to her lips and stayed there long enough to make the point that they could find out how repressed or unrepressed she was right this second if she wanted. Her eyes skittered to his lips. She blinked first and looked away. When she looked back, his gaze was unflinching.

"In a dress like that, lots of people are going to want to find out, *is she, or isn't she?* You aren't going be lonely for very long at all."

Since the whole idea of putting on the dress had been to look passionate, why did she want to smack him again? And badly. She could tell this apology was premature. She had to grip her clutch extra tightly to keep her hand from flying free and hitting him across his handsome, smug face.

No, she didn't want to smack him. That wasn't the truth at all. The truth was exactly as he had said. She was a boiling cauldron of repressed passion, and she wanted to throw herself at Connor and let all that repressed passion boil out.

Isabella was absolutely appalled with herself. She took a step back from him and turned away. "Have a good evening, signor," she said formally, the prim little schoolteacher after all, a child playing dress-up in her red finery.

"Yeah. You, too."

She turned and walked away. And just because she

knew he was watching her, or maybe to prove to herself she wasn't just playing dress-up, she put a little extra swing in her step and felt the red dress swirl around her.

She glanced over her shoulder and caught him still watching her, his eyes narrowed with unconcealed masculine appreciation.

Surprisingly, given that unsettling encounter with Connor, Isabella did have a good evening. Sixteenth birthday parties for young women were a huge event in Monte Calanetti. It was a coming-of-age celebration, probably very much like a debutante ball in the southern US. The party signified the transition from being a child to being a woman.

While looking at the giggling young woman, Valerie, flushed with excitement in her finery, Isabella was struck by how extremely young and innocent she was. She was no more an adult that Isabella was an astronaut.

And yet Isabella had been sixteen herself when she had first declared her undying love for Giorgio. And how adult and sophisticated and sure of herself she had felt at that time. Now, watching this young woman, it seemed it would be laughable to make a lifelong declaration of love at that age, and then to feel bound by it.

The pensive thoughts did not last long, though. Isabella had been seated with some of her coworkers, and the talk turned to preparations for the spring fete and anticipation of the royal wedding being held in Monte Calanetti.

Then there was harmless gossip about who was getting married and divorced and who was burying parents. And, of course, in an Italian village, what was loved more than a pregnancy?

Nothing. But with each pregnancy revealed, Isabella

felt happy and yet crushed, too. She did not think envy was an admirable emotion, and yet the thought of someone holding that beautiful, wiggling, warm bundle of life filled her with a terrible sense of longing for the life she did not have. And would probably never have. Not now.

"Have you heard? Marianna is pregnant."

Again Isabella's happiness for Marianna was laced with her own sense of loss. She listened halfheartedly as the circumstances around Marianna's pregnancy were placed under the microscope of the small, close-knit village. They were not ideal.

Italy was still mostly Catholic, and small towns like Monte Calanetti were very traditional. A pregnancy without the benefit of marriage still raised eyebrows. There was some conjecture around the table about how Marianna's brothers, the staunchly conservative Angelo and Nico, might have reacted to news of a pregnancy.

After it had been discussed to death, it was all put aside and a decision was made.

"We will have to have a baby shower."

This was announced with a sigh of pure happiness and murmurs of delight from the other women. A baby in Italy was always seen as a blessing.

For some reason that made Isabella think of Connor talking about the abandonment of his mother by his father. Marianna's beau looked like the kind of man who would stand by her no matter what. Angelo and Nico, while they might rage and wring their hands, would never turn their backs on their own blood. Never.

Isabella wondered if that was the root of Connor wanting to protect the whole world—a little boy wanting to protect his mother. The thought made her heart ache for him. Not that she wanted to spoil this evening with one single thought about her houseguest!

Though Isabella was careful with the wine, some others were not, and the jokes became quite ribald and the laughter loud. The gathering was around a torch-lit courtyard, and after the dinner the tables were cleared away for dancing, and a live band came out.

The dress made Isabella feel different, less repressed and more carefree. To her astonishment, men she'd known for years were lining up to ask her to dance, and she soon felt as if she was flushed with as much excitement as the young Valerie.

It was after one in the morning before she realized how late it was.

"I have to work in the morning!"

She refused an offer to be walked home, and instead went down the darkened streets by herself. Partway home, she realized her feet ached from all the dancing, and she slipped off her shoes and went barefoot.

A little ways from her house, she saw a figure coming toward her. She knew from his size and the way he carried himself exactly who it was, and she felt her heart begin to race.

But his walk was different, purposeful, the strides long and hard, like a gladiator entering the arena, like a warrior entering the battlefield.

He stopped in front of her and gazed down at her. His eyes were flashing with cold anger.

"Where the hell have you been?"

"Scusi?"

"You heard me."

"I told you I was at a birthday party," she said.

"Well, I assumed a child's birthday party, and I thought it would be over at a decent time."

"What's it to you?" she snapped, angry at his high-handed manner, angry that he thought he could treat her like a child on the night she felt sexy and adult.

Her tone was louder than she intended. In fact, both their tones might have been louder than they thought. A light came on in a window above the street.

Connor stepped back from her, ran a hand through his hair and looked away. "You're waking the neighbors," he said, glancing up at that window.

"Me?" she said, unrepentant.

"Us," he conceded.

"Well, I have an excuse—boiling cauldron of repressed passion that I am, I am now shrieking like a fishwife in the streets. What's yours?"

"Good question," he said.

"You rescued me this afternoon. That does not put you in charge of my life!"

"You're right," Connor said. The anger had faded from his face. Instead, he looked faintly confused. Her own annoyance at him ebbed away a little bit.

"Are you out here looking for me?" she asked, astounded.

He could barely look at her, but he nodded.

What remained of her anger drained away. "But why?" She remembered thinking earlier tonight, with the news of Marianna's pregnancy, of the burden he had placed on himself of looking after the whole world. She remembered wondering if the first person he had felt protective of was his mother.

Almost against her will, something in her softened toward him.

"Hell, I started thinking about you bumping your head. It can be such a tricky injury. I should have checked more for signs of concussion."

"You were worried about me," she said. It was not a question.

"It's just that you'd had quite a bang on the head, and you were dressed like that, and I started thinking you might not be making the best decisions."

"I'm thirty-three years old!"

"But you'd had a head injury. And you said you were lonely… I thought you might be…" His voice trailed away uncomfortably.

She looked at him silently. She should be insulted. He thought she might be what? Getting carried away with the first man who looked at her with avarice? But poor Connor looked tormented. His expression stole her indignation away from her.

"Vulnerable," he continued.

That was so true. She did feel very vulnerable. But it seemed he felt vulnerable, too.

"It's not that you wouldn't make good decisions under normal conditions," he said hastily. "But a bump on the head can cause confusion. Alter judgment slightly. I'm sorry. Am I making a fool of myself?"

"No," she said softly, "you are not. I am quite touched by your concern for me."

"I'm not sure it's rational," he said. "It's just that, unfortunately, I've just seen a lot of people get themselves in trouble before they know what's happened to them."

"I wasn't in trouble. But the party wasn't for a child. Not really. For a sixteen-year-old. It's a big deal in Monte Calanetti. Almost like a wedding. A meal and dancing. The party could go on all night."

"I hate it when I act from emotion," he said gruffly.

"Do you?"

He stepped one step closer to her. He lifted her hair off her shoulder with his hand. "What are you doing to me?" he asked huskily. "I feel as if I'm not thinking straight."

"Ah."

"I find you very beautiful. It's hard for a man to think straight around that."

"It's just the dress," she said.

"No, Isabella, it's not."

"It's not?"

"There's something about you that makes me think with my heart instead of my head."

"Oh, dear," she said, and her tone was playfully mocking.

"Here's what I think," he said firmly, as if he had it all figured out.

"Yes?"

"I should take you on a date."

CHAPTER FIVE

ISABELLA STARED AT CONNOR. He should take her on a date? But was that his head or his heart talking? Because the way he said it, it was almost as though he hoped to get her out of his system.

"You should?" she asked.

"Sure. I mean, if you'd like to."

There was something very endearing about seeing this big, self-assured, superconfident Texan looking so unsure of himself.

"I'd like to," she said softly. "I'd like to, very much."

And then it seemed slightly and wonderfully ridiculous that they turned and walked home together.

Only it didn't seem ridiculous when his hand found hers.

It felt not as if she was going to go on a real date for the first time in her life, but as if she was coming home.

"I've gone and done something really stupid," Connor whispered into his phone.

"Huh? Who is this?"

"Justin, it's me."

"Connor?"

"Yeah."

"What the hell is going on?"

"There's this girl."

Something relaxed in Justin's tone. "This better be good—it's two o'clock in the morning here."

Connor contemplated that. Was there one rational thing left in him? No, that's why he was consulting his friend. That's what SEALs did when they were in a pickle, they relied on each other.

"She's not really a girl. A woman."

"Uh-huh?"

"I asked her out."

"That sounds like it's worthy of a two a.m. phone call."

"The thing is, I didn't really ask her out for me. I asked her out for her. She's a widow. She married really young. She's missed a lot. She's never been on a real date before."

Silence.

Connor sighed. "I'm the wrong guy for this, aren't I?"

Silence.

"I mean, I'm just the wrong guy to try and show her how it can be."

"How what can be?"

"You know."

"You'll have to spell it out for me. I'm having that two-o'clock-in-the-morning brain fart."

"How it can be, uh, when two people like each other. A lot."

"You mean falling in love?" Justin asked. He sounded wide-awake now.

"No!" Connor had to backtrack. He was sorry he had admitted liking her. A lot. His mission was one of altruism, and he wanted to make Justin understand that.

"I mean maybe falling in love," Connor said carefully, "just not with me. I just want to show her life can be fun. I want to show her she's missed something, and not to be afraid to embrace it. That it is not too late for her."

"From the embracer of all things romantic," Justin said wryly.

"You're not helping! I guess I want to show her what she should be looking for in a guy. Not me. I mean, I'm leaving. I'm here for the short term only. But if I could just give her an idea how a date should feel."

"Very altruistic."

"Are you being sarcastic?"

Justin sighed. "Okay. Ask me a specific question, and I will try to help you with it."

"What should I do with her on a date? I was thinking dinner and a movie."

"So, basically the same thing you've done on every single date you've ever been on?"

"Yes."

"Hmm."

"What does that mean?" Connor demanded. "I hate it when you say *hmm* like that."

"It just seems to me if you're trying to show her life is good, and trying to encourage her to embrace the great adventure, and trying to show her what a good date would feel like, you should put a bit more thought into it."

"I've been thinking of nothing else!"

"Just a sec." Connor could hear Justin talking to someone, the sound muffled as if he had stuck the phone under his pillow. Connor was pretty sure the other voice was feminine. He strained his ears. Justin came back on a moment later.

"Be original. A picnic in the moonlight. Something like that."

"That is the hokiest thing I've ever heard."

"Well, then, don't ask."

"Okay, I won't." And Connor contemplated the fact that Justin was with someone. Justin really was getting on with his life. It occurred to Connor that the wheelchair Justin used was holding Connor back more than it was his friend.

"Don't hang up, Connor. The red line is going off."

The red line. That was the dedicated line for emergencies for their company.

Justin came back on the phone. His voice was completely different, the sleep stripped from it. This voice, crisp, take-charge and take-no-prisoners, was a voice Connor recognized. He was a warrior now, and Connor shifted into that role easily, aware he was far more at ease with this than the places of the heart that he had very nearly gone to.

"How long would it take you to get back to Azerbaijan?"

Connor was already opening a different screen on his phone, looking up flights. "I could be in Baku in under six hours if I can make the connections."

"A vulture has landed. Go."

A vulture had landed. It was their code for a bad guy, known to them. In a similar code, Justin and whoever was on the ground in Azerbaijan would text the details to Connor's phone as they had them. Connor was aware as he threw things in his bag that he felt a sense of purpose and mission. This was the world he moved in with absolute ease. This was where he belonged.

He scrawled a note for Isabella, sent a quick text to

Nico and slipped out the door, back into the comfort of all that was familiar.

It was ironic just how safe danger made Connor Benson feel.

Isabella was aware, as soon as she woke up the next morning, that Connor was gone. She could feel his absence in the house, as if some energy that was necessary to life was gone.

She found his note on the kitchen table but was not comforted by it. Was it convenient that he was suddenly called away at the same time things were taking a turn between them? Was he deliberately cooling things off?

Isabella nursed the hope that he would call, and it increased her tension when he did not. He *was* cooling things off.

Still, she could not believe it was possible to miss Connor so much. In the short time he had been part of her life, his presence had made a big impact on her household without her really realizing it at the time. There was something about having a man in her house—even though they had mostly avoided each other—that made her feel safe. That in itself was not really rational—he had attacked her the very first day.

So, no, her acute sense of missing him had very little to do with a sense of safety. Maybe even the opposite. There was a sense that very *unsafe* things could unfold between them. And that made each day have a delicious sense of anticipation.

She looked at his note, over and over, trying to glean any emotion from it, trying to discern which way the compass was swinging. His handwriting was no surprise, strong and bold. The message was to the point:

"Called away on business. Will pay for my room for days I am not here. Please hold for my return."

Given their middle-of-the-street conversation of the night before he had written that note—given his invitation to go on a date—it seemed very impersonal and businesslike. He had signed it only with his first name, no term of endearment.

What would she expect? *Love, Connor.* No, definitely not that. *Hugs?* That was laughable. How about *best wishes*? Or *can't wait to see you again*?

Despite all her misgivings, Isabella could feel herself anticipating his return like a child anticipating Christmas, even though she chided herself not to.

He had asked her on a date. If he followed through, she wondered what he had in mind. She felt excited about it, when really, that was the most unsafe thing of all.

Or maybe she really did not know the first thing about safety. Because she turned on the news one night, and it was focused on Azerbaijan. Normally, Isabella did not watch the news, and she would have flipped by the station. But tonight, she recalled that first morning Connor had said that was where he was coming from. Was that where his business had called him back to?

And indeed, the story was about an incident that had happened at the World Food Conference. Members of an unnamed private security organization had apprehended someone who had made threats against one of the delegates. Details were sketchy, and there was no footage. Had Connor's company been involved? Her gut said it had been.

When the story was over, Isabella shut off the TV,

but she sat there until the room grew dark, thinking about what she had seen.

She was aware her stomach was in a knot. She was aware that *this* would be the reality of tangling your life with a man like Connor Benson.

Six days after he departed, a knock came on her front door. It was dinnertime, and Isabella was not sure who would come calling at that hour.

She swung open the door to see Connor standing there.

He looked so wondrously familiar. Her heart began to pound unreasonably. Her anxiety about the kind of work he did left her in a rush of warm relief to see him standing there, so obviously unharmed.

"Oh!" she said. She could feel herself blushing as she stepped back from the door. "You didn't have to knock. You live here."

He cocked his head at her, lifted a brow.

"I mean, you're a guest here. I want you to feel you can come and go as you please."

"I know that, but I also knew you didn't know when I would be back. I didn't want to startle you. Again."

She regarded him. His face was deeply etched with exhaustion. But there was something else there, too. It was as she had suspected when she read his curt note— he had bought himself some time and now he seemed remote, as if they wanted different things. It was as if he had thought about that late-night meeting in the street and decided he wanted something different than what she wanted. He wanted them to be strangers. She wanted them to be friends.

Or more than friends?

Her anxieties were realized. Isabella could feel the

excitement that had been building about his return leaving her like air hissing out of a pricked balloon.

"Come in," she said. "It's hot outside. Are you hungry?"

He hesitated. Isabella had the feeling they were not back at square one, they were somewhere even before square one. Was he going to pretend he had never even asked her on a date?

"Come eat," she said, more forcefully than she intended. She felt as if she did not want to give him room to retreat, physically, to his room, or emotionally, away from her.

She suspected it was because Connor was a soldier, and he responded to the command in her voice. He dropped his bag inside the door and followed her into the kitchen. He took a chair at the table, and she moved to get him some of the pasta she had made for her own dinner. Now, passing it to him, she could see even more clearly the exhaustion in the lines of his face. His mouth had a stern set to it, as if smiling was foreign to him.

She felt guilty. Whatever he had just come from, it had been hard, and it had taken a very obvious toll on him. What was she thinking, making this all about her?

"Where have you been?" she asked, lowering herself in the seat across from him.

"Just a job."

"Ah. Azerbaijan?"

He frowned at her.

"The World Food Conference?"

"The conference is over now. Everything went fine." He dug into the pasta like a starving man. It did her heart good to see him eat like that, even if he was doing it to avoid her.

"I saw something about it on television one night. Was there some kind of threat made against some of the delegates?"

His voice was cool, it didn't invite probing. "Everything went fine," he repeated.

"Someone was apprehended."

"Really?"

"Really. By the private firm that looked after security for the event."

He lifted his eyebrows at her. *So what?*

"Were you in danger?" she asked him softly.

He lifted a shoulder. "Not particularly."

She knew then that he *had* been in danger, and that he shouldered the dangers of his job with the ease of long practice. This was not a man you could be timid with. This was not a man you could beg not to go to his world because it would soothe something in you. She found she had more courage than she ever would have believed. Because she felt proud of him, and in awe of his strength.

"Ah, Itus," she said. "Ever humble."

He looked up from his plate, lifted a brow at her. "What do you know about Itus?"

"I know in Greek mythology, he is the god of protection."

"It's just a name," he said. "My business partner, Justin, named the company. He picked that name. I am not a Greek mythology kind of guy."

"I wonder if your business partner was thinking of you when he chose that name."

Connor frowned, uninviting, but she went on anyway.

"Because Itus was very like you," she said quietly.

"Me?" He snorted, self-deprecating.

"Yes, you."

"In what way?" Connor had a bemused look on his face.

"He was a mortal boy, only seventeen when he was chosen to protect the god Apollo. He was given two swords, and he became so good with them that he beat the god Ares in a sword fight, though he would not boast about it. Apollo wanted to make him a god, and Zeus agreed, possibly because he did not want any more of his gods beaten in sword fights with mere mortals. Itus refused the honor. He did not feel he was worthy, but Apollo insisted and made him eat the food that would make him immortal."

Connor actually cast a wary glance down at his pasta.

"Then Apollo released him from his duties, and Itus now spends his days protecting the innocent from those who would do them harm."

"Look—" he set down his utensils, very deliberately "—Isabella, there is no use thinking there is anything the least romantic about me. Or what I do. It's hard, dirty, dangerous work—"

"You forgot lonely," she said quietly.

"—and it makes me a poor choice for a companion. No, not a poor choice. The worst choice. I should have never asked you out on a date. It was stupid and frivolous."

She felt the sharp bite of disappointment, but she was not totally unprepared for it. The crispness of his note had hinted this might be coming. At the same time, she could see it was the result of the events he had just come from that made something so simple as going on a date seem frivolous to him.

"I've decided," he said, his voice curt, "a date between us is out of the question. I mean, we are living together under the same roof for two more weeks. It's just way too awkward."

"I agree," she said soothingly.

That seemed to pull him up short. He regarded her suspiciously and then continued, "I mean, if I'm going to spend time with you, I should make it count. I should teach you something useful."

She found herself gazing at his lips, thinking she had an idea or two what she'd like Connor Benson to teach her. "What would that be?"

"I should teach you how to swim."

"Instead of a date," she clarified.

He nodded vigorously. "It's not good to go through life with fears."

"Ah." It seemed ironic that he would say that when it was more than apparent he might have a fear or two about the date he had asked her on. She decided now might not be the best time to point that out to him.

"Once you know how to swim," Connor said seriously, "it gives you confidence and courage in dealing with all kinds of things that come up in life."

But not dates. Again, Isabella bit her tongue to keep herself from saying it out loud. So, her Itus did not want to date her, but he still wanted to protect her, or give her some tools to protect herself.

"Someday I believe you will have children," he continued sternly. "You can give them no greater gift than comfort in the water."

She could argue with him, of course. It seemed unlikely she would ever have children. But if she did, it seemed to Isabella there were all kinds of gifts parents gave their children, and that the greatest of those was love, not swimming lessons.

But he was in full retreat, and she had a feeling that the mention of the word *love* would probably push him right out her door and out of her life, so she bit her tongue again. It was probably good to learn this tongue-biting skill. You would need it a great deal around a man like him.

"I would be deeply appreciative if you would teach me how to swim," Isabella said.

He looked at her, wary of her demure tone.

She smiled back at him, though she had to bite her tongue, yet again, to keep from laughing out loud. She could so clearly see he was terrified of going on a date with her. His terror made her feel powerful and attractive and sexy. She had never really felt those things before. It was worth facing her own terror of the water dead-on.

A swimming lesson? He didn't know what he was letting himself in for. In fact, Connor Benson had no idea that he was teaching her already, all about the nature of confidence and courage.

"When should we start?" she asked, sweetly. "And where?"

"I'll arrange with Nico to use his pool," Connor said. "An hour, every afternoon from tomorrow, Monday to Friday, should give you the basics."

"I can learn to swim in five days?"

"Well, you won't be trying out for the Italian swim team, but you'll have some basic skills you can practice."

"Thank you," she said, lowering her eyes from his so he would not see the glee dancing in hers. When she looked back up, Connor was eyeing her suspiciously. Then he pushed back from the table and left the room.

"Things are improving between us," she said softly to herself. "I managed to feed him something before he ran away this time."

He probably hadn't considered that little detail when he was planning swimming lessons. No, Connor had probably not given a single thought to how hard it was going to be to run away from her in a swimming pool, especially since she had no love of the water. She'd be clinging to him like a barnacle to the bottom of a boat.

But there was another problem. Where, in a tiny place like Monte Calanetti, on such short notice, was she going to find the right bathing suit for this? Obviously she would have to make do with what she could find for tomorrow.

But he'd said it would take a week.

It was so much better than a date! A whole week.

She went into her office and shut the door. She flipped on her computer and typed the words she wanted into the search engine. Then she narrowed the search by putting in the necessary delivery dates.

By the time Isabella was done, she felt extremely naughty. The way she had felt in the red dress should have been fair warning to her, and to Connor, both.

Isabella Rossi *liked* feeling naughty.

As Connor was waiting in the water of Nico's beautiful pool, Isabella came through the back gate and gave him a quick wave before ducking into the cabana beside the pool.

He was pleased to note she looked particularly understated today in a longish skirt in a dull shade of beige and a baggy blouse in the same color. Her glossy hair was pulled back tightly, and she was carrying a large book bag that she was hugging to her chest. Really? She looked more like a nerdy student than the teacher.

He surveyed the pool while he waited for her. It was nestled in the garden grotto behind the house, and the pool had been made to look like a pond. Ferns trailed fronds in the water, and there was a small waterfall at one end of it.

Lovely as it was aesthetically, it was not really a pool for serious swimming, but it was large enough to do a few strokes, plus it had a deep end. It was about the furthest thing from the pools he had done SEAL training in, but it would do for an introduction to swimming basics.

Connor was feeling enormously pleased with himself. Teaching Isabella how to swim—instead of going on a date—had been a brainstorm. Swimming, after all, was useful. Tackling an irrational fear was useful. When he left this place, he would leave her with a skill that would be practical to her for her whole life. He would leave her with a sense of herself that was different than what it had been before. That sounded quite a bit better than leaving her with the heartache that a date promised.

She was staying here in this idyllic little village in Tuscany, and he was leaving, so what was the sense of exploring the sparks that were flying between them?

Isabella came out of the cabana. She had taken her hair out of the elastic when it would have been more sensible to leave it in. She had on an enormous poncho-like caftan that covered her from her head to her toes. It had hideous wide stripes in a crazy array of colors.

It reminded him of pictures he had seen of what people wore to music festivals in the '60s.

When she stood on the deck he was at eye level with her feet. Her toenails were painted lime green, and as odd a choice as that was, he had to admit it was adorable, and a little less nerdy than the rest of her ensemble.

"What's that thing?" he asked her. He noticed that her face had been scrubbed free of makeup, probably in preparation for her swim.

"What thing?"

"That thing you're wearing."

She looked down at herself. "Oh. My swim cover."

He had to bite back a smile. She had to wear a swim cover to get from the cabana to the pool? The walk might have been twenty yards.

"Well, how about if you take it off and get in the water."

She hesitated. He could see the pulse beating in her throat. She looked past him at the water and gulped.

"Believe me, you can't swim with it on."

"Oh," she said, as if he was breaking world news to her. Isabella reached for the zipper, and closed her eyes. Because she was afraid of the water? Or was she sweetly shy about being seen in her swimming suit?

She bent over to get the zipper undone. Her swim cover was still doing its job. Covering. The zipper stuck partway down, and she tugged and tugged, but nothing happened. Suddenly, in frustration, she gave up on the zipper and pulled the caftan from her shoulders. As she was freed from the bulky covering, it slid down and settled in a lump at her waist.

Connor stared helplessly.

Her eyes locked on his. He looked away, focusing

on those little green toenails, not sure he wanted her to see what he was thinking. She pushed the caftan away from her waist and it floated to the ground, at his eye level, creating a puddle that looked like a burlap bag around her little monster-toed feet.

He was left looking at the length of her lovely legs. Then she stepped out of the fabric puddle and kicked the covering aside.

Connor reminded himself he had seen her in a transparent shower curtain. And a red dress that had made his mouth go dry. Whatever this was, it could not be any worse than that. Isabella was a practical schoolteacher. She would know how to pick a good bathing suit.

Having thus reassured himself, Connor cocked his head upward to see more than her feet and her legs. His mouth fell open. He gulped. He snapped his mouth shut so that the practical schoolteacher would not guess how much she was rattling his world.

A swimming lesson? Whose dumb idea had this been?

She was wearing one of the tiniest swimsuits he had ever seen, if you could call that scrap of fabric—three scraps of fabric—a swimsuit. Isabella was wearing a string bikini in an amazing shade of lime green that made her skin look as golden as the sand at a beach in New Zealand, Kaiteriteri, that he had visited once. Her dark hair spilled over that golden expanse of skin, shiny and beautiful.

"Is something wrong?" she asked. Her tone was all innocence, but he wasn't fooled. No woman put on a bathing suit like that without knowing exactly what she was doing!

Suck it up, he ordered himself. He'd seen her in a

shower curtain. Nothing could be worse than that. Except this was worse than that. It was worse, even, than the red dress.

Isabella Rossi, village schoolteacher, nerdy girl, was smoking hot!

"Wrong?" he choked out, not willing to give her the victory. "What could possibly be wrong?"

"I don't know. You have a look on your face."

"A look on my face?" he demanded.

"Mmm. Like you've been smacked with a frozen fish."

He wiped whatever look he had on his face off. He felt as though he'd been smacked, all right, and not with a frozen fish. Smacked with awareness of her. He had the ugly feeling she wasn't as innocent as she appeared. In fact, Connor had the ugly feeling that she might be toying with him.

He forced himself to find his voice. It had to be addressed. "You really should have left your hair up."

"Oh? Why's that?"

What was he doing talking about her hair? He needed to tell her the bathing suit wasn't going to work. At all. "You don't want to get it in your face."

"I'm not planning on getting my face wet."

"You have to get your face wet. To swim."

She didn't look the least convinced. She dismissed him with a little wave of her hand. "Oh, well, maybe next time I'll get my face wet."

Address it, he ordered himself. "Uh, that bathing suit—"

"Yes?" Her voice was husky.

"—is really nice."

Now, *that* he had not meant to say. At all. Isabella was beaming at him.

"—but, it isn't, er, really made for swimming."

Unless he was mistaken, and he was pretty sure he was not, the little minx was lapping up his discomfort.

"It's called a bathing suit," she said stubbornly.

"Maybe it's for *sun*bathing. I mean, if you were to dive in the water with that thing..."

His voice trailed away.

"I'm not planning on diving today, either," she informed him primly.

Wait a minute. Who was in charge here? He suspected, in that bathing suit, she was. "Well, I wasn't planning on that, either, but—"

"The bathing suit will have to suffice," she said. The schoolteacher voice was very at odds with the drop-dead gorgeous woman standing in front of him. "Selection—"

Seduction? No, no, she'd said *selection*, not *seduction*.

"—is very limited in Monte Calanetti at this time of year. I ordered some other things on the internet. They should arrive soon."

How soon was soon, he wanted to demand. Maybe they could postpone.

"I'm sure it will be fine," Isabella said, "You already said it's not as if I'm training for the national swim team."

She had him there. He wanted to teach her enough to hold her own if she fell out of a boat. Or in the river. Or got carried away unexpectedly by a current. He wanted to teach her enough that being around water did not make that pulse go crazy in her throat, like a rabbit being chased by dogs. The way it was now.

Was that because she was about to get wet? Or was it because she was trying out her bold new self on him?

Connor considered, again, postponing. He glanced at her face. A tiny little smile was playing across her lips before she doused it. She *was* toying with him!

"Get in the water," he snapped. The sooner she was covered up with anything, including water, the better. If the bathing suit fell off, or melted, they'd deal with that when it happened. Just as they had dealt with the shower catastrophe.

But really, how much could one man take?

Isabella stuck her toe in and yanked it back out. She made a face. She hugged herself, either not as confident in the skimpy suit as she wanted him to believe or suddenly aware that she was tackling something she was afraid of.

"I can't just jump in," she decided.

She could sit on the edge of the pool, reach out and put her hands around his neck… Connor gave himself a shake. This was going to be quite hard enough! "There are stairs at that end."

She looked where he was pointing and saw the stairs entering the pool at the shallow end. She eyed her dropped caftan for a second, as if she was considering putting it back on for the short walk to the stairs. Or putting it back on and fleeing.

Instead, she tilted her chin up and went over there, wiggling her hips self-consciously the whole way. It gave Connor plenty of opportunity to study how much of her was not covered by those skimpy green scraps of fabric. It also gave him plenty of opportunity to set his face into a mask of indifference.

At the top of the stairs, she repeated the put-one-toe-in-and-withdraw-it procedure. Still in the water, he slogged his way over to that end of the pool and stood close to the bottom of the stairs.

"At this rate we are still going to be here tomorrow," he groused out loud, instead of saying what he really wanted, which was *get in the water, dammit*.

She held up a hand, a very Italian gesture that warned him not to hurry her, and then Isabella proceeded to get into the water with painful slowness.

CHAPTER SIX

As Connor watched, Isabella got on the first stair leading into the pool. She was acting as if the world was tilting and her life depended on her hanging on to the handrail.

The world was tilting, and Connor felt as if his life depended on her getting in the water. With the water at her ankles, she paused there, allowing him to wallow in the full impact of that bathing suit. Was that a piercing, right below her belly button? Was his jaw clenched?

"The easiest way is just to jump in," he told her. Yes, definitely clenched. He deliberately relaxed it.

"Never let it be said I'm easy."

He contemplated her. Her command of English and all its nuances and slang was not good enough for her to have meant that the way it sounded. Though the beautiful young widow was probably about the furthest thing from easy that he had ever met.

She went down one more step. Now she was up to her knees. She had both hands on the handrail. Her knuckles were white.

"I thought the water would be warmer," she said.

"It's perfect." His jaw was clenching again.

She wrinkled her nose, letting him know their ideas

of perfect were different, which would be a very good thing for him to keep in mind, because a bathing suit like that made a man think he could make anything work out, even against impossible odds.

And the odds were impossible. Everything about them was different. He was large, she was tiny. He was powerful, she was fragile. He was cynical, she was innocent. They were culturally a million miles apart. He's seen colleagues fall for the seemingly exotic girls of foreign lands. It never worked.

He tried to hold those thoughts as, finally, Isabella was at the bottom of the steps, up to her cute little belly button in water. It was a little dark mole under her belly button, not a piercing. He was not sure which was sexier.

Isabella was still holding onto the handrail as if her life depended on it. He tried to remember why he had thought getting her in the water would be easier on him. It was not.

"Let go of the handrail and walk over to me," he said.

"Not yet." Her voice had a little quaver to it.

And that changed everything. Because it reminded him this wasn't about him. It wasn't about recalculating impossible odds. It was about her, giving her a few tools to deal with the harsh realities of life. And he could not let her scanty little bathing suit distract him from that. That's one of the things he was trained to do. Sift through information very quickly, ignore the distractions, focus on the mission.

So he crossed the distance that remained between them and pried her hand, ever so gently, off the handrail. He placed himself right in front of her and held out his other hand. She hesitated and then placed her hand in his.

Their hands joined as they faced each other, they were like two dance partners who had never danced together sizing each other up. It occurred to him this was going to be like no swimming lesson he had ever given before.

"Don't even look at the water," he said softly. "Just look at me."

Her eyes fastened on his face as if she was drowning and he was the lifeline. Her gaze was as disconcerting as the bikini. Maybe more so. It made the mission waver a little more.

"See?" he said, forcing himself to speak, keeping his voice soft, and taking a step back, "No danger. No crocodiles. No chance of falling over a ledge. No current to sweep you away."

No danger. Ha-ha. Her hand, small but strong in his, felt like one of the gravest dangers he had ever encountered. Had he really thought getting her in the water was going to be better than watching her on the deck?

Now, added to his physical awareness of her hands in his, she was so close to him he could smell that spicy perfume that was hers and hers alone. It felt as if he was being swept away by the absolute trust in her eyes fastened on his, the way she was holding his hands. She took her first tiny step through the water toward him.

He backed up. She took one more. He backed up two. And then they were doing a slow waltz through the water. He was careful to stay in the shallows, even though it wasn't nearly deep enough to help him deal with the worst of the distractions. Was that tiny bathing suit top sliding sideways just a touch?

Connor repeated his command to himself.

Suck it up.

"See?" he said softly. "It's not so bad, is it? Just stay in the moment. Don't think one thought about what could happen."

She actually closed her eyes. A tiny smile touched her lips. He ordered himself not to look at her lips and definitely not to think about what could happen. Connor felt the purity of the moment—water on his skin, her hair shining in the sun, her small hands in his, the rapturous look on her face—seducing him.

Somehow, he'd had this utterly foolish idea that he was going to pretend she was a raw recruit and be able to keep professional distance from her as he taught her the basics of swimming. He was not sure how he had deluded himself. He had never had that much imagination. He'd always prided himself on being such a realist.

"The water does feel amazing on my skin," she breathed. Her eyes remained closed in wonder.

Connor cleared his throat. "So now you've seen the water in this end of the swimming pool holds no danger to you," he said, trying desperately to stick to the business at hand and not think one single thought about her skin. "So, let's try the next step."

Her eyes flew open and that pulse in her throat picked up tempo. "What is the next step?"

"I'd like you to learn the water will support you. Human beings are buoyant. They float."

She looked doubtful about that—the pulse in her throat went crazy.

"Isabella, you will float."

"I'm scared."

"I know."

His life's work had presented him with this situation, again and again. He'd had plenty of encounters with people, civilians, who found themselves in difficult situations. Families who, through no fault of their own, found themselves in war zones. Hostages, in the wrong place at the wrong time, who didn't know the rule book, who had spent their entire lives blissfully oblivious to the fact there was a rule book.

Connor had led people from burning buildings, evacuated the terrified, navigated the fear of others in a thousand different ways. He'd dealt with people who were scared. He did it all the time.

He excelled at this: at infusing his abundance of confidence and calm into panicky people through his voice and his actions.

It felt different this time, way too personal, as if that enemy called fear was hovering at the edges of his own awareness. But that was his fault, not hers, bikini notwithstanding. He took a deep breath, gathered himself, formed a plan.

"I'm going to stand beside you," he said quietly, "with my hands like this. You are going to lie down in the water, on your back, and let my hands support you."

"Oh, God," she said in Italian. "I don't think I can. Could we just walk around some more? I was getting the hang of that. Walking in water. I think it's biblical."

"I think that may be walking *on* water."

"It's good enough for me. For today."

"Swimming lessons, heavy emphasis on the swimming."

"My hair isn't right. And the bathing suit won't work. You already said that."

"We'll figure it out. Together."

Together. He did not excel at figuring things out *together.* It had been his greatest weakness with the

SEALs. He was not a good team player. He had a tendency to go maverick. The last time he had done it, against orders, Justin had followed him...

"Are you all right?" Her hand, wet, warm, was on his cheek.

He shook his head. How was it she could see what no one else ever saw? "Yeah. I'm fine."

She didn't move her hand. He didn't move it, either. He had to stop this craziness. He shook his head again, trying to be all business. But droplets of water flew off his hair and rained down on her face, emphasizing the compassion there.

"Lie down in the water." His voice had a snap to it, like a flag caught in the wind.

Isabella's hand dropped to her side, but Connor could feel the warmth of it on his face as if it still rested there.

"No, I—" She twisted and looked at the stairs.

"Trust me," he said in *that* voice, firm, the voice of a man who was used to being in charge of everything, including the safety of others.

She dragged her eyes back from the staircase and looked at him for a long moment. Her eyes, with the water reflecting in them, looked more green than gold.

"Okay," she whispered.

"So just lean back," he coaxed her.

She leaned back an inch.

"Maybe a little more."

She leaned back another inch, so stiff-spined she looked like a tree bending over. He sighed and moved into her swiftly, before she could guess what he was going to do. Maybe he didn't even know what he was going to do himself until he had done it.

He scooped Isabella up and held her against his chest.

"Oh," she sighed with surprise. She would have weighed about as much as a feather under normal circumstances. With the water taking most of her weight, it was like holding a puff of air.

Except that her skin was warm and sensual, like silk. She blinked up at him and then twined her arms around his neck.

What part of the Swimming 101 manual was this in? he demanded of himself. He pried her fingers from around his neck and put her away from his chest, supporting her body on his hands, at right angles from his own.

"Okay," he said. His voice was faintly hoarse, not completely his talking-a-hostage-away-from-the-bad-guy voice. "Just relax. That's it. Now straighten out your legs. I've got you."

Tentatively, she did as he asked, her forehead wrinkled with anxiety as she gave herself over to the water. Her hair floated out in the water around her face, like dark silk ribbons. The small of her back was resting securely on his hands. Her skin was warmer than the water, and he felt a primal awareness of her that he did not want to feel.

At all.

"You're a bit tense," he told her. He heard the tension in his own voice and took a deep, steadying breath. "Relax. I won't bite."

"Yes," she said. "So you've said."

"Focus on your breathing. Put your hands on your tummy—no, you don't need them, I've got you—and breathe until you feel your tummy rising instead of your chest."

Shoot. Did he have to mention her chest just as his voice was returning to normal?

"This is quite amazing," she said after a moment.

"Amazing," he agreed. His jaw was starting to hurt from clenching his teeth so tightly. "So, just try moving your legs a bit. Kick."

She did a little kick.

"Very good," he encouraged her. "Harder, both of them."

She kicked tentatively. And then harder. The splash hit him in the face, which seemed to motivate more strenuous kicking on her part. She giggled.

That giggle helped him turn a page. Connor pretended to be worried about getting wet, ducking the worst of the splash while never letting her go. She giggled some more.

"Now straighten your legs out. Think of a pair of scissors opening and closing and kick like that. That's perfect. That's why it's called a scissor kick. Now, instead of just standing here, I'm going to let the kick propel you. I'll move with you, though. You see how it works? Your legs are amazingly strong."

What he meant was that everyone's legs were amazingly strong, that this particular movement used the gluteus maximus, the largest muscle in the human body, but he didn't clarify, since she looked so pleased. And there was no denying her legs were amazing!

He supported her and guided her until she had kicked around the pool in a large circle.

"Now," he said, "my hands are still here, but I'm moving them away from you, so you can see it's the water supporting you, not me."

"No."

"Yes."

She glared up at him.

"Don't be nervous. The water's only three feet deep here. You can stand up at any time. Just relax. I'm going to—"

"No! Don't let go of me. I'm not ready."

He'd heard it again and again, looking into the eyes of a terrified civilian who was being asked to do something that required more of them than had ever been required before.

"Yes, you are," he said, "you are ready."

Slowly, he slid his hands out from underneath her. Her eyes grew wide, and then she got nervous, and her body folded at the center, legs and head going up, abdomen and torso going down, under the water.

"Ahh," she yelped.

His hands were floating inches below her, and so he supported her again, very quickly.

"Try and keep your body stiff."

"I thought I was supposed to relax!"

"Well, relaxed stiffness."

"There is no such thing."

"Maybe not in Italian. There is in English." He managed to say it with a straight face.

She smiled in spite of herself, and then he let her go, and she tried again. Again, she got nervous and began to fold; again he used his hands to steady her. The third time, she got it. She kicked on her own and he shadowed her.

"Am I swimming?" she demanded. "Am I swimming all by myself?"

He smiled at her enthusiasm, and she seemed to realize she was swimming, unaided, on her back. The realization ruined it, of course. This time he wasn't quite quick enough, and her head went under the water. She came up sputtering, her hair spilling rivulets of water down her golden skin. She grabbed for him and clung to him.

He realized he was enjoying that way too much and put her away from his chest, though he allowed her to hang on to his forearms.

"That wasn't so bad, was it?" he asked her.

She shook water from her hair. "No," she said, surprised and then delighted. "No, it was fine. I just held my breath when I went under."

There was a moment when people reached deep inside and found out who they really were that was awe-inspiring. It could happen as you sneaked them across a border or pushed them out of a plane, or it happened in those moments, large and small, when people required just a tiny bit more of themselves.

And so it could happen just like this, a woman in a swimming pool on a warm spring day when everything seemed suddenly infused with a light that was not the sun.

It was always an amazing thing to be a part of this moment. She was grinning ear to ear, which increased Connor's sensation of basking in the light. He had to force himself to move away from that moment and back on task.

"And that brings us to part two," Connor said. "For some reason, people have a natural aversion to getting their faces wet."

"I told you not today," she said. The grin disappeared.

"Let's just ride this wave of discovery," he suggested.

For a moment, she looked as if she intended to argue, but then, reluctantly, she smiled again. "All right. Let's ride this wave."

Both of them had said it—let's. Let *us*. Us. A duo. A team. Sheesh.

"So, before you dunk again, we're going to work on getting your face wet," Connor said. There it was again, slipping off his tongue naturally. *We*. "Lie on my hands again, this time on your stomach."

She flopped down on her stomach, and he supported her, his hands on the firm flesh of her belly. "Good. Now put your face in the water and blow air out of your mouth. Make bubbles. The more the better. Think of yourself as a motorboat."

Whatever reservations she might have had up until this point now disappeared. Isabella gave herself over to learning to swim with unreserved enthusiasm. With Connor supporting her stomach, she blew bubbles and then they added a scissor kick. She managed a few kicks without any support before she went under and came up laughing.

Isabella laughing.

Isabella soaking wet, in the world's skimpiest bathing suit, laughing.

It was probably one of the most dangerous moments of Connor's entire life, and he had had a life fraught with danger.

It wasn't dangerous because she was so beautiful, or even because she had lost her self-consciousness and she was so sexy in her teeny bathing suit. It wasn't dangerous because she was finding her inner resources of courage and strength.

No, what made the moment beautiful was her joy.

What made the moment astounding was the serious expression gone from her face and the sorrow completely erased from her eyes. No matter what the danger to himself, Connor was glad he had given her this moment.

"I think that's probably enough for today," he said gruffly. "We'll start some basic arm work tomorrow, moving toward a front crawl. And we'll do work on your legs with a kickboard. By the end of the week, you'll be swimming across this pool by yourself."

"Really?"

"You are a complete natural."

"I am?" she asked, so pleased.

"Absolutely."

"What an amazing afternoon." She cocked her head at him. "What do the American teenagers say? Awesome!"

She was standing facing him. She leaned a bit closer. He had plenty of time to move away from her. But somehow he didn't, frozen to the spot, like a deer in headlights, not able to back away from where *awesome* could take them.

She stood on tippy toes. Her body, slippery and lithe, came in contact with his in a far different way than it had when he was using his arms to buoy her up in the water. She kissed him, a tiny brushing of their lips.

He, of all people, knew how little time it took to change everything. A millisecond. The time for a bullet to find its way from rifle to target, the time for tires to crunch across the trigger device on an explosive, the time for a school to go from rooms of laughing children to completely engulfed in flames. He, of all people, knew how quickly everything could change.

But maybe he hadn't known this: as quickly as you

could be sucked into darkness and everything could shatter around you, just as quickly you could be thrust toward the light, propelled into a world that promised love was stronger.

Love? He felt furious with himself, and not too happy with Isabella, either. But then she was backed away from him, still laughing, that delightful, carefree, water-over-rocks laughter, as if she had no awareness at all how badly she had just disrupted his well-ordered world.

"Thank you, Connor. I can't wait for tomorrow."

And then she walked away from him, through the water, by herself, the woman she had been an hour ago—clinging to the handrail and then to him—gone forever.

Isabella got out of the pool without the benefit of the stairs. She put her hands on the deck and levered herself out, wiggling her bottom at him in the process. And then, free of the pool, she gathered up that voluminous caftan but didn't put it on. She scampered across the deck to the cabana, not once looking back.

Thank goodness she did not look back. Because she would have seen him, still standing in the water, stunned by the power of that one tiny little brush of lips. To change everything.

The man he had been an hour ago might have been gone forever, too. Because the thing about a kiss like that? It opened a door. It opened a door that was pretty darned difficult to wrestle shut again once it had been opened. It changed everything in subtle ways.

Connor sucked in a deep breath. He said a word under his breath that he would never say in Isabella's presence. He dived under the surface of the water. His momentum carried him to one end of the pool. Though there was hardly room to get going, he began to do furious laps, butterfly stroke.

But by the time Isabella emerged from the cabana, he was aware that swimming had not defused what he was feeling. Even that most challenging stroke did not begin to burn off the fire that brush of her lips against his had stoked within him.

CHAPTER SEVEN

ISABELLA CONTEMPLATED THE fact that she had kissed Connor Benson. Really, as far as kisses went, it had been nothing. A peck. A thank-you.

But even in Italy, where people were passionate, a thank-you kiss might normally be placed on the cheek, not the lips.

Connor's lips looked so firm. And yet, giving under the pressure of hers, they had felt soft and pliable. His lips had tasted of something, but she wasn't sure what. It had been pure, like holding out your tongue to catch raindrops.

Heaven. That's what they had tasted of. The problem was, after tasting something like that, a person could spend her life in pursuit of it. It had really been a foolish thing to do, reckless, especially with them living under her roof together.

But in that moment, after the lesson, she had just felt so bold, so ready to do just as he suggested, to ride the wave of discovery instead of fighting it. It had been wonderful tackling the water, doing something she had always been afraid of. It had made her feel free in a way she never had before.

From the moment she had chosen that bathing suit

over the far more conservative ones available, even with the limited selection in Monte Calanetti at this time of year, Isabella had felt she was saying yes to life.

The swimming lesson itself had made her feel so alive and so bold and as if the world and this day were plump with possibilities instead of just one day following the next, safe and routine.

Isabella came out of the cabana and saw that Connor was swimming like a man possessed. The stroke he was using was amazing, his powerful arms and shoulders lifting his torso and propelling him out of the water as if he had been shot out of a cannon.

He noticed her, she was not sure how, and he stopped and stood up. He folded his arms over the lines of his chest. Her awareness of him rippled through her like a current that could sweep her away.

"I forgot to tell you, I found another place to stay," he said.

She knew instantly he was lying. He hadn't found another place to stay. He had tasted the reckless danger, too, as soon as her lips had touched his, and decided to find different accommodations.

He was acknowledging something was going on between them. Something more powerful than he could control. And even though he had told her to ride the wave of discovery, he was not prepared to do that himself.

She held her breath. Was he going to cancel swimming?

"I'll see you tomorrow. And I'll pay you for your place for the agreed dates." he said. He dived back under the water before she could let him know she was not going to help him assuage his guilt by allowing him to pay her for a room he wasn't going to occupy.

Isabella had never really felt this before: an acute awareness of her feminine power.

She walked home by herself, aware that the buoyancy of the water seemed to have infused her. Even though Connor had said he was moving out, her steps were light, and she felt as if she was walking on air.

She got home to discover a parcel had been delivered. It was one of the bathing suits she had ordered online, from Milan. She was pleased it had been delivered so quickly, that overnight delivery had meant just that.

And she was even more pleased when she opened the parcel and slipped the fabric from the tissue paper. So tiny! How could it possibly have cost so much money? Still, she hugged the scraps of fabric to her and went to try the new suit on. It was no more a *swim*suit than the lime-green bikini today had been.

But she had given herself permission, with that first bold choice of a bathing suit, to start exploring a different side of herself. More feminine. More sexy. Deeply alive within her own body. Deeply appreciative of herself as a woman, and of the power that came with acknowledging this new side of herself.

Isabella was choosing the bathing suits of a woman who wanted a man to be very aware she was a woman. Not to just tease him, but to let him know he was not going to be able to shunt her aside so easily, just because he'd switched from a date to swimming lessons.

She thought of the way Connor had been swimming when she left Nico's garden area—like a man possessed, or at the very least, like a man trying to clear his head—and allowed herself the satisfied chuckle of someone who had succeeded beyond their wildest dreams.

Still, when she heard him come in later, pack his

bags and leave, she avoided him. Already her house felt empty without him. If she went and saw him, she was not at all certain she could trust herself not to beg him to stay.

She would not beg him to stay, but she was not above making him sorry he had left.

The next day at the pool, she wore the same over-size caftan out onto the deck. Connor was in the pool tossing a blue flutter board into the air and catching it, pretending he'd barely registered her arrival.

But when she dropped the caftan, he registered her arrival—he missed his catch on the kickboard.

If it was possible, her new bathing suit, black and shiny, was even skimpier than the one she had worn yesterday. She really took her time getting into the water, savoring the scowl on his face.

When she reached the bottom stair, he shoved the kickboard at her and snapped some instructions.

"Aren't you even going to say hello?" she asked, petulant.

"Hello," he snapped.

"Your new accommodations must not be very nice."

"What would make you say that?"

"You seem like you haven't slept well or something. You have grumpy lines." She touched the sides of her own mouth to show him where. He stared at her mouth. His grumpy lines deepened.

"We're going to work on your kick today." And so they did. There was a lot less touching this second day of instruction. It was shameful how disappointed she was by that. He announced the session was over from the opposite end of the pool. Isabella was fairly certain this was to discourage thank-you kisses.

Though, even without the kiss, his swimming seemed even more furious when she left than it had the day before.

The third day, another bathing suit had arrived. It was not a bikini. It was a leopard-patterned one-piece with a plunging neckline and the legs cut very high. It was so racy—and not the competitive swimming kind of racy—that Isabella actually debated not wearing it at all.

But she was so glad she had when they sat side by side on the pool deck, legs dangling in the water for lesson number three. His mouth set in a grim line, Connor demonstrated the arm movements for the front crawl. Really? Him showing off his arm muscles like that was no more fair than her showing off in her bikini!

They ended the lesson in the water. With him at her side she managed to swim across the width of the shallow end of the pool, once on her back and then once on her front.

The only reason he touched her at all was because she swallowed some water and came up choking. He slammed her on the back a few times before ordering her back to work.

When she emerged from the cabana, she noticed that Connor was churning up enough water to create a tidal wave.

The fourth day, not wanting it to be too obvious she was enjoying driving him crazy, she put the lime-green bikini from the first day back on. He got her into the deep end. He taught her to tread water, arms doing huge swooping circles, legs bicycling.

"You don't work hard at it," he warned her. "You relax. It's something you should be able to do for a long, long time."

And then he made her do it for half an hour, treading water right beside her without ever touching her. Once again, when she left he was covering the pool in length-eating strokes.

The fifth day, she arrived at the pool in her newest bathing suit. It was too bad he'd left her house and she'd refused his money. It would have helped her afford all these suits.

This one was a simple black one-piece, a tank style. The most suitable for swimming, it made the light come on in his eyes just as the others had done.

"Today," he announced, "we'll do a quick review of everything we have learned, and then we're done."

Done. Isabella thought of that. No more seeing him every day, unless she caught glimpses of him in the village, going about his business. Her life would be as empty as her house.

And then the wedding would come and go, and he would be gone from Monte Calanetti for good. Forever.

She got in the water and stood at the bottom of the stairs.

"Don't stand there gripping the rail like that," he snapped. "You've come farther than that."

The tone! As bossy as if she was some green recruit he had authority over. A beach ball, rolling around on the deck, pushed by the wind, plopped in the water beside her. On an impulse, she picked it up and hurled it at his head.

He caught it easily and squinted at her. For a moment she thought he was going to ignore her protest of his high-handed ways. But then he tossed the ball high in the air and spiked it at her. She swiveled out of the way with a little squeal. The ball missed her, and then she grabbed it. She threw. He dived under the water.

Connor resurfaced and grabbed the ball. He threw it hard. She, who a week ago had been afraid to get her face wet, ducked under the water. She came up and grabbed the ball. He was swimming away from her. She waded in after him, threw the ball when he stopped. It bounced off his head.

"Ha-ha, one for me," she cried.

He grabbed the ball and tossed it. It hit her arm. "Even. One for me, too." He swam right up to her, his powerful strokes bringing him to her in a breath. He grabbed the ball and let her have it from close range. "Two for me."

"Oh!"

Just like that, all the tension that had been building between them for a week dissolved into laughter. They were playing. The last lesson was forgotten, and they were like children chasing each other around the pool, shrieking and laughing and calling taunts at each other.

And then she missed a throw and the ball bounced onto the deck. Neither of them bothered to get it, and now they were just playing tag without the ball between them. The air filled with their hoots of laughter. She tagged him with a shove and swam away. He came after her hard and splashed her, then tagged her and was off. She knew she couldn't possibly catch him, and so he was letting her shove him and splash him.

An hour went by. They were breathless, the air shimmering with their awareness of each other.

Reluctant for it ever to end, Isabella finally gave in first and hauled herself up on the deck and lay there on her tummy, panting, exhausted. A shadow passed over her. He was standing above her.

Isabella was aware she was holding her breath. He had moved out of her house to avoid her. But then, after a moment, he lowered himself to the deck, on his stomach, right beside her. He wasn't touching her, but he was so close she could feel a wave of warmth coming off the outer part of his arm.

He closed his eyes, and she unabashedly studied him. She could see how the water was beading on his skin, droplets tangled in his eyelashes, sunlight turning them to diamonds. She could see the smooth perfection of his skin, the lines of his muscles, the swimmer's broadness of his shoulders and back.

She had never, ever been more aware of another human being than she was of Connor, lying beside her. She sighed with something that sounded very much like surrender, and closed her eyes.

Lying there on the pool deck beside Isabella, Connor felt as if the whole world came to a standstill. When danger was near, he always felt this—his senses heightened until they were almost painful. And he felt it again right now, as he had never felt it before.

He could feel the gentle Tuscan sun on his back and the heat rising up through the pool deck and warming every cell of his skin. He could hear the birds singing, but more, he could separate their songs, so he could hear each one individually. She sighed—a contented sound like a kitten's mew—and he could feel the puff of air from that sigh touch his lips, as life-altering as her kiss had been.

He could smell the flowers that bloomed in abundance around the pool, the faint tang of chlorine and most of all Isabella. The spicy scent had been washed away and replaced by an aroma that was dizzying in its feminine purity.

He had only one sense left to explore. He opened his eyes and gazed at Isabella stretched out on the pool deck. Her hair hung thick and wet and luxurious down the narrowness of her back. Her black bathing suit clung to her like a second skin, caressing the curve of her back and the swell of her firm buttock. Her skin was as flawless as porcelain. The roundness of her cheek was pressed into the deck, and her lashes were so thick and long they cast a faint shadow there. Her lips had not a hint of lipstick on them, and yet they naturally called to him, full and plump and sensuous.

As if she sensed him studying her, she opened her eyes. He unabashedly threw himself into the color of them—it felt as if he was swimming in cool pools of sun-filtered greens and golds and browns.

A few days ago, he had gone to the chapel at the palazzo. It had been strictly work. If he was a bad guy, where would he hide? What were the weak places both in the chapel and around it? He'd taken some pictures and made some notes of the exterior and then moved inside.

Logan Cascini, the project manager for the whole restoration, had come up to him. Connor had been touching base with Logan on and off since he arrived, and there was an affinity between the two men.

"You have to see what has complicated my life today," Logan had said wryly.

"That's gotta be a woman," Connor had muttered.

"That sounds like the voice of experience," Logan said, raising a quizzical eyebrow.

"Show me your complication," Connor said, not following Logan's implied invitation to elaborate.

"This is the final wall we're working on. We're just pulling off that old wood paneling."

Connor followed Logan over to a side wall of the church. The workmen were absolutely silent, their normal chatter gone.

As they uncovered it, Connor, who considered himself no kind of art lover, had stood there, frozen by the beauty of what he was seeing revealed.

"It's a fresco," Logan supplied, "probably centuries old, and probably by one of the lesser Renaissance painters."

"I've never seen anything so beautiful," Connor said when he could find his voice. The fresco was the Madonna and child. The expression on the Madonna's face was so infused with love that Connor could feel an uncomfortable emotion closing his throat.

"And like all beautiful women," Logan said, "she is complicated."

"Now *you* sound like the voice of experience."

For a moment something pained appeared in Logan's eyes, but then he rolled his shoulders and ran a hand through his hair. "You don't find something like this and just keep on as if it's normal. I'll have to notify the authorities. Depending what they decide, the wedding could be delayed."

Connor had let out a long, low whistle, loaded with the sympathy of a man who knew firsthand how the unexpected could mess with a guy's plans.

Then, taking one more look at the fresco, he had said goodbye to Logan and left the chapel.

Now, days later, lying side by side at the pool with Isabella, with the sun warming their backs, he was feeling that again.

Paralyzed by almost incomprehensible beauty. When Isabella saw how intently he was looking at her, she smiled and didn't look away. Neither did he.

The danger he was in came to him slowly. He'd tried to fight this attraction every way that he knew how. He'd tried to create distance. He'd tried to nip it in the bud. He'd even moved out of her house.

But still, he was falling in love with Isabella Rossi. Or maybe he already had. That was why he had felt such an urgent need to cancel that date, to get out from under the same roof as her. It was why he was in this state of heightened awareness and had been for days. The fact that he could see beauty so intensely was connected to what he was experiencing with this woman.

She reached out and touched his shoulder, and again, because of his heightened awareness, he felt that touch as though he had never been touched before, had never felt so exquisitely connected to another human being before.

"I've gone from being terrified of the water to loving it," she said huskily.

"I know, you have been a great student." He was the wrong man for a woman to love. He had always known that. His childhood had left him wary of relationships, and his choice of work had suited that perfectly. He had told himself he was protecting women from the potential for loss, but in fact he had been protecting himself.

Because he'd always known only the bravest of women could handle what he was dishing out.

True, he wasn't in active service anymore. But what had just gone down in Azerbaijan was plenty of evidence he still had his knack for finding danger.

It seemed to him this little slip of a woman lying on the deck beside him was the bravest of women.

"Connor?"

"Huh?"

"I've never had that before, what I had just now."

"What?"

"Just fun," she said. "Just good old-fashioned fun. Even when I was a child, Giorgio was my best friend. He couldn't run and play like everyone else, and so I stayed with him. We read and drew pictures, but I've never really had this. Just to let go of everything, to play until I'm so out of breath I feel as if I can't breathe.

"I mean, I do it with my students. I have fun with them, but it's not the same. I have to be the adult. I have to maintain a modicum of control. I don't ever get to be this carefree."

His awareness of her deepened yet again. Her beautiful eyes were sparkling with tears.

"So, thank you," she said. "I'm never going to be able to thank you enough. Never."

His awareness of himself deepened, too, but not in a good way. An unexpected element inserted itself into the pure and sizzling awareness of the moment. Connor suddenly felt ashamed of himself. He'd backed out of that date out of pure terror of what she was doing to him. He'd left her house because he couldn't trust himself around her without wanting to taste her lips again.

But when he'd challenged her to embrace what terrified her, she had done it in a heartbeat. She had shown incredible bravery.

And now she was telling him she'd never had fun. That fooling around in the swimming pool was the most fun she'd ever had. She'd given her whole life to looking after others. Her husband, and then the kids at school.

It seemed to Connor he was being given an opportunity to do something good. Maybe the best thing he'd ever done. It wasn't about whether or not he was comfortable. It wasn't about that at all. That feeling that maybe he was falling for her deepened in him. Didn't that call him to be a better man? Didn't it ask him to be more than he had ever been before. Braver? Stronger? More compassionate?

"You know that date I canceled?" His voice was so low it came out sounding like a whisper.

She went very still.

"You want to give me another chance?"

"Yes," she said, her voice low, too, as if they were in a church. "Yes, I do."

"What about tomorrow night?"

"That would be perfect."

Isabella looked at her bed. It was covered with every single item of clothing that she owned. She had tried on the red dress and then taken it off. He'd already seen it. It wasn't the message she wanted to give. Nothing was the message she wanted to give.

Suddenly, frustrated, exhausted from trying things on and ripping them back off, she threw herself down on the bed, falling backward into the heap of clothes. Isabella lay there, staring at the ceiling.

She thought back over their week of swimming lessons. There had been the most delicious sense of getting to know Connor, of connecting with him. There had been the most delicious awareness of him physically, a yearning to touch him and taste him that was astonishingly powerful. That small kiss had shown her what was going on between them was like riding a wild horse. It wasn't going to be controlled.

She had never felt that for Giorgio.

A stab of guilt pierced her heart. And she had a terrible moment of self-awareness. Giorgio, despite the fact he was dying, had been the safest choice she could make. He had been her friend, and she had loved him as a friend.

But that other kind of love? The kind that was filled with passion and excitement? Hadn't she known from the time she was a little girl that that kind was unpredictable and hurtful and destructive?

Connor would never be unfaithful. After you knew him for ten minutes, you knew that of him. That he was a man of complete honor.

But he had pitted his formidable strength against the wrongs of the world. He had warned her that he sought out danger, and that he found it. She had seen that for herself when she had caught the tail end of that news clip out of Azerbaijan.

To allow herself to love Connor Benson would be to open herself up to pain such as she had never felt, not even when she was a little girl and had seen her father in a café with a woman who was not her mother.

From the second she had spotted him, Isabella had begun working on an elaborate story: it was someone from work. It was a friend. It was a cousin. And then her father had leaned forward and kissed that woman on the mouth with unmistakable passion.

Then there had been the different pain: watching Giorgio die, every day a series of losses for him, and for them, until she was feeding the man she married baby food from a spoon.

And so, this week Isabella had tackled one of her fears. She had learned to swim. And she had deliberately fanned the fire she had seen in Connor's eyes.

But without considering the consequences. In a way, she had won. He had given in. He had asked her out again after canceling the first time. But was she really ready to open herself to more pain?

Isabella realized, sadly, she had used up all her bravery. She did not have any left. She certainly did not have the kind left that you would need to go on the wild ride that was love.

Not with a man like Connor Benson.

The next morning, she caught up with him on the edge of town. She had known he would be there, heading out for his early morning swim.

"Connor."

He swung around and looked at her. His smile held as much promise as the sun that was just beginning to touch the rooftops of Monte Calanetti.

"I'm sorry. About tonight?"

His smile faded.

"I can't. I realized I have a previous obligation."

He cocked his head at her.

She should have thought of the previous obligation before now! She blurted out the first thing that came to her head. "My students are putting on a skit for the spring fete. I'm not ready. The costumes aren't finished. I haven't started the props."

He was looking at her quietly.

"So, clearly a date is out of the question. For right now."

And in a while, he would be gone, anyway. If she could just hold off for a few more days, she would be what she most liked to be. Safe. She would leave that woman she had been introduced to in Nico's swimming pool behind, a memory that would fade more with each passing day, and then week, and then year.

Besides, neither of them had addressed where a date would be leading—down that dark road to heartbreak? There were so many different routes to get to that destination.

So, if she should be so pleased with herself that she was taking control of a situation that had the potential to get seriously out of control if she let it, why did she feel so annoyed that instead of looking dismayed that she had canceled their date, he looked downright relieved.

"Is it the swimming lessons that put you behind the eight ball?" he asked.

She frowned at him. "What is this? Behind the eight ball?"

"Have you ever played pool?"

"Isn't that what we just did all week?"

He threw back his head and laughed. Oh, of all the things he could have done, that was the worst. It filled her with an ache to live in a state of playful days of hearing him laugh. But of course, given what he did for a living, that was unrealistic.

There would be far more days of waiting for him, of anxiety sitting in her stomach like a pool of acid, of uncertainty and fear.

"In America, we play a variation of billiards called pool. Guys like me who spend ninety-nine percent of our lives bored out of our skulls become very good at it. There's a game in pool called eight ball," he said. "The eight ball is black. You can only touch it when it's the last ball on the table, otherwise you lose. So, if it gets between you and the ball you are aiming at, you are in a very difficult predicament. That's what 'behind the eight ball' means."

"What about the one percent?" she asked. She didn't care about the eight ball.

"Huh?"

"You spend ninety-nine percent of your life bored out of your skull—what about the one percent?"

"Oh, that."

She waited.

He grinned at her, devil-may-care. "It's one percent of all hell breaking loose." He held that smile, but she saw something else in his eyes, as if he held within him shadows of every terrible thing he had ever seen.

"And that's the part you love, and also the part you pay a price for."

He did not like it when the powers of observation that he had encouraged her to hone were turned on him.

"Weren't we talking about you?"

"Yes, we were," she said. "I think that would be an accurate description of how I feel right now, behind this eight ball. I have much to do, and not enough time to do it."

"My fault. Because of the swimming. I'll help you get ready for your skit. I'm winding down on the recon for the wedding anyway. I'll be wrapped up in a couple of days."

And then he would be gone.

CHAPTER EIGHT

"You won't like it," Isabella said with all the firmness she could muster. "You won't like helping me. I'm making paper sunshine cutouts."

Connor laughed again, but she could hear a faint edge to it. "Lady, my life has been so full of things I didn't like it would make your head spin."

Again, that hint of the dark places he had been that he carried within him. "What is this, make your head spin?"

"I'll explain it to you over paper sunshines."

Isabella was ashamed of her weakness. She could not give up what he was offering. She could not give up an opportunity to spend time with him. It seemed to her that she had caught a glimpse of his world when they went swimming. Now she had an overwhelming desire to see how he would react to hers.

No doubt with utter boredom. But at least it was not a date, that event that was so loaded with romantic expectation and foolish hopes.

"All right," she said stiffly. "Come after school. Class gets out at one."

"Okay," he said. He sauntered away, into the magic of Monte Calanetti's dawn, whistling. Whistling! It confirmed that he was not the least distressed that she had canceled the date. The exact opposite, in fact.

He was very punctual, and Connor Benson showed up just as her students were swarming out the door of her classroom. He looked like a ship plowing through the sea of bright blue uniforms. Luigi Caravetti, who always had too much energy, was walking backward, catcalling at one of the girls.

Connor sidestepped him easily, but at that very moment, Luigi swung around and smashed into him.

Connor barely moved, but Luigi fell down. With absolute ease, Connor went down on his haunches, helped the little boy up, picked up the homework Luigi wouldn't do anyway and handed it back to him. Luigi said something to him and then wound up and kicked Connor in the shin and ran off before Isabella could reprimand him.

Rubbing his shin, he turned to her and grinned ruefully.

"I'm sorry," she said, "Luigi is a bit of a handful. What did he say to you?"

"I don't know. He said it in Italian. I'm beginning to pick up a few phrases, so I think he told me to watch were I was going. And then he switched to English."

"He doesn't know any English."

"Ah, well, there's a universal word that all little boys—and most big ones—love to use."

"Oh! I will speak to him tomorrow."

"No, that's okay. He kind of reminded me of me at that age. And if I was going to guess something about him? No dad in the picture."

Again, Isabella was taken by Connor's incredible powers of observation. "That's true. In fact, his poor mother had to get a court order to keep the father away from them. He's not, apparently, a very nice man. But still, Luigi is troubled about it all. Children are always troubled about difficulties between their parents."

The last of the children clattered down the stairway to the main floor of the school, and they were cloaked in sudden silence. Then Connor Benson was in her classroom.

"So," he said, putting his hands in his pockets and rocking back on his heels, "this is your world."

"Ninety-nine percent boring," she told him. "One percent all hell breaking loose."

Connor gave her an odd look that she interpreted as *you don't have a clue what all hell breaking loose looks like.* But then he shrugged it off, as if he had given himself a mental order to lighten up. "I'm going to guess that one percent is largely your little Luigi."

"You would be guessing right."

"Nobody asked me what I was doing here when I came in," he said.

"Sorry?"

"When I came in and asked for your classroom, no one at the office asked me what I wanted or what I was doing at the school. They didn't even ask to see identification."

"Obviously we are in need of a security expert!" she said brightly, but he didn't seem amused. She became more serious. "We haven't experienced the kinds of problems here that you have in America."

Did he mutter *yet* under his breath? He removed his hands from his pockets and turned away from her and wandered around her classroom. At first she thought he was looking at drawings and pictures, and she was pleased that he was curious about her world. But then Isabella realized that Connor actually seemed to be looking for something else. She was not sure what.

He stood at the front, taking note of both the doors into the room. Then she saw him go to the windows, open the lock on one. He slid the window open and leaned out, looking at the ground.

He came to the table at the back, where she had the project laid out. He seemed faintly uneasy, but he lifted a sun with the hole in the center and put his head through it, attached the elastic around his chin.

She had planned to be so reserved, professional, accepting his help as a volunteer, but nothing more. Instead, she giggled at the picture this big self-assured man made with his face poking through a hole in a cardboard sunshine. The wall came tumbling down as she joined him at the art table at the back of the room.

How could he wear that silly thing with such aplomb? That's what confidence did, she supposed. "Boys are sunshine," she said.

"And girls?"

She picked up a pink flower and put her head through the center of it and attached the elastic. "Girls are flowers."

He smiled at her, but she still thought she detected faint uneasiness in him. Well, was that so unusual? Many men seemed uneasy in classrooms. The furniture was all in miniature, after all. The spaces were too tiny for most men, and Connor was even larger than most men.

"These are done," Isabella said, resting her hand on one stack, "but we have seven sunshines remaining to cut out and thirteen flowers. The children drew their own, but the cutting part can be quite difficult for little hands. The cardboard is a bit thick." She gave him a pair of scissors.

He sank into one of the little chairs. She actually wondered if it would break under his weight.

"That doesn't look very comfortable."

"I'm used to discomfort." Connor picked up a particularly messy-looking sun drawn on yellow construction paper.

"Luigi's?" he guessed.

She lifted a shoulder—*yes*.

When they had been swimming, that task had occupied them and filled the space between them. There had been no need for conversation on a personal level.

Now, tongue caught slightly between his teeth as he tried to fit his hands in the little scissors, Connor said, "So, tell me everything."

"What?"

"Where you grew up, how many kids are in your family, what your favorite color is and what your most secret dream is."

Again, she had the feeling he might be trying to distract her from some uneasiness he was feeling. Still, she was happy to do that and so, with his encouragement, she talked. It was amazingly comfortable sitting at the little table, cutting with little scissors, the sun pouring in around them. She marveled at how good it felt to be with him like this, at ease, and yet not at ease the way she had been with Giorgio.

With Connor, something sizzled in the air between them. All that time in the pool together had increased her awareness of him, and that did not change now that they were sitting in her classroom, in chairs too small for them, fully clothed.

She answered all his questions except one.

He didn't miss that, of course.

"And is there a secret dream?"

She thought of the way she had felt when she had learned Marianna was pregnant. Happy for Marianna, of course, and yet...

"No," she croaked.

His scissors stopped moving. He looked across at her. "There is," he said.

"I've given up on the secret dream thing."

"Ah." He obviously did not believe her, but he didn't press. They finished all the costume pieces, and he helped her build a simple set.

How could it be both so easy and so difficult to be with him? He came into her world of paper and glue and paint as easily as she had gone into his world of water. And he did the same thing to it.

An existence that had seemed mundane suddenly sparkled. There was laughter everywhere.

Except as he got ready to leave. He was suddenly very serious. "Can you request a different classroom?" he asked.

"What? Why?"

He shrugged and shoved his hands in his pockets. "You should just ask for one on the first floor, if you can."

"I like this one," she said, feeling stubborn.

"I'm sure you do. Unless there's a fire." His voice, which had been laughter filled only moments ago, was suddenly very grim.

Now, a few days after they had begun, they stood

back from her completed set, costumes and props. The set was lightweight cardboard so that it could be moved easily to the village square the day of the fete.

She sighed with contentment. With his help, it was so much better than anything she could have ever done alone.

He stood beside her. "It's done to your satisfaction?"

"Yes. A whole two days before the fete. I am officially out from under the eight ball."

"That's good," he said. "Because now we can have our date."

She slid him a look. He was covered with splotches of blue paint from painting the sky. He had a relaxed smile on his face.

She was so aware of him. It was dangerous. But she had no fight left in her. She did not want to fight anymore. She wanted to see what would happen between them.

Even if it was the most dangerous thing of all.

"Did you have something in mind?" she asked. Her voice sounded like a mouse squeaking.

"Oh, yeah," he said.

"What?" She hoped he would say something safe, something not that different than watching television at her house. A movie, maybe.

"I want to surprise you with it."

"How do I know what to wear for a surprise?" she asked.

"Anything you wear will be fine."

Did he not understand women at all? "If you could give me a hint," she suggested.

"It will have something to do with the chapel."

"The chapel?" Isabella could not imagine what he

had in mind. The last time she had seen it, the chapel had looked like a construction site, surrounded by scaffolding.

"Trust me."

"All right."

"I'll pick you up just before eight."

"All right."

It was complete surrender, and she knew it. And looking at his face, so familiar to her now, she realized it was a surrender for him, too. It was a surrender to what had been building between them like a thunderstorm on the horizon.

Looking at his face, Isabella wondered when exactly this had happened. When had he come to feel beloved to her?

Had it been as he painted the sky on cardboard or cut the head hole from yet another sunshine? Or had it been before that, when he had drawn her into the swimming pool and taught her to embrace what frightened her most?

Maybe it was before even that. Maybe it had begun that morning they had walked through the dawn to the river and she had felt the mud ooze up between her toes.

Or maybe it had been from the very first moment, when she had put his breakfast outside his door and been assaulted by him in her own home, the beginning of the waking up that had led to this: how she loved her life with Connor Benson in it.

It was a warm evening, so Isabella wore a simple white sundress of eyelet cotton, with narrow straps and a ribbon at the waist and a wide skirt. It did not sing the siren song that her red dress had, but it showed off her coloring and her figure, and it was more her, somehow.

It was as if, with Connor, she was exploring herself and slowly arriving at what that really was.

She saw she had chosen exactly the right ensemble when he arrived at her door. She could see it in his eyes even before he told her that she looked beautiful. Connor looked extraordinary. She had always seen him looking quite casual. Tonight he was in pressed dark slacks and a cream-colored linen dress shirt.

He went down her narrow walk before her and held open a car door. It was a very sleek, sporty car.

"Did you have a car before?" He hadn't ever parked one when he lived with her.

"I had one at my disposal, if I needed it. I prefer to walk. It gives me a better sense of a place. You notice more."

"Is this the car you had?" she asked.

He shook his head. "I traded up."

"Why?" she whispered, looking at the sleek gray convertible with awe.

"It seems to me, my lady, you have missed a few things on the road to romance. Your man wants to show you new worlds and impress you."

Her man? On the road to romance? Was she really ready for this? Isabella could barely breathe as he held open the door for her. It seemed like a long step down into the low-slung sports car, and he took her hand and helped her. She settled back in a deep leather seat.

The car was a dream to ride in, and she loved the way Connor handled it in the narrow streets. There was nothing about him, she realized, that was inclined to show off. And yet he was obviously extremely confident and capable handling the very powerful car. She loved the way one hand rested lightly on the wheel, his other on the knob of the gearshift. The ride seemed over way too soon. When she reached for the door handle, he gave her a meaningful look and she let her hand fall away.

He opened the door for her and then went around to the trunk and opened it as well. He looped the handle of a large wicker basket over his left arm and offered her his right. She threaded her arm through the crook of his elbow and they went up the well-worn path to the palazzo's chapel.

It was as she had remembered, almost completely engulfed in scaffolding.

"It must be American," she said out loud.

"What?"

"A date at a construction site."

"What? Italians don't date at construction sites?" He shook his head, teasing her. "I thought you people had perfected the romantic gesture."

"Why would you think that?"

"My mother calls Italy the land of *amore*."

The land of *amore*. She lived here, and she had missed it! Not that she was going to admit that to Connor.

And then he led her around the back of the chapel.

Isabella gasped. There was a table set up there with a white tablecloth on it. It faced out over a view that seemed to show the rolling, vineyard-covered hills of the entire valley.

Connor placed his picnic basket on the table and pulled back a chair for her. "The sun will be setting—" he glanced at his watch "—in seven minutes. Do you want a glass of wine?"

How could she refuse? He took a bottle out of his basket, dewdrops of condensation running down it. He popped the cork with complete ease. While the wine breathed, he took long-stemmed glasses, plates and cutlery from the bag.

He glanced at his watch. She could see the sun beginning to lower to the edges of the hills. The light was changing, softening all around them.

"What I want to share with you is this way," he said. "I'll let the wine breathe for a moment before I pour it."

What did he mean? The sun would go down over there, in front of them. Was that not what he had brought her here to see, a most wildly romantic gesture? She turned and looked at him. He held out his hand to her, and she took it. Could she ever get used to the feeling of a hand like his closing around hers?

He led her around the chapel and in a side door.

The light inside was suddenly drenched in color, golds and pinks. It was almost as though the chapel had been designed for this moment in time: the setting of the sun. Despite much evidence of work and restoration, when it was suffused with light like this the space seemed sacred.

"I wanted you to see this," he said, and with a sweep of his arm directed her gaze to the side wall of the chapel, by the family pews.

She saw a fresco on the wall of the chapel. Even without the amazing addition of the light from the setting sun, the fresco took her breath away. She moved toward it as if in a dream, staring at the scene before her with utter awe.

The detail of the Madonna and child was stunning: as if each hair on their heads, each eyelash, had been painted individually.

"The color is astounding," she breathed. Connor was

standing right beside her, gazing at the fresco. "Their skin, the color of her robe, the child's lips."

Both Madonna and child had enormous, expressive eyes turned to the heavens, where the clouds parted and a beam of light illuminated them.

"Do you think I can touch it?" she whispered.

"I think so."

She placed her hand on the wall. The sun was touching the wall, and its warmth had seeped into it, making the fresco seem even more like a living thing. "I don't think I've ever seen anything as beautiful as this."

His hand covered hers. "I know. I felt the same way when I saw it. It's been covered all these years. I can't imagine why, and yet it probably preserved the magnificence of the colors. You know, Isabella, I have seen the world at its ugly worst, and I'm not sure why but this restored something in me."

"I understand."

"Do you?"

"Yes, it's like it holds a message. That beauty survives, or wins. It's like it is saying, when all else falls away, the best, the good, will remain."

"That's exactly what I felt when I saw it, not that I could articulate it like that."

"The best," she said quietly, "a mother's love for her child. The Madonna radiates love. Maybe not just for the child. Something bigger. For the world." She could feel the tears clogging her throat, and she bit them back. Even so, he seemed to know what an emotional moment this was for her, because his hand came to rest on the small of her back.

Time slipped away as they explored the fresco together, pointing out incredible details they thought the other might have missed.

Finally, when darkness had fallen so completely that the church was pitched in blackness, Connor ushered her back outside.

He poured the wine and took some candles out of the basket, placed them carefully on the table and lit them. And then he took a dish of still-hot pasta out, wrapped in a tea towel. When he took the towel off, the spicy fragrance of the lasagna made her mouth water. She was not sure if it was because of the painting or because of him that the food tasted as if the angels themselves had prepared it.

"Tell me now about your secret dream," he said softly.

The night was so perfect. Seeing the fresco had brought her secret dreams to the forefront of her mind. It felt right to give him all of her, to hold nothing back.

"Once, I dreamed I would have babies," she confessed.

"Not now? I can picture you with babies. I can picture that look on your face, exactly like the one on the face of the Madonna in the chapel."

"I'm getting very old for this dream," she said, her voice small.

"You think thirty-three is old for having babies?"

"Isn't it?"

He actually laughed. "My mother had my half brother Sammy when she was thirty-six, and my sister, Amelia, a year later. The baby of the family, Henry, arrived when she was forty."

"Thank you for telling me that. It just feels as if everyone having babies is so much younger than me.

Marianna's shower is tomorrow night, and I was trying to think of reasons not to go. Of course, I could not think of a reason not to go that would not raise eyebrows. In Monte Calanetti, celebrating the coming of a baby is mandatory, like giving kisses to strangers on New Year's Eve. But it is very painful watching others have what I wanted."

"You are not kissing any strangers on New Year's Eve," he teased.

Isabella shivered. Would it be reading too much into the teasingly possessive statement to think she could count on Connor to still be part of her life as the village welcomed the new year?

His teasing tone was gone when he spoke again. "Isabella, you and your husband could not have children?"

She shook her head. "He was already too sick by the time we married."

"Aw, Isabella."

"Please don't say that as if I'm to be pitied."

"I'm sorry, that wasn't my intention."

"I wanted to try, even though I knew I would be raising a child alone. Is that selfish?"

"It makes me wonder why you wanted one so badly that you would be willing to raise it alone. That is the hardest thing. I know, because I watched my mom do it. Even if there had been financial security, which I am sure you would have, the emotional burden is huge. The responsibility is a lot to carry alone."

"I see that every day in Luigi," she said.

"And yet?" Connor heard the unspoken as clearly as if she had said it.

She drew in a deep breath. The stars and the wine

and the gaze of Connor, steady and strong, drew her every secret out of her soul.

"And yet, I have always craved a family. A real family."

"Yours wasn't?"

"Oh, my mother and my father stayed together, but only because they both considered it a sin to split up. Our family was a sham. My father always had girlfriends, mistresses. My mother lived in a state of wounded pride and furious anger."

"I'm sorry."

"It's no matter," she said. "Not now. I have my students. They are all my children now. I am lucky in so many ways. And you, Connor? What are your thoughts on children?"

"My own?" he asked. His voice broke in pretended terror, and she laughed, but she was unwilling to let him off the hook so easily.

"I think you would make a wonderful father," she said.

"How, when I have never had that modeled for me?"

"Yes, you have, by men you admired, if not by your own father. I can tell by how you taught me to swim how good you would be at it."

"That's what my mom says, too, when she sees me tussling with my new brothers and sister, that I'd make a great daddy."

"You enjoy being with them?"

"Don't tell anyone, but it's one of my favorite things."

"And why would you not want to tell anyone this?"

"Kind of spoils the whole warrior image. But seriously? I don't think my lifestyle is very conducive to children."

"I think you're wrong. Your lifestyle is about honor, and about standing strong for what you believe. I am not sure you could give a child any greater gift than that."

"Until you come home in a box."

"What is this? Come home in a box?"

"It means to not come home at all."

Isabella wanted to shudder at the harshness of the expression, but she reminded herself there was no room in this man's life for a woman who shuddered at harsh realities.

"And just like that," he continued quietly, "you've made a lot of pain in the world. You've made a Luigi."

"Or maybe, if the love was strong enough, you've left a legacy that is not like the legacy poor Luigi has inherited."

"Maybe," he said, but he did not sound convinced.

The wind came up suddenly and lifted the tablecloth and blew out the candle. By the time they had rearranged the cloth and relit the candle, the serious mood was gone. They joked back and forth while they ate, and when silence fell it was comfortable, soaking up the beauty of the night skyline and the immense sky overhead and the stars that studded it.

Then he slipped his phone from his pocket. She was almost relieved he had made such a wildly inappropriate gaffe in the evening, because she thought to believe in perfection was probably an invitation to fate to prove you wrong. But then Connor searched through the phone and found some music. He put it on, then pushed another button. The phone glowed softly.

"How did you do that?" she asked.

"It's an app—it turns your phone into a light."

"Americans," she teased.

"Yes, we have to have all the state-of-the-art toys."

"If it brings you happiness."

"Isabella, stuff does not bring happiness. This brings happiness." He rose from the table, and he set his phone on the table and held out his hand to her.

"Dance with me?"

She rose from the table and went into his arms with a sigh.

"No words," he said of the music choice. "Not English, and not Italian. I think music and art can speak the language of the heart."

With the stars watching them and tears spilling down her cheeks at the absolute and complete wonder of this moment, Isabella Rossi luxuriated in the feeling of Connor Benson's arms closing around her. Her cheek was pressed into his chest, and she could feel the steady beat of his heart in her skin.

It was homecoming.

It was as if every event of her entire life had served only one purpose and that was to lead her to this moment, dancing under the stars of a Tuscan sky with Connor swaying against her, his hand on the small of her back, his breath fanning the hair on the top of her head.

One song became another. She kicked off her shoes. So did he. The grass was sweet and cool under their feet.

And then, in one smooth movement, he released one of her hands and bent down and retrieved his phone. He shut off the music and the light, plunging them into darkness and silence.

Only it wasn't really silent. She could hear the sounds of the night insects chirping and rubbing their wings, the call of a night bird. She could hear her own breath.

And his. She was certain she could hear the beating of her own heart.

It was no more completely dark than it was completely silent. The houses in the vineyards on the hillsides were matched by the pinpricks of light that shined brilliantly in the black velvet sky above them. His face was illuminated in a sliver of moonlight. She reached up and touched his features, running her fingertips along his forehead and his temples, the bridge of his nose, the faint scrape of whiskers on his cheek.

And then her fingers found the silky plumpness of his lower lip, and he reached out and held her hand there, kissed her fingertips and moaned with a sound of such yearning and longing it sent a wave of tingles up her spine.

His eyes on hers, he turned her hand over and kissed the palm, and the inside of her wrist, and up the length of her arm, feathery little kisses that the stars that watched over them would have approved of. He put that hand away from him and took up her other one and kissed it, just as thoroughly.

And then he tugged, urging her against the length of him.

She went willingly. She'd had hints of what this would feel like—accidental brushings at the pool, going by him in a narrow hallway—but she could not stop herself from sighing at how they fit together so perfectly, how the hard wall of him felt with her body pressed against it. She wrapped her arms around him, melding herself into his contours.

His hands moved her hair away from her face, and then his right index finger went to her chin and tilted it up.

He scanned her face, drank it in. She saw the same look of reverence that she had seen when he looked at the fresco.

"Would it be all right if I kissed you?" he asked huskily.

CHAPTER NINE

OF COURSE IT would not be all right if Connor Benson kissed her, Isabella thought dreamily. Her world would never be the same. It would open places in her that could not be forced shut again. But already her body was trembling in anticipation of welcoming him, and so instead of answering with words, she rose up on the tiptoes of her bare feet and took his lips.

They tasted of wine and starlight and pure masculine perfection. Connor's lips tasted of everything that was beautiful about the world. Everything.

He tangled his hands ever so gently in her hair and tilted his head over hers. The plundering was sweet, his lips claiming her lips, his tongue probing the curves and hollows of her lips and then of her mouth. She could feel the gentle scrape of his whiskers against the tender skin of her face.

She was rocketed into a different world. She was not so much Isabella, and he was not so much Connor. It was more as if they were part of some enormous energy that fused. That energy had been fusing since the dawn of time, drawing men and women together in a way that guaranteed the future of the human race.

That's how big what was between them was: the

whole human race relied on this fusion that was searing, delightful and painful by turns.

It opened up a cavernous hunger in her, to know more, to be more, to be filled to the top. It left her with an aching awareness that until this moment, she had been empty.

She released him and staggered back a step, touching her lips, her eyes wide and searching on his face.

"What?" he whispered.

"I didn't know." And then she was crying again, the night pregnant with overwhelming emotion. "I didn't know that it could be this beautiful."

He reached out over the distance she had created between them, pulled her back gently against his chest, stroked her hair as her tears soaked his shirt. "Shh," he said. "Shh, it's going to be okay."

A star a million years away fell through the night sky, leaving a stunning trail of light behind it.

And she thought that was what she had never really believed. Not in her whole life. She had never really believed it could be okay.

She went to take his lips again, but he shook his head, tucked her head to his chest and continued to stroke her hair.

"I don't think we should start again," he said huskily. He released her, turned to the table and began to pack their things back in the basket.

She hugged herself. A whisper of a breeze touched her, and she felt chilly without the protection of his embrace.

"Why?" Her voice, in her own ears, sounded like a mew of pure need.

"I don't want you to look back and regret an impulse."

"I won't."

"If it's not an impulse, you will still feel the same way tomorrow night," he said.

"I resent that you are choosing now to show off how disciplined you are." She went up behind him and pressed herself into his back, reached around and ran her hand over the marvelous strength of his forearms.

He went very still, and then he turned from the table and caught her up. He kissed her again, but lightly this time, before putting her away from him.

"Tomorrow," he promised her huskily. "Tomorrow night. We could have a second date."

"There is no tomorrow night," she said, aware her tone was sulky. "I have to go to Marianna's shower. As much as I would like to get out of it, I cannot."

"Well, then Sunday. Your day off, correct? We could spend the day together."

"It's the fete."

"Ah."

"Will you come watch?"

"I wouldn't miss it for anything. And after the fete? Are you free?"

"Yes." She felt shy and pleased. She actually felt grateful to him that he had stopped the runaway train of their passion, slowed it down. She thought it showed enormous respect for her.

"Would you let me plan something for after? That will be our second date."

"Yes," she said, and her sigh of happiness felt like that star she had watched fall from the sky.

* * *

When Connor woke the next morning, it seemed to him his whole body was smiling. And that was even though he did not really like his accommodations.

There had not been much available when he had taken his hurried leave from Isabella's house, a small, dark room at the back of someone's house. But it had its own bathroom and a separate entrance and compared to some of the places he had laid his head in his life, it was a palace.

And last night he had been more than grateful that he was not staying under Isabella's roof. Where would that have gone?

Where was it going, anyway? Apparently, at his instigation, it was going to a second official date.

How was he going to live up to the first date? Because really, in the date department, he was pretty sure he had scored a perfect ten, following Justin's instructions to be original.

He wondered what he should do next. But then that question pestered him again. Where was it going, anyway?

He realized, stunned, that he knew where it was going. He knew exactly. It was why he had refused to follow that kiss everywhere it had wanted to go.

He wanted to marry her.

Connor knew he would never feel right about having her in the way he wanted her without doing everything right. She was that kind of woman. Without saying a word she demanded a certain standard. Yes, she had a passionate side, and yes, that was easy to coax to the surface.

She would never be a quick roll in the hay. Underneath that passion, she was old-fashioned and traditional. She was the kind of woman who demanded a man's respect without ever saying a word out loud. With Isabella Rossi, you would either be committed for life or you shouldn't even be playing ball.

Committed for life. He mulled that over. The very thought a month ago would have put him on a plane for anywhere.

But now he was thinking how easy it would be for him to adapt to life in Monte Calanetti. With phones and computers being so high-tech, with global travel being so easy, there was no reason he could not work with Justin and Itus from here.

He even thought that children, whom, with the exception of his half siblings, he'd always found mildly repulsive, would be something he could manage with Isabella guiding him through the pitfalls. Maybe they could have a little girl who looked like her. What if the little girl looked like him, though? Maybe they would be better off to have a little boy.

He got up out of bed, filled with restless energy. He knew how to deal with restless energy, or thought he did. Connor gathered his swim things.

But somehow he never made it to the river. He was stopped by wildflowers that grew by the road. He wasn't going to see her tonight. She was going to a shower. He wouldn't repeat his performance from last time she had gone to a function—he wouldn't be chasing through the streets looking for her.

He would leave the flowers for her to find after school. He wanted her to know he was thinking about her. Bonus: they would make her think of him, too.

Though, when he thought of the reluctance with which she had broken away from their first real kiss, he was happily aware she might not be thinking of much else except him! Being romantic—the thing he'd run in terror from his whole life—had the potential to be all kinds of fun.

He began to plan their second date in earnest. Connor wanted to do even better than he had done on the first one. She would want to relax after all her hard work on the fete. And so he spent the next few hours figuring out where to get a canoe. They would explore the river and find the perfect place, a secluded meadow of wildflowers that could only be reached by the boat.

They would have a picnic supper there. He planned an exquisite menu. He thought of introducing her to the mystical experience of swimming in the dark. And then he would paddle them home, the water so inky dark it would reflect the stars. He hoped he could create the illusion they were paddling through the heavenly night sky.

He left a second vase of flowers on her doorstep, where she would find it immediately after the shower. It contained a note telling her to bring her swimsuit for their second date after the fete. He underlined *swim* so that she wouldn't get any ideas about tormenting him with one of those bikinis.

But then, on thinking about it, he did not want to be in a secluded meadow with her in a bikini. So he tore up that note, and made a new one that simply said what time he would pick her up. He hesitated a long time. Should he conclude with *I love you*? He tried it. And then felt foolish. He tore up that note, too.

On the other hand, he wanted her to know he was

serious. He wanted her to know the whole course of his life felt as if it was changing. He tried a third time.

> *Dear Isabella,*
> *Life is a river, with calm places and turbulent places. I wonder if you would like to join me on this wild and unpredictable ride? If you are willing, I will pick you up tomorrow evening, after the fete, and we will explore the river.*

Instead of signing it with "love," he drew a clumsy heart and signed his name.

He stuffed the note in the vase of flowers before he could change his mind.

And then he went shopping for a swimsuit for Isabella, uncaring of the raised eyebrows and giggles as he went through the selection of women's bathing suits, noting the selection in Monte Calanetti at this time of year was quite a bit better than Isabella had claimed it was.

He purchased a particularly dowdy suit, put the wrapped package under his arm and went back to his humble quarters. He could not wait for tomorrow to come.

As Connor arrived at the town square the next night, it was already filling up with people. A makeshift stage had been set up at the far end of the square, and someone was testing a sound system.

For the first time since he had started planning the second date, he came down to earth. Connor could feel some nervousness tickle along his spine at the number of people in the square. As far as he could see, there was absolutely no security for the event. Didn't the good people of Monte Calanetti know that there were no safe places anymore? Not in the whole world?

He scanned the crowd and relaxed marginally. Really, it was just a family event. The chairs set up in neat rows in front of the stage were nearly full already, but no one seemed to mind. Farther back from the stage area, families were setting up picnic blankets. There were grandmothers and grandfathers, women holding babies, and children threading through the crowd screaming their delight. Young men stood in defensive huddles trying to pretend they did not notice the young women who sashayed by them in their spring clothes.

For all that it seemed benign and happy, Connor could not make himself go into the square and that crush of people to look for one of the remaining seats. He found a tree just on the very edge of the square, leaned his shoulder up against it and watched from a distance.

He could see the kids from Isabella's school, already seated cross-legged on the ground up front, in front of the rows of chairs. He spotted her class easily, their sunshine and flower headdresses making them stand out from the others.

There was Isabella, pacing up front, bending over to adjust a headpiece here, to tap a shoulder there, to smile encouragement or to listen to what one of the children was saying.

She looked extraordinary in a simple shift.

He realized there was no hope at all that the bathing suit he had chosen for her was going to dim her light. She could have been wearing a burlap sack today and she would have looked beautiful.

She was absolutely glowing.

Was that because she had feelings for him that matched his growing feelings for her? Did that light that shined forth from her like a beacon of hope have something to do with him? Did it have something to do with that kiss at the chapel? It felt like quite something to be responsible for a light like that one.

She turned suddenly, as if she could feel the intensity of his gaze on her. Her eyes scanned the crowd and then she saw him.

Despite all the noise and motion that separated them, it was as if the world went still. Her eyes locked on his. She lifted a hand in shy acknowledgment. He lifted his back. She smiled, and the glow about her deepened. She turned back to her responsibilities.

And he turned back to his. He tried to relax, but it was not in his nature. He simply could not be in a situation like this and not be scanning, watching for trouble. It had been a part of his life for too long.

A band took the stage and began to play boisterously, if without great talent. They received wild applause and launched into their second number.

Connor noticed something. His eyes rested on a man who, like Connor, was on the fringes of the crowd. The man was by himself in a sea of families.

The band finished their second number to wild applause, took bows and began to pack up their things. Two of Isabella's children, little girls in matching pink dresses, carried the cardboard backdrop for their performance onto the stage. Isabella's class rose in preparation.

Connor watched, and then his gaze went back to the man. He frowned. It was a very warm day. Why was that man wearing an overcoat? Why was he looking around like that, furtively?

The band had vacated the stage and Isabella's class marched into their places. The boys with their sunshine heads were in the back, the girls in the front. They were so excited, joyous in their moment of being at the center.

Isabella stood off to one side. She darted forward and made a last adjustment and said a stern word to a boy whose sun was looking decidedly crumpled. Connor recognized Luigi, the boy who had run into him and then told him to watch where he was going.

And then she went back to the side again and nodded. She beamed with pride as those innocent young voices filled the air.

Connor did not have to speak Italian to know the song welcomed spring. The suns rose, and the flowers waved happily.

But he was not transported to that place of innocence and hope. In fact, he felt as if the music and the rising suns and the waving flowers were all fading. Because the man was moving through the crowd, snaking his way in and out of the crush of people.

Connor pushed himself away from the tree he had been leaning on. With a sense of urgency, he closed the distance between them, following the man through the crowd. Connor ignored the outrage when he blocked people's views.

The man was nearly in front of the stage now, where the children had been sitting moments ago. He was reaching inside his coat pocket.

Without hesitation, Connor became that huge mountain lion he had been nicknamed for. He went from stalking to pouncing. He launched himself at the man in the coat. They went down in the front of the crowd of people. Everyone was screaming in Italian. The commotion moved like a wave through the crowd until it reached the stage. Isabella, who had been focused on the children, turned, as if in slow motion. Her mouth formed a surprised O. The singing faltered and then ground to a halt.

Connor rolled back to his feet, taking the other man with him. He lifted him up by the collar of the too-warm coat and reached his hand into the pocket. His hand closed around something cold and square.

Wrong shape.

Connor tugged it out and glared at his hand. There was a camera in it.

Connor stared at it. And then, convinced there was danger, he ripped open the buttons of the too-warm jacket. A wrapped birthday gift was hidden in the folds and fell to the ground.

"What's this?" he asked. It looked innocuous, but his training told him it could be anything. The whole point was to make dangerous things appear innocuous.

The man was staring at him with incomprehension. Connor picked up the package, and held it in front of him. "What is this?" he demanded again.

He was hit in the knees from behind and staggered forward a step before whirling to face this new opponent.

Luigi, was there, his face as crumpled as his sunshine headdress. He was screaming in Italian. The man was talking rapidly, both hands raised at his sides, open palmed.

Connor recognized *ma sei pazzo*.

And then Isabella was there, her hands resting gently

on Luigi's shoulders. The little boy turned to her skirt and wept.

She said something to the man in Italian, and seeing her embracing the boy, he thrust the wrapped parcel into Connor's arms and turned and pushed his way through the crowd.

Isabella's eyes, distressed, went to Connor's face. "Luigi's dad," she said quietly. "He wanted a picture of his son in the fete. He wanted to give him a birthday present."

Luigi sobbed something against her skirt, and she stroked his head.

"His dad wasn't allowed to go to his birthday party," she said sadly.

And then a woman pushed her way through the milling, jabbering crowd and grabbed Luigi away from Isabella. The woman turned and marched through the crowd, her chin tilted proudly, half holding Luigi's hand, half dragging him.

"How does this happen?" Isabella whispered. "Presumably they loved each other once. How does it turn to this?"

And then she brushed at her skirt and smiled weakly at Connor. He shoved his hands in his pockets and rocked back on his heels, weathering the dirty looks of the crowd returning to their seats.

"I will see if the children will go on," Isabella said. "I think that would be best, don't you?"

He nodded and watched her weave her way back through the crowd, get onstage and shepherd those distressed children. In minutes, she had comforted them enough that they were able to resume their song.

She had not, Connor noted, said one word of recrimination toward him over his overreaction to what had happened.

But then, she didn't have to. He had enough recrimination for both of them. He made his way through the crowds, holding the birthday present along with the parcel containing the bathing suit for Isabella, which he had retrieved. No one even seemed to notice him.

This was Italy. He supposed there were passionate disruptions all the time. But that did not make him feel one bit better.

What he felt was that he had been living in a fool's paradise. Was he really tangling their lives together when she had no idea what she was letting herself in for?

He went to her house, not knowing what to do with the gift for Luigi except drop it off there. He saw his vase of flowers waiting there for her, and in a moment of pure frustration, he swept them off her stoop with his shoe.

The glass shattered and flowers were strewn everywhere. His note was soaked in water. Annoyed with himself, he set Luigi's gift inside her door. Her door was unlocked, of course—this was Monte Calanetti, and the only person in the whole town who was out of step was him. He found her broom and dustpan and swept up the mess he had made and put it in the bin under her sink.

He told himself to leave. He could do what needed to be done over the phone. It would be better that way.

But he did not leave. He went through her house, stood in the doorway of the bedroom he had used and thought of the journey they had been on since that first morning when he had thought she was an assailant.

Normal people did not think like that. Normal people did not go into schools and look for escape routes and try to figure out how you would get out of the building if it burned. Normal people did not drag men in overcoats to the ground in town squares.

From that first day, he should have backed off. What had he done, pressing forward instead?

He stood for a moment in the doorway leading to the bathroom. The showerhead had been fixed, and a new curtain and rod had been installed. The curtain was no longer transparent, and under different circumstances that might have made him smile. But now, standing here, he could remember her wrapped in her shower curtain, and all he felt was an abject sense of loss.

He went back downstairs and stood in her kitchen, memorizing it and saying goodbye.

And then the door squeaked open behind him.

"Hello, Connor."

He turned and looked at her. He had hoped to avoid her. And at the same time, he had hoped for one last chance to look at her.

Just like looking at her house, he realized he was trying to memorize every single thing about her: the upward tilt of her eyes, the puffiness of her bottom lip, the shine of her hair. He was trying to both burn it into his memory and say—

"Goodbye, Isabella."

She looked as if he had struck her. "Goodbye? But—"

"I have to go," he said.

"Go?"

"I'm leaving Monte Calanetti."

"Leaving Monte Calanetti?" she asked, distressed. "But why?"

She had to ask that? After the mistake he had just made at the fete? After he had overreacted so hugely to Luigi's father? After he had destroyed the performance she had worked so hard on? After he had embarrassed himself and her in front of the whole town?

"I've finished the reconnaissance for the wedding." He could hear the chill in his voice. He put up the shield in his eyes. "I'll be back a week before to put everything in place, and then the day it's over, I'll be gone again."

"But isn't this a bit sudden? I thought..." Her voice drifted away. He hated himself for what he had led her to believe.

But wasn't the truth that he hated himself anyway?

"I'm not who you think I am," he said gruffly.

"I have never met anyone less capable of subterfuge than you!" she snapped. "I know exactly who you are, Connor Benson."

For a moment, everything in him went weak. To have this, to have someone know everything about you, and care anyway? Wasn't that what every man really desired?

Beyond anything else, beyond wealth, beyond accomplishment, beyond success, did not the most humble of dreams live in every man? To be cared about for exactly who he was?

But Connor knew, in his case, that was not possible. When Isabella knew the truth, she would not feel the same about him anymore. How could she? He had never felt the same about himself again.

"Isabella, I need to tell you something."

CHAPTER TEN

I NEED TO tell you something. Isabella felt as if her world was going dark and swinging crazily around her. Hadn't every horrible event of her life begun with those words?

Her father, looking up in that café and seeing her standing there, tears rolling down her face, running across the street to her.

I need to tell you something. This is how it is for a man. It doesn't mean I don't love your mother. And you.

Giorgio, just turned sixteen, *I need to tell you something. I have an illness. I have always known I was not well. I might have ten years. And I might not.*

And now this. Isabella pulled one of her chairs out from the table and sank into it. She was so filled with dread she felt as if she could not breathe.

"What? What do you need to tell me?"

He pulled out the chair across from her. Was she ever going to be able to come into this kitchen, this house, again without seeing him here, remembering him? Because he was saying goodbye.

Connor had a dark secret, just as all the men in her life had had dark secrets. She should have known, should never have left herself open to it. Never.

"It's another woman, isn't it?" she asked, her voice shaking. "Of course! How could I have been so naive to think a man like you could love only me?"

He swore under his breath. "It's not another woman."

"You're dying, then," she decided.

"No. I need to tell you why I left the SEALs," he said.

She perked up. Why he'd left his previous job? That didn't sound as if it could be too bad.

"You need to know what kind of man I really am."

"I already know what kind of man you are," she said.

"No, you don't," he said harshly.

The harshness in Connor's voice made her want to cover up her ears so she didn't have to listen to him. It didn't really matter how bad she thought it was. It mattered how bad he thought it was.

"My team had a tough assignment on the Pakistan-Afghan border." He wouldn't look at her. He was looking at his hands. His fingers kept threading and then unthreading. "It was a hotbed of all kinds of activity. We'd gotten some intel about an event that was supposed to go down. But our intel was wrong, or delayed.

"We got there too late. We arrived just as a bomb went off in a school. Within seconds, the whole place was in flames. There were terrified kids everywhere, running. We helped get as many kids out as we could. I thought maybe everyone had gotten out. And then I saw all these little faces pressed against a second-story window."

She remembered his uneasiness in her classroom. She remembered him telling her to try and get on the first floor. She remembered him saying, "I'm sure you do. Unless there's a fire."

Her heart broke for the look on his face as he remembered this, the helpless agony there. He still wouldn't meet her eyes, as if he carried some unspeakable shame within him, as if somehow this was all his fault. She put her hand across the table and laid it on his wrist.

He looked at it for a moment, as if he understood perfectly what she was offering. Her strength and her compassion.

He shook her hand away.

"We had been ordered to stand down." He was looking at her now. His gaze was aloof. She had liked it better when he was not looking at her, not with this look in his eyes.

"The building was deemed too dangerous for us to go into. Do you understand what an order means when you are in the military?"

She nodded mutely.

"It's not open for discussion. At all. But I couldn't do it. I couldn't stand there and look at those kids and hear their terrified voices coming out the window they had smashed. My mom had just had Henry. I had a little brother and a little sister the same age as those kids."

Isabella had never felt the heartbreak she felt looking into his face. She understood that he was trying to close himself off from her. Connor was a man held in the hell of his own memories. And he was not going to allow anyone to shoulder that burden with him.

"In retrospect, there were other things I could have done. We could have organized something for them to jump into. We could have stood under the windows and tried to catch them.

"But no," he said softly. "I had to be the cowboy,

even though I'm from Corpus Christi. You know, I was a wild kid in my youth. The military managed to tame most of that out of me, but not all of it.

"So, they told us to stand down, and I said those words to my superior that Luigi said to me that day in the hallway, and I think I said them with as much pleasure.

"And I went into that building. If you've never been in a burning building, you have no idea. It's darker than night in there, even though it's the middle of the day. The noise is something that you awake in the night thinking you hear—like the wail of a banshee. It's so hot you can feel your clothes melting.

"But none of that mattered. I was in those doors and up those stairs before I could think it through. What I didn't think through? Once I broke the ranks, they all did. My whole squad, eight men, followed me into that fire."

He was silent for a long, long time.

"Only seven came out," he said. "My best friend was unaccounted for. I went back in one more time. He was trapped under a beam that had fallen. His back was broken. He's in a wheelchair to this day. Because of me. He has burn scars over fifty percent of his body because of me."

"What about the children?" she whispered.

"They made it. Every single one them. To this day, Justin will tell you it was worth it."

"Then maybe you should believe him," she said.

The look Connor gave her was furious. "No. Maybe *you* should believe *me*. I made a decision based totally on emotion. It was unacceptable. When I start coming from that place of emotion, my judgment is clouded."

She saw, instantly, where he was going with this.

"You're saying your judgment is clouded about me," she said.

"Look what happened today. I read that situation all wrong. It's an embarrassment."

"I wasn't embarrassed," she said. "I don't think anything you did could ever embarrass me."

For a moment, it looked as if something in him softened, as if he might lean toward her. But no, he leaned away. He heaved himself up from the table.

She got up and stood in front of him. "Please don't go. Please don't carry this one second longer by yourself."

He stared at her. For a second, once again, he hesitated. She saw so much pain and so much longing in his face. She thought she had him.

But then his face hardened, and he put her out of his way. "Like I need a little chit like you to help me carry my burdens," he snapped. "You'd be squished like a bug underneath them. Like a bug."

And then, casting her one more proud look, he was out the door. She followed him. She could not believe the impotent frustration she felt.

"Connor Benson!"

He swung around and looked at her.

"You are the worst kind of coward," she yelled. "You act as if you are the bravest man alive, but when it comes to matters of your heart? You are a complete coward."

His mouth fell open. Then he folded his arms over his chest and spread his legs apart. A warrior's stance if she had ever seen one. It just made her madder. There was a pot of flowers by her door and, propelled by anger, she picked it up. She hurled it at him. He had to step to one side to avoid being hit. The pot smashed harmlessly beside him. He glared at her, and she glared back, and then he turned and walked away, not once glancing back at her.

She watched him walk down the street, his stride long and confident and powerful, the walk of a warrior, until she could see him no more. And then she closed her kitchen door and leaned against it and wept.

What on earth had gotten into her? She was a demure schoolteacher! She did not scream at people in the streets. Or throw pots at them.

Or slap people. Or wear red dresses. Or green bikinis.

Let's face it. Connor Benson had brought out the worst in her.

Or maybe what he had done was make her lose her hold on control, to find at her center she was not demure at all, but passionate and fiery and alive.

Because despite vibrating with anger at him right now, Isabella had to admit she felt as alive as she had ever felt. Despite the fact he had left her, and she knew he was going to use all his considerable strength never to look back, she still felt on fire with life.

She gathered herself and gathered her broom and dustpan and went out into the street and cleaned up the mess she had made. And then she brought it into her kitchen and opened the dustbin. But before she dumped the broken pot and flowers and dirt in, she noticed there was something in there that had not been in there before.

She set her filled dustpan on the floor and hauled the trash out from under the sink. She found the pieces of a smashed vase, and the broken stems of wildflowers, and a water-stained note. She carefully pressed open its folds with her fist. She would know that bold handwriting anywhere. She read the note.

Dear Isabella,
Life is a river, with calm places and turbulent places. I wonder if you would like to join me on this wild and unpredictable ride? If you are willing, I will pick you up tomorrow evening, after the fete, and we will explore the river.

Instead of signing it with "love," he had drawn a quite adorable heart and then signed his name.

But between the time he had written this note and now, everything had changed. Because of Luigi's father, but not really. That incident had just triggered all of Connor's deepest insecurities.

What a terrible burden to carry through life: to think you were in charge of everything, to want to protect everyone, to not allow yourself any mistakes.

It was a hopeless task, of course, protecting everyone. It was impossible. Connor Benson had set for himself an impossible task, and then he was hard on himself when he failed. What he needed most was not, as she had said, someone to help him carry the burden, though he needed that, too. But what he needed most was someone who could gently tell him when he was being unreasonable, when the goal he had set for himself was too much for one man alone.

What he needed was that safe place, where it was okay to make mistakes, where nobody died or was in danger because you had been wrong.

She knew exactly what Connor Benson needed. He needed her. But how on earth was she going to let him know that?

Over the next few days she tried to find clues to where he had gone, but he had disappeared as if he had never been. He was gone completely, without a trace and without a trail. Her initial fire sputtered out. Isabella sank into the deepest despair of her life.

Where there is deep grief, there was deep love.

It complicated her sense of losing Connor that what she felt now was worse than the loss of her husband. It made the wild tumult inside her worse now that she wondered if she had ever truly loved Giorgio. What had it been, if not love?

She could not eat and she could not sleep. Her whole house was a reminder of Connor—the bed he had slept in, the shower he had saved her from, the kitchen table where they had sat together. She was ashamed with how impatient she was with the children at school. But it seemed she spared Luigi, even though his behavior was worse than ever since his father had come to the fete.

Still, she recognized in the child a great mourning, a great sense of loss. She recognized he was acting out in frustration against helplessness.

And then she was shaken out of her own pity when Luigi disappeared. He didn't arrive at school one morning, and she had received no note from his mother saying he would be absent. The whole town was in an uproar. Had he been kidnapped by his father?

The police were called, and a tense day and night later, Luigi was found asleep under a shrub, a backpack beside him, his face tearstained but his spirit as fierce as ever.

"I am not going to have a life without my papa," he screamed, unrepentant, at his mother in front of the police station.

And this time, she heard him. She wrapped her little boy in her arms and said she understood. That she had been wrong to make him suffer because of her pride. That she would change her stance toward Luigi's father, that she would not stand in the way of them loving one another anymore.

Within days, Isabella could see the changes in Luigi. His father was reintroduced into his life. Luigi was calmer. He was happier. He brought her flowers one day, as if to apologize for all he had put her through.

It was a victory of love, and it made Isabella think.

Was she going to mourn for another six years, then? What if she had been wrong? What if deep love didn't cripple you with grief?

What if deep love made you stronger? What if it made you fight to the death for what you wanted? It was the force that had sent a little boy out looking for his father, knowing what all the adults around him had not known—he *needed* that love.

She needed Connor's love. She wanted to be fully alive. She wanted to feel the way she had felt when she was with him.

She realized there were different kinds of love. There was the kind of love Luigi had for his father. And the kind of love Luigi's mother had for her little boy that had helped her overcome her own bitterness and put what was best for him first.

Yes, there was the kind of love that Isabella had had

for Giorgio. Because she had loved Giorgio with gentle compassion did not mean she had loved him less. It meant that she had loved him differently.

And it was all part of her journey to know love completely.

She had to find Connor. She had to convince him not that she was worthy of his love, because she suspected they both knew that. She had to convince him that he was worthy of hers.

She went back to the chapel, sure she could find there some clue to where he would go. What she found was workmen gone for the day and the fresco, reminding her that beauty was true greatness, and that beauty survived when all else fell away.

She went to the river where she had waded with him. It was warmer now, and there were signs the little boys who had a hung a rope and tire from the tree so they could swing out over the water came more often.

There was no one here now, though, and she took off the cover she had put over the plainest of her bathing suits. She hesitated and then climbed the slippery bank, grabbed the rope with both hands and planted her feet on the tire. She swung way out into the river, where the water was definitely over her head, and even though there was a possibility she could lose everything if she let go of that rope, she let go anyway.

It was exhilarating. It felt wonderful to live life without a safety net. It felt wonderful to take chances. It felt wonderful to be brave.

Life was, indeed, a river, with calm places and turbulent places. It was indeed a wild and unpredictable ride. She had never seen it like that before Connor. She wanted to explore completely the wild and unpredictable ride. She wanted to explore it with him.

It came to her—that incident at the fete. It wasn't just that he felt he had made a mistake. It was the whole thing.

It was the realization he could not stop bad things from happening. He could not stop the tragedy of a marriage not working, children being the victims. He said he had seen that before with his SEAL buddies.

If Luigi's father had had a weapon concealed under his coat, Connor could have stopped that particular tragedy from unfolding, but his work had made him so aware of the next one, waiting. His inability to save his friend had made him way too aware how powerless even the most powerful of men could be.

Isabella suddenly felt drenched in light. She felt as if she was the soldier, not him. She had to go get him. She had to rescue Connor from the lonely world of perfection and protection he had made for himself.

And suddenly, there in that deep pool, enjoying the gift he had given her—a freedom from fear—she knew exactly how to find him.

A day later, her confidence felt more shaky as she dialed the number.

"Itus, Arnold speaking."

The voice was curt and no-nonsense. It shook her that it was not a name she was expecting.

"I'm looking for someone named Justin."

There was a moment's silence and then wariness. "You've got him."

"My name is Isabella Rossi. I am looking for Connor Benson."

"You and half the civilized world."

"What does that mean?"

Silence. "What did you say your name was?"

"Isabella Rossi."

"I'm going to guess you're from Monte Calanetti, aren't you?"

"That is correct."

"Ah. I should have guessed."

"Guessed?"

"That there was a reason he came back from there grumpier than a bear with a sore bottom."

"I'm that reason?" Grumpier than a bear with a sore bottom?

"I'm asking you. Are you that reason?"

"I think I might be," she said with a sigh. "I need to talk to him. You don't know where he is?"

"He came back, checked in, made my life miserable for a few days, then cleared his schedule and disappeared."

It confirmed exactly what Isabella had suspected. He had not gone back home and dismissed all that had happened to him. He was somewhere nursing his wounds. Alone. Her heart felt as if it was breaking.

Not for herself. For him. For Connor.

"So, you don't know where he is?" Her disappointment felt as sharp as shards of glass.

"I don't right this minute. But if there's one thing I am very, very good at? It's finding people."

"Who don't want to be found?"

"Especially people who don't want to be found. Up until this point, I thought I'd leave him alone. And I will. But if you want to go find him, I'm okay with that. More than okay with that."

In two hours he called her back. Two hours after that,

she was on a bus to the city to catch a plane, a ticket for the first flight to Switzerland clutched in her hand.

Connor stared out the window of the mountain cabin. There was really nothing as glorious as the Alps in springtime. He wasn't sure why he had picked a place to hide where he couldn't swim, though.

No, that choice had not been an accident.

His whole life he had chased away strong feelings. It was what his military training had taught him to do. Emotion always got him in trouble. He could swim it off, shake off nearly anything with enough punishing physical activity.

So he couldn't swim, but the mountains all around beckoned. He could hike or climb mountains, or go down to that little public house in the village at the bottom of the mountain and drink himself into oblivion.

But it was the oddest thing that had ever happened to him.

Connor *wanted* to feel this. He wanted to feel the devastating loss of Isabella. He wanted to feel the consequences of his actions. He wanted to wake up in the morning and wonder what the point of life was, to feel his all-encompassing emptiness.

He wanted to remember, in excruciating detail, every second they had spent together. He wanted to remember her joy in the pool, and the way her face had looked when she saw the fresco of the Madonna and child.

He wanted to miss her.

He wanted to feel it all intensely. That was his mission. Miss Isabella. And then be over it, completely, and get back to his life.

Except he had expected the getting-over-it part to

be much faster. He was beginning to think the completely part was out of the question. He might have to settle for getting over her a little bit. Enough to function. After all, he'd been in his little cottage in the Alps for a week and if anything, he felt more morose than when he'd begun.

And that did not bode well for whoever knocked on his door. He'd specifically told his landlady he was not to be disturbed under any circumstances.

But of course, she could not control a lost hiker at the door. Or the Swiss equivalent of a Girl Scout selling cookies.

So he swung open the door in a bad temper, ready to be equally unwelcoming to Heidi selling cookies or the lost hiker seeking refuge.

The shock reverberated up his spine when he saw who was there. For a moment, his heart was so filled with gratitude to see the face he had told himself he would never see again that it felt as though he might fall on his knees.

But then he straightened his spine and drew in a deep breath.

He needed to protect her. From himself. From the damaged person he was. From the incomplete person he was. She deserved so much better.

"Isabella." He heard the coolness in his voice and saw the purpose in her posture falter just a bit.

"Connor."

Again, his knees felt weak at the way she said his name. It came off her lips like a blessing, as if she saw all of him and accepted that completely.

"Why are you here?" he asked harshly.

"I'm here to rescue you. I tried to send a Saint Bernard with a cask of whiskey around his neck, but apparently they don't do that anymore."

He did not want to be charmed by her!

"You look horrible," she said softly.

He already knew that! He had looked at his own reflection this morning in the mirror, made the decision not to shave, again. His hair was uncombed, his clothes were rumpled—he looked like a wild man, as if he was holed up in a cave, not in a perfectly civilized cabin.

"Can I come in?"

"There's no point."

She ignored him and slipped under his arm into the cottage.

"Hey!"

"Wow," she said, looking around.

He turned and saw the place through her eyes. It was an absolute shambles. Clothes on the floor, dirty dishes on every surface. There was a bag of groceries by the small kitchen that he had not even bothered to unpack. A trail of cookie crumbs went across the floor and disappeared under a pair of socks.

It was as if it was the first time he'd really noticed it in days. Who had he become? He was a fastidiously neat person.

Undeterred by how the mess spoke to his character, Isabella went over, frowned at the couch and then delicately moved two newspapers and an empty container of chocolate fudge ice cream out of her way. She sat down as if she planned to stay.

"What do you want?" he asked, folding his arms over his chest. He tapped his foot and glanced at his watch. She looked so unperturbed by his show of impatience that he felt almost panicky. He was going to have to be mean to her.

To Isabella? That was impossible.

But it was for her own good. He took a deep breath, soldiered himself. This was what he did. He did hard things. He did impossible things.

"Look, you've traveled a long way for nothing," he said. "If you're going to tell me you can't live without me, forget it. I'm not moved by emotion."

"Hmm," she said, again unperturbed.

He frowned at her.

"I think I came to tell you that you can't live without me," she decided. He contemplated the awful truth of that, and he contemplated the fact she had seen it so clearly. This was not about her. Not in any way. It was about him.

"Well, I can. Live without you. And I will."

"Quit being so damned strong," she said softly. "You've had to be so strong your whole life, Connor. You started working when you were eleven years old to help look after your mom."

"That's hitting below the belt," he said, "bringing my mom into it."

"What is this, below the belt?"

"You're an adult woman—I think you can figure out where men don't like to get hit."

She nodded, mulling that over, but then kept on talking as if he hadn't warned her. "So you've always felt protective of your poor mother, who had you very young and was abandoned by the people who should have supported her. Is it any surprise you were drawn to a profession where you protect people, where you try and fix things? Everything?"

"Look, Little Red Riding Hood, just skip on home. You're playing with the Big Bad Wolf here, and that story does not end well, if you recall."

She cocked her head at him. She didn't look even slightly intimidated. He considered the possibility he was losing his touch.

"You have carried the weight of the whole world for way, way too long," she decided softly.

"Says you."

She sighed as if he was no more irritating to her than Luigi Caravetti yelling swearwords. "I thought we should have a discussion. About the river of life."

He groaned. "Have you no pride? Picking through the garbage?"

"None at all," she said. "Not when it comes to you. It's your turn, Connor."

"My turn?" he said warily.

"Your turn to be rescued."

"You've already said that. Saint Bernards on strike, you have come in their place, without the cask."

"I brought something better than the cask."

He went very still. He knew what she had brought. He could see what she had brought shining from her eyes. He could see it shining from the very fiber of her being.

He could fight anything. That was what he had been trained to do. To fight. And he was so good at it.

But he was not sure that he could fight this. *Don't ask her*, he begged himself, *don't ask her what she brought. You aren't strong enough, Connor, you aren't.*

"What did you bring?" His voice was a rasp.

"You know," she said softly. "You already know what I brought."

Even before she said the words, he could feel his every defense beginning to crumble, like a dam made out of mud and sticks giving way after holding everything in for way too long, so long that its strength had already been compromised.

"I brought love," she said. "I brought my love to rescue you."

"No, please. Isabella, don't do this."

She was up off that sofa in a heartbeat. She navigated the mess on his floor and stood in front of him. She shined with a fierce light.

So, love could be this, too. Not just gentle and sweet and quiet and compliant. But this: as strong as steel forged in a fire.

She put her hands on both sides of his face and forced him to look her in the eyes, look into those great green-and-gold pools of strength and compassion.

"You be whoever you need to be," she said softly. "You be a warrior going to do battle. You be the man who rushes into burning buildings. You be that man who seeks out danger like a heat-seeking missile seeks warmth. You be the man who sees the potential for bad things on a beautiful spring afternoon in the village square. You be the man who would lay down his life to protect a bride on her wedding day. You be those things."

Her words were like the final drops of water adding pressure to the already compromised structure of the dam. Her words broke Connor wide-open. He felt as if he had waited all his life for this one moment, for these words of acceptance, these words of someone seeing him exactly as he was and moving toward him anyway.

She continued to drop words, like healing raindrops, into the brokenness inside him.

"And then you come back to me," she said, and her voice was a promise that he could feel himself moving toward, that every ounce of his strength could not have stopped him from moving toward.

"And you show me all the bruised places," Isabella said, her voice fierce and true, "and the brokenness of your heart. You show me, and me alone, what it has cost you to be these things. And you let me place poultices on your bruises, and you let me knit my love around your wounds.

"Connor, I will be the place where you lay down your sword. I will be the place where you see that beauty wins. I will be the home that shows you that love survives all things, and makes all things possible."

He was staring at her. His heart was pounding as if he had run a race, and he could see the finish line. She, Isabella Rossi, was the finish line, and he reached out for her.

He reached out and scraped his hand down her cheek. He realized she was crying, and he was pretty sure she did not know that herself.

"You look just like her right now," he said, his voice soft.

"Who? Who do I look like?"

He gazed at her, feeling as if he could never get enough. When he spoke, his voice was hoarse with emotion. "The Madonna in the fresco. You look just like her."

He stared at her, not able to look away, held by the light that had infused her face, aware that he was in the presence of the purest and most powerful thing in the world.

Rarely, like in the fresco, someone captured the essence of this power, the heart of it, the spirit of it. An unknown Renaissance artist had followed inspiration, obeyed it and been allowed to capture it.

It was love.

It was all that it was to be human at its highest and its best. It was what Connor had fought his whole life for, without ever being able to give it a name.

He realized he was like the man in Greek mythology, just as Isabella had said, a long time ago. He *was* like Itus. He was being offered the opportunity to walk among gods. For that was what it was for a man to know love. It was to walk in glory. It was to experience things beyond what a mortal man had a right to expect.

He did not deserve this. He knew that. And he also knew that it didn't matter. That he was not strong enough to refuse what was being offered to him.

Connor Benson did what he had never done, not in his whole life. Even when he was a child, he had stood strong, he had been ready to fight for what he felt was right. But now, standing here before Isabella, drenched in the light, he bowed before her, and before the presence of a force greater than himself.

He laid down his weapons. He laid his head on her shoulder. He surrendered. He ate the food that was offered to him.

He felt Isabella's hand, cool and strong, on the back of his neck. He felt her tears anoint him. And he drew her into the warmth of himself and held her in a way that reflected the truths he had just learned.

He held Isabella as if he would never let her go.

He was a man who had crossed deserts, navigated jungles, climbed mountains. He was a man who had fought to give others something that he had not named. But now that he was there, in the circle of its light, he recognized the name of it.

Home.

Connor Benson was home.

* * * * *

"You got some hang-up about a man touching you?"

"I most certainly do not," Margot retorted before realizing she'd played right into his hands. "I don't know you. I don't particularly like you. That's why I don't want you touching me."

His gaze met hers. "Liar."

"What are you talking about?" Margot sputtered.

"You want me to touch you," Brad said as if speaking the gospel from the pulpit. "But you're scared of what might happen once I do."

"Oh for the love of—" She reined in her emotions. "You are so incredibly arrogant. You think every woman is interested in that hot body of yours."

A grin spread across his face, like a kid opening a present at Christmastime. "You think my body is hot?"

"Let's get a few things straight. I'm not interested in touching you. I'm not interested in sleeping with you. I *am* interested in getting you out of my house."

"*My* house," he corrected. "And you *are* interested in sleeping with me. You just won't admit it."

"Delude yourself all you want." Margot kept her face expressionless. There was no way, *no way*, she was letting him know that she found him the teensiest bit attractive.

* * *

Montana Mavericks:
What Happened at the Wedding?
A weekend Rust Creek Falls will never forget!

BETTING ON THE MAVERICK

BY
CINDY KIRK

Published in Great Britain 2015
by Mills & Boon, an imprint of Harlequin (UK) Limited,
Eton House, 18-24 Paradise Road, Richmond, Surrey, TW9 1SR

Special thanks and acknowledgement are given to Cara Colter for her contribution to The Vineyards of Calanetti series.

© 2015 Harlequin Books S.A.

Special thanks and acknowledgement to Cindy Kirk for her contribution to Montana Mavericks: What Happened at the Wedding? continuity.

ISBN: 978-0-263-25173-9

23-1015

Printed and bound in Spain
by CPI, Barcelona

From the time she was a little girl, **Cindy Kirk** thought everyone made up different endings to books, movies and television shows. Instead of counting sheep at night, she made up stories. She's now had over forty novels published. She enjoys writing emotionally satisfying stories with a little faith and humor tossed in. She encourages readers to connect with her on Facebook and Twitter, @cindykirkauthor, and via her website, www.cindykirk.com.

To Renee Ryan and Nancy Robards Thompson,
my writing buddies. I love you, guys!

Chapter One

It was nearly 3:00 a.m. when Margot Sullivan stepped out of the brisk October wind and into the darkened foyer of her family home. She sniffed appreciatively. The ranch house where she'd grown up smelled different, cleaner than her last visit six months earlier. Though battling dust was a constant challenge in rural Montana, her mother had always worked hard to have a clean house. After her death, everything had been let go.

It appeared her father was once again taking pride in the home.

Pausing on the rug covering the weathered hardwood, Margot bent to take off her boots. She froze when Vivian, her blue heeler, snarled. The growl grew louder and Vivian crouched into a fighting stance, the fur on the back of her neck standing straight up.

Following the dog's gaze to the stairway leading to the second floor, Margot gasped.

A bare-chested man wearing only jeans stood on the steps, a baseball bat in his hands. Tall with a thatch of brown hair and a dark stubble of beard on his cheeks, his hair was mussed as if he'd just run his hands through it. The eyes riveted on her were sharp and assessing.

"What are you doing here?" he demanded, but his expression was more puzzled than menacing.

"I'll ask the questions." Margot rested a trembling hand on Vivian's head. "Where's my father?"

Without answering, the man lowered the bat and started down the stairs toward her.

"Not one more step," she ordered. "Or I'll give my dog the command to attack."

He paused, cocked his head, grinned.

That's when she recognized him. Brad Crawford, of the illustrious Crawford family. What the heck was a Crawford doing skulking around her father's house half-dressed in the middle of the night?

"Little Margot Sullivan." He shook his head and flashed a smile that had been winning him hearts since he'd been old enough to walk.

Despite herself, Margot relaxed slightly. Given the choice, she'd take Brad with a bat over a stranger in the same pose. Though she still had no clue what he was doing in her house.

"Didn't expect to see you here," he added.

"This *is* my house."

"Well, now." He rubbed his chin. "That's debatable."

"Where's my father?" Margot's heart froze as she imagined all the things that could have happened to a man pushing eighty. Without waiting for an answer, she called out. "Dad! It's Margot. Where are you?"

"Save your breath." Barely giving a second glance to Vivian who'd continued to growl low in her throat, Brad meandered into the living room and plopped down into an overstuffed chair. "Boyd isn't here."

Vivian's eyes remained trained on Brad.

"Friend," Margot said reluctantly, then repeated. "Friend."

Friend might be carrying it a bit far but the Crawfords were well-known in Rust Creek Falls, Montana. Although Brad was a good ten years older than her—and had quite the reputation as a ladies' man—there was no denying his family was respected in the community.

While he wasn't exactly her friend, Brad wasn't a dangerous enemy, either.

With Vivian glued to her side, Margot moved to the sofa and took a seat. Questions over her father's whereabouts fought with an unexpected spike of lust at the sight of Brad's muscular chest. She'd already noticed he hadn't quite secured the button on his jeans. Just like she noticed he smelled terrific: a scent of soap and shampoo and that male scent that was incredibly sexy.

Trying to forget the fact she'd driven ten hours today with the windows down and that her red hair was a messy tumble of curls, Margot leaned forward, concern for her father front and center. She rested her arms on her thighs and fixed her gaze on Brad. "Tell me where my father is."

"I don't know."

A cold chill enveloped her in a too-tight hug. "What do you mean you don't know?"

"He left town right after the Fourth of July," Brad said in a conversational tone. "Hasn't come back."

It was now October. *Three months*. Her elderly father had left the family ranch not long after that last argument between them. A horrible conversation that had ended with him hanging up on her after telling her to not come back or call again.

"Everyone knows he has a daughter, yet no one in this town thought to let me know he'd up and taken off for parts unknown?" Fear sluiced through Margot's veins and panic had her voice rising with each word.

"The sheriff confirmed he left by train with a ticket to New York City."

"Wow. That makes me feel so much better." Sarcasm ran through her voice like thick molasses. Then the anger punched. "Did anyone even try to get a hold of me?"

"Initially everyone thought Boyd had gone to see his sister, who—"

"Who lived in New Jersey, not New York City. My aunt Verna has been gone almost two years. She died six months before my mother passed away."

"That fact wasn't known until later." Brad waved a dismissive hand. "You know your dad. He wasn't the kind of guy to share personal stuff."

Margot clasped her hands together. "That still doesn't explain why no one called me."

"After the sheriff discovered his sister was no longer living, he attempted to contact you. He discovered you'd been injured and were no longer competing. No one knew where to find you."

After sustaining a serious skull fracture shortly after that last conversation with her father, Margot had left the rodeo circuit to stay with a friend in Cheyenne. But when a week or two of recuperation stretched into several months, Margot decided to return to the only home she'd ever known. "My father has my cell number."

"One problem," Brad said. "He wasn't around to give it to us. And it's not like you've kept in touch with anyone else in town."

Where would her father have gone? None of this made any sense. Margot wasn't certain if it truly didn't compute or if her head just wasn't processing the information correctly. Boyd Sullivan was a smart man who, despite his age, knew how to handle himself. When he was sober, that is.

"Was he still drinking before he left?"

"He was," Brad said quietly.

Margot sat back abruptly. The head she'd injured ten weeks earlier began to ache. The strain of travel from Wyoming to Montana had taken its toll, but it was the tension of the past few minutes that now had her head clamped in a vise.

She rubbed the back of her neck with one hand, trying to ease the pressure. With every syllable Brad uttered, the story worsened.

"What are you doing here?" she asked bluntly.

"I live here."

"You're watching the place while my father is away?" she asked cautiously, her admiration for him inching up a notch.

Unlike in many large cities where people could live side-by-side for years and not really know each other, in Rust Creek Falls neighbors took care of neighbors.

Not to say there weren't feuds. The bad blood between the Crawfords and the Traubs over the years was a prime example.

But on the whole, you couldn't have asked for a better place to grow up, or in her father's case, to grow old.

Brad shifted uncomfortably in the chair. "That's not exactly the case."

Margot frowned. "If you're not watching it for him, what are you doing here?"

"Well, you see, your father put up the deed to the ranch in a poker game." A sheepish grin crossed his handsome face. "He lost. I won. The Leap of Faith is now mine."

* * *

Brad left the pretty redhead fuming in the downstairs parlor as he headed upstairs for his shirt and shoes. He was concerned about her father, too—if he wasn't he wouldn't have used some of his own money to hire a PI to search for the old man. But right now he had Boyd's daughter on the brain.

Sitting across from Margot Sullivan with that white shirt gaping open and those green eyes flashing fire had been a huge turn-on. Especially when he'd told her she could stay the night. It had been like tossing kerosene onto a burning fire.

The hellcat had been so angry she'd sputtered and stammered, her breasts heaving in a most delectable way as she informed him that this was *her* house and if anyone was leaving, it was him.

Damn. There was nothing that excited Brad more than a woman with spunk.

That fact was firmly evident in the sudden tightness of his jeans. He grinned, more than a little relieved.

Though he'd dated his share of women since his divorce four years earlier, in the past six months there hadn't been a single female who'd caused his mast to rise.

Not that his seeming lack of libido worried him. Not in the least.

Brad had been more puzzled than anything by the occurrence…or rather the non-occurrence.

Tonight had illustrated he'd been foolish to give the matter a second thought. Obviously it had just been that none of the women he'd taken out recently tripped his trigger.

Odd, as the saucy redhead had only to step through the front door to capture his interest.

Brad jerked on a flannel shirt, buttoned it but deliberately left the tail hanging out. Even being on a different floor in a far-removed room hadn't, ah, cooled his interest. Still, there was no need to advertise the fact.

Of course, he reminded himself as he pulled on his boots, that interest between a man and a woman needed to be a two-way street. The fact that, in her eyes, he'd—oh, what was the phrase she'd used—"stolen a grieving old man's ranch" almost certainly ensured she wasn't likely to get naked with him.

At least not tonight.

He clambered back down the rickety steps and felt one bend beneath his weight. After making a mental note to fix it before it collapsed, Brad traversed the last few steps, then crossed to the parlor.

Margot stood at the darkened fireplace, her gaze riveted to one of the photographs on the mantel: a family picture of her parents and a skinny girl with rusty hair and freckles. But that gawky little girl had grown into a real beauty. Worn Levis hugged her slender legs like a glove and a mass of red-gold hair tumbled down her back like a colorful waterfall.

His body stirred in appreciation of such a fine female figure. Brad tried to recall how old she'd be by now.

Twenty-two? Twenty-three? Definitely old enough.

All he knew for certain was that the spitfire who at age six had once tossed a bucketful of rancid water on him when he'd mentioned her freckles had grown into a lovely young woman.

A flash of teeth from the dog standing beside her brought a smile to his lips. It wasn't only the white-and-black coat tinged with silver or those large ears that alerted Brad to the breed. The protective stance was pure heeler.

Rather than resenting the animal, Brad found himself grateful Margot had such a companion. A woman traveling alone could be a target for the unscrupulous. But first they'd have to get through—what had she called the animal... Viper?

The name didn't sound exactly right, but it certainly fit.

Viper emitted a low growl as Brad entered the room.

Margot didn't growl like her dog, but when she turned her face was composed and icy.

"I'm calling Gage Christensen first thing in the morning," she said, referring to the sheriff of Rust Creek Falls. "You and I and the sheriff will hash out this matter tomorrow."

"Anyone ever tell you you're pretty cute when you're angry?" Ignoring the dog's warning growl, Brad stepped closer. "You growed up real fine, Margot Sullivan."

Though Brad was a recipient of a solid education from the University of Montana, most of his days before and since graduation were spent with ranch hands who delighted in slaughtering the English language. When necessary, he could play the good-ole-boy card with the best of 'em.

He shoved his hands into his pockets, rocked back on his heels and let his admiring gaze linger.

Instead of blushing or simply accepting the compliment as her due, she glared at him.

"You think you're pretty hot stuff."

Brad waited, inclined his head, not sure of the point she was trying to make.

"While you may have a face that doesn't send children screaming away in the night—" she paused, whether for effect or to gain control of the emotions that had brought the two bright swaths of color to her cheeks, he couldn't tell "—you don't impress me. You showed your true character when you stole this ranch from my fath—"

"Hey, I won it fair and square," Brad protested. Crawfords might be many things—just ask a Traub if you wanted a laundry list of sins—but they didn't cheat. Not at cards, or anything else, for that matter. Not even to protect an old coot from himself.

It was obvious Margot wasn't in the mood to listen to him, so it hardly seemed the time to divulge that he planned to sign the ranch back over to her father when he returned.

Once he played that card, she'd kick him out immediately.

And Brad was much too entranced to go.

The man had showed her to her own room!

Margot held on to her temper when he insisted on carrying her battered suitcases up the stairs. They'd tussled briefly until Vivian became so distraught Margot feared the stress would push the dog into early labor. Gritting her teeth, she'd acquiesced, but not before letting go so abruptly the move had sent Brad stumbling backward.

He deposited the suitcases next to her bed then just stood there like a bellman expecting a tip.

"Thank you," she murmured when he made no move to go. She told herself she should be grateful he hadn't chosen her bedroom to make his own.

Instead, on the way down the hall, he'd motioned to the room across from hers—the guest room—as being his.

She was relieved—and a bit puzzled—he'd left her parents' room undisturbed. The master bedroom was by far the largest of the four. Still, having him stay in the guest room was appropriate. He *was* a guest, albeit an uninvited and unwanted one. His story about winning the ranch in a poker game only managed to anger her further.

Once Gage came out tomorrow and they got this whole mess straightened out, the "guest" would be gone.

For now, Margot wanted nothing more than to shower off road grime and collapse into bed.

"If there's anything you need—" he began.

"If there's anything I need," Margot said pointedly. "I think I know where to find it. I did, after all, grow up in this house."

At the sudden intense emotion filling her voice, Vivian stiffened beside her.

"Are you always cranky when you're tired?" Brad asked with an innocent air that neither of them bought.

"Bite me," Margot snapped, her head now throbbing in earnest.

He murmured something under his breath, but she missed it. She sank down at the end of the bed covered by a quilt her mother had made for her sixteenth birthday and placed her head in her hands.

The blows just kept coming.

First the injury when a horse she'd been mounting had spooked and she'd been pushed back, slamming her head against a trailer. Her head had hit just right...or, as the doctor said, just wrong. The skull fracture she'd sustained had been serious enough for the neurologist to warn that another concussion before she was fully healed could leave her with permanent impairment.

All that paled in comparison to worry over her father's whereabouts. He could be sick. He could be injured. He could be...dead.

Margot buried her face in her hands.

"Are you okay?"

The concern in his voice sounded genuine but thankfully Brad didn't move any closer.

She knew she was in bad shape when she only exhaled a breath and nodded. "We'll get this settled in the morning."

That was his cue to leave. But he remained where he was. When she finally gathered the strength to lift her head, she found him staring at her with the oddest expression on his face.

"If you need anything, anything at all." His hazel—or were they green?—eyes held a hint of worry. "I'm just across the hall."

What should she say to that? Thank you for taking over my home? Thank you for stealing the ranch from a drunken old man?

Yet he was obviously *trying* to be nice so she cut him a break. "Okay."

Then he was gone, taking his handsome face, impudent smile and the intoxicating scent of soap, shampoo and testosterone with him.

She stretched out on the bed and let her muscles relax. Eyes closed, she offered up a prayer for her father's safety and well-being.

It was the last rational thought Margot had that evening.

Chapter Two

Margot awoke the next morning to sunlight streaming through lace curtains and birdsong outside her window.

Vivian lay on the woven rag rug next to the bed. The dog lifted her head when Margot sat up, still dressed in the jeans and shirt she'd worn last night.

If that wasn't bad enough, her eyes were gritty and her mouth tasted like sawdust.

Though having to walk down the hall to the bathroom had never particularly bothered her, for the first time Margot wished for an adjacent bath. The last thing she wanted was to tangle with Brad before she had her morning shower or coffee.

But she'd learned several hard lessons in the past couple of years and one of them was wishing didn't change reality.

With a resigned sigh, she unlatched her suitcase and scooped up all the items she needed, then slipped down the hall to the aged bathroom with cracked white tile on the floor and a mirror that made her look like a ghost. She pulled her gaze from the disturbing image and listened. The house stood eerily silent.

Brad isn't here.

It was too much to hope that he'd packed up his stuff and left. Though Margot had no idea where he'd gone, there wasn't a single doubt in her mind that he'd be back.

She was familiar with the type. Add a swagger and you could be talking about three-quarters of the cowboys on the rodeo circuit. Most of them only had two things on their mind; scoring enough points to make it to the rodeo finals in Las Vegas and getting into as many women's pants as possible.

Her dad, a successful bareback rider back in the day, had warned her shortly before she'd left Rust Creek Falls to pursue her dream of one day making it to the PRCA National finals. She'd listened respectfully to everything Boyd Sullivan had said but it was a classic case of too little, too late.

Even at nineteen, Margot had been no shy virgin facing the big bad world. She'd lost her virginity—and her innocence—her junior year in high school.

Shortly after that momentous occasion in the backseat of Rex Atwood's Mustang, she learned Rex had been bragging about "bagging" her to his fellow rodeo team members. Margot vividly remembered the day she'd confronted him and her fist had *accidentally* connected with his eye.

Both of them had learned a valuable lesson that day. He'd learned what happened when you crossed Margot Sullivan and she'd learned not to believe a guy who says he loves you in the heat of passion.

The bright autumn day dawned unseasonably warm, which was lucky for the calf that had been born last night. After checking on the rest of the cattle, Brad fixed a troublesome area of fence and reined his horse in the direction of the house.

Before leaving the house at dawn, he'd opened the door to Margot's room to see if she needed anything. Viper stood guard at the side of the bed. Golden eyes glowed with a malevolent warning. Of course, the bared teeth and the growl weren't all that welcoming, either.

A fully clothed Margot lay sprawled across the bed, facedown in the pillow. He'd known she was alive from the cute little snoring sounds. Though he'd never gotten the impression she and her dad were particularly close, he had to admit she *had* seemed concerned when she'd discovered him MIA.

Brad had been uneasy when he'd first learned Boyd didn't have any family back east. But anyone who knew the old guy knew Boyd could take care of himself, drunk or not. The man reminded him of a badger, solitary and not all that pretty but damned determined.

Thankfully, his daughter took after her mother in the looks department. Though, he had to admit, last night she had shown a few badger tendencies. For a second, he'd thought she might try to rip a piece out of his hide.

Having him in her family home definitely had her all hot and bothered. Or maybe it was him without his shirt.

Brad grinned and relaxed even further in the saddle. There had been a potent sizzle of attraction between them. She'd done her best to ignore it. But he'd seen how her gaze had lingered on his bare chest and then dropped lower for an instant before returning to his face.

She might want him out of her house, but she also wanted him in her bed. A place where he wouldn't mind spending a little time.

The sex would, of course, likely be a short-term kind

of thing. It would be like one of those fireworks on the Fourth of July. Brilliant and hot, they'd light up the sky then everything would fizzle.

That was fine with him. His marriage to Janie had confirmed what he'd always known. He wasn't a happily-ever-after kind of guy. Though Brad liked and respected women, he could never seem to make them happy. At least not out of bed.

The house was still quiet when he entered after putting his horse in the stable. Normally, he'd have stayed out most of the day, trying to get everything ready for winter. But he and Margot had a few things to square first.

Until they came to an understanding, he didn't trust her not to toss his stuff into the yard and lock him out of the home. Thankfully, the doors didn't have deadbolts and he'd been smart enough to drop a key into his pocket before leaving the house—just in case.

People in this part of the country barely locked their doors. If he had a mean-ass dog like Viper, there'd be no need to lock anything ever again.

Pulling the door shut, Brad glanced around. No sign of Margot. Or Viper.

Brad set the coffee to brew, then pulled out a heavy cast-iron skillet and went to work.

Several minutes later, when the eggs were frying in bacon grease and two slices of his mother's homemade bread had just popped up in the toaster, Brad was distracted from his culinary pursuit by a voice from the doorway.

"What the heck do you think you're doing?"

Ignoring the outrage in the tone, Brad wrote off the impressive anger to an as-yet-no-coffee morning.

"What does it look like?" He focused on plating the food. "I'm making breakfast."

"Why?"

"Because I'm hungry. I assume you are, too." He turned to glance at her.

It was a mistake. Hair still slightly damp from the shower hung in gentle waves past her shoulders. She'd pulled on a green long-sleeved tee that made her eyes look like emeralds and showed off her breasts to mouthwatering perfection. The jeans, well, the way they hugged those long legs should be outlawed.

Though Brad told himself not to go there, he imagined stripping off her shirt and filling his hands—and his mouth—with those amazing—

"What's the matter with you?"

Brad blinked and the image vanished. He resisted the urge to curse. Barely. "What do you mean?"

His innocent tone had her green eyes flashing.

"You looked like you were plotting something."

Oh, she was perceptive, this one. He had indeed been plotting. Plotting what to do once he got her into bed. The thought made him grin.

"I was just thinking about feasting on—" he stopped himself in the nick of time "—eggs. And bacon."

"We need to talk."

"Eat first. Then talk." Brad placed the plates of food on the table then expertly filled two mugs with coffee. He cocked his head. "Cream?"

"Black."

"A woman after my own heart."

She took the cup he handed her then met his gaze.

"I'm a woman," she said, "who is determined to get you out of my home."

Viper, whom he'd up to now tried to ignore, growled as if in agreement.

"Drink your coffee," he said mildly.

"Coffee won't change my mind." Still, she brought the cup to her lips and exhaled a blissful sigh after the first gulp. She looked up. "What is this? The cheap stuff my dad always had on hand did double-duty as a drain cleaner."

"I order it online. It has chicory in it."

Those wide lips of hers curved up. Though she wouldn't admit it, Margot Sullivan looked as though she might be starting to soften toward him.

He thought about pulling out her chair, but decided that would be overkill. Brad pulled out one for himself and sat down.

Sunlight streamed in through the window, filling the small eating area in the country kitchen with warmth. He supposed some people found the wallpaper with dancing teakettles appealing. At first they'd bothered the heck out of him. Now he barely noticed them.

Though he'd moved in two months earlier, Brad had focused on the outdoor needs and had left the inside alone.

When Boyd had first left town, Brad felt sure the old guy would be back any day. Then he'd learned about the ticket to New York. Brad had asked around and discovered the old guy hadn't requested any of the neighbors to watch the ranch. Of course, that may have been because he now considered it to be Brad's.

After almost two months, Brad had grown weary of making the trek to the ranch every day and decided to move in.

Though the decor wasn't to his liking, the only change he made was to the guest bedroom. He refused to sleep under a pink, blue and yellow quilt with ruffles around the shams.

The scrape of a chair against the linoleum had him looking up just in time to see Margot finally take a seat in the chair opposite him, her steaming mug gripped tightly in one hand.

"Your dog might be hungry," he said. "Her kibble is in the bowl over there."

Brad gestured with his head toward a weathered enclosed back porch that doubled as a storage area.

"I put some water out for her, too."

Margot paused, coffee mug poised near those tempting full lips. "Where did you get the food?"

"From your truck." He shrugged and shoved a forkful of eggs into his mouth. "I brought in your other stuff. It's sitting in the foyer."

"Thanks." Still, she looked at him suspiciously, as if trying to figure out the catch.

Well, she could look all she wanted. There was no catch. If the dog didn't eat, it'd get meaner. And Brad prized his ass. His brother Nate had always accused him of being soft on animals. Nothing could be further from the truth, unless feeling that any living being deserved to have fresh food and water qualified as soft.

While he'd briefly considered leaving her stuff in the truck as a way of saying hit-the-road-Red, he couldn't do it. Despite what the deed said, the place still didn't feel as if it belonged to him, and he wasn't sure it ever would.

They ate in silence for several minutes. Though Brad considered himself a social guy, he'd enjoyed the solitude of this house, this ranch. When he'd worked his parents' spread there was always someone around, his brothers and the other ranch hands. Until he could hire some help, he was on his own. Or he had been, until Margot had showed up.

Brad wondered what it said about him that he found himself enjoying the suspicious looks Viper shot him while chowing down on her food and the scrutiny in Margot's emerald eyes from her spot across the table.

Her hand returned to her coffee cup and she took another long gulp, an ecstatic look on her face.

Would she look like that after sex, he wondered? He let his gaze linger on the large breasts evident beneath the clinging fabric of her tee.

When he lifted his gaze, Brad found icy green eyes fixed on him.

She set her mug down with a bam. "If you're through staring, I suggest we get down to business. Gage is busy so he's sending a detective or something. I didn't even know we had those in this town. He should be here any minute—"

"You really called the sheriff?" Brad wasn't sure why he was surprised. He hadn't expected her to follow through on her threat made in the dark of night. Then again, though he barely knew this woman, it seemed like something she'd do. Still, he realized he'd hoped they could become better acquainted before she brought in the law.

Now that she was home, Brad supposed he could just turn the Leap of Faith over to her. But he hesitated to voice that option. From what he could tell, she and Boyd had been estranged, at least for the past few years. Once he signed the deed over to her, she could do with it what she wanted. Which might not be what Boyd would want...

"I felt it best to move swiftly." Margot relaxed back in the metal chair, circa 1950, and peered at him over the top of her mug. "You understand."

The challenge in those eyes stirred something inside him.

He shot her a sardonic smile. "I'd have taken exactly the same step."

The look of surprise that flashed across her face pleased him. But before he had a chance to revel in this minor victory, Viper returned from the back porch, those narrowed piercing gold eyes never leaving him as she ambled past him to sit beside Margot's chair.

The sound of a truck pulling up in the drive had Viper forgetting all about him to focus her attention on a new target. She gave three short high-pitched barks but quieted instantly at Margot's command.

"I'll get—" he began, shoving back his chair.

"I'll get it." She was already on her feet and moving toward the foyer. "This *is* my house."

Brad moved to the counter, pulled out another mug and filled it with coffee, then topped off his and Margot's cups.

He'd barely finished dumping the breakfast dishes in the sink when Margot and Viper returned with Russ Campbell.

Brad had met Russ when he returned to Montana after three years in Colorado. A police detective from Kalispell, Russ had recently been doing some consulting detective work for Gage Christensen in Rust Creek Falls.

"Mornin', Russ." Brad handed the guy a cup and then quickly performed introductions. "What made you stop by?"

"Margot, here." Russ took the cup gratefully then glanced at the woman. "Called the station and asked Gage when we started allowing squatters."

"I called because I need to know what's been done and what you're doing now to find my father." Margot spoke slowly and distinctly, her eyes flashing. "That's my first priority. Getting rid of him—" she pointed to Brad "—is secondary."

Brad found it interesting she seemed so concerned about locating her dad now. According to what she'd said last night, they hadn't spoken in months.

Once the deputy asked his questions, Brad had a few of his own.

Chapter Three

"Let's sit." Russ gestured to the table and took a gulp of coffee.

Brad topped off his mug. Instead of sitting, he leaned back against the counter.

His actions didn't surprise Margot. Cowboys were an independent breed who didn't like to be told what to do.

Russ took a seat at the table. He was a good-looking guy: around six foot two with broad shoulders, wavy brown hair and hazel eyes.

Margot wondered if the detective had grown up in the area but couldn't place him. Russ was older enough that if he had, she wouldn't have known him.

She remembered Brad because everyone knew the Crawfords. When Brad went off to college, she was still playing with dolls. By the time he was back, he was running with an older crowd and then he was married.

She forced her thoughts from Brad and back to the question that Russ had just asked him.

"Is it that you like hearing me repeat myself?" Brad frowned into his coffee before lifting his gaze. "We went through all of this right after Boyd left."

"Miss Sullivan wasn't here then." The detective slanted a smile in her direction. "I'd like to catch her up to speed. Perhaps she can shed some light on the situation."

"Please call me Margot," she told Russ with a smile.

"Margot, then. You can call me Russ."

Brad gave a snort of disgust. "Now that we've got that settled," he said with a sarcastic drawl, "can we move this along? I have fences to mend."

Russ merely smiled and inclined his head, obviously an indication that the ball was still in Brad's court.

Margot watched him square his shoulders.

"It was the Fourth of July. I went to the wedding—of Braden Traub and Jennifer MacCallum," he clarified for Margot. "They had a reception in Rust Creek Falls Park. The usual barbecue and this wedding punch that lots of people couldn't get enough of…including your father."

"Go on," Russ prompted.

"Several of us guys, including Boyd, ended up at the Ace in the Hole saloon. We played a little poker. Had some drinks." Brad looked as Margot. "The bets were getting a little out of hand. Your father was really betting like crazy. For a while he was winning. Then his luck changed. He lost everything he'd won…and then all the money he had on him."

"My father was," Margot paused and took a deep breath, "*is* an alcoholic. He quit drinking around the time he met my mother and had been sober ever since. After she died, he went to the bottle for comfort. It was as if he had nothing more to live for since she was gone."

"He had you," Brad said quietly.

"I guess he didn't see it that way." Margot tried to force a smile to her lips but it wouldn't slip into place.

"On that particular day, most of the town was drunk." Russ jotted down some notes, glanced back up at Margot. "What about gambling? Was that an issue for him, too?"

She thought for a moment. "I can't say for certain. During my childhood, he never gambled. I remember my parents had friends who were always asking them to go to the casinos in Kalispell with them, but they'd never go."

Russ asked for their names and added their contact information to his growing notes. "I'll check with them to see if a gambling addiction was ever mentioned."

Margot shifted her gaze to Brad. "You said he ran out of money. What happened then?"

"The pot was large. Everyone seemed to think they held the winning hand, so it kept growing." Brad shifted from one foot to the other. "Then it was just me and Boyd. He grew frantic when it was time for him to ante up. He had no more money and he didn't want to drop out. He put up the deed to the ranch so he could stay in. Insisted upon it."

Margot raised a skeptical brow. *"Insisted?"*

"Yes," Brad said flatly. "You know how bullheaded your dad can be. I tried to talk him out of it, but let's just say his, ah, response made it clear I was to mind my own."

It rang true. Margot had been on the receiving end of her father's sharp tongue. When he was in one of his black moods, you couldn't tell him a darn thing.

She took a breath and exhaled. "So he lost the hand—" she added, more to neatly tie up the incident with a bow than because she had any doubt of the outcome "—and the ranch."

"The punch at the wedding was spiked," Russ interjected.

Clearly annoyed, Brad pinned the detective with his

gaze. "I've admitted—numerous times—that while I may have had a few glasses, I wasn't drunk. What I've told you is accurate."

Margot's gaze turned speculative.

"I had a full house," Brad explained. "He had three queens. Normally a winning hand. Just not this time."

"You didn't have to take it." Even she could hear the recrimination in her tone. "The ranch, I mean."

"You think I wanted to take it? You know your dad. He shoved the deed in my face the next day." Brad lifted his hands, let them drop. "Then he was gone. No one has seen him since."

"One-way ticket to New York City," Russ confirmed.

"He was out of money." Margot's head swam. None of this made any sense. "Yet he had enough to buy himself a train ticket all the way across the country?"

Brad shrugged. "Apparently."

"We're thinking someone bought him that ticket." Russ cast a pointed glance at Brad.

"I didn't buy it," Brad answered with a cold stare of his own. "I made that very clear."

"Who would do something like that?" Margot's voice rose then broke. "Who would put a drunken old man on a train to New York City, a place where he doesn't have any friends or family? Where someone could hurt him or—"

She closed her eyes briefly and fought for control.

"We initially assumed he'd gone to see his sister—"

"Until you found out she lived in New Jersey, not New York, and has been dead almost two years."

"That's right." Russ looked surprised but his tone remained carefully controlled. "How did you know—?"

"I told her," Brad said. "And I also mentioned how we've been trying to track her down ever since Boyd disappeared."

"I'm sorry about that. I should have stayed in closer contact."

"Why didn't you?" Russ asked bluntly, his shrewd hazel eyes fixed on her.

Margot resisted the urge to squirm under that penetrating gaze. Instead she squared her shoulders. "We argued the last time I called."

Russ's gaze narrowed on her face. He lifted his pencil over his notepad. "What about?"

Out of the corner of her eye, Margot saw Brad pull out the chair and take a seat on her right. He wrapped both hands around his mug and leaned back.

"About everything." Margot gave a humorless laugh. "I told him I won second place in Cortez. He reminded me that 'second place is the first loser.' I could tell by how he was slurring his words he'd been drinking. I confronted him."

"What happened then?" Russ leaned forward, resting his arms on the table, his intense eyes never leaving her face.

"He told me if I was going to be on his ass every time we spoke, not to bother calling again." She blinked away the tears that flooded her eyes. "He'd had a hard time of it since my mother died. He told me numerous times how hard it was to be here without her. I thought if I gave him some space…"

"There was no way for you to know he'd take off." When Brad reached across the table and gave her hand a squeeze, Margot didn't know which of them was more surprised. He quickly pulled back.

"Then I got injured." Margot relayed the events of that day. "I ended up in the hospital. I called him but he didn't answer and there was no voice mail. He refused to set it up. I must have tried to reach him at least fifty times. I was angry. I was hurt."

"Were you worried?" Russ asked.

"I would have been, if we hadn't had that blowup." Margot blew out a breath and closed her eyes. Once she had her rioting emotions suppressed, she lifted her chin and fixed her gaze on Russ. "When the doctors told me I was out for the season, I stayed with a friend in Cheyenne for a bit but she had a small apartment and a roommate. I was in the way. I decided to come home. I planned to heal my hard head and hopefully mend fences with my father."

Vivian nudged her hand with her nose and Margot patted the dog's head, grateful for the show of support.

"When I got here, my dad was gone." She gestured with one hand toward Brad. "He was here, acting as if he owned the place."

"Well, I'm afraid he does own the Leap of Faith." Russ cast a censuring glance in Brad's direction.

Emotions rose hot and hard, nearly suffocating Margot with their intensity. "You—you can't win a ranch in a card game."

"Boyd signed the deed over to him." Russ shot her a sympathetic look. "We've checked and it was a legitimate business transaction."

"It was a poker game," she said so loudly Vivian swiveled her head and growled.

At Russ? At Brad? Did it even matter?

Later, she would deal with the ownership of the ranch. For now, Margot would focus on what was most important…finding her dad.

"Tell me what steps you've taken to find him."

"We've notified the New York City Police Department as well as the police departments of every stop between here and there." Russ spoke in what she thought of as a police voice. "Because of your father's age and questionable cognitive ability, we were able to put him out there as a 'Missing Vulnerable Adult.'"

"How is that different than simply being a missing person?" Margot asked.

"More attention," Russ told her. "More focus."

"Has *anyone* spoken with him since he left Rust Creek Falls?" she asked. "Or have there been any sightings in any of the cities on the train route?"

"No." Russ gentled his tone. "That doesn't mean we quit looking. I check in weekly with the departments in the towns where the train stopped."

Margot shoved back her chair with a clatter and began to pace. "He can't have vanished into thin air. I should go to New York, see—"

"New York City has a population of over eight and a half million." Russ rose and moved to her, his voice calm. "The best thing you can do is to wait here. Let us know if he contacts you."

Margot blew out a breath, raked her fingers through her hair. She returned to the table and dropped down in the seat she'd vacated only moments earlier. "You're right. It's just that…he's my dad. He's old and he's out there alone."

And there was a man living in her house who, despite what the detective said, had no right to be here.

This was *her* home. *She* was the one who belonged. If Brad Crawford thought she would move out because of a poker hand, he would soon learn differently.

Brad watched Russ drive off from the front porch and hoped he'd seen the last of the deputy. The man obviously still had it into his head—just like many others in town—that Brad had something to do with Boyd's mysterious disappearance. That, for an unknown reason, he wanted the old guy out of town so badly he'd purchased a train ticket.

Even though it made no sense, the rumor persisted. Brad had heard the whispers and seen the sidelong glances. He'd paid them no mind, telling himself it really was no different than the gossip that flourished whenever one of his relationships came to an end.

Rust Creek Falls was a nice little town but people clearly had too much time on their hands to speculate and draw erroneous conclusions.

He glanced around, wondering where Margot had gone. She'd said her goodbyes to the deputy but then disappeared when Russ stepped outside.

The sound of a dog barking came from the stables so Brad headed in that direction. The saddle was already on her gray Arabian when he stepped inside. The dog was there too, baring her teeth in welcome.

"Hey, Viper, the mean-dog act is getting old," Brad told the animal, ignoring the growls.

Margot turned, her brows slamming together. "What did you call her?"

"Viper. That's her name."

"That is not her name." Margot scowled. "Her name is Vivian."

"Seriously?"

Her chin lifted. "What's so strange about that?"

Brad paused, considered, grinned. "My mother has a friend named Vivian. That woman has a certain bite to her so perhaps it's not so strange. Come to think of it, Mom's friend also has those streaks of gray in her hair."

"Har, har. You're hilarious, Crawford." Margot reached down and gently rubbed the top of the dog's head. "Sometimes I call her Vivi."

He made a gagging sound. "That's even worse."

"Deal with it. That's her name."

"I'm going to call her Viper," he said, settling the matter.

"You most certainly are not." Her voice snapped like sheets hung out to dry on a windy day.

"Try and stop me." He shot her a wicked smile, enjoying the banter.

She rolled her eyes. "I don't need to stop you. You're moving out, so you won't be around to call her anything."

"Wrong again, Red."

She leaned forward, giving him a good view of her lace bra. He tried to think of something else that would irritate her but there was only one thought in his head.

If she'd only lean closer...

Not only would he be interested in seeing more, he wanted to immerse himself in her, in her scent. She smelled like wildflowers. Not the sickening over-the-top fragrance his grandma wore, the kind that made his eyes water, but a light, airy scent that enveloped him, made him want to draw closer.

Her boot barely missed his gut as she swung into the saddle. "I'm going to check the property."

"I haven't sold any of it off since your dad hightailed it out of town," he assured her. "If that's what you're thinking."

"How reassuring." Her eyes were cool. "Actually I plan to check the fence line. It's October. The weather could change any time. There were some sections that needed—"

"Already done." Brad smiled when he saw the shock on her face then turned and quickly saddled his own horse, a three-year-old roan called Buck.

"What do you think you're doing?"

He grinned, kicked the horse gently in the sides and headed out of the stable. "Enjoying an autumn day with a beautiful woman."

Chapter Four

Despite the worry over her father, Margot relaxed in the saddle. She'd grown up riding before she could walk. The fact that she couldn't compete until next season was a blow, but she was thankful the doctor said she could still ride at a slow walk. Exploring these meadows and valleys on horseback under the big Montana sky had been a huge part of her childhood.

Though she'd never given much thought to the matter, she realized now that the land she assumed would always be there for her was in danger of slipping away.

A poker game.

It was a good thing her mother wasn't here. Giselle Sullivan would have kicked her husband's ass nine ways to Sunday if he'd pulled a stunt like this when she was alive. Of course, Boyd would never have gambled or drank or ordered his only daughter to stay away if her mother was still alive.

He adored the pretty city girl he'd married when he was fifty-three. Married once in his early twenties, then quickly divorced because of his drinking, Boyd had long given up hope of finding his own happily-ever-after.

Margot recalled how his face glowed whenever he spoke of the day he'd run into Giselle in New York City. Though her father rarely left the ranch in later years, apparently he'd once loved to travel. Running into the pretty career woman had been a fluke, but for both of them it had been love at first sight. He'd quit drinking right then and there, knowing Giselle deserved better.

Sobriety had stuck. They'd stuck. When Margot made an appearance two years later when Giselle was forty-three, both her parents had shed tears of joy.

Margot's heart tightened remembering the angry words between her and her father the last time they'd spoke. If she could only be granted a do-over, she'd respond differently.

"I'm going to hire a private detective," Margot announced, though why she felt the need to make Brad aware of her plans she wasn't certain.

Perhaps it had to do with the fact that he'd respected her need for silence. The interaction with the detective had brought all her fears bubbling to the surface. While she'd kept her composure, by the time he left and she reached the stable, her control was ready to snap.

The ridiculous conversation about Vivian had actually helped. Thankfully Brad didn't feel the need to fill the silence between them with inane chatter. Instead he'd showed her the parts of the fence, answered her questions regarding the price of hay and otherwise remained silent.

"No need to hire a PI," Brad said.

"If you're thinking just because Russ said he's following up that's enough—"

"I'm thinking," he said pointedly, "that it isn't necessary because I've already hired one."

"You have?" If Margot had been a less experienced rider, she'd have fallen off her horse in shock. "Why?"

"Crawford land has butted up to the Leap of Faith for generations. Boyd went to school with my grandmother. Besides, I kind of like the guy. I want to find out what happened to him, make sure he's safe."

Tears stung the backs of Margot's eyes. But a sliver of distrust remained. It would be so easy to say he'd hired a detective—so no one else would—and then have the illusive detective find nothing. *But for what purpose?*

She wasn't sure if it was the sun, the lingering effects of fatigue from the long drive yesterday or remnants from the skull fracture and concussion, but her head started to swim.

"I'm going to take a break," she announced, pulling her horse under a tall cottonwood near a creek. "You go on."

After dismounting, she moved to the tree and sat, resting her back against the massive trunk. Vivian, who'd been trotting along beside the horses, took a stance near her feet, her amber gaze firmly focused on Brad.

She wasn't surprised when he got off his horse and tied the animal to a smaller tree nearby.

"That hard head of yours hurting?" he asked in an insolent tone.

"What's it to you?"

"Just wondering if I'm going to have to strap you across the back of my horse to get you back to the house."

"In your dreams," she shot back, relieved he'd responded with cocky arrogance rather than sympathy.

"Viper looks thirsty."

Margot glanced at Vivian. Though the temperature was a mild sixty, the heeler visibly panted. With so much going on and despite the fullness around the dog's midsection, it was easy to forget Vivi was pregnant.

Though Margot hadn't thought to bring any water with her, there was a creek nearby. She pushed to her feet, discovering that the short break had eased the headache into the manageable range.

"I can—" Brad began.

"She won't go with you," Margot said in a matter-of-fact tone. "And she won't leave me."

"Then I guess we take a walk together." He reached out to take her arm but after seeing her pointed look, dropped his hand. "You got some hang-up about a man touching you?"

"I most certainly do not," Margot retorted before realizing she'd played right into his hands. "I don't know you. I don't particularly like you. That's why I don't want you touching me."

His gaze met hers. "Liar."

"What are you talking about?" Margot sputtered.

"You want me to touch you," he said as if speaking the gospel from the pulpit. "But you're scared of what might happen once I do."

"Oh, for the love of—" She reined in her emotions. "You are so incredibly arrogant. You think every woman is interested in that hot body of yours."

A grin spread across his face, like a kid opening a present at Christmastime. "You think my body is hot?"

"Let's get a few things straight. I'm not interested in touching you. I'm not interested in sleeping with you. I *am* interested in getting you out of my house."

"My house," he corrected. "And you are interested in sleeping with me. You just won't admit it."

"There's nothing to admit." She flung her hands up in

the air, drawing Vivian's watchful gaze as the dog lapped up crystal-clear water from the bubbling creek.

"Come on," Brad teased. "This attraction between us is so strong it's a wonder we haven't both burst into flames."

"Delude yourself all you want." Margot kept her face expressionless. There was no way, *no way*, she was letting him know that she found him the teensiest bit attractive. "I have a compromise I'd like to propose."

"No touching below the waist?"

"Shut up." She fought to hide a smile. The guy never gave up. "I'm talking about the house."

She inhaled deeply, that crisp scent of autumn in the air. It wouldn't be long before the temperature would drop and the cool breeze would turn frigid. The cattle would need to be fed. She'd have to fire up the tractor and attach the blade so she could plow the lane once the snow came. With four-wheel drive, at least her truck would get around.

How had her dad managed these past few years, she wondered? Even before her mother passed, it wasn't as if Giselle was the outdoorsy type. He had no sons to help, no family nearby and he'd told his only daughter to take a hike. Had there been a growing sense that the ranch was becoming too much for him to handle? Had he secretly considered the land a burden?

Certainly she'd seen a few signs that she'd chosen to ignore. Because every time she confronted him he got belligerent.

Her dad had always been proud of how he'd maintained the ranch. But, even before her mom died, Margot had noticed that some things were being neglected. Last year he hadn't even gotten up the snow fence and the drifts had blocked the lane until he'd been able to get the tractor out and plow.

Once her mom had passed, it was as if she'd taken any

drive he'd possessed with her. Of course, most of that lethargy could be due to the alcohol.

"We need to get back," Brad said abruptly.

"We haven't finished our talk."

"If you're not interested in making out, there's nothing keeping us here."

"Is everything about sex with you?"

He paused, considered. "Yeah, pretty much."

Not sure how to respond to such a comment, Margot said nothing, merely returned to her horse and mounted. "Forget a compromise. Once we get back to the house, I want you to pack up your stuff and go back to the Shooting Star. Once my dad returns, we can sort out what he owes."

"Good try."

"What's that supposed to mean?"

He mounted the roan with an ease that spoke of long years in the saddle. "I'm not going anywhere. I don't know how many times I have to say this, but this is my home now. Legally."

"Oh, so you're saying *I* have to leave?"

That would happen when hell froze over, she thought to herself.

"Absolutely not." He gave her a little wink. "I want you to stay."

"You do?"

"How else are we ever going to become, ah, intimately acquainted, if you're living somewhere else?"

The invitation to accompany Brad to his parents' house for dinner that evening surprised her. She was ready to say no when she realized that this might be an opportunity. As she'd had no luck in convincing Brad to move out, perhaps she could get his parents on her side and they could convince him.

Margot dressed carefully for the dinner though she knew she'd probably have been properly attired in jeans and a nice shirt. But this wasn't neighbors getting together for a barbecue; this was a business meeting of sorts. With this fact in mind, she'd pulled out a pair of black pants and topped them with a green sweater. Instead of cowboy boots, she pulled on a pair of shiny heeled ones. She even took a little extra time with her makeup.

Though she was most happy in jeans, she had just enough of her girlie mother in her to enjoy dressing up occasionally.

Her fingers moved to the horseshoe necklace around her neck. It had been a gift from her mother when she was ten and had participated in her first big rodeo. Though many of the girls were older, she'd been excited to get second place.

Her father had been less than impressed. It was the first, but certainly not the last, time she'd heard his "second place is the first loser" speech.

Margot's fingers tightened around the horseshoe. Her mother's faith in her ability had never faltered and Margot was determined not to disappoint her now. She would find her father, bring him home and get the deed to the ranch back, one way or the other.

She gave Vivian a scrub on the top of her head. "You'll have the whole house to yourself tonight, Vivi. Relax and enjoy."

Suddenly cognizant of the time, Margot rushed out of the bedroom and slammed into Brad.

"Whoa, there, filly." His strong hands steadied her.

She inhaled sharply and breathed in the intoxicating scent of his cologne. As her gaze took in his dark pants and gray shirt, she realized she wasn't the only one who'd done a little dressing up. "We're going to be late."

The second the words slipped past her lips she wished

she could pull them back. "We're" made it sound too much like they were a couple, which they weren't, not at all.

"Plenty of time," Brad said easily, his appreciative gaze studying her from head to toe. "You look nice."

He sniffed the air. "Smell good, too. Did you put on that flowery perfume for me? I definitely approve."

"Why you—" For a second Margot was tempted to rush back in her room and wash off the scent she'd impulsively sprayed on after her shower. But that would only make her look like a gauche sixteen-year-old. And she hadn't been that for an awfully long time. So instead she laughed and patted his cheek. "Oh, you poor deluded man."

Margot wondered whether they should drive separately just in case his parents convinced him to turn over the house to her. Though the chance of that happening was a long shot, it *could* happen.

She felt him study her as she slipped past him and headed down the steps. He caught up with her at the door, reaching around her so quickly she had no choice but to let him open it for her.

"I have no idea what's on the menu tonight," he told her, then pinned her with those amazing green eyes. "Unless you're talking about something other than—"

"Forget it."

When they reached his truck, she paused, then heaved a resigned sigh and opened the door. Even knowing the man as little as she did, the odds that she could persuade him to stay at his parents' home tonight were slim to none.

"Let's get back to the point I was making. The menu."

"No worries." She settled into the leather seat, fastened the belt. "I'm not particular."

"I wasn't speaking about food." Brad turned over the engine and cast a sideways glance in her direction. "You didn't accept my invitation for dinner because you wanted to see my parents or because you wanted to spend time with me."

"Give the guy a bubblegum cigar."

"Seriously, something is going on in that devious mind of yours. I want to know what it is."

Margot simply smiled and reached forward. "Mind if I change the station?"

Before he had a chance to respond she'd already changed it to a classic country station. As Merle started wailing about love gone wrong, she poised herself for Brad's next volley.

Vivian ran along the truck barking her displeasure at being left behind. When Brad turned onto the gravel road in the direction of town, Vivian stopped running but continued to bark.

In the cab of the truck the subtle spicy scent of Brad's cologne mingled with her perfume. A watchful waiting filled the air.

Instead of being disturbed by it, Margot felt a thrill of exhilaration. The same feeling she got before she entered the ring on Storm and started the race around the barrels.

"I'm on to you, Red," he said after about a mile.

Now *this* was interesting. She lifted a brow. "Really?"

"My parents aren't going to side with you," he told her. "Trust me. If that's why you came, you'll be heading home tonight disappointed."

Chapter Five

The Crawford home on the Shooting Star property was beautiful, a two-story white clapboard on a double lot. As it was early October, the grass in the yard surrounding the house with its wraparound porch had already gone dormant. Someone, likely Brad's mother, Laura, had put up an autumn display that included stalks of corn, colorful gourds and a huge pumpkin.

Though Margot couldn't recall ever being inside the house, she remembered attending several outdoor barbecues when she was young.

Margot had always been envious of the Crawford family with their six kids. Brad's youngest sister Natalie was three years older than Margot, so they'd run in different social circles. But she knew Natalie and liked her quite a bit.

"Will Natalie be here?" Margot asked as Brad pulled the truck to a stop behind a car she figured must belong to one of his parents.

"It's Friday night," Brad said as if that answered her question.

"Thanks for orienting me to the day of the week." Margot shoved open the door to the truck, even as he was still rounding the front. "But that wasn't my question."

Brad shot her an easy smile. "She's young, single and it's Friday night. You connect the dots."

"Well, I'm young and single and I'm having dinner with your folks. What does that say about me?"

He grinned. "That you're holding on to the false belief that you can get me out of the house by luring my parents over to your side."

"Oh, look," Margot said, grateful for the distraction, for *any* distraction. "Your mother came out to greet us."

"Great," Brad muttered. When he'd asked if he could bring Margot, he'd made sure to clarify to his mother that Margot had just gotten into town. He hoped his parents would convince her that running a ranch was too much for a woman recovering from a head injury.

Sometime during the course of the evening, he would pull his matchmaking mother aside and make it clear he wasn't interested in Margot Sullivan, other than as a casual bed-partner. Even though, to his way of thinking, that fact never belonged in any mother-son discussion.

"Margot." Laura Crawford moved forward holding out both of her hands in welcome. "I'm so glad you could join us."

Seeing Margot warm to her instantly, Brad had to admit his mother had a way. Laura was a pretty middle-aged woman with blond hair cut in a stylish bob, blue eyes and a friendly smile.

But Brad knew from personal experience the woman could be tough if the situation warranted it. You didn't raise four boys and two daughters without a spine. The eyes in the back of her head helped immensely. Of her six children, only Natalie resembled her, both in coloring and in stature.

Tonight his mom wore khakis and a blue checked shirt. Though in her late fifties, she looked much too young to have grown children. When his dad had snagged her, he'd gotten himself a gem. Nearly forty years later, they were still happy together.

That lifelong love, devotion and trust had been what Brad had hoped to have in his marriage with Janie.

"Where's Dad?" he asked as he followed his mother and Margot up the steps to the porch.

"Inside changing. He wanted to wear jeans and that old flannel shirt." Laura smiled at her son. "I said that while that may be good enough for dinner with you, it's not appropriate when we have guests."

"Oh, Mrs. Crawford, jeans and a flannel shirt would have been fine."

"Please call me Laura." His mother patted Margot's arm. "Believe me, it doesn't hurt any of us to go outside our comfort zone every now and then."

They'd barely stepped inside the front door when Todd Crawford came clomping down the stairs in navy pants and a sweater, grumbling with each step.

The disgruntled look on his face was replaced with a smile when he caught sight of Margot.

"Well, this is a pleasure," Todd said. "It's been years since you paid us a visit."

"Hello, Mr. Crawford."

Todd gave a laugh. "It's Todd, honey. When I hear Mr. Crawford I always think of my granddad."

Too bad, Brad thought, they didn't have any bees hovering around. The honey couldn't melt in his parents' mouth. It bordered on sickening. But he wouldn't complain.

He thought of how differently his parents—his mother

especially—had reacted when his sister Nina had begun associating with Dallas Traub and his kids. Thankfully, now that Nina and Dallas were married, both of his parents had come around.

"What's for dinner?" Brad asked. "I'm starving."

"We're having pot roast," his mother said easily, but he caught her warning glance. "I thought it'd be nice if we had a glass of wine in the living room before we ate."

Because he'd been warned and because, small though she might be, his mother was definitely a force to be reckoned with, Brad didn't say he preferred beer to wine. And his hunger would be put on hold, until his mother deemed it time to eat.

He almost wished Natalie was here to run interference. But then he realized that would be playing with fire. Nat was likely to side with Margot and then his mother would join them, leaving him and his father outnumbered. At least this way, if it came to choosing sides and they went by gender, it would be a draw.

"Would you like a glass of wine?" Laura asked Margot, already lifting a bottle they'd had breathing on a side table.

"Absolutely." Margot took a seat in a chintz-covered chair, leaving Brad no choice but to sit on the sofa beside his father, who didn't smell nearly as good as Margot.

"Margot has a blue heeler," Brad said to no one in particular, once they all had their wine.

"Really?" His dad actually looked interested. "Now, that's a dog. Not like—"

"Watch it, Todd," Laura warned.

Margot took a sip of her wine, watching the interaction with undisguised interest.

"We're babysitting my friend Lucille's dog. Lucy lives in Missoula and she's very ill," Laura explained. "We promised to keep the dog—"

"*You* promised to keep her," Todd said pointedly.

The remark earned his father a scowl. Brad wanted to empathize but he kept his expression impassive. He'd quickly learned no one, but no one, dissed the Maltese.

"Brandie Sue," Laura called out in that sugary sweet voice usually reserved for young children and the elderly… and white balls of fluff.

Seconds later, tiny toenails could be heard clicking across the hardwood. A small dog that couldn't weigh more than five pounds trotted in. Her pristine white hair was long and flowing and a pink ribbon adorned the top of her head.

"There's my baby girl," Laura simpered.

"She's adorable," Margot said, sounding surprisingly sincere.

For some reason Brad hadn't expected a woman who rode horses, had a blue heeler and seemed more comfortable in jeans and boots to be into frou-frou dogs.

Brandie Sue paused and cocked her head, ignoring him as usual, her gaze totally riveted to Margot. If there were justice in the world, the animal would bare those little white teeth at her.

Instead BS, as Brad privately thought of her, swished her plume of a tail from side to side and approached Margot.

"She likes you." Laura couldn't have looked any more pleased when the dog sprang into Margot's lap. "She won't go near Brad or Nate."

A hint of a smile formed on Margot's lips. "I believe animals can sense whether you truly like them."

Laura nodded. "What does your dog think of Brad?"

Margot stroked Brandie Sue's fur and gave what Brad thought of as a Mona Lisa smile. "No comment."

Laura laughed, clearly delighted. "What's your dog's name?"

"Viper."

Margot shot Brad a disapproving look. "Vivian."

His mother frowned.

"Her name is Vivian," Margot repeated. "She's a real sweetie."

Brad hid his snort behind a cough when both women stared at him.

"She's about two weeks from having a litter of pups. Father unknown."

"Once they get older, if you need any help finding homes, I can ask around," his dad offered. "Herding dogs are always in demand."

"Thanks." Margot took another sip of her wine.

"Have you heard anything from your father, dear?" Laura asked, her blue eyes filled with concern.

"Not a word." Margot lowered the glass, her expression now troubled. "I called Gage. He sent that detective of his—Russ, I guess?—out checking, but he had nothing new to report."

"Did they ever find out who purchased the train ticket for your dad?" Todd asked.

Margot shot a sidewise glance in Brad's direction before answering. "No leads."

"I don't know who'd do such a thing." Laura reached over and patted her son's knee. "I'm proud of Brad for keeping the place going while your father is gone."

Todd nodded. "A ranch doesn't run itself. The Leap of Faith has been limping along ever since your ma died."

"I didn't realize how bad things had gotten," Margot said, but something in her downward glance told Brad she'd suspected and felt guilty over staying away.

"Brad has done a lot of work these past couple of months, getting it ready for winter." Todd winced when

Brandie Sue hopped off Margot's lap, pranced a few feet then hopped into his.

"Looks like she's taken to you, Dad," Brad said.

"All the women like me," his dad drawled, then grinned at Laura. "But there's only one woman for me."

Brad and Margot exchanged glances.

"Speaking of the Leap of Faith…" Margot paused as if gathering her thoughts.

"How long will you be staying, dear?" his mother said, pulling her besotted gaze from her husband.

Laura would have been horrified to realize Margot hadn't yet finished speaking, but Brad could have kissed his mother.

Margot blinked, clearly caught off guard. "Six months," she said. "Or less."

"Brad said you'd had some sort of injury," his father interjected.

"Yes." She folded her hands in lap and relayed the story she'd told him, including more detail.

"Oh, my dear, a skull fracture is serious." Laura breathed the words.

"Should you have been on a horse today?" Brad asked, more sharply than he'd intended.

"I'm to avoid any activity where I could fall and hit my head." Her lips quirked up. "I haven't fallen off a horse since I was a toddler. I tried to tell the neurologist that the risk in the ring is also minimal for injury but he insisted it would be unwise."

"You must be relieved to have Brad around," Laura said. "I can't imagine doing all that heavy ranch work would be good for you, in your condition."

"What condition is that?" Natalie asked, breezing into the room.

She was pretty and blonde, an angelic face with a mischievous streak a mile wide. Brad adored her.

"Hey, brat," he said in lieu of greeting. "I thought I was going to be able to get in and out of this place without seeing you."

Natalie stuck her tongue out at him then smiled at Margot.

"Ohmigod," she shrieked the second she recognized their guest, moving in to give the redhead a hug. "It's been ages."

Margot blinked, appearing stunned by the effusive welcome. "It's nice to see you."

Brad was seized with the sudden urge to protect, to step between his sister and Margot. Recognizing that as a ridiculous impulse, he remained seated.

Natalie, dressed in a jean skirt that showed way too much skin—what was his father thinking, letting her go out that way—and a blue shirt at least one size too small, studied Margot through lowered lashes.

Brad was suddenly seized with a bad feeling, the same type of feeling he got years ago just before she beaned him over the head with one of her Barbie dolls.

"Rumor is you're shacking up with my brother." Natalie offered a sympathetic glance. "Sweetie, you could do so much better."

"Natalie," Todd ordered. "Apologize this instant."

His sister's head jerked back, her eyes widened. "Why?"

"You've insulted a guest in our home, and your brother."

"I did no such thing." Natalie gave her blond hair a little shake.

"Natalie." His father's voice held a warning.

Brandie Sue, who'd been napping, chose that moment to awaken. Almost immediately she began to bark, as if wanting to add her two cents to the fray.

His father started growling at his mother to shut the dog up while his mother cast censuring glances in her daughter's direction.

"What?" Natalie threw up her hands. "I was teasing. Letting Brad and Margot know what's being said around town."

"I appreciate it." Margot sounded surprisingly sincere. "I can't believe the gossip has already started. I haven't even been here twenty-four hours. Up to now, I've only seen Brad and Russ."

Her gaze shifted to Brad. "Do you think Russ said something?"

Brad considered, nodded. "Probably mentioned to someone you're back. They would have asked about me, or where you were staying. And the story took off from there."

Natalie inclined her head. "Are you really going to stay out there with my brother?"

"It's my home," Margot insisted. "If anyone should leave, it should be him."

"You could move back in with us," Laura told her son and hope flared in Margot's green eyes.

"That isn't feasible." Brad forced a reasonable tone. "Not with winter around the corner. I need to be there to see to things."

"You could drive over every day." Margot's voice took on a hint of desperation. "It's not all that far."

Brad knew that he had to put a stop to this kind of thinking right away. Before his mother or—God forbid—his dad jumped on that bandwagon.

"You're a Montana girl," Brad said with feigned nonchalance. "You know what the winters can be like. Ten miles away might as well be across the continent when drifts close the road. If anyone should live somewhere else, it should be you."

From the way her eyes flashed and that stubborn chin tilted, it was exactly the wrong thing to say.

"I'm not moving out."

"Well, neither am I," Brad shot back.

Natalie grinned, bent over to kiss her mother's cheek. "I'm almost sorry I have to leave. This is getting interesting."

Brad scowled.

Natalie laughed and wiggled her fingers. "Ciao."

The four sat there in silence while the door slammed shut.

"I'm thinking it might be nice to have a second glass of wine," Laura offered finally.

On this point, it seemed, everyone could agree.

Chapter Six

"It appears," Margot said when she and Brad were finally back home and standing in the living room, "we've reached a stalemate."

"Appears so." Brad kept a wary eye on Viper. He didn't trust her any more than he trusted BS.

"You're not going anywhere. Neither am I." She put her hands on her hips, looked him up and down. "We're going to have to figure out a way to peacefully coexist until my father returns."

Though her tone was confident, the look of worry was back, furrowing her brow and darkening her eyes.

"I'm afraid I don't have much cash to contribute to running the household, but I'll pay back what money you spend," she said when he didn't respond. "I want to use what money I do have for a private investigator. Someone needs to be actively searching for my father. I can call

all his old friends, any family, but I want someone out in the field."

"Not necessary," Brad said.

"Of course it's necessary," Margot said, those almond-shaped eyes now flashing green fire.

"Paying a PI isn't necessary," he clarified, "because I already have one on the case. I told you that when we were riding."

For a second she looked confused. "Did you?"

"How can you not remember?"

Margot flushed. "The doctor told me cognitive impairment isn't uncommon after a traumatic brain injury."

The fancy words and the look of guilt on her face told him all he needed to know. The injury she'd sustained was more serious than she'd led any of them to believe. "Well, the man I hired is on the job."

"You didn't mention hiring a PI to Russ."

"I figure he'll work harder if he thinks no one else is looking." Brad shrugged. "Once the guy finds something, I'll let the sheriff's office know."

"He hasn't found *anything*?"

Brad shook his head. "It's like your dad vanished into thin air."

"He could be lying dead in a ditch somewhere." She closed her eyes and a few tears slid down her cheeks.

Without thinking Brad closed the distance between them and pulled her to him. Instead of pushing him away, she buried her face in his shoulder and cried as if her heart would break.

His shirt was wet by the time she drew a shuddering breath and stepped back.

"I'm sorry." With the back of her hand she swiped the last of the tears away, her face now red and splotchy. "I don't know what got into me."

"Don't worry. Boyd is a tough old bird." Brad forced a tone filled with more confidence than he felt. "It'd take a lot to bring him down."

She lifted her gaze to meet his. "Is that what you really think?"

He'd have to be the worst kind of jerk to not respond to the bald hope shimmering in her eyes. "That's what I think."

She sniffled and visibly brought herself under control. "Your parents and sister are nice."

"They're okay."

"I liked Brandie Sue."

He had to smile. "You would."

She wiped her eyes and smiled back. "Well, I guess I better go to bed."

With any other woman, Brad would have gone for broke and kissed her. But as she'd just cried all over him, making a move now felt as if he'd be taking advantage.

"Thank you, Brad."

Before he quite realized what was happening, she stepped close, plunked her hands on his shoulders and pressed her lips against his. Then she turned and headed up the steps, Viper at her heels.

"Hey," he called out just as she reached the top step. "What was that?"

"That was for not being a jerk."

Brad could only stare as she disappeared from sight.

His revving body reminded him of the time he'd gotten a chance to drive a sprint car around the track at the Chicagoland Speedway several years ago. Back then, his foot had been heavy on the accelerator and his hands firmly on the wheel with a set destination in mind.

With Margot, he'd gone from zero to sixty the second he'd felt those sexy lips on his. He'd wanted to devour her, to race with her all the way to the finish line, which in his mind was the bedroom. But she'd simply walked away. *After thanking him for not being a jerk.*

The way Brad saw it, things flowed more smoothly in his life when he was the one in control. Tonight, Margot had been in the driver's seat. While it felt uncomfortable, it hadn't been so terrible.

Brad ambled into the kitchen, still puzzled over the evening's turn of events. The refrigerator door had barely opened when he heard toenails clicking on linoleum and turned to see Viper. For once the dog wasn't growling or snarling.

Instead, the animal strode to her dish and gave it a shove with her nose.

"You're hungry. Is that it?" Brad crossed to the bag of kibble Margot had brought with her.

Viper's eyes lit up.

Brad held the bag out for her to see. "If I give you food, will you promise to be a good girl and do everything I tell you?"

The dog emitted a low growl.

He supposed that *could* be a yes.

After filling the dish, Brad topped off the water bowl then turned his attention back to the refrigerator. Though his mother had served a good meal, he was in the mood for something. Even as he opened the refrigerator door, he knew it wasn't food he wanted.

He wanted Margot. He wanted to go upstairs and see if they could continue what she'd started.

Brad pulled a beer from the cool depths and took a seat at the table. There was a method to Margot Sullivan's madness but darn if he could figure out what it was...

Possibly she was waiting for him to make a play so she could go to his parents and say she couldn't trust him to keep his hands off her. While his parents didn't run his life and tell him what to do, if it came to something like that, he'd definitely get the pressure to move out.

That, he figured, was the most logical reason for her action. She could be upstairs now, chuckling to herself and just waiting for him to come to her.

Brad took a long pull from the bottle and smiled. Well, she could just go ahead and wait.

Brad Crawford was nobody's fool. No matter how much he was tempted, his hands were staying off her…until this whole mess with the house was resolved.

Or, at least for tonight.

By the time Margot came downstairs the next morning, Brad was already in the kitchen, a mug of coffee in his hands. While the sun had started its ascent, darkness still filled the sky.

Though she could have easily slept another couple of hours, Margot figured this was her ranch and she needed to establish that fact from the start. Plus, the longer she went without seeing Brad after last night's kiss, the more difficult facing him would be.

Pressing her lips to his had been a simple gesture, but a mistake. There was no getting around that fact. What had she been thinking?

Margot had spent a good hour last night considering how best to handle the attraction between them. It was simply there. Even now it simmered in the air.

He looked up from the paper spread open on the table in front of him. "Help yourself to coffee."

"Don't mind if I do." She sashayed past him and poured herself a mug.

"You're up early." Even as he gathered up the paper and folded it neatly, she felt his gaze on her.

"Life on a ranch starts early." She took a sip of the dark brew with a bite and felt herself begin to wake up. "What's on the agenda for today?"

He lifted a brow. "What agenda would that be?"

"The ranch duties?"

"Oh, that one." He offered a lazy smile. "I plan to clean out the chicken coop and make some repairs. It promises to be lots of fun."

Margot resisted the urge to grimace. Cleaning the coop had never been high on her list of favorite chores. "My dad got rid of the chickens right after my mother died."

"Perhaps when he's back, he might get a hankering for fresh eggs again. This way the coop will be ready to go. If he doesn't, he'll have an extra building in good repair for extra storage."

Having chickens had been her mother's idea. Giselle had loved the birds. One of Margot's first memories was of her mother showing her how to fetch the eggs in the mornings. Like her mother, Margot adored the hens, gave them names and often sang to them. When her father had caught them midsong one morning, her mother had told him she'd discovered hens produced more eggs when you sang to them. He'd laughed, tugged Margot's ponytail, given her mom a kiss and told them to carry on.

"We'll start right after breakfast." Brad gestured to a couple of boxes of cereal on the counter. "Help yourself."

The fact that he was giving orders as if the place was his didn't escape her notice. Yet he'd spoken of redoing the chicken coop so it would be ready when her father returned...so perhaps there was some hope here.

Margot dumped cereal in a bowl, poured in a good amount of milk and stood at the counter to eat while Brad remained at the table.

She'd eaten half of her Cheerios when she caught him staring. "Something on your mind, cowboy?"

Margot cursed the flirtatious edge that kept finding its way into her voice when she spoke to him.

"You've made it clear you want to pull your weight." His gaze searched hers. "I just want to make sure that's okay with the doctor."

"Worried about me?"

"It would slow me up if I had to take time to call an ambulance and wait with you until they arrived."

"Understood." She put down the cereal bowl and took a long sip of coffee. "I'm cleared to do anything that doesn't result in a blow to the head. As long as the coop doesn't collapse on top of us, I should be fine."

"My sister-in-law Callie works at the Rust Creek Falls Clinic. I could take you there and she could check you out—"

"Seriously, I know what I can and can't do."

"If you're sure…"

"I'm positive."

By midafternoon, Margot remembered just how much she detested cleaning the coops, especially when routine maintenance had been ignored for several years.

Both she and Brad wore gloves and masks as they shoveled the floor and emptied the roosting boxes. Then it was time for the bleach and soapy water. While Margot continued to work inside the coop, Brad caulked the cracks around the perimeter of the floor and nests.

Her head had begun to ache when he suggested they call it a day. She noticed that, in addition to caulking he'd also scraped the exterior of the building.

"Are you planning to paint it?" she asked as they walked to the house.

"It needs a good couple of coats." He reached around

her to open the door to the back porch. "Your father really let things slide around here."

"He lost his wife." She whirled, in full defense mode now. "He's an old man."

"Facts are facts." Brad motioned her inside. "If you want first dibs on the shower, I can wait."

Margot gave a jerky nod, her anger deflating like an untied balloon.

When her father returned home they were going to sit down and have a heart-to-heart. In the past Boyd had employed several ranch hands. Like the chickens, he'd sold off most of the cattle after her mother's death. The hands had taken positions at other ranches.

She might not like to admit it, but Brad was right. Facts *were* facts.

Could it be he'd grown tired of ranching? Was that why he'd been so willing to leave? For a man who'd once loved the land so passionately, it hardly seemed possible.

The fact remained he'd need help if he wanted to continue ranching. And smaller herds. She'd insist on him hiring help, not only for ranch work but for normal maintenance around the place.

"That'll go over like a lead balloon," she muttered. Was there a rancher on the face of this earth who wasn't hardheaded?

"Did you say something?" Brad asked.

She glanced down at her filthy clothes. "First dibs on the shower."

He just smiled and when his gaze slid down to the tips of her boots and slowly made the journey back up to her face, she had the distinct feeling he was imagining her with those clothes stripped off.

Tit for tat, she thought. She'd had a few lascivious thoughts of her own earlier today when he'd been working and his shirt had stretched tight across those broad shoulders.

Fueled by warmth that had nothing to do with hard work, she scampered up the stairs to the shower.

Twenty minutes later she was in her room, dressed and blow-drying her hair when she heard the water turn off. Had he taken his change of clothes into the bathroom as she had? Or would he soon be emerging from the small steamy room with nothing but a towel around his midsection?

Stop it, she told herself. Stop it.

The irritating preoccupation with Brad Crawford only pointed out the fact that she'd gone a long time without a man in her life, or in her bed. It had obviously been *too* long if she was entertaining thoughts of jumping the man who was squatting on her father's property.

Not that she would act on the impulse. Kissing a handsome cowboy was one thing. Having sex with him was quite another.

Instead of tying her hair back, Margot let the wavy strands hang loose. She pulled on a black skirt and a sweater of vibrant gold. Standing in front of the dresser mirror, she took a few seconds to add mascara and lipstick before wandering out in the hall and heading down the steps.

Vivian followed close on her heels, a silent shadow. As best Margot could calculate, the heeler was due to deliver her pups in the next few weeks. Which meant she needed to make sure Vivi didn't overdo and that she had adequate food and water.

Earlier today she'd noticed Brad had set out fresh water for the dog. Margot thought of the people in town who gossiped so disparagingly about Brad. Did they know how thoughtful he could be? She doubted it. Brad seemed like the kind of guy who loved to make people think the worst of him.

I wonder why that is? She shoved the thought aside as of no consequence when he strolled into the kitchen.

Like her, he'd changed into fresh jeans. Instead of the worn flannel shirt he'd had on earlier, he now sported a long-sleeved button-down shirt with thin stripes. His hair still held a hint of moisture from the shower. If her nose wasn't mistaken, he'd dabbed on a little of that spicy cologne.

She rested her back against the counter and forced a nonchalant tone. "You look nice."

"I'd say we both look—and smell—a heckuva lot better than we did an hour ago." He headed to the back porch and pulled a jacket from the hook.

She stared, puzzled. "Are you going somewhere?"

"Saturday night poker with friends." He shrugged into the jacket.

"What about dinner?"

Surprise flitted across his face.

She flushed, regretting even mentioning it. Obviously the guy wasn't hanging around expecting food since he'd already put on his coat.

"I'll grab some wings," he said, then paused. "You have plans for tonight?"

"Not firm ones." Margot forced a cavalier tone. "One of my high school friends mentioned on Facebook that she's back in Rust Creek Falls visiting family. I plan to give her a call. See if we can reconnect."

"Sounds like a solid." He gave her a wink. "Don't wait up."

"You don't wait up either," she called after him. But he was already out the front door.

When she heard his truck roar to life, Margot reached

into her pocket for her cell phone and punched in a number, praying Leila came through.

After all, Brad shouldn't be the only one with plans for a Saturday night.

Chapter Seven

"Just as good as I remembered." Leila Dirks exhaled a dramatic sigh even as she dipped her spoon for one more taste of the salted caramel ice cream.

The two women had taken a road trip to Kalispell for dinner. With pizza on the brain, due in large part to Brad's comment about *his* dinner plans, Margot and Leila had stopped at an old haunt on Hilton Ranch Road for wood-fired pizza. They'd gone with a favorite, the "Crazy Mountain," which included spicy sausage, pepperoni, genoa salami, black olives and jalapeños.

Splitting a small pizza should have been enough food. But when Leila suggested they satisfy their sweet tooth with a stop at an ice cream shop on Main, Margot had enthusiastically agreed.

"You're going to have to roll me out of here," Margot groaned.

"Wimp," Leila shot back with a grin.

"Guilty." Margot glanced across the table at the brunette with eyes so blue they almost looked violet, and returned the smile.

When Leila picked her up, she'd been struck by the change in her old friend. Gone was any hint of the country girl. Everything from her stylish razor-cut bob to her Jimmy Choo shoes screamed big-city girl. As a news reporter for an Atlanta television station, Leila's lifestyle had done a one-eighty from her days growing up in Montana.

Over pizza they caught each other up on details of their lives they hadn't chosen to share on social media. By the time they were at the ice cream parlor, they'd pretty much covered the four years since high school.

"I still can't believe you're living with Brad Crawford." Leila rested her chin on her hand, returning to the topic that appeared to pique her interest the most. "The guys in that family are total hotties."

Though she'd already clarified the point a thousand times this evening, Margot once again set her friend straight. "Under the same roof is not the same as living with."

"It's certainly a lot closer than I ever got to him or any of his hunky brothers."

"I'm hoping to convince him to move out soon," Margot confided.

"Before or after you have your way with him?" Leila raised an eyebrow and both women laughed.

"Granted, the man is attractive." Margot then went on to explain how Brad's shirt had tightened across his back when they'd been working on the chicken coop, bringing to mind how he'd looked when she'd first seen him with his shirt off. "He's got some serious muscles."

"You and I need to make a deal, honey bun. I want to hear all about Brad's hotness—especially what he looks like with his clothes off—but," Leila paused and swallowed, wrinkling her face as if tasting something foul, "no more talk about chicken coops or cows or manual labor."

The request didn't come as a surprise to Margot. So far this evening her friend hadn't had a single good thing to say about Montana or Rust Creek Falls.

Margot stared thoughtfully at her high school buddy. "You don't plan to ever come back."

A look of puzzlement crossed Leila's face. "Did you think I did?"

Margot shrugged.

"What about you?"

"When I first left, I'd have said no." Margot took one last bite of the ice cream remaining in her dish before pushing it aside. "Now I think after I'm done with the rodeo circuit, I'll probably settle here."

"This part of the country is a wasteland." Leila shot Margot a disbelieving look. "They don't even have a Starbucks."

"I enjoy small-town life." On the long drive from Wyoming to Rust Creek Falls, Margot had done plenty of thinking and come to a surprising conclusion. "I like walking down the street and knowing everyone who passes by."

Leila pointed a perfectly manicured finger in Margot's direction. "And every single one of those people has their nose in your business."

"That's a definite downside," Margot admitted. "But every last person would be there to help me if I needed anything. Besides, there's nothing like riding across the meadows on horseback, skiing cross-country on pristine white snow and breathing in clean country air."

"They should hire you to do a tourism ad campaign." Leila chuckled before her expression turned serious. "I bet you don't leave."

"You mean once my head is healed?"

Leila nodded.

"I'm not ready to settle down yet," Margot told her friend. "I still have goals I haven't met."

"Making the National Finals Rodeo in Las Vegas." Leila winked, took a sip of her cola. "Three barrels. Two hearts. One dream."

"You got it."

Leila might not be a country girl anymore but she'd spent time in rodeo club in high school and knew the passion that gripped barrel racers.

"For now," Margot said. "I'm going to enjoy my time back in the great outdoors."

Even as she said the words, Margot felt guilty. How could she even think about having fun when she didn't know what had happened to her father? Still, what was the alternative? Sit in her room and worry?

"You're going to enjoy jumping Brad Crawford's bones."

"It might help pass the time." Margot pushed back from the table and stood. "Now that we've totally pigged out we need to hit a hot spot and work it off. Since you're only here for two weeks—"

"An eternity," Leila grumbled.

"Hey, your sister's baby only gets christened once, and how many times will your parents celebrate their thirtieth anniversary with both of their children present?"

"I suppose."

"What I'm trying to say is it's your choice where we spend the rest of the evening." Margot tried to recall what she knew of Kalispell's nightlife. "We could go to the Pub on East Center? Or check out the saloon just down the street?"

"I've got a better idea." Leila's lips lifted in a smile. "I know a place that can always be counted on to provide a good time."

"Well, then, I'm in." Margot felt a surge of excitement. "Lead the way."

Though it was barely ten o'clock, Brad found himself bored by the card game. The nachos were mediocre, he'd let his beer get warm and the music from a local country band came in at a few decibels below earsplitting.

Brad had been a fan of the Ace in the Hole bar since he'd been old enough to down his first beer. But since the card game on July Fourth, the place held too many memories.

Like the odd look on Boyd's face when he realized the pot was building and he was running out of money. The way the old man's hands had gripped his set of cards. The tone that brooked no argument when he'd insisted they accept the deed to his ranch so he could stay in the game.

Most of all, Brad remembered the way Boyd had stared at the pot in the center of the table when he realized he'd lost the hand...and his legacy. The old man had surprised everyone when he'd shoved himself back from the table and left.

The next day, Margot's father had been on an eastbound train to New York City, leaving Brad holding the deed to the ranch.

"In or out?" Anderson Dalton asked.

In answer, Brad tossed some chips into the pile.

"You seem distracted." His brother Justin shot Brad a sly smile. "Are we keeping you from something more interesting? Or should I say *someone* more interesting?"

Brad narrowed his gaze. "What do you mean by that?"

"Nothing." If anything, his younger brother's smile only widened. The innocent expression he'd pasted on his face didn't suit him in the least.

"Ante up, Justin." Pointing to the center of the table, Travis Dalton—Anderson's younger brother—took a long pull from his bottle of beer.

Justin shot him a sour look. "Can't you see my brother and me are having a conversation?"

"If you want a tea party, find another table," Anderson said. "We're playing poker at this one."

Justin tossed down his cards. "I'm out."

The game continued but Justin appeared disinclined to let the subject drop. "Mom mentioned Margot Sullivan is back in town."

"Does she still have those big boobs?" Travis asked.

Brad's fingers tightened around his cards. What did Travis know about Margot's breasts?

"Butt out, Dalton." Justin smiled sweetly at his friend. "We didn't invite you to our tea party."

The other man snorted and the topic was temporarily forgotten, until a low wolf whistle split the air.

"Fresh meat," someone at an adjacent table announced.

Brad tipped his cards down and turned in his seat. His heart slammed against his rib cage.

Margot, looking decidedly uncowgirl-like in a black skirt, heeled boots and gold sweater, glanced around the room. Her friend, a striking brunette in a red wraparound dress and boots, grabbed Margot's arm and tugged her inside.

The two women sauntered over to the bar and took a seat at a couple of empty stools on the end.

Brad tried to place the woman Margot was with but came up blank. "Who's the brunette?"

"Leila Dirks." Justin slanted him a sideways gaze. "She's hot but I prefer the redhead."

"Leave Margot alone," Brad warned in a tone that brooked no argument before he refocused on his cards.

Both of the Dalton brothers were skilled poker players, and Brad wasn't about to lose this hand to his younger brother. Still, his gaze kept sliding in the direction of Margot and her friend. Out of the corner of his eye he saw various men approach, chat and then mosey on their way.

Justin pushed back his chair. "I believe I'll go over and welcome the beautiful ladies to this fine establishment."

Brad had no doubt Justin could score some serious points. Though Brad couldn't understand it, most of the women in the area appeared to find his younger brother charming.

As far as Brad was concerned Justin would always be the pain-in-the-ass younger brother determined to tag along with him and Nate. When Justin didn't get his way, he could be a real jerk. Like the time he put snakes in Brad's boots.

Brad clamped his hand on Justin's arm when he started to rise. "Sit."

"Sorry, bro." Justin appeared amused. "Not my keeper."

"You play out my hand," Brad told him. "Keep the winnings."

Justin thought for a second then grinned. "Wait until I tell Nate. He'll never believe it."

"Shut up and play the cards," Brad said mildly, deliberately bumping against Justin when he stood.

He crossed the room, feeling less sure of himself with each stride. This uncertainty was a new feeling. From the time he'd been fifteen, Brad had known just what to say to girls and then, as he grew older, to women.

He and Nate used to joke they'd grown up being irresistible to the opposite sex. Now Nate was married and the owner of the new Maverick Manor hotel. Two years ago he'd even run for mayor of Rust Creek Falls. He'd lost to

Collin Traub, a fact that had only fueled the fire between the two families.

Now that their sister Nina had married a Traub, a truce of sorts had come to pass.

"Well, if it isn't Brad Crawford." The brunette—Leila—served up a sunny smile. "We were just talking about you."

"Is that right?" Brad felt his natural ease returning under the warmth of her admiring gaze.

"Were you talking about me, too?" a voice behind him asked.

Brad turned to find Justin standing there. He frowned. "I thought you were playing my hand."

Justin shrugged. "I folded."

"I had four kings." Brad had to restrain the impulse to wrap his hands around his brother's neck and squeeze tightly.

"If you thought it was such a good hand, you should have stayed and played it yourself," Justin said in a matter-of-fact tone before flashing the women an enticing Crawford smile. "Margot and Leila. Right?"

Brad gritted his teeth. "My pain-in-the-ass brother, Justin."

"Oh, we remember Justin." A trill that some men might find sexy filled Leila's voice. "He was an über-hot senior when Margot and I were lowly freshmen."

Margot's gaze met Brad's but he couldn't tell what the glint in her eyes meant.

"Why don't I snag a table?" Justin suggested, his gaze returning to Margot. "We can get reacquainted."

"Forget the table." Leila swiveled on the stool and stood. "I didn't come to sit and talk. I came to dance."

The brunette smiled seductively at Brad, just as Justin took a step closer to Margot. Utilizing the swift footwork he'd once displayed on the ball field, Brad stepped in between the two, took Margot's hand and pulled her to him. "Good idea. Let's dance."

Once they were out of earshot, Margot gave a little chuckle. "Aren't you the smooth one?"

"I *am* the big brother."

Margot tossed back her head and gave a throaty laugh. There was no time for silly chitchat as the band launched into a series of songs practically demanding a raucous two-step. By the time the set ended, Brad and Margot weren't the only ones breathing hard. To slow things down, the quartet chose a love song to lead off the next set.

Sometimes, Brad thought, *you just know there is a God.*

His arms wrapped around Margot and they moved together in time to the music. She fit perfectly in his arms, her body soft and molding to his. The light flowery scent of her perfume mixed with the fresh aroma of her shampoo created an enticing combination.

"I didn't realize you were playing poker here this evening." She sounded almost apologetic. "I thought you played at someone's house."

"It's easier to meet here."

"Do you come every Saturday night?"

"Usually." Brad deliberately kept his answers short and sweet. Though he didn't mind talking poker, this discussion had to remind Margot what happened the night before her father disappeared.

Out of the corner of his eye, Brad caught sight of Leila and Justin on the other side of the dance floor, their bodies glued together. "Looks like those two are getting acquainted."

Margot turned in his arms. "Leila was hoping for some action this evening. Appears she's headed in that direction."

"Perhaps I should have asked her to dance." The second the words left his mouth, Brad knew they'd been a mistake.

Margot stiffened in his arms.

"It may not be too late." The green eyes that met his were edged in ice. "I'm sure you can figure out a way to make the change. You are, after all, the big brother."

For some reason, the comment made him laugh and in seconds Margot was laughing, too.

"I'm right where I want to be." Brad kept his tone light.

When she glanced curiously up at him, he offered a benign smile. "No one can two-step like a cowgirl."

"I love to dance," Margot admitted.

When the band launched back into another series of fast-moving songs, they stayed on the sawdust strewn floor for another set, before collapsing into some seats at a recently vacated table.

Brad gestured to the server for two beers then settled his gaze on Margot. This seemed the perfect opportunity to find out more about her. "What did you and Leila do this evening?"

She told him about their trip to the pizza place in Kalispell, which he admitted was one of his favorites and then about the ice cream store.

"Did you try the s'mores flavor?"

Margot thought for a moment then shook her head. "I didn't see it on the menu. If it had been there, I definitely would have given it a try."

"They don't have it all the time." He smiled, thinking how nice it would be to share ice cream with her.

He pulled himself up short, barely stifling a snort. Yeah, and maybe they could go pick flowers together, too.

Still, he did approve of her choice of pizza. They chatted easily, the conversation flowing like a freshwater stream. They'd just made the leap from food to horses, when Justin and Leila appeared at the table.

"I'm going to show Justin my father's new hunting cabin."

Margot lifted a brow. "In the dark?"

Leila's lips curved slightly. "There's a full moon tonight."

Margot glanced from her friend to Justin. "Don't worry about coming back for me. I can find a ride home."

"You can ride home with me," Brad said, then turned to Leila. "If you can take Justin home."

Leila and Justin exchanged smiles.

"I can do that." Leila elbowed him. "But if he's not good, he might have to walk home."

"Oh, baby, I'll be good," Justin promised.

It was all Brad could do to stifle a gag. Still, as he walked Margot to his truck and opened the door for her, Brad couldn't help thinking he owed his brother. This couldn't have worked out better if he'd planned it.

Now, he just had to figure out a way to snag himself a little honey in the form of a good-night kiss or, if he was really lucky, something more.

Chapter Eight

On the drive back to the Leap of Faith Ranch, Margot was pleased to discover her head didn't ache from all the dancing and the noise. Perhaps the glass of wine she'd had with the pizza and the few sips of beer had relaxed her more than she realized.

Or perhaps it was Brad's company. The realization surprised her. Though she hesitated to describe him as a restful kind of guy, he was accomplished in the art of small talk and kept the conversation flowing with seemingly little effort. After spending the past few years around cowboys who could only talk rodeo, this was a refreshing change.

"Do you think you'll be seeing Leila again before she heads back to Atlanta?" Brad slanted a sideways glance at her as he turned onto a gravel road that would eventually lead them to the ranch.

"I can't say for sure since she has her niece's christening

tomorrow and her parents' anniversary party the day after that, but the odds are good." Margot leaned back, a slight smile curving her lips. "She's already going stir-crazy and she hasn't even been here forty-eight hours. She asked me how one can be expected to exist without a Starbucks."

Brad smiled at that. "Sounds as if she won't be moving back."

Margot laughed and shook her head. "Not a snowball's chance."

"Big-city life can be seductive," he said in a low tone that made something in her belly quiver.

It wasn't the comment, she knew, but the way those smooth, firm lips lingered over the word "seductive" and the way her mind immediately leaped to all that the word implied.

"Mmm-hmm," she murmured, remembering that brief taste of his lips when she'd planted that kiss on him and surprised them both.

"Once you finish with your rodeo career, do you see yourself coming back?"

It was virtually the same discussion she'd had with Leila earlier this evening.

"I'd like to settle here." Her gaze turned pensive. "I've thought about offering a series of barrel-racing boot camps. The majority would be designed for the serious rider who wants to increase their speed and proficiency. Others could be like a dude ranch introduction to the sport."

Surprise widened his eyes. "You've given this a lot of thought."

"Not really." Margot gazed out her window into the darkness. "I've just discovered I like to teach. If that possibility was off the table, I'm not sure what I'd do if I did come back."

"Work the ranch," he said almost immediately.

"My dad could use the help," she admitted, "and I'd be happy to do what I could to make life easier on him. But growing up, we were always tangling over one thing or another. I bet we'd drive each other crazy."

She found the thought that there just might not be a place for her on her father's ranch disturbing.

"Maybe you'll find someone and settle down," Brad suggested in a casual tone.

Margot gave a snort. "I've perused the inventory in this area. While it's possible there might be a diamond in the rough out there that I've missed, it's not likely."

"Do you have a boyfriend on the circuit?"

"What is this?" She rolled her eyes. "Twenty questions?"

He smiled easily. "Just curious."

"Next you'll be asking me the last time I slept with a guy."

A quiet hum filled the air.

"I'm guessing it's been a while," he said after a long moment.

"What gives you that idea?" She didn't even try to keep the indignation from her voice. "I'm an attractive—"

"It's been a while for me, too."

"No way."

He lifted a shoulder in a slight shrug and steered the truck into the long drive leading to the house. "You know how it is, Margot. People like to talk. They believe what they want. I like women. That sure as hell is true. But I don't sleep with everyone I date."

Her skepticism must have shown on her face because he laughed. "Scout's honor."

"You're too...hot," she said finally, unable to come up with a better word, "to go without sex for long. Testosterone oozes from your pores."

He looked startled then pleased.

"I could say the same for you," he said. "Except for the testosterone part."

"It's hard to get involved with guys you see every day." Margot considered. "The circuit is its own little microcosm. It's one thing if you're together and happy. It's quite another to be there bumping elbows when things go south."

"It's not any better here," Brad admitted with a rueful smile.

"You're right." She rested her head back against the seat and expelled a heavy sigh. "We're both screwed."

"People are going to continue to talk about you living here with me."

"I've got an idea. You could move out."

"Good try." The truck came to a stop in front of the house.

Margot frowned. "Why don't you park in the garage?"

"Have you seen all the junk in there?" he asked then stopped. "Not to disparage your father's stuff…"

"It probably is junk. Mom controlled his pack-rat tendencies when she was alive but I'm sure he's been accumulating all sorts of useless stuff ever since." She slanted a questioning glance in his direction. "I'm surprised you haven't cleaned it out by now."

"I wasn't sure what he'd want to keep or toss."

"That's sweet."

He killed the engine, but made no move to get out. "I'm a sweet guy."

Inside the house, Vivian barked wildly.

When Margot's hand moved to the door handle, Brad's hand closed over her arm. "What's your hurry?"

She tilted her head questioningly.

"When you went on a date in high school and the guy

took you home, did you ever just sit in the car and make out before going inside?"

"With my dad?" Margot laughed. "If I tried anything like that, he'd be out with his shotgun."

"I had several brushes with protective dads back in the day." Brad leaned close, brushed a kiss as light as a feather across her cheek. "But the only one in the house right now is Viper. Unless we open the front door I should be safe."

He lifted one of her curls and tucked it behind her ear. "Of course, the way I'm feeling right now, I'd risk it."

Margot held herself very still. Her breath hitched. "What are you saying?"

"I'm asking," his voice low and smooth as cream, "if I may kiss you."

She tapped her cheek with her index finger. "I think you already did."

Brad shook his head slowly from side to side, a slow and lazy smile tugging at his lips. "That was nothing."

The moment her gaze linked with his, something inside Margot seemed to lock into place and she could not look away. She moistened her lips with the tip of her tongue. "Perhaps you could illustrate the difference, cowboy..."

He reached out and touched her cheek, one finger trailing slowly along her skin until it reached the line of her jaw. "Happy to be of service."

The words barely left his mouth when he shifted and gathered her close against him, kissing her. Gently, he stroked her back, cradled her head.

Margot wasn't sure what she expected but it wasn't this slow sensual onslaught of her senses. His mouth teased, planting warm sweet kisses on her lips then moving to her cheeks and neck, sending shivers all the way to the tips of her toes.

She loved the way he smelled, a woodsy mixture of cologne and soap that brought a tingle to her lips and heat percolating low in her belly.

They kissed gently, sweetly, for the longest time. But a fire had begun to build and the kisses grew longer and more intense. Her pulse became a swift tripping beat. When his tongue teased the fullness of her lower lip she opened for him and when it penetrated her mouth it was as if he was inside her.

A smoldering heat flared through Margot, a sensation she didn't bother to fight. He tasted like the most delicious, decadent candy and she couldn't help wanting more.

She yearned to run her hands over his body, to feel the coiled strength of skin and muscle sliding under her fingers. She wanted him to touch her in the same way.

She planted a kiss at the base of his neck, his skin salty beneath her lips.

Brad folded her more fully into his arms, anchoring her against his chest as his mouth once again covered hers in a deep, compelling kiss.

Then he sat back, his hands dropping to his sides. "We should go in."

Margot felt like a child whose new toy had just been snatched from her grasp. For a second she wondered if *going in* meant they'd go in and go to bed…together.

Something in his eyes told her that wasn't the plan.

Her stomach curled with nervousness.

With a sigh he looped his arms around her pulling her closer against him. "I want to take this slow."

"Why?"

"I don't know." For a second, he sounded as confused as she felt. Then he blew out a breath and the cocky look was back in his eyes.

"You're right," she said with a studied nonchalance that deserved an award. "Too much kissing is gross."

His eyes widened with surprise then he laughed.

Though her heart performed another series of flutters, she laughed, too, and opened the door.

Had he friggin' lost his mind?

In his bedroom—*alone*, because he was a certifiable idiot—Brad pulled off his coat and flung it on a nearby chair. What had he been thinking? Calling it quits just when the action was heating up?

He had no doubt it would have taken very little effort to get Margot into bed. They were both on fire…until he'd thrown a bucket of water on the moment.

Though he suspected not many people saw that side of her, Margot was clearly a sensitive woman. And it didn't take a rocket scientist to know she was going through a rough patch. She faced not only the abrupt end to her rodeo career—at least for now—but the loss of her mother and now her father's craziness.

The last thing Brad wanted was to do anything that would add to her burden and take advantage of her situation. He'd chosen to play the role of gentleman, instead of a randy cowboy out for what he could get.

But darn it, being a randy cowboy was so much fun.

"Brad."

The fear in Margot's voice broke through his thoughts like a well-thrown knife. With several long strides he was at the door, shoving it open. He rushed into the hall.

She stood, wide-eyed and trembling, just outside the open bathroom door. Like him, she was still fully dressed.

He immediately moved to her side. His worry skyrocketed when he felt her trembling. "What's wrong?"

"It's Vivi."

Brad suddenly realized that despite the earlier bark-fest at the window when they'd first driven up, the animal hadn't been there snarling a greeting when he'd walked through the door. He'd been so lost in being an idiot he hadn't noticed. "She's around here somewhere."

"She's in the bathtub."

He exhaled a frustrated breath, thinking of the cold shower he needed if he was going to have any chance of falling asleep. "Tell her to get out."

"I can't." Margot clasped her hands together. "She's having her puppies."

"You said she wasn't due for a couple of weeks."

"That's what I thought, but I wasn't sure exactly when she got pregnant."

Margot looked so distressed he wanted to pull her into his arms, but restrained himself.

"Dogs have puppies every day."

She worried her lower lip. "I don't want anything to go wrong."

"Would you like me to take a look?" Over the years Brad had delivered his share of calves and foals so this certainly wasn't new territory.

"I'd appreciate it. My father never let us have a dog, so I don't have much experience in the puppy arena." Her eyes remained filled with worry. "I can't lose her."

Brad stepped into the bathroom. It was immediately apparent he'd be showering in the downstairs facilities tonight. Viper was on her side, stretched out in the tub. Margot must have placed a towel nearby and one puppy had already been born.

Thankfully Viper seemed to have some motherly instincts as she'd done a good job of cleaning the pup that was making squeaking noises.

"So far, so good." Brad offered Margot a reassuring smile.

"There's more." Margot's fingers clamped his arm with the force of a vise. "But they're not coming."

True statement, Brad knew, from the way Viper was breathing. But she didn't appear to be in any distress... unless you counted her obvious displeasure at having him in the room. The instant she saw him she curled her lip and growled. He had no doubt if he decided to do something crazy like reach inside the tub, he'd lose a hand.

"This could take all night." Brad spoke in a reassuring tone. "Heelers can have ten or twelve pups."

He closed his eyes and nearly shuddered, imagining a dozen little Vipers roaming the house.

"You think she'll be okay?"

"She seems to have it under control but I believe me being in here is stressful."

Margot glanced at the tub. There was no way she could miss the way Viper reacted to him.

"You're right." She shot him an apologetic smile. "Go to bed. We'll be fine."

"You're going to stay up."

"I can't leave Vivi. I want to be here in...in case she needs me. You understand."

Just like that she'd slid under his defenses...again.

"How about I make coffee?" he asked. "It may be a long night."

"Thank you." She lifted a hand, cupped his cheek. "You're really a sweet guy."

"No, I'm not. I'm doing this in the hopes of getting to second base once this is over."

She rolled her eyes heavenward and chuckled as if he'd made a joke.

Brad took his time with the coffee, knowing Margot would call out if she needed him. And knowing, just as surely as he knew his own name, that he'd come running the second she called.

By the time he returned to the Viper's nest with a couple of to-go cups filled with steaming brew, there were three more pups in the tub.

Margot smiled when she saw him. "Vivi is on a roll."

The heeler glanced up and growled low in her throat.

"Good to see you, too, Viper," he said.

Margot took the cup from his hands and sipped. "Thank you."

Because Viper was now more focused on spitting out another pup than snarling at him, Brad remained in the room, leaning against the sink. "What a way to end a date."

"We didn't have a date," Margot clarified. "You played poker with your friends. I went to dinner with Leila."

"Apologies. It must have been the make-out session in the truck that conjured up the word *date.*"

Her eyes softened. "You can go to bed now. I'm confident Vivi and I will do just fine."

Wishing the night could have ended differently, Brad went downstairs, took a cold shower and went to bed. Alone.

Chapter Nine

By the time the tenth, and last, puppy was born, it was close to 3:00 a.m. Margot almost knocked on Brad's door to tell him mother and puppies were fine, then decided the good news could wait until morning.

She'd had to troop downstairs for her shower and afterward considered stopping by Brad's room on the way to hers. But sleep beckoned and she heeded the call. The clock read nearly ten by the time she pried her eyes open.

Jumping out of bed, she pulled the chenille robe from the hook on the door and raced out to check on Vivi and the puppies.

Her heart dropped. The tub was empty. Then her ears registered sounds coming from the first level. With her heart in her throat, Margot bounded down the steps in her bare feet.

She found Vivi in the parlor with two bowls, one of kibble and the other filled with water, near a box that Margot had never seen before. Made of plywood, it wasn't anything fancy, but it kept the puppies contained while giving Vivian easy access in and out.

A lump rose to her throat. Though she wasn't sure how Brad managed to move the puppies and Vivi, he had to be the one responsible. With the box's close proximity to heater vents, the puppies would remain warm even when the nights turned cold.

She took a couple of steps closer then stopped at the warning glint in Vivian's amber eyes. From where she stood, Margot counted all ten puppies.

Realizing the new mother had what she needed, Margot headed to the kitchen. She found a note on the counter from Brad. He'd gone out and would be back this afternoon.

Which meant she was on her own.

Margot fought a surge of disappointment. While Brad was an interloper, he kept her from feeling alone in the big house.

For the first time she truly comprehended her father's repeated assertions that she didn't understand how hard it was for him to be in the house without her mother. When Margot had returned to the rodeo circuit after her mother's funeral, he'd been utterly alone.

Boyd had never been very social. Her mother had loved card parties, church events and socializing with friends. Boyd always grumbled that Giselle was always dragging him one place or another.

But it was his wife's outgoing personality that had kept Boyd connected to the community and filled his life with meaning. Once Giselle was gone, the connection vanished. Not long after she was laid to rest, he'd returned to his first love, the bottle.

A heavy weight settled over Margot's heart. She'd failed

her dad. In the process, she'd failed her mother, who counted on Margot to take care of the man she loved.

Well, Margot would do whatever it took to find Boyd and bring him home. Then they'd go from there. There was no point in worrying if he'd stop drinking or if he'd order her away. Finding him, making sure he was safe and bringing him back to Rust Creek Falls where he belonged were good first steps.

Margot dressed quickly, pulling on a favorite pair of jeans and a lightweight gray sweater with colorful threads running through it. She thought about skipping makeup entirely but took a few minutes to dab on some mascara and lip gloss.

As she smoothed the color onto her lips, she thought about what had almost happened last night. If Brad had been willing, she'd have made love with him.

The fact that she had so easily considered having sex with a man she barely knew should have shocked Margot. But it didn't. Not that she was promiscuous.

In fact her first two sexual encounters had been boys/men she'd had feelings for and who she thought had feelings for her. She'd been wrong both times.

By the third, she decided if she had an itch that needed scratching, trusting someone enough to get naked with them was good enough.

But number three had been well over a year ago and in the end they'd only been intimate a couple of times. Still, going without sex for this past year had hardly been a burden.

She worked and trained hard, which left little time for anything else. Margot meant what she said to Brad. It wasn't wise to become involved with guys you saw every day. And she'd been okay with celibacy...until she'd caught sight of Brad with all those rippling muscles and that ultra-sexy "don't mess with me" scowl.

One look and all her pent-up sexual energy had exploded. He was just the type of guy her mother—and father—had warned her against, a good-looking cowboy who thought he owned the world.

Even though Brad was older and Margot had only been home for brief snatches of time in recent years, she'd heard the talk. Brad had married only to split with his wife several years later.

Though Margot hadn't known Janie Delane personally, she remembered the woman's vindictive behavior. Before Janie left town, the woman had trash-talked her ex, painting Brad in vivid brush strokes as an egotistical, self-absorbed jerk.

As if determined not to be drawn back into the drama, Brad had said nothing.

It was the jerk part that didn't ring true for Margot. Not when she recalled Brad's kindness to an animal that distrusted him.

Egotistical and self-absorbed…probably. But not a jerk.

Besides, everyone had flaws. And it wasn't as if she was looking at the guy as a potential boyfriend or husband.

The thought made her smile as she ate a quick breakfast then refreshed Vivi's food and water dishes before heading out to the garage.

Margot gazed at piles of empty cardboard boxes, multi-packs of paper towels tossed on top of stacks of newspapers interspersed with garden hoses and books. Coating it all was a thick layer of dirt.

The gray sweater she currently wore was a favorite and hardly suitable for the cleaning and clearing out she had planned.

After changing into a tan sweatshirt she'd picked up in

Cheyenne with the words "Ride it like you stole it" emblazoned across the front, Margot traded her good Levis for a pair so worn it was a wonder the threads still held. Pulling her hair back with a covered band, she grabbed a pair of brown gloves and went to work.

By the time Brad pulled up to the house early that afternoon, most of the boxes and newspapers had been reduced to ashes. He hopped out of the truck looking incredibly handsome in dark brown pants, a cream-colored shirt and a leather jacket the color of dark chocolate.

"What are you doing?" Without waiting for an answer he hurried over and helped her maneuver several long strips of cardboard into the burn barrel.

"Be careful," Margot warned. "Don't touch the sides. You don't want to get soot on your clothes."

"Don't worry about me. This is a big project. You need help."

Margot shook her head. "Not until you change."

Surprise flickered in his eyes at her determined tone. Then, unexpectedly, he grinned and gave her a mock salute. "Aye, aye, sir."

He returned in a matter of minutes, dressed casually in jeans and a chambray shirt. He lugged several large trash cans out from behind the stable.

Margot's pulse quickened with excitement. She'd already filled the garbage cans she'd been able to locate, but hadn't realized there were more.

When he released the barrels, she grasped his hands with her gloved ones and gave them a squeeze. "Thank you."

Brad looked down at his now-sooty hands.

"Ohmigod, I'm so sorry." Margot glanced around for a rag. "I forgot—"

"No worries." Brad's eyes danced with good humor

when they met hers. "You've been away from ranch work too long if you think a little dirt is a big deal."

He was right, of course. Ranchers' hands found their way into a little bit of everything.

"It's just that I appreciate the help," she said with a good-natured smile. "I don't want to turn you off."

"Darlin', there isn't much you could do to turn me off."

Her sweatshirt now had streaks of dirt and soot. What was on her shirt had to be on her face as well. She couldn't believe any man could find her attractive in her current state.

Yet the look in Brad's eyes reminded her of a predatory cat that had just spotted something of extreme interest.

He took a step closer.

Margot didn't move an inch, her gaze firmly fixed on those glittering green eyes. In the background, a rousing rock classic, courtesy of her iPad, followed the beat of her heart.

The sound of a car engine and a horn honking startled them both.

Brad swore. His gaze held hers for the briefest of moments before he pivoted and sauntered over to the truck. His brother Nate, as well as Anderson and Travis Dalton, emerged from the pickup.

In seconds Margot had caught up to him. These guys might be his brother and friends, but this was still her family's ranch.

"Hi, guys." Margot pulled off her gloves, wishing she could rid her face of grime so easily.

Brad's stance wasn't quite so welcoming. "What are you doing here?"

Anderson looked amused. "You asked us to come."

"You must have forgotten." Nate cast a pointed glance

in Margot's direction. "Understandable. You have other things on your mind. More important things."

"Yeah." Brad's sarcastic drawl drew his brother's attention back to him. "Like cleaning the garage."

"What about the cattle?" Travis asked.

"What about them?" Margot responded.

"You mentioned culling the herd. We said we'd help." Nate spoke to Brad as one would a dull-witted child. "Today."

Recognition dawned on Brad's face. He swore again.

"The garage can wait." Margot knew separating the animals on the cull list into the corral would take all their efforts. "I'll put everything away so we can get to work."

The men exchanged glances.

"You stick with the garage," Brad instructed. "The guys and I will take care of the cattle."

While there was really nothing particularly offensive in his words or tone, Margot bristled. Doggone it, this was *her* ranch and if anyone should be giving orders, it should be her.

"I appreciate you coming by to help." Margot smiled at the four men. "Why don't we get started now, so you can get back home?"

As they headed to the stables, Margot heard one of the men—she wasn't sure which one—tell Brad he had a spirited filly on his hands.

Margot only smiled to herself. It was obvious to anyone with half a brain they weren't referring to one of the horses.

They were wrong. Brad hadn't *had* her. Not yet.

Her heart launched into a ramshackle rhythm.

She wanted him. She'd accepted that fact. But all in good time. For now, they had a herd to cull.

By the time Brad's brother and friends left it was past suppertime. They declined Margot's offer to stay for a meal.

"I could use some food right now." Brad lifted a hand, watching as the truck disappeared down the lane in a cloud of dust before following Margot inside.

"I'll toss something together." She rubbed her temples with two fingers. "Let me pop a couple of ibuprofens first then I'll see what's in the fridge."

"Is your head bothering you?" Brad asked in a deceptively casual tone.

"A little," she admitted. "Nothing drugs won't fix right up."

Margot opened a cupboard and pulled out a bottle of pills, popping four into her mouth. She chased them with a long drink of milk.

When she looked up, glass still in hand, Brad was beside her.

He wasn't smiling.

"I want you to go upstairs and rest. I'll pull something together for us to eat."

Her smile vanished. "You're not in charge of me, mister."

"Someone needs to be."

Margot's head snapped back so suddenly it was a wonder she didn't get whiplash.

Before she had a chance to speak, he rested a hand on her arm. "You've been in an accident. You worked as hard as the rest of us today. Rest. Please. Just for a little while."

She hesitated.

He flashed that oh-so-charming smile. "If you feel better and want to do something, I'll let you do the after-dinner cleanup."

The innocent look in his eyes didn't fool her. But it did make her laugh.

An hour later, Brad had thrown together a spaghetti dinner complete with green beans—from a can—and garlic

Wonder Bread. Everything was ready when Brad headed up the stairs to get Margot.

He found her sprawled across the bed facedown. She'd clearly showered and changed out of her work clothes. The black stretchy pants she now wore hugged her derriere like a man's hand, and the oversized tee had ridden up to give him a good view of an impressive amount of ivory skin. It took every ounce of self-control not to touch her.

All day he'd been in a state of arousal. Who knew watching a woman separate cattle could be so stimulating? He stood at the foot of her bed pondering his options.

Letting her sleep seemed a no-brainer. Except she hadn't had any dinner and, if he had to hazard a guess, she likely hadn't had any lunch, either.

Though resting was all well and good, a woman who worked as hard as she had today needed nourishment.

Fifteen more minutes, he decided. If she wasn't up by then, he'd wake her.

In the meantime, he'd grab a quick shower and try not to think about sliding his hand across that bare patch of skin and up under her shirt.

Twenty minutes later, Margot jerked up at the light touch on her arm, her heart pounding. Though the light was off, moonlight streamed in through the window.

She heard Brad whisper her name almost at the same time she smelled the clean, fresh scent she was beginning to associate with him. "What are you doing in here?"

He smiled and sat beside her on the bed. "Waking you for dinner."

"How long have I been sleeping?"

"Not long. How's the headache?"

Margot paused, turned her head to one side and then to the other. She smiled. "No pain."

"Good news." When he stood, Margot fought a sudden urge to pull him down beside her. "I've kept everything warm in the oven. Come down when you're ready."

"You're a good guy," Margot called out when he stepped from the room.

"Not really." He turned and winked. "Although I do have my moments."

Chapter Ten

An hour later, with her dog resting in the parlor, Margot pushed back her chair and gave a contented sigh. Though she'd just consumed her daily allotment of carbs in one sitting, even the garlic toast made out of Wonder Bread had been, well, wonderful.

While Brad seemed determined to keep the conversation light and easy, at her insistence he'd now gone to pull up the PI reports off his laptop. As Margot knew she wouldn't be able to fully relax and study the reports with a tableful of dirty dishes, she got up and began to clear the table.

By the time Brad strode into the kitchen with his laptop under his arm, the dishwasher was happily humming away. She straightened from the tabletop, Lysol wipe in hand. "Perfect timing."

"Wow." Undisguised admiration showed in his green eyes as he glanced around the kitchen. "You work fast."

After giving the table one last swipe, she tossed the wipe into the garbage. "I prefer to tackle the tough stuff, rather than procrastinate and feel guilty."

"Good to know." He glanced at the garbage can. "Speaking of procrastinating, I'll take that out while I'm thinking of it."

"I'll start a fire. It feels like the temperature is dropping outside."

The words had barely left her lips when a gust of outside air rattled the kitchen window.

"Storm is coming in." Brad shrugged. "The forecasters are saying we could get a couple of inches of snow."

"It's the beginning of October." Margot heard the whine in her voice and pulled back.

"Have you forgotten you're back in Montana?" Brad shot her a good-natured grin. "It's not supposed to stick around. Temperatures should be back in the lower fifties by Thursday."

"I like winter. It's just that there's so much that needs to be done—"

His hand touched her shoulder and his eyes met hers. "We'll get it done."

We.

As he left the room, Margot was once again struck by the power in that simple little word.

Once again, she was forced to admit she was glad Brad was here. With her father gone, facing all that needed to be done before bad weather set in would have been overwhelming. With her injury, she wouldn't have had the ability to handle the physical labor. And then there was the worry...

Her gaze settled on the laptop Brad had placed on the table. She hoped something in the reports would lead her to her father.

It didn't make sense that her dad would buy a ticket to New York City. Though he'd always loved the state, his sister—the only one he knew who lived in the region—had died two years ago. Verna never married so it wasn't as if he had nieces or nephews to visit.

Since arriving in Rust Creek Falls, Margot had called everyone she could think of whom her parents had ever known, no matter where they currently resided. Just because Boyd's train ticket had been to the east coast didn't mean he hadn't gotten off and exchanged the ticket for one to a different destination. Unfortunately, no one had heard from him.

Troubled, Margot picked up the laptop and ambled into the parlor. A low growl greeted her when she stepped into the room, stopping immediately when Vivian saw that it was her.

Vivi's head relaxed back down while the puppies nursed, gathered close around her. Aware of the dog's protective nature, Margot didn't approach the box. Instead she spoke soothingly to the heeler while she focused on getting a fire started in the hearth.

Years of practice made the task easy and quick. In a matter of minutes, flames danced merrily, filling the room with warmth. Margot straightened and stared into the fire, praying that wherever her father was tonight, he was also safe and warm.

"Penny for your thoughts." Brad spoke softly, coming up behind her.

He stood close, but didn't touch.

"I was thinking about my dad." Margot turned to face Brad. "I hope he's okay. The thought of him being hurt, lying alone in some cold, dark alley..."

She shivered.

Brad pulled her into his arms and held her for several

moments. He lifted a hand and stroked her hair, a surprisingly gentle and soothing gesture. "Boyd was going
through some hard times but he's a tough son of a gun.
I know he's pushing eighty but he's still very capable of
taking care of himself."

"Not when he's drinking." Margot voiced her greatest fear. "He's vulnerable then because he doesn't think
clearly."

"Even when he drinks, Boyd is nobody's fool," Brad
insisted.

"How can you say that?" Margot pulled from his arms
and began to pace as worry churned inside her. "The man
got on a train to New York City. A place where he knows
absolutely no one. That's hardly thinking clearly."

"Unless he didn't buy the ticket for himself," Brad mused.

"Russ thinks you bought it."

"Well, I didn't," Brad said flatly.

Though not a hint of emotion was reflected in his gaze,
she knew her remark had stung.

"I know you didn't." She closed her eyes for several seconds in an attempt to gain control of her rioting emotions.
"I only wish I knew where he is tonight. And why he left."

"Let's sit." Without waiting for her reply, Brad took
her elbow and led her to the sofa, bringing a low warning
growl from Vivian.

"Don't worry, Viper." Brad's mild tone seemed to soothe
the dog. "I'm not interested in you or your mini-vipers."

"Hey." Margot plopped down on the sofa. "Be nice."

"Just telling it like it is, sweetheart." He settled down
beside her and opened the laptop.

Since he didn't look in Vivian's direction, the dog soon
quit growling, although her golden eyes remained firmly
fixed on him.

Margot hid a smile. She'd like to say Vivi was all bark

and no bite, but she had a feeling if Brad got too close to those babies, she might nip.

Brad pulled up the reports the PI had been sending him ever since he'd hired the man. As Margot flipped through them, she saw lots of contacts, but not a single piece of good information.

"Why did you wait until August to hire someone?" she asked then realized that was a silly question. Brad wasn't family and hadn't been particularly close to Boyd. A better question would be why he'd hired anyone at all.

"Those first weeks after Boyd left, we all assumed he'd taken off to see his sister." He could see Margot about to remind him of Verna's passing, and held up a hand to stop her. "One of your mother's friends returned from vacation the end of July. When she heard about Boyd leaving and the assumption of where he was, she set us straight." Brad gazed unseeing at the computer screen. "Everyone had been helping out with the cattle and the ranch as we looked for Boyd, but as the place was legally mine, I moved in and hired the PI."

Margot sat back, discouraged. "Who has found zip."

"Not entirely true. We learned your dad hasn't contacted or visited any known friends."

"I've made some calls, too," Margot told him. "I can put together a list so we can give it to your PI and the sheriff. That way we're not duplicating efforts."

"Makes sense."

Margot rested her head against the back of the couch. "I've reached out to everyone I can think of, but I have to be forgetting someone."

"Write down any other names as they come to you."

"I don't have time to let them come to me." Margot heard the frustration in her own voice. "Remembering could be the key to finding my father before anything bad happens to him."

Brad gave her shoulder a squeeze then pushed to his feet. "I'll get us a bottle of wine."

"You think drinking will help me remember?"

Brad's answering smile did strange things to her insides. In the firelight glow, his dark hair glimmered like polished oak and his eyes looked mysterious.

"A glass of wine might relax you." The soothing tone of his words wrapped around her. "I don't know about you, but sometimes not trying so hard works for me."

"That philosophy would never have passed muster in our household." Margot gave a half-laugh. "Giving 110 percent was the expectation. Nothing less was tolerated."

"Interesting," was all Brad said. He returned moments later with a bottle of merlot and two glasses. He handed one to her.

"Tell me about Boyd." Brad's tone encouraged confidences. "I know him as a rancher and a poker player, but I'm sure there's more to him."

Margot took a sip of the wine and considered where to begin. "My father was married once before, when he was in his early twenties. No kids. I'm not exactly sure why they divorced but I got the feeling his drinking played a part."

Brad nodded.

"He'd given up on love, or so he thought." Margot's lips lifted as she remembered how her father's eyes would shine when he'd tell the story of the first time he'd seen her mother. "He was back east visiting his sister when he ran into my mom on a sidewalk in New York City. He literally knocked her down."

"That's one way to get a woman's attention."

"He said she took his breath away." Margot swallowed

past the lump in her throat. Would any man ever love her so completely? "They started talking. He bought her a cup of coffee at a nearby shop. At the time he was divorced, fifty-three years old and a Montana rancher. She was forty-one, never married and an executive with an ad agency in New York City."

"They couldn't have been more different."

"On the surface. But somehow they just fit." Margot recalled the pride in her father's voice when he'd told of going to AA and getting sober because Giselle deserved the best. "He stopped drinking. They married within six months. She quit her job and moved to Montana to become a rancher's wife. Two years later, I was born."

"Like a Hallmark movie." Brad took a drink of wine, his brows pulling together in thought. "Does your mother have any friends or family we could contact?"

Margot shook her head. "She didn't maintain any friendships and her parents were older. They died shortly before she met my father. She was an only child, like me."

"So there's no family on her side to call."

"None. My mom used to say she and Dad were two lost souls who'd found each other at the perfect time in their lives. They were happy together." Margot sighed. "Truly happy. He was a good husband."

Margot twirled the wineglass back and forth between two fingers. Yes, her parents had been happy. So happy that growing up she'd often felt like a fifth wheel.

"How was he as a father?"

The glass stilled between her fingers. "Tough. But fair."

Brad inclined his head but didn't comment.

"He enjoyed a good amount of success on the rodeo circuit," Margot told him. "Made it all the way to the top."

Brad merely watched her intently over the top of his wineglass.

Though she'd long accepted the fact that her father expected nothing less than perfection, a chill traveled through her body. Margot grabbed the cotton throw draped over the side of the sofa and wrapped it tight around her.

Margot took a deep breath, let it out slowly. "His favorite saying is 'second place is the first loser.' Taking first place, winning the event, is all that matters."

"He wants you to do your best."

"Doing my best isn't good enough." Her fingers stole to the horseshoe necklace that hung around her neck.

Brad's gaze narrowed on her fingers. "Where does the necklace fit in?"

"My mother gave it to me when I was ten." Margot knew she'd never forget that day. "I got second in the first big competition I entered. On the way home all my dad could talk about was that I should have tried harder, done better. By the time we walked through the front door I felt as if I'd botched the ride completely."

Brad muttered something she couldn't make out.

"The next day my mother took me out to lunch in Kalispell and gave me the necklace." Margot's heart swelled at the memory. "She told me I'd always be number one in her heart. That doing my best was all she expected."

"Wise woman."

"I still don't feel I've had a good ride unless I come in first. Before I fractured this," Margot tapped the side of her head with two fingers, "I was on track to have my best year since I began competing."

"You plan to go back."

"It's my life. It's what I do. It's who I am."

As if bored with the topic, he nodded and changed the subject. "Any other names pop into your head while we've been talking?"

Margot realized the brief trip down memory lane *had*

jogged loose several names. "I did think of a few from those early rodeo days."

She leaned close and watched as Brad keyed in the names she gave him and the locations. God, why did the man have to smell so terrific?

"Enough about me," she said. "Why don't you tell me about yourself?"

"Not much to tell that you don't already know." He grinned. "I'm an open book in this town."

"Tell me about your divorce."

The smile dropped from his lips and a watchful look filled his eyes. "What do you want to know?"

"Why did you and Janie split?"

Brad sat back, poured himself another glass of wine. "We married too young."

"Lots of people marry in their early twenties and stay together."

He was silent so long Margot thought he might not be aware she was waiting for a response.

"Janie wanted me to make all the decisions then resented me when I did."

"She wanted you to make all the decisions?" Margot lifted a skeptical brow. "Seriously?"

He nodded.

"That's all? She wanted you to make decisions then resented you?"

Brad's jaw jutted out and his green eyes flashed. "We argued. All the time. About everything. We couldn't seem to talk about issues without it turning into a screaming match or her walking out. Then she decided she wanted a baby. She thought it would bring us closer. I said no. I might not have known how to fix my marriage but I sure as hell knew a baby wasn't the answer."

"You were smart. A baby would have complicated everything."

He scrubbed a hand over his face. "The day I signed those divorce papers was one of the worst days of my life. I felt like a failure. I kept asking myself if I'd done everything I could to make the marriage work."

"I know the feeling. Not about a marriage but I keep thinking I should have tried harder to keep in touch with my dad," she murmured. "Even though he ordered me to stay away, I shouldn't have listened. If I'd been a little more available, maybe he'd have turned to me instead of leaving town."

"It's easy to look back and say what we should have, could have, done." Brad gave her arm a comforting squeeze. "But that serves no purpose other than to drive us crazy."

"I suppose…" She sat down her glass and leaned back, wrapping the throw tightly around her.

"Did I tell you it was starting to snow when I took out the garbage?" He tugged the blanket from her. "It's time I warm you up."

"Is this you taking control?" she asked, watching him drop it to the floor.

"It is."

Her heart tripped over itself. "Won't we need the blanket?"

His gaze met her and he offered a wicked grin. "Not for what I have in mind."

Chapter Eleven

Brad wanted to devour her. One greedy bite at a time. But Margot had just finished baring her soul about her father so jumping her bones seemed a little crass.

Not to mention, talking about Janie had stirred up some emotions of his own, making him feel raw and vulnerable. Neither feeling he cared to explore. But kissing was practically a national pastime, so he felt no guilt in pulling Margot to him and sealing her lips with his.

The simple touch of those lips was like tossing a lit match on a puddle of gasoline. His body erupted like a blast furnace and his decision only seconds before to take it slow was forgotten. Slow was no longer a word in his wheelhouse.

When his tongue swept across her lips seeking access, Margot eagerly opened her mouth to him, pulling him on top of her, her tongue fencing with his.

Slow? Did such a word even exist, *ever* exist? It was

as if he was galloping full-out across a flat field. The exhilaration that always gripped him in those moments held him in its clutches now.

Brad wanted her in a way he couldn't remember wanting any woman. He slid his palm under her shirt, up the silky smooth skin. Her body quivered. His fingers skimmed the curve of her breast before he allowed the tips of his fingers just the barest of contact with her flesh.

An almost overwhelming need to rip off her clothes and bury himself inside her had him fighting for control.

The problem was Margot didn't appear to have gotten the memo about going slow. She pressed herself more fully against him, against the erection straining against the front of his jeans.

"Someone," she said in a husky voice that reminded him of naked limbs entwined and sweat-soaked sheets, "wants to come out and play."

"We should take it slow," he murmured in a guttural tone as the offending appendage reared up in protest.

"I'm not a fan of slow."

Damn it. Neither was he. Not usually. Certainly not in circumstances like this.

"I'm hot," she said.

What a coincidence. So was he...

Somehow she managed to push him back, but instead of getting up, she pulled her shirt over her head to reveal naked skin. No lacy scrap of underwear, just two delectable round breasts.

"I want to touch you." He didn't realize he'd spoken aloud until she gave a little laugh, her lips curving into a pleased smile.

Lying on the sofa with her red hair streaming around her, those eyes darkened with passion, she was irresistible.

He leaned over. As she watched he touched the tip of his

tongue to the tip of her left breast. His lips curved when she cried out in delight.

He circled the nipple before drawing it fully into his mouth. The gentle sucking had her arching against him. At the same time, his hand dipped south, cupping her between her legs.

She parted for him, catching her breath as his fingers slipped inside her waistband, searching for her slick center.

The desire to tug off those pants slammed into him with the force of a Mack truck but he knew once that happened he was a goner. What little self-control he possessed would vanish the second her naked limbs wrapped around him.

When he shifted his fingers slightly and found a single spot of pleasure, she nearly rose off the sofa.

"Oh, Brad," she moaned, "don't stop."

He didn't. He continued to touch her, stroking her, teasing, circling her center as he worshiped her breasts.

Her breathing now came in fast pants until she dug her heels into the sofa and cried out as her release claimed her. Her climax rippled through her and still he touched her, gentling the contact until the last drop of pleasure had been wrung from her body.

Then he kissed her, long and deep and soft, doing his best to ignore his own body's clamor for equal time.

Margot looked up at him, all languid and sated. She reached over for the zipper of his jeans.

He clamped his hand around her wrist. "No."

Puzzlement filled her gaze.

"I don't have any protection." Brad prided himself on never making love without holstering his gun.

Her face fell.

Brad started to set up but she curled her fingers around his arm. "What's the hurry? Don't tell me you're an all-or-nothing guy."

With her gaze firmly fixed on his face, she unzipped his jeans and freed him, her fingers gently stroking the hard length of him.

His breath became ragged as she continued to stroke. When her lips closed over him, he let out a moan.

"That's what I'm talking about," she said with a pleased laugh. "Relax and enjoy. It's time I returned the favor."

Margot and Leila were the only customers in Daisy's Donut Shop on Broomtail Road. When Brad had mentioned that he needed to go into town to pick up a few things at the General Store—the one owned and run by his family—Margot rode into town with him.

She was in the mood for some different scenery but after what had happened between her and Brad last night on the sofa, she wasn't quite up to a face-to-face with his mom and dad.

So on the way she'd given Leila a call and was delighted that her friend had time to meet her for a donut and coffee.

"This place is no Starbucks," Leila grumbled, looking chic in her trim gray pants and white shirt, "but the coffee is at least drinkable."

"And the donuts are terrific." Margot bit into her second cruller.

Leila shook her head. "I don't know how you can eat that much and stay so slim."

"Fast metabolism." Margot spoke around the pastry in her mouth.

"You should be the one in front of the camera, not me." Leila cast a longing look in the direction of the bakery case. "The camera shows every ounce and then some."

"Are you happy you chose a career in broadcast journalism?"

"I can't imagine doing anything else," Leila said, giving

into temptation and taking a glazed-filled out of the sack on the table. "What about you? Are you happy on the circuit?"

"Definitely." Margot licked the spoon.

"This is probably like a little vacay for you."

"Hardly. It's not good for me or for Storm—my Arabian," she said in answer to Leila's raised brow "—to be away from competition for so long."

"Sounds like you had no choice."

"I didn't."

"Did I tell you my cousin Sierra is totally crazy about barrel racing?"

Margot tried to place the child in the Dirks family. "Your mother's sister's girl?"

"That's the one."

"Is she competing?"

"Just started the last couple of years." Leila paused. "I think she's doing pretty well."

"They're the ones who live on the acreage outside of Kalispell, right?"

"Yep." Leila waved a dismissive hand. "Time to move on to something more interesting, like you and Brad Crawford."

Margot leaned forward and rested her forearms on the table. "First, tell me about you and Justin."

Leila's lips curved in a smug smile. "Justin is the perfect guy for one night of fun. We put my father's cabin to excellent use."

"I knew it." Margot hit her fist against the table. "I saw the way he looked at you."

"Speaking of lascivious glances, how about you and Brad? Did you and he...?"

"We fooled around a bit but stopped short of doing the deed." Margot shrugged. "No protection on hand."

"Allow me to be of service." Leila reached into her bag and pulled out several brightly colored foil packets.

"Leila." Margot scooped up the packets and glanced furtively around before stuffing them into her purse.

"I was a Girl Scout. Okay, just a Brownie, but all that stuff about being prepared stuck." She shot Margot a sly smile. "Go forth and sin."

Margot laughed. "God, I'm going to miss you."

It was true. Margot had friends on the circuit, but no one she missed. No one quite like Leila.

"I wish you didn't have to go," Margot added.

"You'll be gone soon enough yourself," Leila said in a matter-of-fact tone. "Unless you're thinking about staying?"

"I won't make it to Las Vegas sitting on my duff here." Margot forced a light tone. "And, as my dear dad is so fond of saying, winning is everything."

Leila picked up her donut. "I'm not sure that's true. But if winning a championship is what you really want, then you should go for it. Life is too short for regrets."

The call from his brother Nate informing him the *Rust Creek Rambler* had printed a blind item implying he and Margot were shacking up—and that she was a "fringe benefit" to the ranch—had taken Brad by surprise. He didn't know whether to punch the wall or laugh.

Him take advantage of *her*? From what Brad had seen so far, no one took advantage of Margot Sullivan. And the truth of it was, he liked her too much to do anything to hurt her.

Not making love to her last night had been one of the hardest things he'd ever *not* done. But if, okay *when*, they finally made love he wanted it to be because it was something they both wanted. Not because she was feeling sad and lonely and guilty because of her father being gone.

And they absolutely had to be stocked up on protection. Not just one measly condom either. As hot as things were between them, one would definitely not be enough.

With that thought in mind, Brad strode down the sidewalk toward Crawford's General Store, a place that had a little bit of everything, including several varieties of condoms. Though paying for them wasn't an issue, paying his mother or father for them was unacceptable.

On the way into town, Brad had formulated a plan, worthy of any high school boy. He'd "pick up" a box from the back stock and pay his parents…later.

As he approached the store, his mind kept circling back to the *Rambler*'s column. One part had been totally out in left field. The cowardly columnist—who never used his/her own name—had mentioned his "me first" history and brought up his failed marriage as a classic example.

Though Brad readily admitted he enjoyed a good time as much as the next guy, he didn't promise women more than he could deliver.

Margot didn't seem to expect or want anything more from him than a good time.

For some reason the thought left a bitter taste in his mouth. Was it because she viewed him only as a good-time guy without a whole lot else to offer? Not that he was complaining. He wasn't looking for a relationship. And she was leaving soon.

The bells over the door to the store jingled as he stepped inside.

He'd barely gone three feet when his mother hurried around the counter to greet him. "What a pleasant surprise. I didn't expect to see you this morning."

"Just stopped by to pick up a few things."

"Tell me what they are and I'll get them for you." Laura smiled brightly. "It'll be much faster. I know exactly where every item in the store is located."

How about condoms? Can you grab me a couple of boxes?

It might have been worth the look on her face to ask the question. Then again, she was the mother of three grown sons. He doubted much could surprise her.

"That'd be great, Mom." Brad handed her the sanitized version of the list and glanced toward the storeroom. "Where's Dad?"

"At the ranch," his mother said absently, her gaze focused on the list. She looked up. "Could you watch the register while I pick these up?"

"Sure." Brad shoved his hands in his pockets and rocked back on his heels. "Mind if I grab a cup of coffee from the back?"

"Not at all." She gave his arm an affectionate pat as she brushed past him. "Just listen for the door chimes."

Brad waited until she disappeared before heading into the back. Like all of his siblings, he knew exactly where items of interest were stored. He found the condoms and popped a box in each of his jacket pockets, then poured a cup of coffee and wandered back to the counter.

When the bells over the door chimed he looked up and nearly groaned when he saw Justin walk through the door.

"Didn't realize Ma had put you to work," Justin said with that cocky arrogance that Brad occasionally found entertaining. Today, there was something about the gleam in his little brother's eyes that put him on guard.

"Just holding down the fort until you showed up, little brother," Brad said with an easy smile.

He knew for a fact there was nothing Justin liked more than to get his brothers riled up. It drove the youngest

Crawford male crazy when his older siblings simply ignored him.

Justin smirked. "Read all about you in the newspaper."

Brad feigned a bored expression. "I didn't know you were into gossip. I thought only girls liked that kind of stuff."

If the red rising up his brother's neck was any indication, Brad's comment hit the bull's-eye.

"Everyone is talking about it." Justin's eyes turned razor-sharp and Brad knew he was looking for any sign, no matter how small, that his needling was connecting. "Just like when Janie walked out, you're once again at the center of town gossip, bro."

"Whatever."

It was the wrong response. Brad sensed it immediately when Justin sauntered closer. He should have laughed or made some joke. But the failure of his marriage remained a sore spot.

"I have to tell you, I envy you." A gleam filled Justin's eyes. "She caught my eye right away. I wouldn't mind getting a piece of that action—"

Brad's fist shot out, connecting with Justin's jaw and sending him to the floor.

"You hit your brother?" Margot gave a horrified laugh when he finished telling her the story as they left Rust Creek Falls for the ranch. "Over a silly newspaper article?"

"There was a little more to it than that, but yes, I punched him." Brad didn't see any need to go into what Justin had said about her. Knowing his brother, the guy was just trying to get his goat. Unfortunately, this time he'd succeeded.

Brad had expected her to be upset when he told her the news but he'd discovered Leila had already filled her in. "Don't you understand," he said, feeling the need to impress upon Margot the gravity of the situation. "The article implied you and I are shacking up."

"We are shacking up."

When he opened his mouth to protest, she held up a hand.

"Think about it, Brad." Her expression held amusement rather than distress. "We live under the same roof. No, we're not sleeping in the same bed," she hurriedly added when he opened his mouth to speak, "but we both know that's just a matter of time."

What could he say to that? The boxes in his pockets were lumpy pieces of evidence to that hope.

"There is one thing that bothers me, though…" She exhaled a breath that sounded suspiciously like a sigh. Or suppressed laughter.

"What?"

"We're getting all this press and we've only made it to third base." Even as her eyes twinkled, she shot him a mournful look. "It's really quite depressing."

Chapter Twelve

Knowing Brad planned to pick up condoms while he was in town, Margot fully expected them to start shedding their clothes the second they reached the ranch. But on the drive home an overwhelming lethargy had wrapped tight tentacles around her. Granted, she hadn't been sleeping well the past couple of nights but she was only twenty-two. If she was in college, she'd be pulling all-nighters.

At first she thought it might be due to the temperature being too warm in the cab. She hurriedly stepped from the truck into the crisp autumn air, hoping the cool breeze would make a difference. Instead, her head began to swim. She grabbed the door and held on tight, praying for the world to quit spinning like an out-of-control Tilt-A-Whirl.

In seconds Brad was at her side, concern blanketing his handsome face.

"No worries." Despite her death grip on the door, she swayed slightly. "I'm just a little dizzy."

"You're white as your shirt."

When he scooped her up into his arms, she didn't fight. She couldn't. The dizziness made her sick and she had to keep her eyes firmly shut to keep control of the nausea.

He'd removed his coat in the car, so only a layer of flannel separated them. She felt his heartbeat galloping as he laid her gently on the sofa.

Vivian gave three short barks as if letting Brad know she was on duty.

Ignoring the dog, he pulled the cell phone from his pocket. "I'm calling the doctor."

"No, Brad, please. There's nothing he can do for me."

Something in her tone must have gotten through because he moved to her side, crouched down beside the sofa and took her hand. "Your concussion was months ago. This isn't normal, Margot."

"I didn't just have a concussion. I fractured my skull and had a traumatic brain injury." She hated reliving the time immediately after the accident but knew if she didn't explain fully, Brad would have the doctor at the ranch in a heartbeat. "I had all kinds of specialists look at me. They told me to expect this, especially if I don't take it easy."

Brad frowned. "You said you were cleared to do everything other than an activity where you could hit your head."

"That's true." While she may have glossed over a few of the additional instructions, or omitted them entirely, she hadn't lied. "They simply told me to pace myself and make sure to get all the rest I needed. The doctors said if my symptoms got worse, or if I noticed new ones, to consider it a sign I'm pushing myself too hard. How I feel right now tells me I need more sleep."

"You've been working too hard." He brushed a strand of hair back from her face with a gentle hand, his brow furrowed in worry. After a long moment, he pocketed his phone. "Have you told me all of it now? No other forgotten details?"

He took her hand, played with her fingers while his gaze remained riveted to her face.

Margot closed her eyes, the warmth of his concern as soft and soothing as any embrace. "You know everything. I'm absolutely certain that after a few minutes of rest I'll be good as new."

The fact that she honestly believed she'd get up after an hour and go back to work illustrated she didn't know how Brad Crawford operated.

The rest Margot had planned to last an hour max lasted much longer. For two straight days Brad refused—absolutely refused—to let her help him with *any* of the outside chores. He'd been solicitous and kind but firm.

Worse, he'd brought out the gentleman card. Since they'd arrived home on Sunday, he hadn't touched her in any intimate fashion. Not unless you counted an occasional squeeze of the hand or a touch on the shoulder, actions that only fueled the flames of desire burning inside her. The mulish expression he wore whenever she pressed for more told her protesting was pointless.

Resigning herself to being pampered, Margot used the time to sort through her dad's papers. Tasks that made her miss her father more and spiked her worry. Although Boyd could be self-centered at times, she'd begun to fear something bad had happened to him. Otherwise, he'd never have stayed away so long.

When the mountain of paper and the sadness began to close in and feel overwhelming, Margot pulled out her laptop and opened her blog. For several minutes she worked on a new post titled "Good to Great: Improving Your Riding Skills." As the words flowed, she felt her emotions begin to settle.

She'd barely finished the post when Brad strolled into the room.

He gestured to several brown sacks overflowing with paper on the floor next to her chair. "What's all this?"

"More of the same. I went through another drawer of my dad's file cabinet." Margot shook her head. Her mother had handled the family's financial affairs. It was apparent her dad hadn't known what he should throw away so he'd saved everything. "These sacks are primarily filled with old bank statements, utility bills and receipts for every transaction he's completed since my mother's death. Everything can be burned."

The barrel out back had been kept busy the past few days incinerating all the needless records her dad had kept. Margot knew once Boyd returned, he'd refuse to let her touch any of his papers so she had to make the best use of his absence.

"I'll get a fire started in the barrel after lunch." Brad's curious gaze settled on the laptop. "What are you working on now?"

"My blog." Margot scheduled the post she'd just finished and swiveled in her seat to face him. "I offer barrel-racing tips and other information to those who share my passion for the sport."

"Impressive." Brad grabbed two Cokes from the fridge, handed one to her then sat down. "You like doing stuff like that?"

Margot started to shrug but stopped herself. She loved to blog. Why not admit it? "I do."

"Maybe that could be your next career," he said in a casual tone. "That and running boot camps."

"It's a definite possibility." Margot popped the tab on the can and took a long drink. "You should have heard my dad the last time I was back when I mentioned I believed teaching was in my future plans."

The look on Brad's face was almost comical. Knowing how Boyd could be, he was clearly struggling with whether to ask for further details. He finally gave in to curiosity. "What did he say?"

"Gave me the old 'those who can't do, teach' lecture." Brad rolled his eyes.

For some reason his response made Margot feel better.

"Anyway, all that is a ways down the road." Margot took another sip of soda. She hadn't realized she was so parched. "Once I'm healed, Storm and I have unfinished business. Number one or bust."

"You'll be a success in whatever you do." Brad leaned back in his chair and studied her. "You've got brains, talent and incredible drive."

"Thank you," she stammered, touched by the look of respect in his eyes.

"Now that you've got your five-year plan solidified, let's talk food. I'm starving. How does wings from Buffalo Bart's sound for lunch?"

"Sounds good," she said. "As long as we have something more nutritious this evening."

We.

There it was again, the ubiquitous "we." More and more the word found its way past her lips. Though Margot had shared quarters with plenty of females over the past few years, she'd never had a male roommate. She thought men would be more difficult. Not Brad. To her surprise, he was surprisingly easy to live with...at least so far.

She shifted her gaze and found him staring. Her body began to hum, even though she knew with absolute certainty nothing was going to happen.

She needed to *rest. Recharge.* Margot had heard him say

those words so often since Sunday she had his response to her overtures memorized.

His lips lifted in a slight smile as if he read her thoughts. "Feel like going out this evening?"

For a second, Margot thought she must have misheard. Hallucinated. But he gazed at her so expectantly it was apparent he had posed the question. "What do you have in mind?"

She didn't know why she asked. She really didn't care where they went or what he had planned. After being homebound the past two days, even the possibility of a trip to Wal-Mart made her heart race with excitement.

"We have several options. Oh, I almost forgot." Brad pulled out the rolled-up stack of letters and advertising circulars protruding from his pocket and dropped them on the table. "I got the mail from the box."

Margot glanced at the pile. She'd almost decided to leave sorting through it until later when an iconic torch peeking out from between two envelopes caught her eye. She gave the glossy paper a tug. It was a postcard with a picture of the Statue of Liberty.

"Don't worry about that stuff now." Brad's voice seemed to come from far away.

Her breath clogged her throat. She had to swallow several times to summon enough moisture to speak. "Brad. Look."

Something in her tone must have alerted him because he immediately leaned close, his brows pulling together. "What is it?"

"It's from my father." Her heart pounded so hard in her ears she could barely hear herself speak. With trembling fingers she lifted the postcard so Brad could see the picture. She'd have known the handwriting on the back anywhere. "No return address but it's clear that he's alive. Or at least he was when he wrote and sent it."

Margot was glad she was sitting because the relief that washed through her had turned her knees to jelly.

Brad's hand, which had been lifting a can of soda to his lips, stilled. "About time he wrote you."

But Margot had seen the name and address on the card. Her heart stumbled because her joy was laced with pain. "It's addressed to you."

"Me?" Brad choked on the soda. "Why would he write to me?"

Without a word, she held out the postcard.

His jaw set in a hard tilt as he lifted it from her fingers.

"Brad," he read aloud. "Take care of the ranch. I wanted you to have it. I won't be back. I'm settled and content. Boyd."

"He's alive." A war raged inside Margot, the overwhelming relief fighting a losing battle with rising anger. "He has settled somewhere and is *content*."

The word tasted foul on her tongue.

Brad held up the card. "This doesn't make sense."

"Content," Margot spat. "While I've been worried sick about him, he's been somewhere enjoying life and being all…content."

"This doesn't make sense," Brad repeated. Puzzlement blanketed his face. He reread the postcard, checked the name and address. "Why write to me and not you?"

"He must still be angry at me." Margot blinked back tears, the knowledge that her father held her in such little regard a dagger to the heart. All she'd done was express concern about his drinking and urge him to get help. For that horrible act, he'd cut her out of his life.

She blew out a breath and forced herself to focus on the positive. "He's alive and safe. That's what matters."

"He put you through hell and he sends *me* a postcard," Brad ground out, tossing the missive to the table.

The anger on Brad's face didn't surprise her. She was feeling pretty steamed herself. What surprised Margot was that the anger was for her.

Margot scrubbed her face with her hands but her eyes remained dry. Her emotions were far too tangled for tears. While part of her was relieved her father was alive and apparently well, there was a profound feeling of loss. Not only for the love he obviously didn't feel for her but for the life they'd once shared on the Leap of Faith.

When her mother died, Margot had been devastated. The person she'd loved most had left the ranch one afternoon to pick up supplies in town and never returned.

Her mother's car had slid off an icy road and tumbled down a ravine. It had been two days before the search team found the car. Margot had been grief-stricken but also angry. How dare her mother leave her? It wasn't rational to feel abandoned. Logically she understood her mother hadn't chosen to leave.

Not like her father. He'd deliberately walked out on her and the life he'd worked so hard to build. Leaving had been a *choice* for him.

"Honey." Brad pulled her to her feet and wrapped his arms around her. "It's going to be okay."

The comforting warmth of his embrace barely touched the chill that permeated every atom of her being.

"I'll pack up my things." Her voice sounded flat and lifeless even to her own ears. But it mirrored how she felt inside. Though her father was alive she was on her own. Because he didn't want her. "It'll take me a few days to find a place to stay, so if you could give me to the end of the week, I'd appreciate it."

"What are you talking about?" Brad's voice was rough

with emotion as he held her at arms' length, his puzzled gaze scanning her face.

"This is your home now, not mine." She tried to smile but her lips were trembling too much to hold it for more than a second. "I'm sure you'll be very happy here."

"You're not moving out." His jaw was now set and his face had taken on that mulish expression she'd seen so often the past two days.

"I was only here because I thought this was my home." She tried to take a step back but his arms remained locked around her. "Now we both know for certain that the Leap of Faith belongs to you."

"We don't know squat." His eyes flashed green fire and the look on his face dared her to disagree. "You're not moving out on the basis of a few scribbles on a postcard. I'll let the sheriff know what we've discovered but that doesn't mean we won't keep looking for your father. In the meantime, you're staying put."

"Since when are you the boss of me?" Margot countered.

She wasn't Brad Crawford's latest charity. From an early age she'd been taught to pull her own weight, to stand strong and make her own way. Perhaps her dad had been preparing her for the day he'd walk out of her life without a backward glance or a single word of explanation.

Unexpectedly, the tears that had been frozen inside her broke free and filled her eyes.

"I care about you, Margot." Brad's soft words were like a balm on her shattered heart. "We'll figure this out... together."

"There's nothing to figure out."

"You're not leaving."

All of a sudden, all the fight went out of her. She swiped

at her cheeks. "If I stay—and it'll only be while I'm looking at other options—I'll pay for my room and board."

"You don't need—"

"That's the only way I'll remain under your roof." She lifted her chin.

He opened his mouth as if to argue but closed it at the determination in her voice. "If that's how you want it."

Of course that wasn't how she wanted it but this whole situation left her with little choice. "That's how it has to be."

His gaze turned thoughtful. "I can see if my parents need someone to help out in the General Store."

"Thanks." She placed a hand on his arm. "I have something else in mind. But for it to work, I'll need your help."

The gaze that locked on hers didn't waver. "Whatever you need."

Chapter Thirteen

The postcard set several wheels in motion almost immediately. Fortunately, Margot didn't need to waste any time developing a plan to raise enough cash to pay for her room and board. She already had the pieces in play. The best part was it involved earning money doing what she loved.

By the time Saturday rolled around and Leila stopped over, Margot felt steadier. And while the thought of her father's actions still stung, she no longer felt like crying every time she thought about him.

The day was a pretty one for October, offering up a brilliant blue sky. The snow from last week had pretty much disappeared with only scattered patches remaining in shady spots.

Leila, who'd stopped over to say goodbye, would have no difficulty making the drive to Kalispell tomorrow to catch a flight back to Atlanta. Her time in Rust Creek Falls had come to an end. While Leila was champing at the bit to get back to the big city, Margot was sad to see her leave.

"I'm going to miss you," Margot told her friend, buttering a slice of pumpkin bread.

They were seated at the kitchen table. Slices of the bread Margot had made that morning sat between them, along with a carafe of coffee.

When Leila had first arrived, Margot had made them both hot cocoa—Leila's favorite—then brewed a pot of the chicory blend to enjoy with the bread.

"The time went by so quickly." Margot sighed and sat the bread knife down. "Too quickly."

"For you, maybe," Leila said then chuckled. "Anyway, I'll be back at Christmas."

"Forgive me if I don't believe that tall tale," Margot said in a dry tone.

"I realize it's hard to believe—okay, impossible to believe—that I'd willingly return in a couple of months, but it's true." Leila held up her fingers in the Brownie salute. "I promised the folks I'd try to swing it. My father was thrilled. You know how dads are with their daughters. He wants me—"

As if remembering Margot's situation, Leila paused. Two bright spots of color dotted her cheeks. "I'm sorry."

"Don't be." Margot kept her tone light. No way was she spending her last few minutes with Leila whining about her father not loving her. If she let it, the realization would suck all joy from her life.

Boyd was alive and safe. He was even *content*.

Knowing that had to be enough.

Margot shook the cobwebs of emotion from her head and changed the subject. "I really enjoyed meeting your cousin. She's a real sweetie."

"Sierra? The family contacted you about lessons already? That was fast."

"Her mother called and her dad brought her over yesterday." Margot smiled, recalling the young girl's eagerness. "She was so excited. And she adored Storm."

Leila picked up another piece of bread, although she'd already told Margot two was her limit. But unlike her hostess, she ignored the butter.

"You let her ride Storm?" Leila asked then took a bite.

Margot nodded. "It's important for Storm to stay in top shape. I can ride him uphill at a walk. We can trot, especially if Brad isn't around."

At Leila's quizzical glance, Margot smiled.

"He's afraid I'll fall." Margot gave a snort of amusement. "If I fell off a horse while it was simply trotting I'd deserve to get my head cracked open."

"I saw the barrels in the corral," Leila said slowly.

Margot could see by the confusion in her eyes that her friend still didn't understand. "The doctors told me I couldn't race. That's where Sierra comes in. It's good for Storm to keep in practice."

"Did you set the barrels up yourself?" Leila asked, a little too casually for Margot's liking.

She shook her head. "Brad set them up for me."

"That was nice of him."

Margot ignored Leila's speculative gaze. She wasn't sure what to think—much less do—about her growing feelings for Brad. He was starting to matter to her and the realization scared her. "He's a nice guy."

Leila pushed her mug and bread plate aside. She leaned forward and rested her arms on the table. "How is he?"

"Doing fine," she told her friend. "He thought he was getting a cold but he must have knocked it because this morning he woke up feeling great."

Leila expelled a frustrated breath. "I wasn't referring to how he is physically...well, okay I was, but in a deeper sense."

The wicked smile her friend shot her did the trick. Suddenly all was clear.

Leila was asking about her sex life. Her nonexistent sex life. Although the sizzle between her and Brad was definitely still there, he'd been keeping his hands to himself and frustrating the heck out of her. "We, ah, still haven't…"

"I gave you the condoms." Clearly puzzled, Leila studied her. "Have things turned cold?"

Actually, Margot thought, things were hotter than ever. She found herself struggling to explain something she didn't fully understand herself. "I told you about my episode on the drive back from the ranch."

"That was almost a week ago," Leila pointed out.

"Brad was concerned about me." Margot found herself rising to his defense. "For a couple of days afterward he insisted I rest and recharge."

"Okay, that enforced rest was over, what, on Wednesday?"

"The day the postcard came." Margot saw no need to go into more detail. When her friend had first arrived, she'd explained the situation to Leila.

"Oh." As if not knowing what to do with her hands, Leila eyed the cup. She picked it up and took a sip. "In a way getting it was good, right? You know your father is safe."

"He's settled and content." Margot tried to keep the bitterness from her voice. She wasn't sure why that last word continued to irritate rather than soothe.

Shouldn't a good daughter be happy her father was content? But she knew what scraped her heart raw was the impression the postcard had given that Boyd didn't care how the months of silence had affected her or his friends. Even Brad had been worried.

"I realize I said this when you told me about the postcard earlier, but none of this makes sense." Leila lifted a hand with perfectly manicured nails and let it drop. "It almost sounds as if your father just wanted to get away and start fresh somewhere new."

It was a possibility. Margot had considered so many possibilities in the past couple of days she refused to speculate further. Any of the scenarios could be the truth, or Boyd's actions could be attributed to something else entirely.

"His behavior is a complete mystery to me, Leila. Who moves away from the only home they've ever known when they're nearly eighty? Who leaves their family and friends behind as if they don't matter? As if they never mattered?" Margot's voice rose and cracked. She clamped her mouth shut.

Leila inclined her head. "What did the sheriff say when you told him?"

"Not much. He thanked us for letting him know." Margot pressed her lips together. "It was obvious he was angry. Sheriff Christensen spent a lot of money and resources looking for my dad."

"Hang in there, sweetie." Leila reached across the table and gave Margot's hand a squeeze. Her eyes were filled with sympathy. "You're still worried about Boyd, aren't you?"

Margot nodded. "Not like I was before the postcard came, but yes. Brad has kept the PI he hired on the case. He says we'll keep looking until we find my dad."

"We?"

"It's just a figure of speech." Margot raked back her hair from her face with her fingers, expelled a heavy sigh. "I don't know what's going on with me and Brad. He— he doesn't seem to want to make love to me. We kiss. We hug. But he stops it at that. Maybe I just don't appeal to him in that way anymore."

"Not a chance." Leila's admiring gaze settled on her. "If we both weren't straight, I'd be jumping you."

Margot laughed. She had to admit she'd dressed this morning with special care, pulling on her favorite skinny jeans and a clingy royal blue sweater, hoping to tempt Brad—not Leila.

Leila tapped a finger against her lips. "Maybe you could—"

Before her friend had a chance to offer any words of wisdom, the back door scraped open. Brad burst into the room.

He'd been out checking cattle when Leila had arrived and Margot hadn't seen him all morning. Though a bit dusty and windblown, he looked delectable in worn jeans and a sturdy jacket.

"I think I have another student lined u—" He paused and whipped off his cowboy hat. His gaze lingered on Margot for a second before he smiled at Leila. "Margot mentioned last night you might drop by today. How've you been?"

"I'm great. Heading back to Atlanta tomorrow." Leila pushed back her chair and stood. "Actually I was just leaving. Walk me to the door, Margot?"

"Don't hurry off on my account," Brad protested. "I can get lost. Give you two ladies your space."

"Thanks, but I promised my sister I'd stop over. The visit will give me one last chance to kiss and coo over my new niece." Her gaze met Brad's. "Take care of my friend while I'm gone."

His gaze never wavered; the look in his eyes was as much a promise as his words. "Count on it."

After the briefest of detours to show Leila the puppies,

which she dutifully admired, Margot walked her friend outside.

"Don't worry about the sex," Leila whispered in Margot's ear on the porch, hugging her tight.

"What?"

"From the look in Brad's eye, your sexual fast is about to come to an end."

Brad paced the kitchen while he waited for Margot to return from bidding Leila farewell. Though he'd been ready to take things to the next level physically on Wednesday, those plans had been shot to hell because of the postcard.

If Boyd was here, Brad would kick him nine ways to Sunday for putting that sadness in Margot's eyes. He knew the old coot cared about her, but Boyd's actions hadn't showed any love, much less respect, for his only child.

Several times in the past few days when Brad had kissed Margot, he'd sensed she wanted more. Hell, he'd wanted more, too. But Brad couldn't recall ever feeling so protective of someone. Sometimes he felt like Viper, standing guard, determined not to let anyone or anything hurt Margot…and that included him.

Maybe he was making a big deal out of nothing. It had seemed to him that moving on her so quickly would be taking advantage of someone whose emotions were in a tailspin.

He'd seen the look of devastation in her eyes when she'd told him the postcard was addressed to him, not her. Brad had found himself going to the mailbox every day hoping a letter or postcard from Boyd to Margot would have shown up in the mail by now.

Each time she mentioned moving out, he'd been able to change her mind. How could he take care of her if she wasn't here?

"Can I tempt you with a cup of hot cocoa?" she asked when she strolled back into the kitchen, looking tempting in tight-fitting jeans and a V-necked sweater that made his mouth grow dry. "I made some for Leila and me. With the chill in the air, it really hit the spot."

"I'm fine. Thanks." Brad quit pacing. He tried, he really tried to avoid looking at her chest. Was it just his imagination or had her breasts grown even larger in the past couple of days? He blew out a breath and focused on her face. For a second those full, sensual lips distracted him before Brad focused on her beautiful green eyes. "So like I was saying before, ah, I may have another student for you. Jilly is eight. I ran into her dad at the General Store this morning. He sounded very interested."

Margot leaned back against the countertop, making her chest stick out even farther. Or so it seemed to Brad.

Focus, he told himself. Focus on business.

"Jilly?" Margot shook her head. "I don't know any Jillys. Who is her father?"

Brad gave her Roger's full name but could see by her blank expression that the name wasn't familiar. "I gave Rog your cell number. I hope that's okay."

"No problem," she said, those sensuous full lips curving up. "I mean it's not like you're posting my number on the bathroom wall at the gas station...or on the internet."

"I'd never do that," he hastened to assure her.

"I know you wouldn't."

Why did he get the feeling she was teasing him? That was okay. It was good to see her smile. "Rog said he'd have his wife call and set it up. Her name is Shelley."

"Thanks. I appreciate you pumping up my business." She adjusted her sweater and heat shot straight to his groin. "I really enjoyed my time with Sierra yesterday."

"You're a good teacher. You not only have the knowledge, you have a way with kids." Brad had watched her work with the girl. Though he wasn't always able to hear what Margot said, he saw how the child responded to her. "That's what I told Roger."

She inclined her head, a question in her eyes.

Heat spiked up his neck. "I watched you work with Sierra for a few minutes."

"Next time, if you have a few minutes, come over and join us," she said. "I can always use an extra hand."

"Oh," he teased, "is that what I am to you? An extra pair of hands."

"You do have nice hands." She grinned. "And, if I'm remembering correctly, some stellar moves."

She seemed surer of herself today and much happier. Or maybe that was hopeful thinking on his part. Still, the warmth of her smile wrapped around him and he let himself bask in the glow for several moments before getting down to business.

"Speaking of your new business venture…" Okay, so maybe it wasn't the smoothest transition but the way she looked in that sweater was creating havoc in his brain and in other parts of him, as well.

A dimple he hadn't even known she had flashed in her left cheek. "I thought we were talking about my teaching skills."

"Whatever." Brad waved a dismissive hand. This wasn't the time to split hairs. He had something to ask her and the words were burning a hole in his tongue. "It's time we celebrate the successful start of your new business enterprise."

He paused. Had he just said those same words or…? He pulled his gaze from her chest.

She looked amused. "One student is not a successful start to any business."

"Two," he reminded her.

She brought a finger to her mouth and his own went dry. "What do you have in mind?"

For a second, he went blank. Then he rallied.

"A night in Kalispell." Though he couldn't read her reaction, he continued on. "It's Glacier Jazz weekend."

As Margot had grown up in the area, she'd be familiar with the yearly event that featured bands and guest artists performing everything from jazz to ragtime. The event was a big deal in the entire region.

She studied him for a long moment.

Brad began to sweat. When he'd first decided to suggest the outing, it was with the attitude that he didn't care one way or the other about going. But now he realized just how much he wanted her to say yes.

"Sounds like fun," she said in a light tone.

Without giving himself a chance to back down, he plunged forward with the ferocity he'd once shown on the football field. "My mother has a friend in Kalispell who runs a B&B. She has a room open tonight. We could spend the night and drive back tomorrow."

Margot hesitated for only a second but it was long enough.

"It's no problem. I can cancel." He should have known better than to bring it up. After all, it had been less than a week since her fainting episode and only a few days after that damned postcard had knocked her world on its axis.

"No. Don't cancel." Margot spoke hurriedly, as if he had the proprietress on the phone and was ready to give the room away. "I was just wondering what we'd do about Vivian and the puppies."

"I've got that covered." When he'd decided to ask Margot if she wanted to head to Kalispell, Brad had tried to cover all bases. "I told my father we were thinking about going and he said Jesse could check on the cattle. My dad will take care of Viper, er, Vivian, and the pups."

Margot frowned. "That seems an awful lot to ask of your dad and brother."

"Not at all." Brad waved away her concerns. "They were excited to help us out."

Chapter Fourteen

"Did you see how Viper took to my dad?" Brad asked Margot later that afternoon as they pulled up in front of a massive home in the East Side Historic District in Kalispell. "Not a single growl. Dad said if we wanted to stay longer, just to let him know."

"That's nice of him," Margot murmured. For this evening, the last thing she wanted to think about—or discuss—were fathers, even Brad's very nice and very helpful one.

He shut off the engine and for a second they simply sat in the truck, gaping at the home in front of them, the one where they would be spending the night.

The massive structure, built sometime in the early twentieth century, featured a steep roof with several tall chimneys and a dramatic curved porch made out of native rock.

"Wow." Margot couldn't take her eyes off the home. "The place looks amazing."

"Let's hope the inside is equally amazing."

Thunder crackled overhead and the air was thick with moisture. Though the yard seemed to go on forever, the walk to the front of the house was relatively short by country standards. Yet the wind had a bite. Margot buttoned up her wool coat, hoping she wouldn't regret not bringing her down-filled one instead.

Brad took their overnight bags from the back seat of the truck, and when she reached for hers, he held on tight.

When she looked at him quizzically, he winked. "At least let me look like a gentleman."

"If you insist," Margot said, but sprinted up the steps when they reached the porch and opened the screen door before he had a chance.

She shot him a triumphant grin and he chuckled.

"Mrs. Driscoll," Brad said easily as the middle-aged proprietress greeted them at the door. "It's nice to see you again. Thanks for putting us up."

"It's my pleasure. Please call me Debbie." The woman was somewhere in her fifties, almost as round as she was tall with brown hair streaked liberally with gray. But it was her bright blue eyes and welcoming smile that Margot found mesmerizing. "Welcome to the Rogers House."

She glanced curiously at Margot when Brad made the introductions. "Why, you must be Giselle and Boyd's daughter."

"Yes, ma'am." Margot stared curiously at the woman. "Did you know my parents?"

"My husband, Gene, he's been gone three years now." The woman's eyes grew misty for a second before she blinked the moisture away. "Gene knew your father quite well. They shared a love of travel."

Travel? Margot couldn't recall the last time her father had left the state before he'd gotten on that train in July.

She felt embarrassed for the woman. Debbie had obviously gotten her dad confused with someone else.

"Over the years, my husband and I would run into your parents at various events in Rust Creek Falls that we attended." The older woman's voice held a twinge of nostalgia. "I moved here after high school, got a job and fell in love with an older man. Your mother and I had the older-man thing in common."

Margot simply nodded, hoping Debbie would let the subject of her father drop. She soon realized she needn't have worried. As they moved deeper into the lovely home with its gleaming hardwood floors and beautifully woven rugs, it was apparent that the proprietress had a house filled with guests and lots to do.

Brad's palm rested against the small of her back as they climbed the steps to the second floor.

Debbie stopped in front of a heavy oak door, a metal key in her hand. Her gaze shifted between Brad and Margot. "How long have you two been seeing each other?"

The hand pressed against Margot's spine flexed. She supposed she could have told the woman it was none of her business, but there was motherly concern in the blue eyes that gazed at her, not censure.

"It feels as if I've known Brad forever." Margot kept her tone light, hoping Debbie didn't notice she hadn't really answered the question. It was too complicated to explain that she and Brad weren't seeing each other, not in the traditional sense anyway.

"I had to wait for her to grow up a bit," Brad said with a hint of gallantry. "Being the older man has its downfalls. You understand."

The two lines of worry between Debbie's brows disappeared. She flashed a smile and matching dimples in her cheeks winked. "Oh, I do indeed."

"I put you in our blue room." Debbie unlocked the door and handed Brad the key, then stepped back to let them enter.

The room Debbie had given them was aptly named. It was awash in shades of blue, from tiny bluebells in the vintage wallpaper to a hand-stitched quilt with a blue wedding ring pattern. Like the downstairs, the hardwood floors were polished to a rich gleam. A large circular rug covered part of the floor and lace curtains with old-fashioned pull shades for privacy, hung at the two large windows.

Fresh flowers spilled from a decorative blue pitcher on the dresser and brought the light fragrant scent of spring into the room.

"This is a gorgeous room." Margot spoke almost reverently, sliding her fingers across the top of the antique Hepplewhite dresser.

Brad nodded his approval.

"I'm glad you approve." Pride filled the woman's voice. "We like to make things nice for our guests."

Leaving Margot's side only long enough to place their overnight bags on the luggage rack that had been conveniently set out, Brad returned and placed a proprietary hand on Margot's shoulder.

The light that flared in Debbie's eyes told Margot the woman had a good grasp on everything going on in her B&B.

"I realize you'll be heading over to the jazz festival," Debbie said, moving toward the door, "but I want to make you aware that we'll be serving complimentary appetizers and wine, as well as non-alcoholic beverages, in the downstairs parlor in fifteen minutes. The bell will ring when they're ready. We'd love for you to join us."

"We'll try. Thanks for—" Brad paused and gestured to the room "—all this."

The grandmother's clock on the dresser began to chime and Debbie gave a little yelp. "Rosa will have my neck if I'm not down there to help her get the food out."

The woman was gone in a flash, leaving Brad and Margot alone.

"Nice place." Brad's gaze flickered to the bed before returning to Margot.

"Cozy," Margot murmured as she drew back the curtains to look out the window. "It's raining."

"The forecast was for clear skies all weekend." Brad joined her, standing close as they watched sheets of rain sweep across the streets. The intoxicating scent of his cologne wrapped around her. "Rain wasn't even mentioned."

"Better than snow." Margot shivered, suddenly conscious of his nearness and the desire bubbling up inside her.

His arm went around her almost immediately. "Cold?"

"Not really." She leaned her head back against his shoulder and contentment seasoned the desire. "Just a reaction to seeing the rain."

Some of Margot's eagerness over the evening's festivities diminished at the thought of going outside in the weather. Because of the clear forecast she hadn't even thought to bring an umbrella. "I'm starting to worry about myself."

Brad's arms were now fully around her. He held her loosely enough that she only had to tip her head back to look in his eyes. Green eyes as tumultuous as the weather outside the window met her gaze. "Tell me."

She smiled at his commanding tone. "Tell you what?"

"What has you worried?"

"Maybe it's all the drama of the week, but I fear I'm becoming antisocial," she said in a whisper. "I look at the rain and find myself wishing I could stay inside with a glass of wine by the fire. How crazy is that?"

"Not so crazy." He tucked a strand of hair behind her ear then kissed her neck. "I feel that way, too."

Her blood turned to fire at the warm moistness of his lips against her skin. Her brain short-circuited, making it difficult to think.

"We didn't drive all this way to hang out in a B&B all night," she pointed out.

"We came to listen to jazz," he said as he nibbled on her ear making her knees grow weak and her breath come in short puffs.

"That's right." Margot could scarcely hear the words over the pounding of her heart.

"I can pull up jazz on my phone. We can enjoy wine and appetizers in front of the fire. We won't have to battle the weather and I guarantee it'll be more peaceful than being at the Eagles Club."

"Eagles Club?"

"Where Glacier Jazz is being held this year."

"Oh."

He took her arm and led her to a small Victorian love-seat barely big enough for two. When he sat beside her, his thigh pressed against hers and she was supremely conscious just how male he was...

Brad captured her hand and studied it for a moment before his thumb began caressing her palm in a way that made her mouth grow dry.

She forced her final protest out that dry throat. "But you like to party."

He laughed softly as his gaze melded with hers. "Who says we're not going to party?"

Chapter Fifteen

Brad cocked his head when a bell sounded. It reminded him of something you'd hear on a ship. He knew what it meant. And he also knew if he remained in this cozy room with Margot alone for even five more minutes, there would be no appetizers and wine by the fire.

Still, the thought of what would happen had him hesitating. Telling himself they would both need sustenance to survive the night he had planned, Brad took Margot's hand then tugged her from the room and down the stairs.

She didn't protest but the look of surprise on her face made him smile. Obviously just when she thought she had him all figured out, he'd surprised her.

A fire glowed cheerily in the parlor and trays of pretty hors d'oeuvres had been set out on a large oval table draped with a lacy tablecloth. Bottles of wine were scattered around the room and crystal glasses gleamed in the chandelier's glow.

Though Margot was clearly the youngest in the room, there were several couples who appeared to be close to his age. Still, the majority of those mingling in the beautiful parlor looked close to retirement age.

Brad remained at her side as they enjoyed bits of bacon-wrapped shrimp and munched on goat cheese poppers. Though most of the conversations were superficial, Margot found it difficult to concentrate. Such a lack could be a symptom from her head injury, but she knew that wasn't the reason.

Each time he glanced in her direction and their eyes locked, all she could think about was the bed waiting for them upstairs. They'd only been downstairs for fifteen or twenty minutes when Margot took the bull by the horns.

She squeezed his hand and stared hard into those beautiful, sexy green eyes.

There was no need for words. He refilled their wine-glasses while she put together a plate of appetizers. Though she wasn't all that hungry now, she had a feeling she was going to be ravenous later.

Debbie stopped them on their way out of the parlor. "Leaving for the Eagles Club?"

"We're going to relax a bit before heading out." Margot jumped at a large crack of thunder overhead.

"Be careful tonight," Debbie warned. "The temperature has dropped twenty degrees in the last hour. The forecast has now gone from clear to rain to thundersnow."

Margot knew what the revised forecast meant; lots of wet, heavy snow.

Though she couldn't wait to get upstairs, she didn't want to be rude. She and Brad visited with Debbie for several minutes before heading up the steps.

Margot paused at the door to their room while Brad

pulled out the key. "This sort of reminds me of that Christmas song, 'Oh, the weather outside is frightful…'"

"Being inside you will be so delightful." As soon as the door opened, he tugged her inside and pressed her up against the wall, almost upsetting the plate of food she held in one hand.

Her breath caught in her throat. "I don't think those are the words."

"They should be." He kissed her firmly then stepped back. "I need to set these glasses down before I pour red wine down the front of that shirt and you're forced to take it off."

Margot placed the appetizers on a side table, then moved to the fireplace where a fragrant fire simmered in the hearth. She smiled to herself. "Something tells me it'll be off very soon anyway."

"You say the nicest things." Brad came up behind her and wrapped his arms around her, making her squeal.

"What nice things?" Her voice sounded breathless.

"Offering to take off your shirt."

She laughed. "Where's my jazz? If I'm going to get naked I need seduction music."

Brad pulled out his phone, swiped a few buttons and Louis Armstrong's distinctive voice filled the air. The melody and romance of the song wrapped around her like a pretty ribbon.

It seemed oh-so-natural when Brad held out his arms as if ready to sweep her across a ballroom floor. "May I have this dance?"

She stepped into his embrace then tilted her head back. "Who are you and what have you done with Brad Crawford?"

He smiled a bit ruefully, his eyes now the color of jade. "You bring out the romantic in me."

"First time I've heard that."

"I have a question for you," he began then hesitated.

From the look in his eyes, it appeared he was waiting for some encouragement. Though Margot had no idea what he might say, she offered a smile and a light tone. "Don't let that stop you."

Still, he hesitated for several seconds before speaking.

"You said once that it had been a while since you'd been with anyone." His gaze searched her eyes. "Did you have a bad experience? Did some guy hurt you, Margot?"

Now she saw the worry in his eyes and rushed to soothe.

Her lips twisted in a wry smile. "Not unless you count the guy back in high school who bragged to his buddies about bagging the redhead with the big boobs."

Brad's jaw set in a hard line and a muscle in his jaw jumped.

Uh-oh. She waved a dismissive hand. "That was eons ago."

"Who is he?" Brad demanded. "Is he still in Rust Creek Falls?"

"What are you going to do?" Margot inclined her head, kept her tone light. "Beat him up for me?"

Brad's hand tightened around hers. "Maybe."

They were barely moving now, swaying slowly back and forth in time to music that had switched from Louis to Ella.

She could almost feel his fury simmering in the air. Margot gave a little laugh, hoping to ease the tension. "Don't tell me you never kissed and told."

"Never," Brad said flatly.

Since appealing to logic obviously hadn't worked, Margot tried distraction. She twined her fingers through his hair, raised herself up to her tiptoes and pressed her mouth against his for a brief kiss.

His smoldering gaze settled on hers and then he lowered his head. Her kiss had been a momentary meeting of the lips. This was a melding of the souls.

When she came up for air, Margot felt dizzy with desire. The fingers of both of her hands were tangled in his hair and the spicy scent of his cologne surrounded her. His hands cupped her backside, pressing her tightly against his arousal, leaving no room for misunderstanding about his desire for her.

"Shall we get more comfortable?" Margot asked in a breathless voice.

Brad took a step back, his gaze never leaving hers. Instead of tackling the buttons on his shirt, he reached for the ones on hers. "Let me help you."

She kept her gaze firmly focused on his face, on green eyes that glittered like a thousand emeralds. Margot's heart skittered as he unfastened each button slowly until her shirt hung open in the front. He tugged the tails from her pants then slipped the garment off her shoulders. It fell to the floor to pool at her feet.

If the flash of heat in his eyes was any indication, the black lacy bra she'd chosen specifically with this moment in mind met with his approval.

Instead of unclasping the front hook as she expected, he turned his attention to her pants. In a matter of seconds, they too were at her feet. Margot stepped out of them, then slipped back on her heels. She stood before him, clad only in her bra, matching panties and black heels.

"Do you approve of my outfit?" She asked with a coquettish smile, striking a pose. "I dressed with you in mind this evening."

"I like it very much." His eyes had turned dark and unreadable in the firelight's glow.

"What about you?" She reached for his belt buckle but he pushed her hands aside and nuzzled her neck.

"In a minute," he murmured, his lips moving to her ear.

"Nah, uh." Margot shook her head and stepped back when he attempted to pull her close. "Down to your boxers or briefs first."

"You drive a hard bargain." Yet those emerald eyes danced and he made quick work of slipping the sweater over his head and shrugging out of his pants.

His chest was broad with a slight smattering of dark hair, his hips lean and his legs long and muscular.

"Look." She pointed to their image in the full-length beveled mirror. "We match."

He stood slightly behind her, clad only in black boxers. The tan he'd gotten from long days in the summer sun still lingered and had turned his skin a soft shade of gold.

Her ivory complexion provided a startling contrast when set against the black lace.

He smiled approvingly at their reflection, her in front and him half a step behind her.

"You're right," he murmured in a husky whisper that sent warm licks of desire up her spine. "We do match. Perfectly."

With their gazes still focused in the mirror, Brad unclasped her bra and eased it gently from her shoulders. His arms slid around her and he cupped a breast in each large palm as his thumbs teased the pointed nipples. "You're beautiful."

While she watched, he leaned around her and took one erect nipple into his mouth and suckled. Margot lifted her hands to his hair and closed her eyes as waves of sensation washed over her.

Then, just when she thought she couldn't stand it any longer he moved to the other breast. She wobbled, her legs threatening to buckle under the onslaught of sensations. But he didn't pull back.

Instead, Brad dropped to his knees in front of her and crooked a finger in the waistband of her panties, easing them all the way down to the floor. He supported her as she stepped out of them. "Spread your legs for me."

She glanced over her shoulder, to the right. "The bed—"

"Spread your legs," he repeated.

When she did as he asked, he pressed his mouth to her center in an openmouthed kiss that made her tremble all over.

Her body responded with breathtaking speed. Feeling his warm breath at her center, seeing him kneeling before her, was the most erotic experience of her life. She cried out in delight.

Though her legs still shook, she parted farther for him. He found her sweet spot and licked it over and over. Tension exploded inside her as her muscles tensed and collected. She tossed her head from side to side, fighting to stay upright as her release claimed her.

He rose and caught her when she swayed. Gathering her in his arms, he carried her to the bed, flinging back the covers with an impatient gesture.

She barely had time to gaze at his arousal before he sheathed it with a condom and settled between her legs.

"Be in me," she whispered as he raised his head and gazed into her eyes.

He was large and stretched her in the best way possible. The need for him grew with each slow thrust. She clung to him, urging him deeper.

The rhythmic thrusting made her pulse against him. She felt her control slipping and she strained toward him, reaching, needing, wanting.

She'd never felt like this before. The desire for him

was a stark carnal hunger Margot hadn't known she was capable of feeling. All she knew was that she didn't want it to end.

They made love several more times that night. The next morning when Margot awoke, tender in places she didn't realize she had muscles, she spent an hour in the whirlpool with Brad.

Margot couldn't remember when she'd had so much fun with any man, in or out of bed. Brad had a sense of humor and a playful side in sync with her own. By the time they dressed, the snow had quit falling outside and the fire was mere glowing embers.

The smell of bacon drew them downstairs, where they sat at a table and chatted with several other couples while drinking copious amounts of coffee and eating a breakfast fit for a lumberjack…or for two people who'd spent the evening in vigorous physical activity.

When the last couple at the table left, Brad's smoldering gaze fixed on hers. Suddenly, she wanted him again.

Maybe it was because she'd gone so long without sex that she couldn't seem to get enough of him. All Margot knew was if she had her way, they'd spend the rest of their time in Kalispell in bed.

"What would you say," Brad said slowly in a low tone, "to spending another night here?"

Margot couldn't keep from touching him another second. She trailed a finger up his arm. "Are you suggesting we stay and actually attend Glacier Jazz?"

"The festival is a possibility. We have other options." He captured her hand, brought it to his lips where he placed a kiss in the palm. "I'm not ready for all this to end."

His gaze shifted around the dining room with its silver platters of food and warm inviting atmosphere. But when his eyes met hers and she saw the fire smoldering there Margot knew they were of the same mind. "I want to stay longer. Do you know if the room is available?"

Margot's stomach flip-flopped at the smile he sent her way.

"I already checked," he said. "It's ours if we want it."

Brad could have easily stayed in the room with Margot all day. Actually that would have been his preference. But despite the hearty breakfast they'd enjoyed, by noon they were both hungry again. The sun shone in a bright blue sky. The three inches of snow the area received last night had already started to melt.

When Margot mentioned checking out some of the little shops on Main Street, Brad had to stifle a groan. But the eagerness in her eyes had him hiding his dismay and agreeing it sounded like a splendid idea.

So far, so good, he thought as they strolled down the street, hand-in-hand with the sun warm against their faces. They stopped for lunch at a little bistro that had popped up in the past year. Once they were finished, Margot declared it was time to shop.

Brad thought he displayed extraordinary control when he smiled instead of groaning. For several minutes, they simply walked down Main, pausing every so often to gaze into a window. If this was Margot's idea of shopping, he found he rather enjoyed it.

Though Brad liked living in Rust Creek Falls, it was nice to be in a town where no one knew him. If he wanted to steal a kiss or loop an arm over Margot's shoulders it wouldn't be reported by the *Rambler* the following Sunday. That fact alone made this day he was sharing with her special.

Margot appeared to be in a good mood, chattering

about Leila and her friends back on the rodeo circuit. She didn't once mention her father and Brad had no intention of bringing up the guy.

"I feel like we're playing hooky," she said with an infectious smile, stopping to linger in front of another store window. Holding true to its name, the All Christmas, All Year store appeared to feature only Christmas items. "It was nice of your father to agree to watch the ranch an extra day."

She looked so happy, so carefree, he couldn't resist. Brad cupped the back of her neck with his hand and kissed her. He couldn't seem to keep his hands—or his mouth— off her.

"He was happy to do it," he murmured against her mouth, pleased by her slightly dazed expression. At least he wasn't the only one affected.

Margot took a deep, steadying breath then grabbed his hand, something she'd done with increasing regularity this afternoon. "Let's go inside."

Brad stood in the doorway for a moment and gazed into the shop filled with anything and everything related to Christmas. "It's only October. Isn't it a little early for this type of shopping?"

The comment earned him a scowl from a middle-aged woman with a woven basket filled to overflowing with an assortment of holiday items.

Margot slipped her arm through his. "Come on, Scrooge. No one is saying you have to buy something."

"I'm not going to buy anything," Brad asserted.

"Your loss." Margot heaved a happy sigh and pointed upward. "I'm thinking your feelings about this shop are going to do a one-eighty pretty darn quick."

She was absolutely right. The mistletoe hanging directly over them practically demanded a kiss. Brad pulled Margot into his arms and by the time they came up for air, he decided this shop did have a few things going for it.

Brad kept his eye out for more mistletoe as they moved deeper into the cluttered store. With Margot stopping every couple of feet to check out various displays, it was slow going.

Pausing once more, Margot's smile turned wistful as she gazed upon an assortment of snow globes. With gentle fingers she caressed the glass top of one, though she made no move to pick it up. "My mother loved snow globes. Now I do, too."

She lifted the one that had captured her attention and held it up. The globe held a couple dancing under old-fashioned street lamps. "Look. This could be us."

Brad studied the globe and was surprised to see just how much the iron streetlights resembled the ones flanking the street where they were currently shopping.

He inclined his head. "Do you have a collection?"

She sat the globe down and her smile disappeared. "My father thought snow globes were the most ridiculous things. My mother and I knew if we bought one for ourselves— or each other—we'd never hear the end of it from him. I sometimes wish…"

Instead of finishing the thought, she turned down another aisle and began flipping through various velvet tree skirts.

He moved close and slid an arm around her waist. "Tell me what you wish."

"I wish I hadn't held back." Margot leaned her head against his shoulder and sighed. "I wish I'd said to heck with my father and bought her one, so she'd know just how much I loved her."

Margot turned into him and tipped her head back, her green eyes swimming with emotion. "I adored my mother.

We fought like a lot of mothers and daughters do during those teenage years, but I always loved her."

Brad's gaze never left her face. His heart ached for her, at the pain he saw reflected in those beautiful eyes. It wasn't fair. In a matter of a few years, she'd lost her mother and now her father. Though Boyd wasn't dead, it appeared he'd written Margot out of his life. He vowed to double his efforts to find the old coot and demand answers.

"Your mother knew you loved her," he told her.

"I hope so." Margot stepped back then turned to tables brimming with an assortment of Christmas items.

They shopped for another fifteen minutes but some of the luster seemed to have gone off the day. Margot purchased a few items, including a small desk calendar with a penguin on the front that she said reminded her of Vivian. Brad thought he showed great restraint in refraining from saying anything negative about Viper.

He waited until Margot had slipped off to the restroom to make his purchase. He added the item to her sack. When she returned, he clasped her hand in his as they stepped outside.

The streets and sidewalks were relatively empty. Brad took in the scene before him and smiled. He had the perfect plan for cheering Margot up. "I have a crazy idea and was wondering if you're interested."

She shot him a suspicious look. "If it involves sex in a public place, I'm going to pass."

He laughed aloud. "No, but it does involve an outdoor activity."

With the hand holding his bag, he gestured to a horse and carriage at the curb down the street. "Want to go for a sleigh ride?"

Chapter Sixteen

Margot had seen the horse-drawn carriages all decked out for the holidays before. With their jingling bells, greenery and red velvet ribbons, they drew everyone's attention. Tourist traps, her father had dubbed them in the same derisive tone he'd used for the snow globes.

When she was young Margot had thought it'd be great fun to ride in one, but sleigh rides had been off her radar in recent years. Now, as she climbed aboard and Brad tucked the red plaid blanket around them, she experienced a thrill of anticipation.

The sun blazed bright in a cloudless sky. The pristine white of last night's snowfall provided a startling contrast to the vivid blue overhead. The horses' hooves made a clip-clopping sound when the driver turned off Main Street onto a cobblestone road. It was as if she'd been transported to a Christmas Winter Wonderland.

Here, snow-covered lawns glittered like diamonds in

the sunlight. Branches of large trees that had been planted over a half century ago arched over the street like a canopy.

When they were seated in the carriage, Brad had put his arm around her shoulders. With her body pressed against his, Margot was reminded just how good they were together sexually.

Settled comfortably under the blanket, Margot felt that desire surge once again. She placed her hand on his thigh. Almost immediately a muscle jumped.

Smiling to herself, Margot began to move her fingers upward until, suddenly, his hand clamped around her hand, stilling the movement.

Margot lifted an innocent gaze to meet his. "Problem?"

"Not playing fair," Brad murmured in a low tone.

"I wasn't aware there were rules." Her tone was deliberately husky, almost a purr.

Margot tossed her hair, sending the red curls scattering. Aware she now had his full attention, she ran her tongue over her lips and watched his eyes grow dark.

"Enjoying the ride, folks?" The driver, clad in a long coat and top hat, asked in a pleasant tone without looking back.

"Very much." Margot squeezed Brad's thigh again and smiled when once again his muscle jerked. "A sleigh ride is a great way to relax and unwind."

"I'm taking you down by the river," the driver called back. "It's a longer way back but, don't worry, I won't charge extra."

"Thanks." Margot gave Brad an impish smile. She knew it wasn't the money, but the time that concerned him.

The look in his eye told her she wasn't the only one eager to get back to the B&B and enjoy some adult time together.

Making love with Brad had unleashed needs that must have been pent up inside for years. Now each time she looked in his eyes, she thought of the way they turned to dark jade every time he saw her naked.

When he spoke and her gaze was drawn to his lips, she could almost feel those lips against her bare skin or around the tip of one of her breasts or at the very center of...

Margot felt a flush creep up her neck and infuse her whole face with heat. She assured herself she could keep her desires under control until they reached the privacy of their room. For now, she'd simply sit back and enjoy the scenery and the fresh...

The feel of Brad's hand on her upper thigh had her inhaling sharply.

This time it was *his* innocent gaze that met hers. "Are you warm enough, honey?"

Before Margot could formulate a response, his hand slid up and inside her waistband. The large callused palm was cool against her fiery hot skin.

Margot supposed she could have reached under the blankets and stopped the naughtiness the same way he'd stopped hers only moments before. But she found herself liking this game.

"Bring it on, cowboy," she whispered in a low tone meant for his ears only. "I can handle it."

The challenge in her tone may have been a bit much. Though Brad had never competed on the rodeo circuit, she recognized the competitive gleam that flashed in his eyes.

"My parents used to bring us to Kalispell every year to go Christmas shopping." His fingers slid down through her curls before one finger slipped inside.

She gasped, brought herself under immediate control. Okay, maybe not immediately, but quickly.

"Is that so?" she managed to stammer, as her body closed in around his finger.

"Yep," he said with a cocky smile. "What about you?"

"How about me what?" Dear God, she'd forgotten the question. Why were they bothering to talk anyway? All she wanted to do was revel in the exquisite sensations flooding her body.

"Did you come here to shop every Christmas?" He added his thumb to the mix and she squirmed at the desire that erupted when he found her sweet spot. She pressed up against his hand, swallowed a moan.

"How often did you come to Kalispell?" The wicked gleam in Brad's eyes told her he knew how his actions were affecting her.

"Now and...then..." She managed to get the words out. While she may have sounded slightly breathless, at least she wasn't panting, which is exactly what she longed to do. His fingers continued to torture and tease.

Under the cover of the blanket, she opened her legs as desire rose as strong and hot as lava inside a volcano.

"Don't stop." She meant to whisper the words but they came out as more of a command.

The driver turned back and Brad's fingers thankfully stilled. "Did you say you wanted to stop?"

"No." Margot screwed on a bright smile. "Just speaking about something else."

The second the man turned his attention back to the front, Brad leaned over and kissed her long and hard.

She plunged over the edge, his mouth absorbing her cries as the orgasm slammed into her. She clung to him as wave after wave of sensation battered her.

When her eyes were capable of focus, she met his gaze. "Your time is coming, mister."

"Bring it on, cowgirl." He nipped her earlobe. "I can handle it."

They drove back to Rust Creek Falls the next day. If Brad didn't know his father was planning to take inventory at the store this afternoon, he'd have tried to get him to watch the ranch another day.

Of course, he wasn't sure he could handle one more night with Margot. He'd gone from being celibate for six months to continuous mind-blowing sex. On the way to the B&B after their sexcapades in the carriage, she'd warned him she'd make him pay once they were back in the room.

All he could think was if that was her way of extracting revenge, she could make him pay anytime. It was as if they couldn't get enough of each other. The feel of her beneath him, the touch of her hands, the taste of her mouth… Brad couldn't remember the last time he'd been so totally mesmerized by a woman.

He enjoyed her company just as much out of bed. Margot was an intelligent woman. She was well-read and her natural curiosity about a variety of things made her an interesting conversationalist.

On the drive back, they'd actually discussed national events and had a lively discussion. He'd never have been able to have such a conversation with Janie. She'd had little interest in anything outside of herself. But then, he'd been equally self-absorbed.

"I should have seen it," Brad muttered.

Margot looked up from programming the radio to a more palatable station. "Should have seen what?"

"Janie."

"What about her?"

Margot looked puzzled. He didn't blame her. He rarely spoke of his feelings. Yet there was something about Margot that made him feel as if he could tell her anything. She was a woman he could trust and Brad found himself wanting to confide in her.

"We had so little in common." He lifted one shoulder

in a slight shrug. "I should have seen that would eventually become a problem."

Apparently finding the country station she wanted, Margot turned the volume down and leaned back in her seat.

"Don't be too hard on yourself for not seeing clearly," she said with a self-deprecating smile. "Look at me and my dad. I thought I meant more to him than someone he could walk away from without a backward glance. I was wrong."

Brad's father appeared touched by the fishing fly that Margot had picked out for him as a thank-you gift. Privately Brad hadn't considered a gift necessary. Helping family, helping neighbors, was simply the Rust Creek Falls way.

But he'd said nothing because her gratitude was sincere and his father had genuinely appreciated the gesture. Brad had stood back while Todd showed Margot the fresh bedding he'd placed in the box when mama dog had been outside.

At least today Viper appeared no fonder of his father than she was of him, growling at both of them when they entered the parlor.

"I want to make sure there's water in the south pasture before I leave." His father cast a pointed glance at Brad. "The windmill didn't seem to be working earlier. Why don't you and me ride out there and see what you think."

Since Brad knew this was something he could easily check himself, it was obvious—at least to him—that his father wanted to talk with him privately.

"You don't have to do that, Mr. Crawford," Margot protested. "You've already done so much."

"I enjoyed every minute of it," he told her. "And, remember, it's Todd."

"Okay, Todd." Even though she wasn't speaking to him, Margot's sweet smile had Brad's heart tripping all over itself. "But—"

"Seriously, it was a pleasure being back in the saddle again." Todd punched Brad in the shoulder. "This trip to the south pasture will give my son a chance to catch me up on your trip to Kalispell."

Though her smile didn't waver, Brad could almost read her thoughts…keep the account PG-rated. She didn't need to warn him. As he'd told Margot this weekend, he wasn't one to kiss and tell. Even if he was, he couldn't imagine ever sharing details of his love life with his *father*.

"If you gentleman don't need me, I'm going to run upstairs and put some of this stuff away." She gestured to the sacks from their shopping spree.

"Let me carry those sacks up for you." Before she could protest, Brad hefted them into his arms. "You can keep my dad company."

As he carried the bags to the bedroom, Brad found himself whistling under his breath. Margot was such an independent woman, it felt as if he'd scored the winning basket whenever he was able to persuade her to let him help. Over the past week, he'd discovered a protective side he didn't even know existed. Whatever he could do to ease Margot's load, to take some of the pressure off her, he'd do it.

When he returned, Margot and his father were laughing over some story involving the miniature vipers. Margot turned when he entered the room and her smile widened. For one crazy second when she stepped forward, he thought she was going to kiss him.

The speculative gleam in his father's eye made him glad she didn't.

"Think about catching a nap." Instead of the kiss he wanted to give her, Brad gave Margot's arm a squeeze.

She rolled her eyes. "We just got back."

"We had a busy weekend," he reminded her. "You're still on the mend."

There was so much more he would have said if his dad hadn't been there watching and listening to every word.

"I'll consider it," she promised.

"Thanks."

Margot's name didn't come up until Brad and his father had made some minor adjustments to the windmill and were on horseback headed back to the house.

"You're different around her," Todd said as they reined the horses back toward the stable.

Although they hadn't spoken of Margot since they'd left the house, Brad had been waiting for the inquisition. "I like her."

"She's a lot younger than you."

Brad heard the censure in his father's voice and stiffened in the saddle. "She's an adult woman of twenty-two."

"She's Natalie's age," his father reminded him. "Be careful with her."

If Brad had been Viper, he'd be snarling right about now. "As I'm not certain what you're accusing me of doing, you'll need to spell it out."

The sharp edge in Brad's voice had his father's jaw tightening. Todd Crawford didn't raise four headstrong young men by being a wimp. "Watch your tone, boy."

Brad inclined his head slightly letting his father know the message had been received.

Todd slanted a sideways glance in his direction. "Since the breakup with Janie, you haven't stayed with one woman for very long."

"That's true," Brad admitted. "Until now, I haven't been looking to settle down."

"Until now?" Todd raised one dark brow. "This girl

is too young to think about settling down with anyone. She's still searching for who she is and what she wants out of life."

Brad felt a slap of cold wind against his cheek. He lifted his head to the ominous-looking gray clouds overhead and wondered if there was more snow in the forecast.

"What are you saying, Dad? That I should move out and let her handle the ranch on her own?" Brad blew out an exasperated breath. "If that's what you're proposing, you can forget it. Margot experienced a bad injury and is still healing. I'm not leaving her."

His father's gaze pinned him and for a second it felt as if his dad could see right through him.

"All I'm saying is that she's in a different place in her life." Todd's tone turned conciliatory as the stable came into view. "If you try to tie her down now, she may end up resenting you for not giving her that time to pursue her dreams."

"Well, you don't need to worry," Brad assured his father. "I'd never keep her from her dreams. I want Margot to have what she wants out of life."

"Even if that's not you?"

Brad gave a curt nod, for the first time in his life knowing what real love felt like. "Even if that isn't me."

Chapter Seventeen

His father had told Brad to give Margot space, warned him not to get too close. But staying away from her proved impossible in the days that followed. Not only were they living under the same roof but their lives intersected in countless ways.

Brad spent every free moment with Margot and each day fell more deeply in love with her. He positioned several large, orange barrels in the corral for Margot's upcoming lesson with her new student, eight-year-old Jilly Grojean.

"That's perfect," Margot called out.

He turned and saw that while he'd been working, she'd climbed to the top of the fence surrounding the corral to watch him.

The last time he'd seen her, barely thirty minutes ago, she'd been at the table wading through more papers belonging to her father.

"Get down." He pointed to the ground. "Before you fall down."

Though he couldn't hear her sigh, the look on her face told him just how she felt. Instead of heading back into the house, she entered the corral and strode over to him, a vision of loveliness in a stylish plaid jacket and jeans.

Though she'd been in an upbeat mood when they'd discussed the upcoming day over pancakes and sausage less than an hour before, the shadows in her eyes told him something was up. It seemed odd that he, who'd never been great at reading another person's emotions, could now tell Margot's moods at a glance.

"What's up?" He leaned over to press his lips to hers.

She let him kiss her but Brad could tell this time her heart wasn't in it. Something was definitely wrong.

He pulled her into his arms and just held her close.

"What's all this?" she asked, her voice muffled against his jacket front.

He didn't answer and after a second she relaxed in his embrace. They stood for a long moment like that until he reluctantly released her.

Margot took a step back and shoved her hands into her pockets. "I feel like going for a walk. Want to join me?"

For mid-October it was a pleasant enough day, Brad supposed. There were only scattered clouds and although there was a slight breeze, it came from the south, which made the fifty-degree temperature feel almost balmy.

The niceness of the day meant that there were a thousand and one things he should be doing before cold weather hit. Margot was a Montana girl. She was aware of what needed to be accomplished, which meant she didn't need a walk, she needed him.

"A walk with a beautiful woman?" He shot her a wink. "I'm in."

She gave a laugh that didn't quite reach her eyes and began to stroll. Since the yard and surrounding areas were still soggy from the recent snow, they settled on a route down the graveled lane leading from the house to the road.

"How's the sorting going?" he asked after a minute of silence. "Shall I get the burn barrel fired up?"

Boyd Sullivan had indeed been a pack rat. It appeared her mother had also shared those tendencies. Every day Margot spent a couple of hours going through ancient receipts and old papers to see what needed to be kept—very little—and what could be discarded, which was almost everything.

"I'll have a barrelful for you by the end of the day." Margot gave a little laugh. "It's been an enlightening experience. I discovered you really can get to know a man by going through his things."

"Is this a confession?" Brad teased. "Are you here to tell me you went through my room and discovered my secret stash of Pavarotti CDs?"

"I'd never snoop through your room," Margot said indignantly. "Though it'd be easy to do since I spend more nights there than in my own."

If Brad had his way, she'd be spending every night with him. It would be *their* room and not his. But cognizant of his father's words, he let Margot guide the course of their relationship. For now.

"You like Pavarotti?" she exclaimed suddenly.

"I do," he admitted, then put a finger to his lips in a shushing gesture. "Let that be our little secret."

The delighted smile that had begun to form on Margot's lips vanished. "I don't like secrets."

Brad reached over and took her hand, found it ice-cold. "You should be wearing gloves."

"I left them in the house."

He took his off and made her take them. Once her hands

were protected, he decided it was time to find out what was troubling her. "Does it have anything to do with your dad?"

She shot him a sideways glance. "Does what?"

"What's got you upset? What has you wanting to take a walk when normally you'd be preparing for your new student?"

"I—" she started then stopped, blew out a breath.

For a second he considered she might not tell him and the thought was a sharp slice to the heart. Janie had never confided in him. She'd trusted her friends with her secrets and her feelings more than she'd trusted him. But Brad had thought things were different between him and Margot.

"Remember how I told you that my father was a champion bareback rider?"

Brad let out the breath he didn't realize he'd been holding.

"Made it all the way to the top at nationals," Brad said, repeating what he'd been told.

"He didn't." The words came out clipped, angry.

Brad blinked. "Pardon?"

"My dad never made it to the top at nationals." Margot came to a halt and he stopped, too. "Today I discovered the best he ever took was third place."

Brad pondered the information. "Perhaps he came in first in a different year than the one you were looking at today."

She shook her head. "I came across an article, 'The Rise and Crash of Boyd Sullivan.' It talked about how my dad had showed such promise but his rise in the bareback world was cut short because of alcoholism. The article stated his highest finish in Vegas was third."

"The reporter could have gotten it wrong…"

"I went back and checked online." Margot's eyes darkened and became unreadable. "Third was the best he ever got."

Brad thought about the way Boyd had pushed Margot to be number one, how he'd refused to see any other placement than first as acceptable. "That's interesting."

"He lied to me."

There was anger and hurt and confusion in her voice. Hell, Margot didn't need a walk. She needed a shot of whiskey.

Brad rubbed his chin. "Do you think your mother knew?"

Margot began walking again and her brow furrowed in thought. "I don't think so. I believe if she'd known, she'd have told me. Especially after one of the many times he got upset with me for not placing first."

There were lots of names that came to Brad's mind but he didn't mutter a single one. The old guy had been a hypocrite, there was no getting around it. But trash-talking her dad wouldn't make Margot feel better.

"I'm starting to believe I never knew him at all," she murmured so softly that if he hadn't been listening intently, he'd never have heard.

Not quite knowing how to respond, Brad settled for putting a comforting arm around her shoulder as they continued down the lane.

Margot didn't speak again until they'd reached the road and turned back toward the house. "Did you hear Debbie mention that her husband and my dad shared a love of travel?"

"Yeah, which surprised me." Brad frowned. That certainly didn't match the man he'd known. "Boyd always stuck close to home."

"When Debbie said that, I thought she had the wrong guy or her memory was faulty." Margot gave a humorless laugh. "Now I'm thinking her husband probably knew my father better than I did."

He hated seeing her so upset. "Margot—"

"No. Listen. Think about all the lies. My dad wasn't a champion bareback rider. He loved to travel. Everyone thought he lost his ranch in a poker game because he was drunk. Wrong. He *deliberately* lost it. Then he leaves town and covers his tracks so no one can find him."

"Do you really think he deliberately covered his tracks?"

"Of course I do," she insisted. "Or the police and your detective would have located him by now."

Knowing how much this line of thinking was hurting her, Brad hesitated to agree.

"There was no return address on the postcard. It was sent from New York City. Impossible to trace." Her chin lifted. "Tell me that wasn't calculated."

"He's old," Brad said slowly. "It could be he's not thinking clearly. That's why I want the investigator to continue. I need answers. More importantly, you need answers."

That was at the crux of the issue. She couldn't move on with her life otherwise. And the life he wanted with her would remain out of reach.

"We'll never find him," she said in a resigned voice. "He'll never let us. I'll never have the answers I seek."

"We will find your father," Brad insisted.

One way or the other Margot needed closure, and by God he was going to make sure she got it.

Margot had always been the cowgirl who'd picked herself up from a bad fall, dusted herself off and moved on. While the situation with her father didn't exactly fall into the same bucket as coming up short at the end of a ride, her response was the same. She focused ahead, not behind. Which meant for now her student had her full attention.

"Great job today, Jilly." Margot clapped a hand on the girl's shoulder as she walked with her and her father to their car.

"It was super fun." The blond-haired girl smiled, showing the gap where a front tooth had once been.

The eight-year-old was a good rider, but as she'd been completely new to barrel racing, Margot had to start with the basics. The girl had caught on quickly and her father, who'd hung around the corral to watch, had been encouraging.

"Can I go back and see the puppies one more time before we leave?" Jilly begged.

Her father patted the girl's shoulder. "I'm sure they haven't changed much since you saw them before your lesson."

Earlier, while she was speaking with Jilly's father about how the lessons would be structured, Brad had taken the girl into the parlor to view the puppies.

Margot had been surprised to discover that Roger and Brad had been in the same high school class. Though they hadn't run in the same circle back then, they seemed friendly now.

They'd almost reached the car when Brad strolled out from around the house. "How'd our girl like her lesson?"

"It was won-der-ful," Jilly announced, singing the word. "I'm coming back Friday."

"She's wanted to do this ever since she started riding." Roger smiled indulgently then shifted his gaze to Margot. "Her mom and I were excited to hear you'd started offering lessons."

"Did you take lessons, too?" Jilly asked, apparently deciding a second viewing of the puppies wasn't going to happen.

Margot paused, remembering the excitement of those

early days. "My—my father had been a bareback rider. He helped me at first, said I had natural talent."

She'd taken the words of praise for gospel, and even now allowed herself to bask in them for a brief moment.

"That's got to be a real plus." Roger's expression turned rueful. "I wish I could help Jilly. I'm a fair enough rider, but my interest has always been in numbers."

"Roger is an accountant," Brad told Margot.

Roger smiled easily. "I told my wife I can put those CPA skills to good use figuring how we're going to buy Jilly a good horse."

"Next spring might be a good time to start looking," Margot said. "You'll also know by then if barrel racing is just a passing interest or something she really does want to pursue."

"I wish you had an indoor arena." Roger wrapped his cashmere scarf more firmly around his neck. "Soon the weather will preclude outdoor lessons."

"Noooo," Jilly protested. "I don't want the lessons to stop."

Margot rested a reassuring hand on the girl's shoulder. "Don't worry. We can get in lots of practices before it gets too cold."

"Promise?"

"Promise." Margot found herself grinning at the child.

Suddenly Jilly was all smiles again.

"Are you certain you don't mind if she rides your horse? We can trailer ours over, although Sheba is more interested in eating than racing around barrels."

His description made Margot smile. "Really, it's no trouble at all. I'll give you some characteristics to look for in a horse if you want to start just seeing what's out there."

Margot glanced at the little girl who'd grown bored

with the conversation and had started to twirl, calling out for Brad to watch her.

"Storm is a beautiful horse. Is she an Arabian?" Roger asked.

Margot nodded.

"I imagine she didn't come cheap."

"I don't know the exact price. My father bought her for me."

"Fathers and their daughters." Roger chuckled. "He must be very proud of your success."

Margot felt Brad's gaze on her. She gave Roger a noncommittal smile.

"What's it like?" Roger asked, motioning for his daughter to get into the car. "Being on the circuit?"

"It's a lot of work," Margot admitted. "Last year I rode in over a hundred events."

"That's so cool." Jilly breathed the words. "That's what I want to do when I grow up."

Margot thought of all the hassles, the fatigue, living out of a trailer. "It can be a lot of fun. But competing has to be something you really want to do."

Margot found herself riding a high from the success of her lesson with Jilly. That is, until the mail arrived the following day and she received a letter from her father.

As she stared down at the brief note from one of her friends on the circuit who'd forwarded the waylaid letter, tears threatened. She swallowed them back. While part of her was happy Brad was out checking on the cattle, another part wished he were here, sitting beside her at the kitchen table while she carefully unsealed the envelope.

She unfolded the page of lined notebook paper and her heart began to beat an erratic rhythm.

Relax, Margot told herself. She took a couple of deep

breaths before lowering her gaze to read the words penciled in her father's distinctive scrawl.

> *Dear Margot,*
> *By now you probably know that Brad Crawford owns the Leap of Faith. I believe he will make something of the ranch.*
> *You love your life on the road. Now you'll be able to choose your own course in life, rather than be stuck with a ranch you don't want and responsibilities you always disliked.*
> *I'm sober again and just got my sixty-day chip in AA.*
> *Don't worry about me. I'm happy. When I am ready, I'll contact you again.*
> *Love,*
> *Dad*

Margot stared at the paper and her fingers flexed. An almost overwhelming need to crumple the letter into a tiny ball and toss it in the trash overwhelmed her.

Because that's just what it was. Trash.

Her father's comments only showed he didn't know her at all. She loved the Leap of Faith. She'd always planned to come back.

Okay, maybe that hadn't been the plan when she'd first gone on the circuit, but it was what she wanted now.

She swiped at the tears that she couldn't hold back another minute. She gave up all control and let the sobs well up from a deep place that she'd held in check ever since she learned he'd gone missing.

Margot cried so hard that she didn't even notice Vivian enter the room until the dog nudged her hand with her cold, wet nose.

"Vivi." Margot turned in the chair and the dog dropped her head into her lap.

The unexpected show of affection made Margot cry all the harder.

She mourned for the mother who'd abandoned her in death and for the father who'd abandoned her in life. Most of all, she cried for the woman now forced to leave the home she loved.

Chapter Eighteen

Brad had a bad feeling in the pit of his stomach when Viper greeted him at the door with a low whine. Although the heeler no longer growled *every* time she saw him, it wasn't as if he and the dog were buddies. But there was one thing they both shared: a protective urge toward Margot.

"Margot," he called out as he moved through the main level of the ranch house.

She wasn't in the parlor. The only signs of life were the rapidly growing puppies, who made little yipping noises when they saw him.

With fear fueling his steps, Brad moved swiftly to the kitchen, pausing at the sight of the mail scattered across the table. One sheet of notebook paper lay on the floor.

The second he picked it up, Brad recognized the handwriting. Though he saw that it was addressed to Margot, he didn't hesitate. He read it quickly, then tossed the letter down on the table, swearing.

Selfish old bastard.

"Margot," he called out again, crossing to the stairs. "Are you up there?"

Despite hearing no response, Brad headed up the steps, taking two at a time. Her bedroom was his first stop. Empty.

With his heart lodged in his throat, he glanced into his bedroom even as he pulled out his phone.

His breath came out in a whoosh of relief the instant he spotted her.

She'd crawled on top of his bed and pulled a blanket over her. She now lay face up, staring at the ceiling, still wearing the jeans and long-sleeved gold tee she'd had on that morning.

When he stepped into the room and the floorboards creaked she turned her head.

"Hi." Margot offered him a wan smile.

"Hey." He crossed the room. The bed dipped when he took a seat next to her. With great gentleness, he stoked her cheek with the side of his finger. "Tired?"

"A little." Her gaze returned to the ceiling. "But I can't seem to sleep."

"I'm tired myself," he lied. "Mind if I lie down next to you?"

"Okay." Though it was hardly an encouraging response, she scooted over to make room for him on the double bed.

Brad kicked off his boots then settled beside her, wrapping an arm around her then pulling her close. "This is just how I like it."

She snuggled against him. "I'm glad you're here."

For a second his heart filled to overflowing with emotion. Love, tenderness and anger at Boyd for making her cry warred for dominance.

He wasn't blind. He'd seen the tear streaks on her cheeks and the sadness in her eyes. As she'd been perfectly happy when he'd left to drop off hay to the cattle, he had to assume it was her father's letter that had made her so unhappy.

"Stupid jerk," he muttered.

"What did you say?" she murmured, turning her head.

The sweet floral scent of her perfume filled his nostrils and he was filled with an overwhelming desire to protect, to soothe. She'd had to endure so much pain in the past few weeks.

"I could spend the whole day like this with you." As he said the words, Brad realized they were true. He loved being with her.

"You'd need to eat." The teasing lilt in her voice told him she might be down, but Margot Sullivan wasn't out.

Some of the tightness in his heart eased.

"Or you'd get tired of cuddling and we'd both end up naked," she added.

There were so many light and funny ways he could have taken the conversation, but instead he spoke from the heart. "It's not about the sex."

"What isn't?"

"You and me."

"I thought you enjoyed making love with me."

Damn. Was that hurt in her voice?

"I do." He stroked her arm. "But I like being with you like this, too. I like having breakfast with you and discussing current events and…everything."

Brad nearly groaned aloud. Could he have sounded any more lame?

"I like all that, too," she said softly.

He tightened his hold around her shoulders and kissed the top of her head. If it made her feel better, he'd spend the entire day with her, like this, just the two of them.

It was then that it hit him. This was exactly how he

wanted it to be between them, not just now, but forever. He wanted to share her joys and her sorrows and be the kind of man she deserved.

He loved her. He wanted her to be his wife, the mother of his children.

Brad only wished he knew if she wanted all those things, too.

Margot snuggled against Brad and realized that her world—which had been off-kilter only hours before—had nearly righted itself.

Being here with him, with his arms around her, made the worries dim in significance.

"I read your dad's letter," he confessed in a low voice.

"Did you?"

He couldn't tell from her response how she felt about him invading her privacy. He hadn't meant to overstep, but the urge to protect her had been overwhelming. "I realize it wasn't addressed to me but—"

"You don't need to explain," she interrupted. "I'm glad you read it. You and I both needed more closure than a postcard could provide."

"We still don't know where he is," Brad reminded her. "I'm not going to stop looking until I find him."

"I'm not sure you should do that," she said in a low voice. "It might be best to just let it go, let him go."

There was resignation in her tone and something else: an emotion he couldn't quite identify.

When he spoke, Brad kept his voice casual and offhand. "Tell me what you're afraid of."

He expected her to laugh or at least say that he was way off-base, that she wasn't afraid of anything. But she didn't. She remained silent for so long he wondered if she'd fallen asleep.

"I'm afraid," she shifted into him as if needing comfort only he could provide, "that once I know where he is nothing will change. What am I going to do? Go to wherever he is and drag him home? Why? So he can be miserable here? Or maybe so he can tell me face-to-face he no longer wants me in his life?"

Brad had no answer and only one comment. "He's a fool."

"No argument here." She expelled a breath that sounded suspiciously like a sigh. "At least we both know now that the ranch is well and truly yours."

"No." Brad rose up on one elbow. "It isn—"

She stopped his words by pulling him down and pressing her mouth to his. The kiss was warm and sweet and gentle and seemed to soothe them both. When it ended she spoke quickly before he had a chance. "Make love to me, Brad."

He shook his head.

"You're upset." He twisted a lock of her hair around his finger. "I don't want to take advantage."

"I need you." Her fingers curved into his shirt. "I want to feel your touch and hear your sweet words. I need you to take me away from my worries and just let me be with you."

He stared into her eyes for several heartbeats, then, reassured by what he saw there, slid his hand under her tee.

When she reached up to tug it off, he stopped her. "This time, we're going to take it slow. Let me take care of you, Margot. All you have to do is relax…and enjoy."

Something in his gaze must have conveyed this was important to him. She nodded and the gentle, persuasive onslaught on her senses began.

In a matter of minutes all Margot knew was Brad: his smell, his taste, his strong arms and those heart-rending sweet words. They took it slow this time and when they both found their fulfillment, Margot clung to him wishing the letter had never come and they could have gone on like they had been, forever.

But she'd lived long enough to know that nothing stayed the same in life or in relationships. Change was the only certainty in life.

Today hers had taken another sharp turn in an unexpected direction. And Margot wasn't quite sure what she was going to do about it.

Later that day, on the pretext of picking up some supplies, Brad got in the truck and met his brother at the donut shop.

He got a coffee and a muffin then sauntered across the small dining area where Nate sat reading emails on his phone. His older brother looked up when Brad plopped down in the seat across from him.

Nate lifted a dark brow and slid the phone into the pocket of his jacket.

For Brad, sitting across from Nate was similar to looking in a mirror. They shared the same brown hair and green eyes, same build and facial features. In fact, those who didn't know them often mistook them for twins. But in the past few years things had changed.

The transformation had occurred when Nate met Callie Kennedy. His brother had fallen hard. Now the popular nurse practitioner was his wife. And Nate was a businessman, managing Maverick Manor, a hotel he'd built last year in Rust Creek Falls.

What Brad saw on his brother's face went beyond the fact that the arrogant cowboy had turned successful businessman. Nate wore an air of contentment as if it was a favorite coat wrapped around his shoulders. That, Brad knew, had nothing to do with the business and everything to do with Callie Kennedy Crawford.

"Something on your mind?" Nate washed down a bite of chocolate donut with a gulp of steaming coffee.

"Of course there's something on my mind." Brad expelled a frustrated breath. "Would I have asked you to meet me at this place if there wasn't?"

Nate took another chunk out of the donut. "You could have just been in the mood for something sweet. Although, you do have something sweet at home."

Brad's gaze narrowed. The comment wasn't about pastries, but Margot. Still, there was nothing lecherous in Nate's gaze, only mild interest.

"I do." Brad took a sip of coffee, warming his hands around the ceramic mug.

"You've grown attached to her." Nate spoke in a conversational tone. He leaned back in his chair and studied his brother. "Is that a problem?"

"It's complicated." Brad sat down his mug, wondering why he was really here and what he wanted his brother to do for him. From the look on Nate's face, he was wondering that, too.

"I'm in love with her," Brad blurted out, surprising them both.

"She's only been in town a few weeks." Nate didn't bother to hide his surprise. Obviously, whatever he'd expected his brother to say, it wasn't a confession of love.

"It is what it is."

"You don't sound too happy about it."

Brad raked a hand through his hair. "I feel as if I'm on a bull and the eight seconds has come and gone and I'm still being tossed around on the animal's back. Part of me finds it exhilarating, part of me is scared to death—and

I'll deny that if you tell anyone—the other part doesn't want the ride to end."

Nate simply nodded and finished off the donut.

His brother had his own share of experience with love and heartbreak. When he was a student in Missoula, Nate had fallen in love with Zoe Baker. They'd married and been happy. Heck, Nate and Zoe had been expecting a child. But the delivery had gone horribly wrong and both Zoe and the child died.

Nate had been inconsolable. For ten years he'd accepted that there would never be anyone else like Zoe. Then, on a cold winter day, nurse practitioner Callie Kennedy had run out of gas on the side of the road and Nate had stopped to offer assistance. The rest was, as they say, history.

"What do you want?" Nate finally asked. "I mean, *really* want from Margot?"

"I want to marry her," Brad heard himself say. "I want her to stay here in Rust Creek Falls. I want to build a life with her on the Leap of Faith."

"Her father's ranch?"

"It's mine now."

"I thought you told me you planned to give it back to the old guy."

Brad took a few moments and explained about the postcard and the letter. "I don't think he's coming home."

Nate shook his head. "The old guy sounds crazy."

"It's impossible to predict what he might do," Brad agreed. "But Boyd is the least of my concerns. If he comes back and wants the ranch, I'll give it to him. I don't need his land. The Crawfords have plenty."

It was true, of course. It was also true that Brad's father had, up to now, refused to parcel off some acres for Brad to have his own place. His dad had said he didn't seem ready, whatever the hell that meant. But he'd been pleased with

Brad's efforts in restoring the Leap of Faith to a well-run spread and Brad surmised if he asked again, the response would be different.

Nate finished off the last of his donut. "So what's the problem, little brother?"

"I don't want to screw this up, Nate. Not like I did with Janie." The admission embarrassed Brad. He was a man used to being in total control of his emotions and his life.

Nate's expression revealed nothing. "Is Margot like Janie?"

Brad knew what his brother was asking. *Is Margot self-centered and spoiled?* Nate had never liked Brad's ex-wife. But Brad knew the failure of their marriage wasn't just on Janie's back, but on his, too.

"Margot is nothing like Janie," he told his brother. "But I played a part in the failure of my marriage. I swept things under the rug. We had disagreements and problems but either we fought about them at the top of our lungs or we ignored them. I'm not proud of that."

"Everything that happens in our lives, good or bad, changes us in some way." Nate gazed down into his coffee mug as if thinking back. "One thing I've learned. The growing comes, not by simply recognizing what you did wrong or where you fell short, it's when you dig deep and make changes."

Brad understood what his brother was saying. The way he'd dealt with Janie, his inability to discuss an issue rationally and his unwillingness to compromise, had been the death knell for his marriage.

He also realized part of the reason he hadn't fought for his marriage was because he'd never really loved Janie. Not in the forever-after-until-death-do-us-part way that a man should love his wife.

His feelings for his ex-wife, even when things were

good, hadn't been a tenth of what he felt for Margot. He'd do whatever it took to make her happy, whether that involved him being in her life or not.

He knew what he had to do.

Brad pushed back his chair with a clatter and stood. "I'm going to be heading to Los Angeles for a few days. I'd appreciate it if you or dad would check in with Margot and make sure she's okay."

Nate studied his brother. "What are you up to, bro?"

"Hopefully making the woman I love very happy."

With those words, Brad strolled out of the shop.

Chapter Nineteen

Margot told herself she was glad Brad had gone into town. It gave her some much-needed time to think, to plan her future.

She took Storm slowly around the barrels. She told herself she wasn't racing. That was against doctor's orders. She was simply walking her horse in the corral. The barrels were like trees in a field, you either plowed into them or you went around them.

The right, left, left turns were as familiar to Margot as tying her shoes. Just walking around the barrels that Brad had set in the standard triangular pattern had her recalling the excitement of those early years.

She remembered teaching Bonner, her first horse, how to do a perfect circle at a walk, trot and lope. They'd progressed from there.

Though her father had been a critical taskmaster, she'd known she had a natural talent for the sport. She also knew he'd never have pushed her so hard if he hadn't recognized that fact, too.

From the beginning, Margot had loved everything about the sport: the cheers of the spectators in the bleachers, the thrill each time she'd cut her time by a second. For many years she and her father had been on the same team, shared the same goal—for her to be the best. For her to be a champion.

In the past year, even before the accident, the lifestyle had lost some of its luster. She'd grown weary of living out of trailers, of competing over a hundred times in the season, sometimes riding twice a night. Most of the prize money she earned went toward entry fees and living expenses.

If she hadn't gotten a few sponsors this past year, with the rise in gasoline prices, Margot had no doubt her expenditures would have exceeded her income. Money hadn't mattered when she'd left Rust Creek Falls. All that had mattered was riding and winning.

Only lately had her dreams begun to morph, to change.

Chasing the win was no longer the life she wanted. She wanted to stay here, work the ranch and teach. She wanted to do all that with Brad.

Storm pulled against the reins and tossed her head, eager for more speed. Margot gave the Arabian a little more lead as her mind settled on the one truth she hadn't been able to accept until this moment. She'd fallen in love with Brad Crawford.

She didn't want to crisscross the country and fight to make it to Las Vegas. Not because she didn't think she was good enough. Margot had no doubt that next year, or perhaps the year after, she'd find herself eyeing a championship.

Yet that goal no longer gripped her and she was smart

enough to know that success at that level demanded not only skill, but total dedication and passion.

Some might wonder if making it to that big stage had been more her father's dream than her own. The truth was, for many years winning on rodeo's biggest stage had been her dream, too. She'd wanted it for herself, just as much as Boyd had wanted it for her.

But now, she wanted what she couldn't have—a life on the Leap of Faith with Brad.

The ranch was no longer hers. And Brad, well, there had been an unspoken agreement between them. Whatever happened would be short-term and fun. He'd never said he loved her, though sometimes she wondered how he could be so tender and gentle if he didn't.

Of course, she knew his reputation and was well aware he didn't stay with one woman for long. There was no reason to think she was any different than the numerous other women who'd flowed in and out of his life in the past few years.

Though he acted as if he didn't want to take the Leap of Faith from her or from her father, it was obvious by how hard he worked that he'd grown to love the ranch. She also knew she couldn't keep it up on her own.

No, she corrected herself as Storm's walk became a lope, if the Leap of Faith was hers she *could* make it work. It would mean long, hard days and watching every penny to make sure there was enough for repairs and feed. It would mean hiring men sparingly to help her while doing the majority of the work herself.

She'd have to give up her blogging and her teaching; there would be no time for any of that if she was running the ranch alone.

Even worse, how could she remain in Rust Creek Falls and watch Brad fall in love with someone else? She couldn't.

No matter how much Margot loved it here, she was going to have to find a new home.

Brad called to Margot when he entered the front door of the house, but got no response. He paused in the parlor.

Viper looked up from cleaning one of the baby vipers and gave him a cool stare. Yesterday, he swore she'd thumped her tail on the floor but that may have been an optical illusion.

Regardless, it appeared he was on the outs again with the blue heeler.

A quick scan of the parlor and the kitchen showed no Margot. He checked the upstairs before heading outside.

His heart slammed against his ribs when he saw her. She was in the corral, riding Storm around the barrels. Even as he admired her form—the way she and the horse moved as one around the barrels in a kind of effortless dance— the speed concerned him.

Brad crossed the property to the corral in long, ground-eating strides. He was ready to call out when she saw him and pulled the horse up short.

"What do you think you're doing?" The fear rising up inside him had his voice sounding harsh.

She took her time dismounting and ambled over to the fence, Storm's reins held loosely in her hand. "How was your trip to town? Did you get your supplies?"

"What are you talking about?" Brad found it difficult to get back the image of her lying on the ground, blood seeping from her head.

"The supplies you went to town to get," she reminded him, a smile hovering at the corners of her lips.

"Oh, yeah." Brad lifted a hand and swiped the air. He couldn't be bothered with discussing such trivial matters.

Not when there was something so much more important to discuss. "What were you doing racing?"

"We weren't racing. Just making a few slow trips around the barrels," she said in a casual tone, as if it was no big deal. "We were barely moving."

He might have second-guessed his first impression if not for the two bright guilty spots of color on her cheeks.

"It's not safe," he argued. "If you'd fallen—"

"I didn't."

"If you had, I'd have come home to find you lying on the ground with no one around to help." The mere thought had his voice rising with anger and fear.

"Well, it's not as if you're always going to be around," she said in a matter-of-fact tone.

The air seemed charged with a curious energy, almost a watchful waiting. Brad wanted to promise her that he'd always be there, but now wasn't the time. Not until he'd taken care of business first.

"Don't do it again," he snapped.

"Is that an order?"

He wasn't sure why she was being so difficult just as he wasn't sure why he felt the desire to argue with her. Instead of giving in to the urge, he smiled.

"It's a request," he said in a conversational tone. "Because I don't want anything to happen to you."

She met his gaze. After a moment she shrugged. "Okay."

"I'll help you with Storm." He hopped the fence and took Storm's reins.

The walk into the stable was heavy with silence.

Brad had just removed Storm's saddle when his phone pinged. Several minutes later, once the horse was settled in her stall, he pulled out his phone and glanced at the readout.

When he looked up, Margot was staring curiously at him. "Something important?"

He hesitated. "I have some business in Los Angeles. Looks like I'll be leaving from Missoula tomorrow. First flight out. I won't be gone long. I'll be back by the end of the week."

She stared at him curiously as she removed Storm's bridle. "What kind of business?"

"Nothing of concern to you."

Though his words were spoken in an offhand manner, Margot felt as if she'd been slapped. He was shutting her out, telling her that his business—which likely had something to do with the Crawford enterprises—was none of hers.

It wasn't that she was all that interested in knowing every single detail of what he had planned on his trip, she'd simply been curious, that's all.

Margot stared at his closed expression and her heart broke, just a little.

She'd been right to start thinking of her future, to begin planning her next step, without considering her feelings for Brad.

By the way he was acting, it was obvious that whatever had been going on between them had been just a temporary thing.

Brad had obtained a meeting with Ryan Roarke the next day at his office in Los Angeles. He'd gotten to know the young attorney fairly well when Ryan had spent time in Thunder Canyon back in July.

He and Ryan were also related, sort of. If you counted the fact that Ryan's sister Maggie was married to Brad's brother, Jesse. Six months ago, the couple had given Brad a niece, Madeline.

Although Kalispell had any number of attorneys and Maggie was also an attorney, Brad chose to deal with Ryan on this particular matter. Better to keep the details from coming out in the *Rambler*'s column.

Done in walnut and teak, the attorney's office was as polished as the man himself. Instead of sitting behind his large desk, Ryan greeted him at the door and showed him to a couple of leather chairs positioned off to the side.

"Sure you don't want some coffee?" Ryan asked.

"I'd be happy to get you whatever you'd like to drink," the pretty blonde who'd shown Brad back offered again.

"Thanks," Brad told her. "I'm fine."

"I'll let you know if we need anything, Tiffany," Ryan said in dismissal.

With his two-hundred-dollar haircut and intense brown eyes, Ryan was the kind of man sophisticated women seemed to prefer. Yet he'd fit right in when he'd shown up in Thunder Canyon.

The attorney studied Brad for a long moment, much the way a scientist would study a bug or how a cowboy would consider a recalcitrant bull. "You must have gotten up at the crack of dawn to catch that flight out of Missoula this morning."

"The dawn hadn't even thought of cracking when I left Rust Creek Falls." The truth of it was Brad hadn't gotten much sleep at all.

Margot had acted strange, distant almost, the entire evening. She'd complained of a headache and had slept in her own bedroom, saying she wanted to get a good night's sleep and hopefully keep the headache from getting worse.

She was sleeping when he left so he didn't wake her, which meant he hadn't had a chance to give her a good-bye kiss. That stung. But this was something he wanted to take care of right away and he didn't want his actions getting around town.

Hopefully, California was far enough away to avoid the Rust Creek Falls gossip mill.

For several minutes, he updated Ryan on local events. Then, when Brad felt as if enough small talk had been exchanged, he decided to tell the attorney the reason he'd come sixteen hundred miles that morning.

Brad started with the wedding between Braden Traub and Jennifer MacCallum that had taken place on the Fourth of July. He moved onto the poker game and the events at the Ace in the Hole later that night.

"Let me get this straight." Ryan leaned forward, his dark eyes riveted to Brad's face. "You raised Boyd Sullivan five hundred. Instead of folding, the old guy puts up his ranch."

"That's correct."

"That's crazy." Ryan leaned back, a look of disbelief on his face. "You said someone had spiked the punch at the wedding."

"There was also a lot of beer flowing at the poker table."

Ryan's eyes sharpened. "Were you drunk?"

"Buzzed," Brad admitted. "But like I told the detective, not blasted drunk."

Ryan steepled his fingers. "That could explain such a reckless action."

"Everyone at the table tried to convince him to fold, but you know old Boyd."

"Actually—" Ryan picked up a Mont Blanc pen, a thoughtful look on his face "—I don't believe I ever met the man."

"I guess I just assumed you had." Brad gave a humorless laugh. "You know how it is. When you live in Rust Creek Falls, everyone knows everyone."

"I like that about the area," Ryan said, surprising Brad

by his admission. "The way everyone greets you on the street. The way they look out for their own, like the guys at the poker table tried to look out for this old man."

"*Tried* being the operative word." Brad shook his head and blew out a breath. "Boyd Sullivan is pushing eighty, but you'd never know it. He's strong as a mule and just as stubborn. Yeah, he'd been drinking that night. We all had. But he could hold his liquor."

Ryan sat back in his chair. "What happened when you encouraged him to fold?"

"The sanitized version is he told us to mind our own."

The attorney laughed. "I'm starting to get a good picture of this guy."

"Like I said, he's a character." He was also Margot's dad and Boyd's recent behavior had caused his daughter much pain. That, Brad found hard to forgive.

"He lost the hand," Ryan interjected when Brad didn't continue.

"He lost and left the game." Brad explained the rest of the details concerning that night to the attorney. "The sheriff did some digging and learned that Boyd had bought a one-way train ticket from Missoula to New York City."

"Hold on a minute." Ryan lifted a hand. "I thought the man was broke."

Brad lifted a shoulder in a shrug. "There's speculation someone bought the ticket for him."

Ryan inclined his head, his brown eyes sharp and assessing. "Did you purchase it?"

"No," Brad snapped.

"I had to ask," Ryan responded in a calm, conversational tone. "Let me see if I have this correct, Boyd willingly signed the deed to the ranch over to you and left town. Now all anyone knows is he's likely somewhere on the East Coast. If he's still alive."

"We know he's alive." Brad told the attorney about the postcard he'd received and the letter Boyd had sent to Margot.

"It's an acquisition route but it sounds to me as if the ranch is yours. He signed the deed and made it clear in two separate pieces of correspondence that he wants you to have it." Ryan stared curiously at Brad. "Have you had the deed recorded? It's not required to make the change of ownership effective, but it's a good idea."

"I haven't done that," Brad admitted. "There's a bit more to me being here, but it all ties in to what I've told you. I believe you have a license to practice law in Montana."

"I do." Interest flickered in Ryan's dark gaze. "Are you in need of an attorney, Brad?"

He nodded. "I want to put the ranch in Boyd's daughter's name. And I want it done immediately."

Chapter Twenty

By the time Margot got up the next morning, Brad had left. She crossed the hall and paused at the entrance to his bedroom before stepping inside. For a full minute she stood staring at the bed where they'd so often made love.

As she moved to plump the pillows and straighten the quilt, she let her hands linger as if she could capture some of his warmth.

Their fun together was over. Brad didn't need to spell it out any more clearly. He'd left her. Just as her mother had, and then her dad.

Well, Margot had her pride. Instead of trying to hold on to someone who didn't want her, she'd take the bull by the horns and move on. She'd only insisted on staying because she was convinced the ranch was her dad's.

Now both the postcard and the letter had made it clear that her father wanted Brad to have the ranch. That branded *her* as the interloper, not *him*.

There was nothing for her here. The only question left to answer was—where to go?

The doctor wouldn't clear her to race until next spring. Margot had a horse, a blue heeler and ten puppies who still needed their mama, and then homes. Hard decisions were needed and she had to be the one to make them.

She mulled the situation over for several minutes then decided to see if Jilly's parents would be interested in boarding Storm until next spring when Margot returned to pick her up. Unlimited access to the horse in exchange for housing the Arabian seemed a fair deal. She only hoped they would agree.

Vivian couldn't be dealt with quite so easily. The thought of leaving town without Vivi had a knot forming in the pit of Margot's stomach. But she couldn't uproot the new mother and her puppies. While Margot had friends who might be willing to let her live with them temporarily, she didn't know anyone who would take her *and* a whole passel of blue heelers.

She wondered if Brad would want...

Immediately Margot shook her head, dismissing the thought. Even though Vivi and Brad had recently formed a tentative truce, he only tolerated "Viper" because of her.

Margot slowly descended the stairs, her mind sorting through various possibilities and rejecting them all. Then she thought of Todd. Brad's father may not be a fan of fluffy white puffballs but he seemed to have an affinity for heelers. The last time he was over he'd even mentioned he might know of some ranchers who'd be interested in the pups once they were fully weaned.

By the time she reached the first floor her phone was out of her back pocket and she was dialing the Crawford General Store. After she ended the call, Margot collapsed on the bottom step.

Though Todd had seemed caught off guard by the request, he'd graciously agreed to board Vivi and her pups. He assured her he'd take good care of the dogs. Even knowing that, believing that, didn't ease the pain.

Lurching to her feet, Margot took a moment to steady herself before entering the parlor. When Vivi looked up and wagged her tail, Margot's eyes filled with tears. She hurriedly blinked them back.

She held out a hand, fully expecting Vivi to come to her. Instead, the heeler jumped out of the box and trotted past her outstretched hand, leaving Margot with the pups.

Margot let her hand drop and crossed to the box. Memories surged of the night Vivian had given birth and how Brad had built the box and placed it near the fire so Vivi and the little "vipers" would be safe and warm.

It had been a sweet thing to do. Margot knew that was the moment she'd begun to look at Brad Crawford in a different light.

Shoving the memories aside, Margot reached into the box and lifted out a fat black-and-gray bundle of fur. As she cuddled the warm little body close, her rioting emotions began to calm. She rocked the sleeping puppy in the ornate chair that had once belonged to her grandmother.

She told herself she should be happy. Everything was falling into place. Except, she still needed to call Jilly's parents. As close as she and Vivian were, she and Storm had been an inseparable team for the past five years.

Of course, if things worked out, both of these separations would be short-lived. Not like between her and Brad. Their separation would be forever.

Cutting the bond that had formed between her and the handsome cowboy hurt the most. Foolishly, she'd let herself believe, let herself hope, for more. She should have known a happily-ever-after between them would be impossible.

He wasn't ready to settle down, at least not with her. That's why the sooner she moved on with her life, the better.

She was scrolling down to Roger's number when the phone rang. Margot was ashamed to admit she hoped to see Brad's name on the readout.

Leila.

"Hey, girl," Leila said when she answered. "How's it going?"

"Good." Margot cleared her throat and forced a cheery tone. "How are you?"

There was a pause on the other end.

"What's wrong?" Leila demanded.

"Nothing. I'm just busy," Margot said quickly. "I'm, ah, getting ready to move."

"Where are you going? I thought you were all settled in."

Margot took a few minutes to explain everything that had happened since Leila had left town, including the letter she'd recently received.

"I barely pass the city limits and everything goes to hell in a handbasket," Leila said with a half laugh before turning serious. "Did Brad ask you to leave the ranch?"

"No." Margot fought the heavy sigh that rose inside her. "But the letter made it clear this is his place now, Leila, not mine."

Margot sensed the reporter in her friend wanted to dig for details. She was grateful Leila refrained.

"What's the plan?" Leila asked after a long moment. "I know you have one."

Margot told her about Todd agreeing to take Vivian and the puppies and her plans for Storm.

"Are you certain this is what you want?"

The quiet question hit a nerve. "What I want? Do you think I *want* to give up Vivian and Storm—even for a few months? I don't have a choice. This isn't my home anymore. I have to find a place to live, then in the spring I'll return to the circuit."

"Is going back *there* what you want?"

"What's with all the questions? Of course it's what I want. I've spent the last five years of my life pursuing that dream."

"We can want something at one time—" Leila's tone turned philosophical "—and decide later that's not what we want, after all."

"It's still my dream," Margot insisted, wondering why she was trying to convince Leila of something she herself no longer believed.

"What about Brad?"

"What about him?"

"I thought you and he might…"

"We had fun while it lasted," Margot told her friend. "That's over now."

Twenty-four hours passed. Margot still hadn't gotten around to calling Jilly's parents. Todd came over and fed the cattle. A couple of men sent by Jesse and Nate put up a snow fence. Before Todd left, she took him in to see Vivian and the puppies. Her heart lurched when the heeler wagged her tail and let Todd pet her.

The entire time Todd was at the ranch he never once mentioned Brad. When he asked how long she planned to stay at the house, Margot told him that since Brad would be back on Friday to take over the ranch chores, she'd stay through Thursday night.

Todd appeared to approve of the plan. Of course, if she

was going to make the timetable work, Margot needed to get on the stick and make arrangements for Storm. She knew Brad would probably agree to keep her, but that would mean seeing him when she came back to pick the horse up in the spring.

She preferred to avoid that pain.

Over lunch, she reread her dad's letter and wondered again at the lack of return address. What was he so afraid of? That she'd show up on his doorstep? Was the idea of making peace with his only daughter so scary? His actions didn't make sense and her continued attempts to figure it out only made her head ache and her heart hurt more.

The night before Brad had left for LA had been a restless one for her. Last night hadn't been much better. When she casually asked his father if he knew what Brad was doing in LA, his father had played dumb. Obviously, she wasn't to be trusted with any Crawford business intel.

After washing the lunch dishes, Margot went upstairs to take a nap. She'd only slept twenty minutes when Vivian began barking. Since she wasn't expecting anyone, the only thing she could figure was Todd had returned for something he'd forgotten.

Margot pushed back the cotton throw and stood. She'd just reached the stairwell when she heard the doorknob rattle. Seconds later, the front door creaked open.

She froze, her mind racing. Brad was out of town and not due back for forty-eight hours. Todd didn't have a key. She distinctly recalled him handing it over when she and Brad returned from Kalispell. Besides, Todd knew she was home. He'd have knocked.

Margot recalled an article in the *Rust Creek Falls Gazette* the week before about a rise in unsolved burglaries in the county. Her heart slammed against her chest.

She reached for her phone intending to call the sheriff then cursed. She'd left the cell downstairs on the kitchen table.

Her gaze settled on the baseball bat perched against the wall. Picking it up, Margot crept down the stairs. The fact that she could no longer hear Vivian barking worried her.

She was on the third to the last step when she caught sight of the intruder. Margot slowly lowered the weapon, unable to tear her eyes from him.

Brad flashed that familiar smile as his gaze settled on the bat. "Guess I can't complain about the welcome since that's how I greeted you the first time we met."

Just hearing that familiar baritone brought a stab of pain. He looked exhausted. His dark hair was mussed from the wind and lines of fatigue edged his eyes, eyes that now were dark and somber.

"How are you, Margot?" His gaze searched hers. "Did you miss me?"

She steeled her heart and sauntered down the steps, setting the bat against the wall. "I've been busy."

He glanced at one of her bags sitting by the door. "Busy packing from the way it looks."

"This isn't my home anymore." Though she spoke normally, her lips felt frozen and stiff. "I don't belong here."

He lowered his duffel to the floor. "How do you figure?"

"My dad signed the place over to you. He made it clear in the letter he wanted you to have it."

"We discussed this before." His voice held a hint of reproach. "I thought we were going to wait to make any decisions until we located your dad and spoke with him personally."

"I—I can't do this anymore, Brad."

He took a step closer.

She took a step back, bumping up against the stairs.

"Can't do what?" Those intense green eyes focused

on hers. There was weariness in the iridescent depths she hadn't noticed before.

She fluttered a hand in the air. "Live in limbo any longer."

"Let's take the topic of you moving out off the table right now." Brad reached inside his jacket, pulled out a legal-sized envelope and held it out to her.

Margot took the ivory envelope, but made no move to open it. "What is in here?"

"It's the deed to the Leap of Faith," he told her. "I had it put legally in your name."

She tossed the envelope down on the sideboard. "Why would you do that?"

"The Leap of Faith is your legacy, not mine." He shoved his hands into his pockets. "I believe if your dad knew how much it meant to you, he'd have given it to you, not me."

Tears filled her eyes. Oh, how she wanted to believe that… "I don't think—"

"You read his letter. He thought you had the wanderlust and wouldn't be happy here. I believe he was wrong. I think you can be happy here."

Margot moistened her suddenly dry lips. She *could* be happy here, but only if she was with Brad. If they weren't together, it would be torture to be in Rust Creek Falls. If only he would tell her he loved her and wanted them to be together.

But no words of love filled the air, only a silent, watchful waiting.

Finally, she couldn't stand the silence anymore. "Keep the ranch, Brad. I'll be going back on the circuit in the spring, anyway."

He opened his mouth as if to say something then closed it. His gaze searched hers. "Is that what you want?"

I want you.

For a second Margot feared she'd spoken aloud, but if she had he showed no response, only stood there breaking her heart with his silence.

"Sure." She managed an offhand tone. "A championship is what I've been working toward all these years."

He slowly nodded. Was it only her imagination or was that disappointment in his eyes? She took another look. Nope, just wishful thinking on her part.

Brad glanced at the bag then back at her. "What's the rush? At least stay until the doctor releases you."

That option still tugged at her. She knew it was why she hadn't yet called Jilly's parents. Margot supposed she could stay and play house with Brad. Yet, if she did that, she knew every day her heart would break a little more until it had been reduced to a handful of shattered bits.

"I need to leave." She waved the protest that sprang to his lips. "I planned to be out tomorrow. It's best I stick to that timetable."

Her voice sounded cold, almost brusque. She was only thankful it didn't quiver.

Tonight, she would make plans for Storm. No more procrastinating. Tomorrow, she would leave as scheduled.

He exhaled a breath. "At least we'll have tonight togeth—"

"Actually, I have plans."

The last of the light in his eyes vanished. His expression turned to stone. "Forgive me for being presumptuous. I thought since it was our last night together, we could have dinner."

Something, a little something she couldn't quite identify in the way he said the words made her wonder if he did care. She opened her mouth to tell him she would change her plans when he continued.

"We could use the time to hammer out the details regarding the management of the ranch."

Margot shut her mouth with a snap, grateful she hadn't bared her soul. He hadn't been thinking of an intimate dinner between the two of them. He'd been considering the logistics of her leaving.

Why should that surprise her, she wondered? He'd obviously already moved on and was looking ahead to the future. A future that didn't include her.

Chapter Twenty-One

Brad spent the next hour alternately cursing himself for being a fool for loving a woman who obviously didn't feel the same and then cursing himself for not having the guts to tell her how he felt.

In some ways it was that last night with Janie all over again. Except he and Margot had never made a commitment to each other.

Which was complete bull.

He'd never have slept with her, never taken advantage of her—his father's words, not his—if he hadn't already committed himself to her and their relationship.

Yet the first time he'd had the opportunity to lay his heart on the line and fight for their relationship, what had he done? He'd taken a step back.

That was bull, too.

He would not give in to fear or pride or whatever it was that had kept him from going after the woman he loved.

He'd fight for her and for what they'd started to build together. This was a battle he couldn't afford to lose.

First step was to figure out where she'd gone this evening. He thought about the penguin desk calendar she'd purchased in Kalispell. She'd started using it almost immediately. He only hoped she'd taken the time to pencil in tonight's appointment.

He found the calendar on the kitchen counter, directly beneath the ancient wall phone that still sported a rotary dial. There was only one entry for today.

Sierra. NILE. 7:00 p.m.

Smiling for the first time since he'd received his father's phone call when he was in Los Angeles, Brad headed immediately for his truck, ready to do battle for the woman he loved.

Margot sat alone on an upper bleacher in the Majestic Valley Arena, a popular venue located between Kalispell and Whitefish.

Tonight the Northern International Livestock Exposition, commonly referred to as NILE by those living in the area, was holding their annual stock show and rodeo. Sierra was competing in the 19-and-under class.

This marked the first time Margot had attended a rodeo since she was injured. A wave of nostalgia washed over her at the familiar sights and smells. The cheers from the crowd when a bull rider stayed on for eight seconds or a barrel racer had a good ride, becoming one with her horse around the turns. The smell of fried foods mixed with the sawdust and sweat. Men in Tony Lama boots, Stetsons and shiny belt buckles and women wearing tight jeans and boots with turquoise trim.

For as far back as Margot could remember this had been her world. Though it hadn't been an easy life, she'd loved it. Still, Margot had to admit that somewhere along the way the desire to reach the top had slipped away. Not to say she hadn't loved winning. Each time she rode into the ring she'd always given it her all.

Yet she realized the promise of a championship no long drove her.

"Sierra Krupicka."

Margot pulled her thoughts back to the present, to her student who sat poised to enter the ring. During their lesson Margot had spent a lot of time working with Sierra and how the girl positioned herself on the horse.

She narrowed her gaze, feeling her own heart race as she watched the girl round the first barrel. Sierra was doing much better, leaning slightly forward and pushing down in the stirrups but she was still a little out of the saddle during the turn.

It's something we'll need to work on…

The thought went no further. There would be no more sessions with Sierra or with Jilly. Margot found it telling that the thought of not teaching bothered her more than the idea of not competing.

She rose to her feet and clapped when Sierra's time flashed. Very respectable. The girl had the makings of a champion.

"Your instruction made a difference," a deep voice beside her remarked.

Margot's heart slammed against her chest. She turned to find Brad standing beside her seat. Wearing jeans and a battered leather jacket, he looked the same as he had back at the house.

No, she realized, something was different. It was the look of determination in his eyes.

"What…what are you doing here?" she stammered.

He gestured with his head toward the ring. "I was watching Sierra race. Now I'm speaking with you."

"Enjoy the rodeo." She twisted her lips into a semblance of a smile. "I was just leaving."

Margot started to slip past him but he grabbed her hand and tugged her back down into her seat, then sat beside her.

She studied his set jaw and that single-minded look in his eyes and sighed. "What exactly is it you want to talk about?"

He took a breath and let it out slowly. "I'm aware you've spent the better part of your childhood and the past twelve years following your father's dream—"

"It was my dream, too," Margot insisted. She lifted her chin, daring him to disagree.

Brad shook his head, the weariness back in his eyes. "Is it really? If you can't be honest with me, at least be honest with yourself."

Margot glared at him, suddenly furious. Who was he to come here and play these games? "You have no idea what I think, what I feel."

"You're right, I don't. Only because you don't trust me enough to share those feelings with me." He blew out an exasperated breath. "You know I had to learn from my father that you were planning to move out?"

"He called you." Margot didn't know why it took her until now to make the connection with Brad's early return.

"Darn right he called me." Brad's jaw lifted in that familiar stubborn tilt she loved so much. "Thank God he did or I'd have come back and you'd have been gone."

"Like I told you back at the house, it's time for me to move on. I don't belong at the Leap of Faith."

Brad took a deep breath in an attempt to control his frustration. He would not, he told himself, lose his cool.

"Why do you think my father stayed in Montana all

those years, Brad? Why do you think he didn't leave a long time ago?"

The sudden change in topic took him by surprise. Was it a ploy on her part to shift the conversation? It seemed likely. Still, she looked genuinely concerned.

"Hard to say," he muttered. Boyd Sullivan and his behavior was a sore subject. "You knew him better than me."

"My mother loved it here, I know that."

"Maybe that's your answer."

She tilted her head. "What do you mean?"

"She loved it here and he loved her." His tone turned pensive. "When a man loves a woman he'll go to great lengths to make her happy. Perhaps staying here was a choice he made for her. Now, with Giselle gone, maybe he's doing what's right for him."

The thought that there had been nothing for Boyd in Rust Creek Falls once her mother died chafed like a too-tight boot. If Margot accepted that explanation, she had to also accept that *she* hadn't mattered enough.

Just like she didn't matter to Brad. She loved him and all he wanted was a casual bedmate. "I need to go."

Margot navigated the steps in a reckless stride. Once she reached the mail level, she didn't even take time to zip her coat before stepping out into the parking lot. She was halfway to her truck before it registered that large, white flakes now filled the air.

Other than the occasional roar emanating from inside the arena, the night was still. The fluorescent parking lot lights shone bright overhead.

Though there were no vintage street lamps and this was a parking lot, not a street filled with quaint shops, Margot thought of the pretty snow globe she and Brad had admired on their trip to Kalispell: the one with the man and woman dancing.

Look Forward With Hope, Not Backwards With Regret

had been one of her mother's favorite sayings. Margot had never really understood what it meant. Now she did.

She should have bought her mother gifts that made her feel loved and cherished. She should have been honest and told Brad how she felt about him.

It was too late to do anything about her mother. But Brad, well, there was still time.

Eager to return to the arena, Margot stopped, whirled and slammed into a broad, firm chest.

"I—I'm so sorry," she began then realized it was Brad's strong hands steadying her. "You...you—"

"I followed you. I can't let you go, Margot. I—"

"It's the snow globe," she blurted out before he could finish. "Being out here reminds me of the one we saw in the Christmas shop. Of course here it's the moon, instead of those streetlamps, giving everything a golden glow."

From the look of confusion in his eyes, her ramblings were making little sense. It was difficult to think, much less speak coherently, with her heart pounding and so much on the line.

"I bought you one."

She blinked.

"A snow globe," he continued. "When you slipped off to the restroom, I purchased the one you admired and then hid it when we got home."

He released his hold on her arms and began to pace.

"I bought it because I want to make you happy." The words tumbled out of Brad's mouth as if a chute holding them in had suddenly been flung open. "I want you to always be happy, Margot. I know winning a championship is important to you. That doesn't mean we can't be together. I can go with you on the circuit, be with you, support you as you chase your dream."

She opened her mouth but he continued to talk as if determined to address any concerns before she raised them.

"We can hire help to manage the ranch when we're on the road. I understand making something like this work won't be easy, but I've spent a good part of my life walking away when things got tough, because it didn't matter enough. *You* matter. We'll make it work because what we have together matters."

Her tremulous smile must have been all the encouragement he needed because he grasped her hands like a drowning man who'd just spotted shore. "I love you, Margot. I can't imagine my life without you. You have my vow that I'll spend the rest of my life making you happy."

No regrets, she told herself.

"I love you, too, Brad." Her voice shook with emotion. "I was on my way back to the arena to tell you just that."

He closed his eyes tight and she swore she heard him murmur a prayer of thanks. Then those eyes flashed open and fixed on hers. Brad jerked her into his arms, kissing her soundly.

She was still reeling when he stepped back, dropped to one knee and pulled out a black jeweler's case from his pocket. He flipped it open to reveal a large oval diamond that flashed brilliant sparks of color. "Margot Sullivan, will you do me the honor of becoming my wife?"

Margot felt as if she was center ring, being awarded the grand prize. Her heart leapt with joy.

"Yes," she said, then again more loudly to make sure he heard, "Yes. I'll marry you, Brad. And I'll love you forever."

Once the ring was on her finger, they kissed again, a warm, wonderful kiss that carried the promise of a future as wide open as the Montana sky. When it ended, Brad stepped back and held out his arms.

Then, under the full moon with the snow falling gently all around them, Margot and Brad danced.

Epilogue

"What do you think of this plan?" Brad spread the blueprints of the equestrian center on the coffee table in the parlor.

Margot smiled at her fiancé's enthusiasm.

"Look." He pointed. "This one has six stalls, a wash rack and tack room. The indoor arena has a fifteen-foot headroom, minimum."

"I do believe you're as excited about finding the perfect plan as I am."

Brad grinned sheepishly. "I like the idea of having several stalls for boarding as well as the facilities so you can teach year-round."

"Want to keep me busy, huh?"

"Not too busy." Brad leaned over and nuzzled her neck.

"I'll never be too busy for this," she agreed, reveling in the closeness.

It had been a week since she'd accepted his proposal.

They'd spent the days planning their future together. Brad had been stunned when she told him that she didn't plan to continue competing. But he understood when she told him she didn't want to spend so much time on the road. She wanted to spend it with him on the Leap of Faith.

Besides, her business was on the verge of exploding. Sierra's much improved performance at NILE had caused the parents of other barrel racers from the area to contact Margot about lessons.

When Brad finally realized she was serious, he'd immediately gotten on board with planning what she'd need in order to help the business grow. Because of the climate in Montana, an indoor arena was a necessity. Adding an equestrian center to the ranch seemed to make sense.

Considering that some students might not want to transport their horse back and forth, while others might want their horse to stay and be trained, making sure the structure had enough extra stalls to accommodate a growing business had become a priority.

Margot tried to focus on the plans before her. But it wasn't easy. Not with a sexy cowboy sitting on the sofa beside her. Brad's hair was still damp from the shower and he'd splashed on some of her favorite cologne.

Focus, Margot told herself, focus.

"I think we should go with the optional stall package that includes the heavy-duty galvanized stall fronts, chew protection, rubber stall mats and Dutch door turnouts." Margot cocked her head. "What do you think?"

Brad's slow grin did funny things to her insides. "I love it when you talk horsey. It's so sexy."

"I'm being serious." She laughed. "Or at least I'm trying."

"I'm serious, too. You are the most beautiful fiancée in Rust Creek Falls."

"I believe I'm the only fiancée in town right now." She tapped his nose with the tip of her one finger. "What are you going to say when I'm your wife?"

He paused, considered, grinned. "Hallelujah."

From the moment Brad had slipped the brilliant diamond on her finger, Margot had known he was eager to make her his wife. But he hadn't pushed for them to firm up plans for the wedding. The date of the nuptials had been left up to her. She could take as long as she wanted to decide.

It was too bad the townsfolk of Rust Creek Falls hadn't gotten that message. Or, if they had, they'd chosen to ignore it.

"Natalie asked me again if we've set a wedding date."

"She asked me, too," Brad admitted.

"What did you tell her?" Margot kept her voice just as casual as his.

"I told her we were waiting to see if Boyd would come back." He took her hand and held it loosely in his. "I'm having the *Gazette* run another article about your dad and mentioning the reward we're offering for any information on Boyd's whereabouts and what happened that night he left."

"Thank you." Margot brushed a kiss across his cheek. "For everything. Including being so patient."

"If I had my choice, I'd have married you yesterday. But, like I said, I'm okay with waiting, if that's what you want."

Margot's lips twisted in a wry smile. "The pastor waylaid me on Sunday and asked when we wanted to reserve the church."

"Don't let anyone pressure you." His fingers tipped her face up and he kissed her gently on the lips. "This is your decision, not anyone else's."

Swamped with love, Margot wrapped her arms around

her fiancé and rested her head against his broad chest. "You are everything to me. You're my friend, my confidant, my biggest supporter and the man I love with my whole heart."

"One day soon you'll be my bride." He gave a contented sigh. "I'm a lucky man."

Margot had never wanted a big wedding. Small and intimate was more her speed. Though she had to admit she'd always imagined her dad walking her down the aisle on her big day. But how could she put her and Brad's life on hold for something she was starting to believe might never happen?

She tipped her head back and stared up into Brad's incredible green eyes. "Two words—Las Vegas."

Momentary disappointment clouded his gaze. "You found the tickets."

She pushed herself upright. "What tickets?"

"The rodeo finals. The tickets were your birthday gift."

"My birthday isn't until December third."

"Which just happens to be the first day of the finals," he said with exaggerated patience.

"I get the feeling we're talking about two different things." Margot put her hand to her spinning head. "What are you talking about?"

"A birthday trip to Vegas." Her words appeared to finally register and a big grin spread over his face. "You want to get married there."

"In December my dad will have been gone six months. I'm not willing to continue putting my life—our lives—on hold. I want to be your wife." As she spoke, Margot's excitement began to build. "We could do a destination wedding. Any family that wanted to make the trip could attend. Hopefully Leila could fly in and be my maid of honor."

Admiration filled his gaze. "You have it all thought out."

"I'm a determined woman and I've got my eye on the prize."

"The rodeo tickets?"

"No, you goof, on you." She grinned. "But the tickets are a great wedding gift."

"Birthday."

"The rodeo finals can be our honeymoon." Margot's gaze met his and her lips curved upward. "*You* can be my birthday gift."

"I like the idea of a December wedding." Brad smiled and looped an arm around her shoulder. "Plus getting married in Vegas seems fitting."

"Because you've already purchased tickets to the finals?"

He grinned. "Because one crazy bet led to the biggest jackpot of all."

As his lips closed over hers, Margot firmly agreed.

* * * * *

15_ST19

MILLS & BOON®

Cherish™

EXPERIENCE THE ULTIMATE RUSH OF FALLING IN LOVE

A sneak peek at next month's titles…

In stores from 16th October 2015:

- **Housekeeper Under the Mistletoe** – Cara Colter
  and **Coming Home for Christmas** – Marie Ferrarella
- **His Lost-and-Found Bride** – Scarlet Wilson
  and **The Maverick's Holiday Masquerade**
  – Caro Carson

In stores from 6th November 2015:

- **His Texas Christmas Bride** – Nancy Robards
  Thompson *and* **Gift-Wrapped in Her Wedding
  Dress** – Kandy Shepherd
- **The Prince's Christmas Vow** – Jennifer Faye
  and **A Husband for the Holidays** – Ami Weaver

Available at WHSmith, Tesco, Asda, Eason, Amazon and Apple

Just can't wait?
Buy our books online a month before they hit the shops!
visit www.millsandboon.co.uk

These books are also available in eBook format!